Rise of the Forest Queen

The Albright Trilogy, Book 1

K. Moongazer

Published by K. Moongazer, 2025.

RISE OF THE FOREST QUEEN

First edition. June 30, 2025.

Copyright © 2025 K. Moongazer.

ISBN: 979-8990893825

Written by K. Moongazer.

Acknowledgements

Thank you to everyone who supported me while I wrote not just one, but two books. I know it was a long journey to get to the skill level I'm at now, and I promise to never stop writing. Thank you to Rein Debrouwer for the royal hammer poem. It's beautifully written and I'm terrible at poems. And a big thank you to my two editors, Ashley and Courtney, for catching the grammar and plot holes I missed. This book wouldn't be half as good without your expertise.

I also want to thank those who provided a name for a character in my book. It helps to feel like those close to me are helping me along the way. And a big thank you to Juan for providing the character of Lorem Epsum. I hope I did her justice.

Cover by Ashley Lokey and K. Moongazer
Chapter Sapling art by Sirius Facts Art Studio
Hammer and Author art by UIDB MGMT
Bob Fan art by Amber Adams
Developmental Editing by Ashley Lokey
Copy Editing by Courtney Umphress Editing

Trigger Warnings

For more information, please visit my website at
https://kmoongazer.carrd.co

- Death
- Skull and chest bashing with a hammer
- Body shaming
- Everything is on fire
- Kidnapping
- Skull headed beast who kills and eats everything it can
- Anxiety
- FMC is hit by a car
- Depression
- Grief
- Crushing
- Carnivorous plants
- Fantasy Violence
- Bullying
- Blood

Author's Note

Please keep in mind that this is MY OWN VERSION of the fae realm. It is not accurate as I have no idea what the real fae realm (if it's real) looks like. This is just my version for the book.

Prologue

Night covered the forest like a blanket, smothering the natural lights of nature. The only noise was a heavy rainfall that made passage through the trees almost impossible. A hooded woman stumbled while running, tripping on an exposed tree root. She clutched a small bundle to her chest, bracing herself against a tree and biting her tongue to keep from crying out in pain when her ankle crumpled under her weight. The pounding in her ears made it hard to listen for the shouts of her pursuers over her heavy breathing and the downpour. Moving the fabric in her arms, she peered at her daughter's sleeping face. This rain couldn't have come at a worse time.

"Almost there, little one," the woman whispered, her voice shaking as she panted. Her child was perfectly content sleeping in her arms; even the fall didn't wake her. She smiled, thinking of how lucky she was to have a child who was a heavy sleeper. The forest could crumble around her and she wouldn't wake up. She started to move a piece of hair from the child's face, when she froze.

"I heard something over there!" The harsh voice of a man cracked through the trees like a whip.

This was no time for a rest, she had to keep moving. Keeping her baby close to her chest, she saw a large oak tree in the distance, the one she was looking for. Putting on a burst of speed, she ran toward the tree, knowing it was the only hope she had of keeping her daughter safe. It looked the same as any other tree from the outside, but the woman had hidden here before. She knew the power this forest wielded.

An arrow shot past her head, and she knew she couldn't stop or look back. They were closing in around her. The woman weaved in and out of the trees, not slowing for a moment while trying to dodge their attacks. With her skin growing clammy and her breaths losing control, she struggled to push the barrage of dangerous thoughts out of her mind. She had to focus all her energy on making it to the oak.

What were the raiders doing in this part of the forest? How could they have found the two of them? They had been attacked countless times, but this time they were forced to flee their home. The woman knew exactly who had attacked them. She also knew that she was not their primary target: Her daughter was. Only a few weeks old now, her daughter would one day have the power to protect everything living in the forest. The baby's survival was important to more than just her mother. Their entire world depended on it.

She paid for the moment of distraction in her own head as one misstep had her tumbling to the ground. She just barely managed to turn her body to land on her side so as not to harm the sleeping child. Could she even stand up and continue to run? The pain in her ankle was shooting up her leg, and it left her wondering why her magic refused to heal her.

An arrow whirred past her head, making her look up at where it had landed on the ground a few feet away to see that it had ripped through the fabric of her hood. Her bright emerald eyes gawked at the arrow with a gasp, and she was horrified to see long strands of curly red hair, *her* hair. She had to move. She had to get up. That arrow was too close.

She forced herself back onto her feet and began to move toward the tree again. The raiders were catching up, and she needed to make it to the tree before she was caught. The raiders were not shooting to wound or capture. Their goal was to kill her and her baby.

Taking a tentative step forward, she nearly cried out in agony as the pain radiated from her ankle through her body. No matter how bad the pain was, she knew she had to make a run for it.

"Over there!" a man shouted as she peeled herself from the shadows of the surrounding trees. She could see the base of the oak now. One hundred feet, fifty feet, twenty feet. They were going to make it. The raiders' voices were getting louder, and someone barked a command to the others before the group separated. They were going to surround her.

It was no use continuing their search. They had reached the tree, and she knew they were safe for now. Even though they wouldn't be found inside, this was no life for a child. Leaving the tree meant the potential of being in danger all the time. She knew if the two of them were seen in the same area for too long, the raiders would eventually close in on their location, and the tree would no longer be safe. Besides, there was no way to stop a crying baby, and the noise could easily be heard from outside the oak. Raising a child in the heat of war was going to be impossible.

The mother looked down at her sleeping child and gently brushed her cheek with the back of her finger, a look of despair staining her features. She had made her decision, though it was the toughest one she had ever made in her life.

The woman reached her hand out toward the tree as soon as it was within view. A green glow came from the insignia that was carved into the tree before a door appeared at the base and opened outward. Ducking through the door, she looked around.

The inside of the oak was hollowed out and looked like a home. It was much bigger on the inside than it should have been. She had used this tree as a sanctuary for most of her life, just as her mother had before her.

Plants and jars filled the space. The shelves were stacked with every imaginable book on plants, fae, and the history of the forest, but there was no time to pick which ones to take with her. She needed to hurry and finish what she needed before the raiders caught up to them.

The mother placed her baby girl in a wicker basket before going to the desk to write up the note that would seal her daughter's fate. It was all she could think to do in the moment to give her daughter a way to find her in the future, to possibly reunite. A quick glance out the small round window in the side revealed the light of the raiders' torches much closer than she'd anticipated.

"Oh no . . ." she breathed.

She grabbed the basket with her daughter and placed the note in the little girl's blanket before leaving the oak. Turning back toward the large tree, she raised her free hand.

"Mighty oak, please conceal our home and keep our enemies out."

Within moments, the door and windows surrounding their hideaway within the tree vanished, returning the tree to its former state. Reaching out her hand to gently touch the still-gleaming symbol in front of her, she traced the outline of the two-leaf sapling, running her fingers along each of the seven circles that came together to form a ring. This small gesture brought her some peace as the symbol faded and left an imprint barely visible to the eye.

That was all she could do for now; they had to leave. Channeling her magic through her core, she made a circle in the grass with her foot, allowing an opening to form and tree roots to sprout up out of it. She climbed onto one of the roots and held on before it pulled her down into the hole. Just as the raiders burst through the bushes they had just cut, the woman was gone and the hole closed up behind her, allowing her to leave the realm. She could hear their angry shouts get further and further away as she shifted to a new plain of existence where she knew her child would be safe.

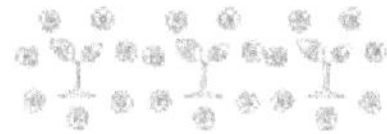

Canton, Ohio, 2006

The sun couldn't have been any gloomier if it tried. Dark gray clouds hung in the sky, marking the first sign of a storm. The ground was covered in morning dew from the night's rainfall.

The woman, dressed in garb that didn't belong in this world, clutched her child to her chest before quickly making her way down the street. Everything was quiet and still. It was a harsh difference from the noises of the forest.

It's around here somewhere, the woman thought as she quickly walked down the sidewalk, looking for a particular house.

There it is.

The gold numbers read 347 against a cream-colored two-story home. She could see a car in front, so she knew that someone would be there.

Three Forty-Seven Forest Lane. This is it.

After walking up the steps, the woman gently set her daughter down by the front door and knelt beside her little girl. She couldn't believe the situation had escalated to where she had to leave her only child on a doorstep in another realm. A tear ran down her face as she tucked a stray hair behind her daughter's ear.

"I will come back for you as soon as I can, my sweet girl. Please stay safe until I can rid our forest of our enemies so we can live together happily once more." She leaned down to gently kiss the girl's forehead. "My sweet Moriana, we will be together again soon."

With that, the mother stood up, rang the doorbell, and stepped behind the bushes where she would not be seen, watching anxiously to make sure her daughter wouldn't be left in the cold.

Only a moment went by before the door opened and a woman stepped outside. She looked around before noticing the sleeping child. Kneeling, she picked up the paper on top of the small bundle and began to read.

"Don't worry, Viviana, I will look after her as if she were my own," the woman said into the dawn, before picking up the child, going back inside, and closing the door.

Viviana could not hold back her tears. She sat in her hiding place and mourned the loss of her daughter, barely able to think.

I know you will, Missy. She will be in good hands.

When she had regained her composure, she stood up and began to make her way back to the hole she had arrived in. Even through the pain in her ankle, she forced herself to run back to the portal, knowing if she looked back even once, she would not have the strength to leave her daughter behind. Every step felt like her heart was being ripped from her chest.

Chapter One

Canton, Ohio, 2024

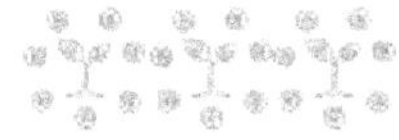

"Hurry up, Mori, or you're going to be late for school!" Missy called to Moriana Albright. She was seventeen years old, but not for much longer; she would be turning eighteen in two days. Finally, she was going to be an adult and would leave this godforsaken high school that felt like a prison. It was always getting in the way of her plant studies and hobbies.

She put on a black T-shirt with her favorite video game's logo on it—a leaf with a small piece missing. It was a really cozy game to play and helped her relax when things were stressful. Then she slipped on her black jeans, a blue sweater, and black socks. Mori walked down to the kitchen and sat at the table, but she barely registered what was going on around her, lost in her thoughts of coming up with a new tea blend. She loved anything in nature, but she had a special knack for brewing teas. Missy always called it her "potion making."

She only looked up when Missy put a plate of food down in front of her.

"Did you finish your math homework last night?" her adopted mom asked.

"It's fine, Missy. It's not like I need to know how to find the value of X in trigonometry. Besides, you know my dream is running Royal-Teas. The only things I need for that is how to convert measurements and weight to portion the tea leaves, and plant knowledge to grow them. I don't see the point of even going back to math class!" Mori explained as she picked up her fork to start eating.

"You need more than just that to get through life." Missy sat down with her own plate of food. "Your birthday is in two days. Eighteen is a big deal. Is there anything special you want to do to celebrate? We could have a small party and invite your best friend. What was her name . . . Jessica?"

"I haven't given it much thought. It's not like I have any friends other than Jessica. She's been nice to me and all, but I wouldn't call her a *best friend*. We barely talk at school and never talk outside of it." Mori sighed a little before taking another bite of her avocado toast.

"Well, we could celebrate. Just the two of us. Jason will be working that day, but I will be around. And your birthday falls on a Saturday this year, so you won't be in school." Missy smiled and took a sip of her coffee.

Mori had been with Missy and Jason as long as she could remember. When she was younger she called them Mom and Dad, but on her twelfth birthday Missy had sat her down and told her about her mom. She said that her mother loved her very much but had something extremely important to do. That day she'd decided to call them by their names because she'd wanted to believe her real mom was out there somewhere, trying to get back to her. Her adoptive parents seemed OK with being called by their names, even though they were the only ones Mori had ever seen as parents.

"Maybe. Can I think about it?" She looked up at her adopted mom. "Was he not able to get the day off work?"

"I'm afraid not, but you know Jason. He's a workaholic. Even if he had the ability to take the time off, he wouldn't." Missy reached over and moved some of Mori's curly red hair from her face. "Some hair was stuck to your freckles. It's too unique of a pattern to cover."

Mori pulled her head away a bit with an embarrassed smile. "Stop. It's fine if they're covered." The kids at school weren't exactly kind about the "crack" running across her face, and it made liking them much harder.

Missy shook her head as she stood up to take care of her plate and the dishes from breakfast.

Mori watched her move around the kitchen, thinking how lucky she was that Missy and Jason decided to take her in. They were wonderful people and amazing parents. She had heard horror stories of other kids in foster care growing up and knew how badly her life could have been if they'd turned her away.

"After school, I'm going to get some new herb seeds for my teas. I've been putting money aside from my sales for a long time, and I'm trying to make a new tea to help with migraines," she explained, before finishing her breakfast and getting up to get ready. If she didn't leave soon, she would be late for her first class.

"That sounds like a good idea." Missy finished the dishes and turned to face her daughter.

After slipping on her black mid-calf boots and grabbing her messenger bag, Mori called back to Missy, "I'm heading off to school."

"Have a good day."

She turned to walk out the door, giving Missy a carefree wave goodbye.

The walk to school wouldn't take too long. She was running late, so she decided to take a shortcut through the park. She paused for a moment to look up through the trees, barely able to see the outline of the brick building. There it was, Canton High School, the bane of her existence.

Mori was just passing through the playground when she felt the hair on her arms stand up. It was like static electricity all over her body. She couldn't explain it, but somehow everything seemed normal but out of place at the same time. It had been windy when she'd left the house, but now the air was still. It was too quiet.

She was absolutely sure she was not alone.

It wasn't abnormal for families to be here at the park, but never this early in the morning. This feeling was different. She felt someone was watching her, studying her. Mori counted to three in her head to reorient herself before turning around to scan her surroundings. Surely if someone was there, she would be able to see them.

Not good.

The only time she got a feeling even close to this was when one of her bullies was about to throw food or mud at her.

She was just about to turn back toward the school, when something flew past her face, missing her by inches. The shock jolted her into movement. She ducked quickly and jumped over the side of the half wall to hide in some bushes and take cover.

"What was that?" Her words were quiet and her heart beat fast in her chest from the sudden movement. Looking through the branches and leaves, she noticed a crossbow bolt sticking out of the top of the swing set frame. One of the chains to a swing had snapped from the force of the bolt, and the swing hung lopsided, now touching the ground. The fact that the metal had been broken so easily by a bolt scared her.

"Did you get her?" a man's voice asked.

She put her hand over her mouth to muffle her breathing. This was definitely not a school bully.

"No, you idiot! Don't you see the broken swing? That means I missed."

Mori had to force herself to remain calm and quiet. She was completely panicking on the inside. This was a second voice, and she could hear what sounded like a string being pulled back, followed by a click. Whatever they were shooting, they were about to try again.

"Maybe I have better aim. Don't forget, we need to bring her back alive," the first man said.

Mori took this as her chance to get a glimpse of what she was up against. She could see the two men fighting over their weapon.

"Tom, you have terrible aim! You wouldn't be able to hit a target one foot in front of you," the second man retorted.

"No I don't, Tim."

If the situation wasn't so serious, she would have laughed watching the two grown men grappling over a crossbow. She couldn't be sure if they were actually after her, but she wasn't going to stick around and find out. This was her chance to make a break for it.

Mori took off running. Thankfully, the grass around her hiding place muffled the sounds of her feet. She panicked when she realized she would have to run across the sidewalk to make her escape. The cement was not as forgiving, and the heels of her black boots made noise as she ran, drawing the attention of the two men who were after her. She wanted to look back and see if they were still fighting with each other, but her main focus had to be getting to safety.

"There she is!" Tim called out.

Mori heard the sound of a trigger being pulled, and another bolt whirred past her head. She wasn't watching where she was going and tripped over a plant, causing her to fall to the ground and land on her shoulder. Without thinking, she rolled to the side just as another bolt pierced the ground right where she was a moment ago. The fear of being impaled by the metal bolt caused her to freeze with fear for several moments, but it gave her a chance to look up at the two men again.

The tall and skinny man, who Mori guessed was Tim, had just stood up and was brushing off his clothes. They both looked like they were wearing peasant costumes from a renaissance faire, but their clothes were completely covered in brown dirt.

"Why did you push me?" the first man demanded.

"You would have killed the girl with your aim! He wants her alive." The larger man was holding the crossbow and trying to load it once more, but Tim still tried to wrestle it away from him. "I won't kill her. I will aim for her legs. Just give me the crossbow, Tom."

Their argument gave Mori another opportunity to run. Standing up, she heard the weapon go off, and another bolt came right at her. Her instincts kicked in, and she closed her eyes and threw her arms up to try to cover herself, trepidation forcing her to stand still. She could sense the air around her start to shift, but she was too scared to open her eyes to see what the cause was. Now was not the time to satisfy her curiosity for nature; she had to keep running.

Has it happened yet? Was I impaled?

She couldn't feel any pain, but she knew it could be from shock. Slowly, she opened her eyes to peek at her arms for blood and a wound, but she didn't see any. She was completely fine, which meant something had blocked what would have been her impending doom. Two thick tree trunks had come out of the ground to form an *X* in front of her, blocking her view of the men chasing her. She looked closer and saw the bolt they'd fired sticking out of one of the trees. As she lowered her arms, the trees retracted back into the ground, and the bolt dropped to the grass two feet in front of her.

Now that the trees weren't covering her anymore, she could see the two men running toward her. She didn't have time to think about what had just happened; she had to keep running. Her mind was racing as fast as her body. *What was that? Trees don't just pull out of the ground like that!* She had to be in shock. That was the only explanation. There was no way that two trees had moved at the exact time she'd raised her arms.

Mori stopped for a moment to steady herself against a tree. It felt like her lungs and legs were on fire as she ran for her life. She'd stopped for only a second or two, but the pounding of the men's feet behind her urged her on. As soon as her hand left the trunk, the tree sprang to life, and she turned her head just in time to see the men knocked back by the branches that were now swinging wildly behind her. When they got up to try to get past the tree again, it grabbed them and lifted them into the air.

What is happening? Trees can't just come to life! She shook off the thoughts swimming in her mind and forced herself to keep going. Should she go home? What if they tried to hurt Missy?

"What the hell is with this tree?" Tom shouted as both men struggled to get free.

"It's her bloody powers. We were warned about this, remember?" Tim responded.

Powers? Did he just say powers? What does he mean by that? She didn't have any powers. Things weren't adding up in her mind, but she didn't really have time to dwell on anything she was hearing.

A car horn in the distance interrupted her thoughts. Mori quickly took off running and turned down an alleyway, making it a good mile away before collapsing between two buildings. She had to focus on her breathing. A sharp pain in her side made her regret not working harder in gym class. She sat herself up against the bricks and cautiously peeked her head out to see if the two were still following her, smiling when she realized she could no longer see or hear them.

The tree must have kept them long enough for me to get away, she thought to herself. Knowing they were no longer behind her gave her the boost she needed to make it the rest of the way home. She needed to talk to Missy and figure out who those men were. She rolled her eyes with a light groan. Knowing Missy, she would have the police at their door as soon as she told her what happened.

Mori burst through the door and closed it behind her before she locked the deadbolt and handle and chained it before turning around to press her back against the oak wood. She knew she was safe now. Sliding down and sitting with her back against the door, she let out a sigh of relief. Home. Home was safe.

"What is going on? Why aren't you at school?" Missy asked as she came around the corner from the kitchen.

"I was going to school and I got this feeling that someone was behind me. When I tried to look, someone shot something at my head. I thought it was just one of the bullies, but it was two strange men. They started chasing me and shooting at me. I lost them in town, but I ran back here as fast as I could!"

Missy dropped the plate she had been washing and ran over to her. Mori rolled her eyes as Missy held on to her so tightly it was a little hard to breathe. "I'm so glad you're safe. We need to call the police." She started feeling around in her pockets for her phone, but when she didn't find it, she stood up and turned to head back into the kitchen. Mori grabbed her by the hand to stop her.

"I managed to get away and I'm fine. Besides, I don't really have a good explanation for how I got away. They were faster than me, and I . . ." Her voice trailed off as she remembered the tree that had ensnared them in its branches, as well as the two trunks that had come up out of nowhere. "Can you just call the school and tell them I'm sick, please?" She looked up at Missy with pleading eyes.

Missy stared at her for a few moments with tears in her eyes before nodding. "Yeah, I can do that. I'm going to call Jason to come home. I understand you don't want to call the police, but we really should report this. He will know what to do; he always does in a crisis." She pulled Mori to her feet and into another hug before wiping the tears from her eyes. "You do what you need to do to get comfortable. I will make you some tea, and we can stay in for today." She walked off to the kitchen and Mori headed upstairs. She could hear Missy crying on the phone and knew she was talking to Jason.

How did my birthday turn into such a mess?

As she walked into her room, she tossed her bag on the floor instead of hanging it up like she usually did. All the running had her exhausted. With a sigh, she took off her sweater, dropped it onto her chair, and fell back onto her bed, finally able to focus on her thoughts. This had been such a strange day. First the men chasing her, then the trees. She couldn't stop thinking about how they moved. It was like a sort of plant manipulation, if she could call it that. She remembered a time when she was running from the football team and a bush sprouted out of nowhere to hide her, and another time she was lifted into a tree to hide by the branch she managed to grab. At the time, she had convinced herself she was seeing things, but with all of this, it made her wonder.

She looked around her room and noticed one of the plants on her windowsill was not doing too good. "Oh no, why are you wilting? You were doing just fine yesterday." Getting up, she went to her window and gently touched the half-dead leaf and stem to examine it. As soon as she touched the plant, it turned green and started to grow rapidly.

"What the—!" She quickly pulled her hand back, but when she did the sudden growth stopped. *What was that?* It was like her touch gave it the energy to grow at an alarming rate. She held her hand in front of her to inspect it, and it looked like it always had.

Mori stumbled back and sat on her bed, trying to keep calm. This was way too weird for her, and her mind was beginning to swirl with confusion. All that stopped when she noticed the plant she had touched was completely healthy and had even started to develop flower buds.

"At least that made you feel better. Maybe I should touch all my sick plants," she joked with a smile as she looked at her plants on the windowsill to see if any others needed a healer's touch.

Mori was about to touch another plant, when Missy knocked on the door and came in holding a tray.

"Are you all right?" she asked as she went to place the tray of snacks on the desk. "I cut up some fruit and cheese for you. I kept the meat slices downstairs for Jason." She was wringing her hands together and for once looked unsure of what to say. "Are you OK, Mori?"

"I'm just having a weird day, that's all," Mori said before walking to her bed to sit down and pull her knees to her chest. "So many weird things have been happening. I'm not sure what to believe or do."

"Did something else happen? Other than you being attacked?" Missy asked curiously.

"Promise you won't think I'm lying?" she asked as she looked at her.

"Promise."

She took a deep breath. "Besides being attacked by two guys dressed in dirty rags, I also brought trees to life. I threw up my arms to block the bolt they shot at me, and two tree trunks came out of the ground and blocked it for me. And then when I ran, this tree in the schoolyard came to life and grabbed them with its branches like they were whips. All I did was touch it." She knew she was talking quickly, but if she stopped and thought about what she was saying, she might not get it all out. Still, saying all this out loud made her feel like a crazy person. Mori looked up at Missy and noticed her adopted mom didn't look back at her with eyes of disbelief.

"Trees coming to life? That is pretty strange, I will admit, but I don't think you're lying."

Missy put her arm around Mori and rubbed her shoulder. Mori's shoulders relaxed as she melted into Missy's arm, feeling relieved that she wasn't judging her. That was something she loved about her adopted mom; there was no judgment no matter what she said.

"Mori, I can't even imagine what you have been through this morning. Jason is on his way home, and we can all decide what to do. We already know you are staying home today, but we will have to see about the rest of this week. Either way, I will have to call the school to report this and make sure there is more security. There is no reason this should have happened close to school property."

"I want to go back tomorrow, but I don't want to run into them again and not have anyone there to help me. Will you drive me to school?" She smiled lightly as the woman nodded. "Thanks, Missy." They hugged each other again, leaving Mori feeling more comfortable. This was the one safe place in this world where she knew there would be no judgment or harm.

Mori was ready to walk into school the next morning, even though it had been a hard night. She'd mixed teas with Missy, and caught up on homework, which was great. With Missy driving her to school, her anxiety levels were down about the possibility of being attacked again.

"Thanks for the ride," she said after closing the car door. Thankfully the window was rolled down so she could hear her.

"I will stay right here until you get inside, just in case," Missy told her.

Mori walked up the steps to the school and looked back toward the park, trying not to relive everything from the day before. She shook her head and pinched herself so she knew for a fact she wasn't back there and she was OK. It really did happen—she had been attacked that close to school grounds and had run for her life. Even though Missy had called the police to report it, she couldn't give enough of a description of the two men for it to be helpful. At least there was a police report in case something happened again. For now, she knew she had to stop thinking about it and go inside the building.

She was so invested in the thoughts swirling in her head, she didn't notice the girl in front of her until it was too late. Mori stumbled when their shoulders collided, and she almost fell but managed to catch herself.

"I'm sorry. I didn't mean to—"

"You should be sorry!" the blonde-haired girl yelled. "I don't want your weird *freak* germs all over me." She shoved Mori, making her stumble once more but not fall over.

Now I'm not sorry. I talked to a bird one time three years ago and no one can seem to let it go.

She rolled her eyes and walked away. A senior in high school still being bullied? To Mori, all of this was childish.

"What a loser," one of the girl's friends said under her breath.

All Mori could do was shake her head and keep walking to class.

Her classes were boring, but she managed to get through the first half of the day. She ended up taking a small nap in math class since it was a review of everything they'd learned the week before.

Lunchtime was usually *so fun*. Almost every day, Mori would be tormented and bullied by the more popular girls, mostly because of her weirdly shaped freckle line and bushy red hair. She looked so out of place for someone who lived in the Midwest. Not that she would know anything else. She had been here her whole life.

"What is with you, carrot top? Why can't you figure out which tables to *not* sit at?" the leader of the popular girls said.

Oh, great, it's Ariana and her posse, Nissa and Danielle. There goes my quiet lunchtime, Mori thought to herself as she looked up at the girls.

"Seeing as how this isn't your usual table, I figured I would sit here." She smiled before turning back to her food. Her mixed green salad was covered in balsamic dressing with tomatoes, carrots, almonds, and tortilla strips. She also had a fruit cup, vegan cookies, and a leftover pasta dish from the previous night.

"Pathetic. No one wants to sit with you, yet you still eat that rabbit food." Ariana huffed.

"You need to eat meat. Humans are supposed to be carnivores, you know." Nissa was Ariana's righthand girl and always backed up her insults.

"Actually, we are omnivores, but no thanks either way. I will stick to my vegetarian lifestyle and will not partake in the slaughter of animals." The last thing she wanted was to have to defend herself to people who didn't want her around, so she just packed up her lunch and stood up. "Enjoy your table, Your Majesty," she mocked with an exaggerated bow and hand wave before walking away. That was when Ariana threw her pudding at her.

"There's no need to be such a messy eater, freckles!" She laughed along with her friends.

Great, now she would have to take another shower today. Instead of confronting the girls, Mori just walked off to the bathroom to wash as much pudding as she could out of her hair. It was pretty hard to do in a small sink when she had so much hair. She always wondered if her mother's red hair was as thick and unmanageable as her own, but she would never get to know. Missy and Jason had told Mori that she'd died along with her father. Neither of them really knew how. All any of them knew was that as a baby, Moriana had been left on their doorstep one morning with a letter from their friend, her mother. The note said that someone was after her and she would return for her child soon. She never returned, so they assumed that she was killed.

After drying her hair the best she could with the hand dryer, she looked at herself in the mirror. Most of the pudding had washed out, but unless she wanted to go home and take a real shower, there was not much more she could do. Damn, her hair was really frizzy now. It looked like a ball of yarn that had been pulled apart by a five-year-old throwing a tantrum. It had taken her two hours this morning to manage the frizzy mass of curls and heavy hair, and now it was a mess. All she could think to do was pull out her large light-blue scrunchie and put her hair up in a messy bun at the back of her head.

Leaving the bathroom, she went to the front of the school and sat on the stairs so she could eat her lunch while watching cars and people go by. Today was not what she'd had in mind after the craziness from yesterday, but the peace and quiet of being outdoors was nice.

She looked over at the park and couldn't help but think about everything from yesterday. The trees that had come from nowhere, and the big one moving on its own. She had never experienced anything like that. Had she imagined it all because of the shock of the moment? No, the plant in her room had definitely grown when she'd touched it. Something very strange was going on.

She laughed to herself before getting up and walking over to the bushes that lined the school steps. Mori reached out her hand to touch it, expecting it to move, but it didn't. Why wasn't it working now? All the plants she'd touched yesterday had seemed to come to life somehow. She shook her head and headed back to her lunch, laughing out loud.

Whatever. I probably hallucinated it anyway. Plants don't come to life, and I can't make them move. She pulled out her phone to check the time and quickly finished her lunch before walking back inside the school to finish out the day.

"How many sales do we have this week?" Missy asked as she entered the garage. Mori had been holed up in there since she'd picked her up from school, making teas for Royal-Teas, her online tea store. All these tea mixes were made by the mother and daughter duo. Mori put all the mixtures of herbs and fruits together, and Missy packaged them.

"It looks like we made twenty sales yesterday, which brought us up to sixty for the week!" Mori handed her the binder where they kept their current orders.

"Wow, that makes this our busiest week yet! I can't believe how much this business is growing. If we keep going at this rate, you will definitely be able to make this a career!" Missy exclaimed with a smile. She had always been supportive of Mori's dream, but hearing her say that made the young girl smile from ear to ear.

Mori was working on a custom order for a woman in Vermont who had constant pain from her arthritis. After adding the ingredients together, she took a scoop of the blend and held it up to her nose to make sure it smelled right before putting it back into the jar. Every herb and berry they used was grown by Mori in her greenhouse in the backyard, and she was always very careful to make sure everything was properly dried out. She kept all her ingredients in little jars that she set aside so they could scoop what they needed later into small bags for the orders. One thing was for sure, the garage smelled amazing now that they had taken it over to run the shop.

"We have joint health, muscle health, bone health, skin health, and digestive health all restocked. We should still have enough of arthritis tea, stomach tea, and common cold tea. Let's get to work." Missy smiled as they both started to package the teas to get them shipped out. They spent a few hours doing this while the two talked about celebrating her birthday, new tea mixes she wanted to try, and even school, but thankfully, there were no more questions about the men or the attack.

Chapter Two

Saturday rolled around faster than Mori was prepared for. She sat up in bed and stretched her arms, smiling when she remembered. Today was her eighteenth birthday. Thankfully it was the weekend, so she wouldn't have to worry about Ariana or her goons harassing her for the way she looked. Most of what had happened to her lately had been out of her control. Today, she was going to get something for her birthday with money from Missy. They were supposed to spend the day together, but her adopted mom suddenly had to work.

She would be headed to a few of her favorite shops. In town was a small flower shop that she ordered seeds through. The owners of Seedlings were always so helpful in finding the specialty seeds she needed for her teas.

She also wanted to stop by the local toy store to see if they had any new plushies in stock. She had been keeping her eye out for a stuffed spider. That was her favorite animal, though if she was talking about the more "normal" animals, she couldn't say she had a favorite. Most people picked dogs or cats, but really she loved all animals. To her, they were all cute. Though, bunnies were up there on the list, for sure.

After pulling on her dark-blue jeans and her favorite oversized gray sweater, it was time to head out. Most of the shops were downtown, so she had to take the bus to get there. The ride was rather relaxing, as there weren't many people on the bus.

Once she got to the downtown shopping strip, Mori walked around to enjoy window shopping until she figured out specifically what she wanted, though she suddenly got the same eerie feeling she'd had the morning she had been chased. She closed her eyes for a moment to focus on the sounds around her and knew someone was following her. Maybe two people, judging by the hurried footsteps that never decreased in volume even as she walked further down the road. She was so panicked that she didn't look over her shoulder; she just kept going, pulling her phone out of her pocket just to be safe. She had Missy on speed dial and was ready to call if necessary.

Making her way into the flower shop, she pretended to look at the merchandise but was really only using it as a cover to try to figure out who was following her. It was odd. She couldn't help but think she was just being paranoid after what had happened a few days before, but when she turned around, the men who had chased her two days ago were standing right in front of her.

"We finally found you," Tim said, and he tried to grab her.

Luckily, all her years of being bullied by Ariana and her friends made her spatial awareness better than most people's. Her reflexes kicked in, and she dodged and ran around him.

"Get her, Tom!" he shouted at the other man.

She ran right into a display of flowers, knocking it to the ground as she tried to escape. Thankfully, a few customers who saw the altercation stepped into the aisle to block their path so she could get away. Mori hightailed it out of the store. She had to think fast. Using the phone in her hand, she dialed Missy's number and hit the button to keep her on speaker while she ran.

Come on, pick up, pick up, PICK UP!

"Hey, sweetheart, how is your birthday going?"

"Missy, they're back!" she almost screamed into the phone.

Now was not the time for thinking. People could see her running. Some moved out of the way when they saw her coming, but she had to sidestep quite a few, slowing her down.

Mori could hear the panic in Missy's voice. "Where are you? Are you OK?"

"I'm downtown at the mall. They're following me! What should I do?"

Mori didn't know when the bus would be back, and she didn't have much choice but to try to hide. She ran down the sidewalk, wishing she had a hood to cover her hair.

"Mori, listen to me. Helena is going to call the police. Don't get off the phone with me, OK? I'm getting in my car now. I'll be right there!" The sounds of movement came through the speaker, as if the phone was being hit by something. Mori could tell Missy grabbed her purse, and heard the car door slam.

Looking over her shoulder, she realized the two men were getting closer to her, physically pushing people out of the way to get to her. Mori ran as fast as she could.

"I think they're going to catch me! *PLEASE* hurry." She was panting now, barely able to get the words out. The pain in her side from running this much was hard to block out.

Mori had no choice but to run across the street and try to lose them in the cars. She ran out into traffic and barely missed being hit by a car that managed to stop in time. What she didn't see was the SUV coming from the other direction. The driver lay on the horn and tried to slow down, but Mori was knocked onto the grill and fell backward onto the ground.

"MORI! Mori, are you OK? Mori, what's happening?"

Her head hit the cement with a sickening crack, and she could feel blood trickling into her hair. Everything around her started to go blurry while Missy screamed.

The driver started to open the door to get out, but Tom ran past and pushed the door closed while Tim picked Mori up and carried her in his arms across the rest of the street. Catching her while dazed was the only way they were going to be able to get her without a fight, and the two raiders had gotten lucky.

"We will make sure she is taken care of. No need to worry. You can go about your business," Tom told the driver before catching up with his partner. Mori was disoriented but could feel the man roughly fling her over his shoulder when they were out of sight of people. She lay limply and could just barely make out that they were walking toward the park.

"We need to get her back to the fae realm. Where is the opening?" Tim asked when the other finally caught up.

"We should be able to use any oak tree since we can make the portal ourselves. I think there is one just over there." Tom started walking in the direction of the tree.

Fae realm? What are they talking about?

They were speaking as if they were in some kind of children's fairy tale. She groggily thought of all kinds of fairies, neighbors, and mythical creatures dancing around a brightly lit forest. Mori was trying to think about how she needed to run, but she kept seeing images of magical beings racing through her mind. She was so absorbed in her thoughts that she didn't realize they had stopped right by a tree.

Tom took something out of his pocket, put it against the tree, and said something in a language Mori couldn't understand.

The tree trunk split open, and the base of the tree exploded with swirling blue light. Time seemed to stand still, and the sounds of nature were silenced, replaced with a low, electrifying hum that radiated out of the light. All Mori could think was how pretty the blue swirly thing was. The taller man stepped through with Mori still over his shoulder. She managed to keep her eyes open long enough to see the silver color of Missy's car pulling up and her rushing out of the driver's side. Missy yelled something, but it was fuzzy and she couldn't make out what it was. The girl reached her hand out toward the only mother she knew as she disappeared into the swirling lights. The other man followed after them, and the portal opening closed. The last thing she saw was Missy reaching for her, being so close but not able to get to her in time.

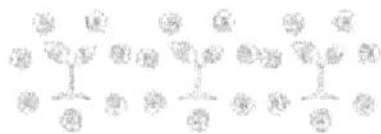

Everything that happened next was a blur for Mori. She was trying to find anything to reorient herself, but it felt like her head and her body were no longer connected. Her body was moving faster than she could comprehend, but her mind was stuck at a standstill. It was almost as if she was watching her body move throughout time without really being a part of it.

Mori's heart pounded in her chest as she desperately tried to make sense of everything she was seeing. The only thing she could make out, apart from the men, was a blend of blues, greens, and purples. She tried to focus on anything specific, but the colors continued to swim before her eyes, which refused to recognize anything comprehensible.

She couldn't tell how long they had been moving. Minutes? Hours? Days? Even the voices of the men with her merged into a cacophony of noises that made her head spin. She closed her eyes, hoping for a moment of respite from the chaos, but the darkness behind her eyelids only intensified her feeling of being lost. She opened them again, blinking rapidly, trying to clear the fog that had taken over her mind.

How would she ever find her way back? Every direction she looked was taken over by the same brilliant colors. The air around her started to grow thick and heavy, constricting her body. Nothing made sense. The world she knew was gone, replaced with a shifting maze with her trapped in the center.

In the time it took Mori to blink, the colors stopped, and she realized they must have arrived where they were heading. She heard a scraping sound before bright light flooded the space they were standing in, and she lifted her hand to her head as the sudden brightness caused a ringing in her ears that drowned out all other sounds. They were outside somewhere. The smells of grass and moss were everywhere around them. The incessant ringing that echoed in her mind moments before slowed, and she found herself able to focus just enough to make out the vague shapes of trees around them.

She jolted when the men began to speak again. Now that her senses were returning to her, it was as if all the sounds around her were magnified. Mori closed her eyes again, forcing herself to focus on their words and any clues that would help her escape from this nightmare they'd pulled her into.

"What should we do with her?" Tom asked. "It's going to be a long trip back to the boss."

"I don't know. I just know neither of us want to carry her the whole way. Maybe we should tie her up before we go any further." Tim gently sat Mori down on the ground, her back hitting something hard. Her elbows rubbed against something rough that felt like tree bark. The sound of things being ruffled around filled her ears, like he was digging for something in the bag.

Mori felt around on the ground at the base of the tree and closed her hand around a rock, knowing she would only have one chance to escape. Opening her eyes a tiny amount, she saw Tim pull a frayed rope from his bag, and when he leaned in to tie it around her feet, she jumped into action, hitting him over the head with the rock with as much strength as she could gather before getting to her feet and making a run for it.

"Get her!" Tom shouted, turning to chase after her. He didn't see Tim on the ground clutching his head in pain, and in his hurry to catch Mori, he tripped over his companion's outstretched leg.

Mori's heart pounded in her chest, each beat a desperate plea for escape. Her vision was starting to return, but things around her were still blurry. She had no idea where she was or where she was running to, but her instincts were screaming at her to get as far away from these men as she could. Shouts sounded behind her as she ran, but she didn't dare stop and look back. The trees around her became a blur of shadow and color as she ran past, hands grasping wildly to make up for her lack of vision. She was allowing the trees around her to guide her, unsure of what else to do.

Her kidnappers drew closer, their voices blending in a menacing cry. With a deep breath, she pushed forward, relying on instinct and sheer willpower to navigate through the trees. Without warning her feet fell out from underneath her, and she was falling, tumbling down the side of a cliff. She would never know where she found the presence of mind to cover her head with her arms and curl her body into as tight of a ball as she could manage.

For the second time that day, Mori felt her body spinning uncontrollably. Rocks and branches scraped against her skin, tearing at her clothes as she fell. Finally, with a bone-jarring thud, she landed in a small clearing, the impact knocking the wind out of her. She struggled to get to her feet as pain radiated through her body. Moving her hands over her arms and legs, she tried to assess any injuries she had. Mostly just a few scratches and bumps that would most likely form into bruises later. The pounding in her head told her she'd probably made her concussion worse as well. She struggled to her feet and looked up at the ledge above her. Thankfully it was only a few yards down the slope.

Mori gasped for breath while she stood still for a moment, realizing how close to disaster she had come. Pain radiated through her body, but she was alive. "Gotta keep going," she said softly, convincing herself to run once more. She knew she would need to find some kind of shelter that could hide her from her captors while she looked for a way to return home.

Mori wasn't sure how long she had been running. Her legs burned from the strain and her muscles screamed for relief. She braced against a tree, giving herself a moment of rest. Her lungs felt like they were on fire. Every breath she took came in a painful rasp, and she doubled over, finally noticing the sharp pain in her side. She never ran this much. Even in gym class she only ran the bare minimum, and her body was paying the price now.

She had made it a good distance away from where she had fallen but was still not really sure where she was going. Everything around her was starting to look the same, and she was worried she was going in circles. The last thing she needed was to get lost in these woods and give those men an easy target. She tried to focus on the task at hand—getting away from them so she could hide.

Looking all around her, she noticed a small, floating green light. It looked like it wanted her to follow it. This was the middle of the forest; how was there a light? Mori thought about all the strange things from the past few days and decided to trust her gut. After a brief moment of imbalance when her limbs refused to cooperate, she urged herself forward.

The light weaved through trees and bushes, but she was managing to keep up. Running out of necessity to escape the bullies made all this running she was doing now bearable. Within minutes she was staring up at a massive oak tree. Looking it over, she couldn't help but think that if she could just climb inside, she could hide from those men who had taken her away from her home. The sounds of her pursuers had faded completely, but she didn't allow herself to hope that she had escaped them. Maybe she could wait to see if they would pass by this area, and then run back to the . . . portal? Was that what that was? Mori shook the thought away before noticing the little light was gone. All that was before her was the tree. Was this what that light had wanted her to find? How could a tree possibly help in this situation? It wasn't like she could *actually* climb inside to hide. She reached her hand out absentmindedly, noticing for the first time the odd symbol that was carved into the tree. A little two-leaf sapling with a ring of circles around it. It was a simple design, but she had no idea what it meant.

Gasping, she quickly pulled her hand back as the symbol lit up a vibrant green color. The tree didn't move at all, but something did happen. It was like a seal was being broken as the seam of a door formed around the symbol, and she felt a strange sense of peace as little four-pane windows appeared and the symbol became part of the door.

Finally, her body betrayed her. Her legs gave out and she collapsed against the door. Every ounce of energy had been drained from her body. She needed sleep, she needed rest. With nowhere else to go, she waited for the tree to stop whatever it was doing and slowly opened the door.

This is no ordinary tree.

Chapter Three

Mori couldn't believe her eyes! The space before her was massive. She would never have assumed all of this could be hidden within a tree. She inspected the outside of the tree, her hand grazing the bark, trying to feel if the walls were solid or some sort of illusion. From the exterior it looked and felt like any other tree, but on the inside, she could barely comprehend what she was seeing.

Stepping inside, she instantly saw the books that were everywhere, bottles of different things, papers with notes scattered along the floor, and even a loft bed. It was definitely bigger on the inside than it was on the outside, similar to a certain police box she had seen on TV.

"Wow!" was all she managed to get out before her head whipped around at the sound of shouting behind her a bit in the distance. *Crap, gotta get inside.*

She shut the door after she got inside and looked around the room for some way to conceal the tree again.

"Hide! Go back to being a tree!" she shouted, but the tree did not budge. Mori put her hands on the door in the spot where she was sure the symbol was carved on the opposite side, and sighed. "Please, just shift back. I need to hide from those guys before they find me."

The tree vibrated beneath her hands as the door and windows started to disappear before her eyes. The door seal connected with the rest of the trunk to make one solid piece while the windows closed up as if they had never been there to begin with, sending her into complete darkness. Thankfully, the inside didn't change size at all. She couldn't see outside anymore, and she was hoping that meant no one could see inside. Reaching into her bag, she quickly grabbed her phone and turned on the flashlight, looking around for a light switch so she wouldn't kill her phone's battery.

Trees don't come equipped with electricity, genius.

She started searching the shelves that lined the room for a candle or lantern of some kind, but her search halted when she heard voices right outside the tree. Panicked, she clicked the flashlight off and pressed herself against the wall of the trunk.

"Her trail ends here," one of the men said. She could hear the shuffling of feet and knew they were checking around the tree for any trace of her. Mori held her breath, afraid to move or make any noise to alert them of her presence in the tree.

"I doubt she was able to climb it. The branches are too high. She must have gone that way," the other man told his companion.

"I'm thinkin' you're right. We should go. We can't let her get away. I for one don't want to have to tell the boss we lost her."

Mori held her ear against the spot where the door stood moments before and listened for the sounds of their footsteps moving further and further away from the tree. Within a few minutes she could no longer hear them. She sank against the tree wall, chest heaving as she tried to steady her breath and mind.

That was too close. I can't let them find me.

The fact that someone out there was trying to kidnap her was terrifying enough. She certainly didn't want to find out who their boss was.

She reached up and touched where the door used to be and spoke once more. "Please open back up and let in the light." The tree did as it was told, and she watched as a seam appeared from the center of the trunk, widening gradually to reveal the door once again. The symbol on the door seemed to pulse with life as the windows formed to allow the soft glow of the sun to illuminate the space.

Now that the danger had passed, she wanted to take in every detail of the magical space around her. It felt like her personal hidden sanctuary, the perfect blend of nature and whatever magical force resided there. She looked down at her phone to see if she had a signal. "Nothing. I can't call Missy at all."

Mori knew she should be scared out of her mind after the events of the day, but she couldn't help but feel calm. She closed her eyes and breathed in deeply. The air was filled with the faint scent of pine, wildflowers, and morning dew, and the window to her left offered a breathtaking view of the forest she had been unable to appreciate while running for her life. Moss and tiny glowing mushrooms sprouted from the branch that served as the windowsill.

A soft golden glow from the sunlight filled the space and made everything within warm and inviting. It was still hard to make out every detail, but something in the middle of the room caught her eye. A string of what looked like festival lights, with little balls every foot, hung around the room. She reached out to touch one, and all the lights turned on in a line along the strings around the room she hadn't noticed before. The brightness was almost blinding compared to the dim lights coming through the branches that composed the canopy above her head. It made everything around that much easier to see.

"I'm pretty sure I could spend all day here." She smiled and started to wander around, looking at the different things on the desk to her right. Beautifully cut pieces of wood created a cozy desk chair that invited her to sit with one of the many books that surrounded her. A small silver tray rested on the desk and held different bottles and jars of plants and herbs. Some Mori recognized, others were completely unfamiliar to her. Each one was labeled with a slip of paper and was attached with some sap on the back. As she reached for one particular jar labeled rosemary, she knocked over a few books onto the floor. An envelope fell out from one of the pages, and when she reached down to inspect it, she realized that it had her full name on it.

Moriana Albright, that's me, but what is it doing here? I have never been here before, wherever here is. She knelt to pick up the letter and sat down on the orange patchwork couch on the left side of the room. After pulling the letter out of the envelope, she unfolded the paper and started reading

My dearest Moriana,

I wish I could have more time with you, be able to raise you myself and teach you all about this land, but alas, I cannot. You were so hard to conceive, and I would give anything to be your mother through all the years of your life. Teaching you about plants, animals, and the fae that live here. For now, I hope this letter will find you once you are born. I imagine you will be quite the fighter since you are kicking my belly all the time.

I want to leave you my entire library and my journals of everything I have learned. It's a custom to pass on knowledge to the next generation so they may learn from our mistakes and the mistakes of the past. This oak tree will house it, and all you have to do to wake it up and put it to sleep is touch the symbol. Anything with this symbol will be of use to you and only you. There will be times when only you will be able to see this symbol, so don't blame those around you for not being able to find it.

My dear Mori, you are the next forest queen. Exciting! I know, I was quite excited when I got that news. As I write this, however, I am being hunted by the raider king. He wishes to take the power by force, but it is not up for grabs for just anyone. Only those in the bloodline of the first forest king can claim this power, and it is passed down to the firstborn child—you. Use this power well. If you don't feel it inside you yet, that means I'm still alive. Find me, Moriana, please find me. I hope I will get to meet you when you are all grown up.

With love,

Your Mother, Viviana

Mori couldn't believe it. Not only did her birth mother leave her a letter, but had asked her to find her so they could meet. Droplets fell onto the letter as Mori began to cry, unable to contain the mix of joy and sorrow. She had always wanted something from her parents, anything that would make her feel connected to them in some way. Missy hadn't told many stories about her mother and knew nothing about her father.

Placing the letter down on the couch beside her, Mori sat staring into space for a few minutes. Her mother's letter had given her some answers, but with all the things that had just happened, she now had more questions than she'd ever had in her life. Where were her parents? Were they still alive? She was trying to wrap her head around everything her mother had written.

Forest queen? That sounds like something out of a fairy tale. Is it too much to ask for a drama-free life?

Mori decided to stand up and explore around some more in the tree. While the oak was big from the outside, there was no way all of this could fit inside the trunk. The only explanation she could come up with was magic, but that was ridiculous.

This isn't a fairy tale and magic isn't real.

Stopping dead in her tracks, she remembered the words her mother had written to her. Symbols only she could use, fae, a mysterious power passed down through generations. Maybe all those things really did exist.

To her left, a dresser stood against the wall, with blue and green fabrics in a mix of textures sticking out of the drawers. Quite a few stones and crystals sat in front of books that each had rich leather-bound covers with intricate gilding on the spine. Below the shelves was a twin-size mattress on the floor that was softly illuminated, creating a comfortable and intimate reading nook.

She stood up and looked at the loft. There was no ladder to get up, just a couch for Mori to stand on and climb up. The bed was king-size, and a small player and a stack of CDs were on the little shelves that lined the walls, along with some empty ceramic bowls that looked handmade. They looked so out of place in a forest, and especially inside a tree.

She picked up a book and spent a little bit of time reading about some medicinal plants that could be found in the forest. They were new to her, definitely not from Earth. The intricate names of some of the plants were hard to pronounce, but she was determined to learn everything she could about them.

Mori stood up and stretched, realizing immediately that she had spent too much time reading by how sore she was from sitting that long. She sighed heavily before slipping the letter into her bag, pulling the bag over her head to rest on her shoulder, and turning off the lights. She stepped outside to look around, wanting to get her bearings and see if she could figure out how to get back home. Placing her hand on the symbol once more, she hid away the house inside the tree before turning, only to be met with the cold, unforgiving feel of a sword pressed against her neck.

The man holding the sword loomed above her, his piercing blue eyes calculating and unyielding. He wore a uniform of all green, with decorative embroidery of leaves and vines trailing down the coat. Sharp and alert, he stared at her intently. The long silver hair he had pulled back into a ponytail looked disheveled where it couldn't cover his long pointed ears. He looked like a typical elf from every fantasy video game on Earth. When he spoke, his voice was low and controlled, carrying an air of authority and menace.

"Who are you and how did you get in there?" he demanded.

Chapter Four

With each passing second, Mori felt the man's sword press closer to her throat. She threw up her hands instinctively, like she had done so many times when confronted by a bully. The reflex to make herself less threatening took hold of her body as she tried to make herself appear innocent.

"I don't know how I did it! I just touched the symbol on the tree, and it formed a door," she answered quickly. Her voice trembled as she tried to shrink away, but her back was pressed against the tree; she had nowhere to run.

The man eyed her up and down again before hesitantly lowering the weapon and standing up straight. "What's your name?"

"Mori."

His eyes narrowed before his body relaxed slightly, though he remained guarded, ready to move at a moment's notice.

"Really? Your name is Mori? How do I know you aren't lying?"

Mori didn't understand what he was getting at or why he seemed so interested in her. She thought for a moment before reaching into her bag, but stopped when the sword returned, only inches away from her again.

"Careful, it would be a shame to spill your blood all over this beautiful foliage because you were foolish enough to take me on." The man's fierce blue eyes never left hers, and the force of his stare caused the hair on the back of her neck to stand on end. Blood coursed through her body, mainly to her legs, ensuring she was ready to run at a moment's notice. The urge to flee was strong, but fear kept her frozen in place.

Mori took a measured breath. "I was just getting my school ID. I can prove my identity," she said while gesturing toward her bag. The man allowed her the space to slowly retrieve the card, which she then held out for him to view. "See? Moriana Albright. That's me."

Mori desperately hoped that by showing the ID, she could prove her real name. She trusted this would be enough to make him leave her alone, but as soon as he skimmed her name, the swordsman's eyes widened. In a flash, he changed from an attacking stance to dropping to one knee before her. She was almost speechless as he bowed his head while his arm crossed his chest.

"Please stand up!" Mori sounded panicked as she reached toward his arm, but he stood up on his own before she touched him.

He managed to gain most of his composure, but shock still overtook his face. "Surely you know you're the next queen." His voice was almost a whisper now.

"What are you talking about? I found a letter inside that had my name on it, and it said it was from my mom, but I have never met her. Who are you? Do you know my mother? What do you know about this tree? Can you tell me anything about my mother or father?" Mori was speaking so fast now it would be a wonder if the man could understand her at all.

"Slow down, Your Highness, you mus—"

"Don't call me that!" she snapped, more out of frustration than anger. "I'm not royalty. I'm just Mori."

"Apologies, Mori. I am Sir Duncan Wynett, and I'm captain of the forest queen's royal guard. Your mother sent me to find you. She said now that your eighteenth birthday has passed, you would find your way to the forest. I have been looking for days." He let out a sigh of relief. "I came to this area because your mother felt a surge of magic in this corner of the forest. She sent me to investigate it. I tracked a pair of footprints for a while, and before I knew it, I was standing in front of the tree house. Something in the forest told me to wait and watch, so I did." The corners of Duncan's lips curled upward slightly, and his facial features softened. "I know Queen Viviana would like to meet you."

Mori's eyes grew wide and her mouth fell open as she tried to process what he was saying. Viviana. That was the name on the letter in the tree house, and the one Missy had used the few times they'd spoken about Mori's birth parents.

"My mom wants to see me? Where is she? Can we go to her now?" she asked, not noticing she began speaking fast again. The possibility of meeting her mom was so overwhelming that Mori was having a hard time containing her excitement. She began to fidget with the hem of her shirt as she nervously looked down at her feet. Nerves took over her as the possibility of meeting her mother became a reality, but she was doing what she could to control her emotions and try not to sweat or fidget too badly.

"That will have to wait for a later time. It's quite far from here. For now, she wanted me to keep you hidden and safe. This tree may be a good hiding spot for now, but it lacks food. Do you know how to hunt or forage?" Duncan asked her.

"I know about plants. I make tea back home . . . Uh . . ." A thought dawned on her as she looked around the area and then back at the man before her. "Where am I, exactly? I was brought here by two men through a tree. There were all kinds of flowy lights, and then we ended up in the forest." She shrugged with a weak and nervous smile, not sure how else to describe what she'd seen and gone through.

"Sounds like you came through The Flow."

"The what?"

"It's the magical portal between worlds. It's called The Flow because all the colors make it look like you're traveling along a magical river from one realm to another." Duncan glanced around them before looking up and pointing. "See how the tree starts as one big trunk but then spans out into the smaller branches? The Flow does the same thing. At each one of the leaves is a different realm. There are only five known realms."

"That actually makes sense. So what realm is this?" Mori asked.

His gaze returned to the redheaded girl. "The fae realm. This is where magic was born." He paused before turning to his right. "I hear voices. We should go. It's best not to use the tree for now in case they decide to linger and never leave." Duncan ushered the young girl away from the area, hoping to avoid whoever was coming their way.

"It's probably those guys who brought me here. They lost my trail when I reached the tree, and left in another direction. When they didn't find me, they probably decided to backtrack." Mori was hoping that wasn't the case and that these voices were from friendly people, but when it came to her own luck, she seemed to be fresh out.

"We better hope not. I have a pretty good idea who those voices belong to. We need to move now."

The two made their way in the opposite direction of the voices, trying to sneak away so they wouldn't be discovered. While Mori had so many questions about what the hell was going on, she knew now was not the time to make a sound. This whole trip had been exhausting so far, and her head was still spinning from all the new things that had happened and everything she'd just learned.

They managed to walk for an hour without being discovered, climbing a cliff that overlooked the entire forest. Mori's eyes widened as she gazed out at the scenery before her. All the trees were tall, green, and filled with different fae life. She couldn't identify any of them, but the multitude of different-colored lights hovered above the trees, lighting up the forest with little rainbow-colored spirits floating around and birds flying overhead. There were a few larger winged creatures flying somewhere off in the distance that looked like fairies, but she couldn't see any detail from this far away. The mountains on the horizon were a vibrant orange and yellow. A river flowed in the distance, a long, deep sapphire blue winding through the trees, cutting the lush green. The beauty of the forest brought tears to Mori's eyes, and she had to wipe them away with her hand. Duncan held out a handkerchief for her.

"Everything you see is yours, Mori. You are the next forest queen," he said softly.

"Why would I be the next forest queen? I'm not even from this place. I'm from Earth and I'm a human." Mori wiped away more tears from her eyes as she continued to stare at the forest. She couldn't pull her eyes away from the beauty of it all.

"You are not fully human. Your mother, the current forest queen, is a fae and was born of the forest. Your father was a human who stumbled into this world. We lost contact with him a decade ago, so we don't know if he is still alive or not. I know your mother misses him terribly, as she does you. It's quite the story, how they met, but I will leave that for her to tell you." Duncan smiled softly, but it didn't last long, as the voices they'd left behind had caught up to them. Mori had been distracted by the forest and hadn't realized their pursuers were closing in.

"Well, what do we have here? It seems we stumbled upon the queen's guard captain. It's rare to see you out here." The gruff voice came from a muscular man dressed in a black-and-gray military uniform with gold accents. His black hair was cut short, and his piercing brown eyes were so dark that they reminded Mori of looking into a void. Several men were behind him, dressed in brown leather, similar to what Tim and Tom had been wearing when they'd kidnapped her.

Duncan drew his sword in defense as he stepped in front of Mori protectively, ready to strike should a fight break out.

"Leave now, Dairus. I just happened upon this girl and want to get her back to her territory." Duncan narrowed his eyes, and Mori did her best to stay behind him.

"Oh, how noble of you," Dairus said sarcastically, making the group of men behind him snicker. "It seems you can't quite grasp the fact that I don't care. My orders are to bring you in dead or alive. The king would like to—"

"There is no king! The forest is currently ruled by a queen!" Duncan yelled angrily.

"Don't get your loincloth in a twist, Duncy. We both know your queen will die soon, and with her offspring in another realm, there is no way for them to claim the throne. The power will transfer to the next of kin, which would be King Yorn. I suggest you get used to it." Dairus grinned widely as he took a few steps forward, causing Duncan to take a few steps back.

Mori grabbed the back of the captain's jacket as her foot found the edge of the cliff.

"I'm gonna fall," she whispered softly to the guard so he would know not to move back further. She peered out from behind the elf and was quickly noticed by Dairus. He studied her for several moments before a wicked grin formed on his face.

"It seems I was mistaken. I would recognize a royal's freckle line anywhere. The heir is here." The men behind him began to murmur among each other.

"Get them both and lock them up. They will make a fine addition to the prison." The raiders' general laughed after giving the command, signaling his men to surround the two by the edge.

Is this really how I die? Some punks will take us and probably will kill me? Now I really wish I had stayed home today.

The men suddenly lunged at them. She had been in fights before, but not something like this. Her body trembled as she gripped the elf's jacket tighter, fear threatening to consume her.

Swords clashed with each other as Duncan did his best to protect them both. He managed to push them off the first time, but that required him to take a step back. Her blood ran cold as she felt her foot start to slide downward. For a brief moment, she felt weightless and everything moved in slow motion. Two more swords were swung toward Duncan at the same time her sweaty hands lost their grip on his clothing. She would fall and there was nothing she could do to stop it. Just as quickly as the world slowed down, it suddenly felt like it sped back up, and now everything was moving too fast.

"DUNCAN!" she cried out. He turned to look at her as she lost her footing on the muddy cliff, arms reaching out for him, for anything she could grab so she could stay upright. Leaving his side was the last thing she wanted.

"MORI!" he called back, kneeling quickly to reach for her hand, but fell short by mere inches. His eyes widened at the realization that he'd missed her hand, panic overtaking his features.

"Follow the sapling to find what you need!" Duncan managed to shout to her before several raiders pinned him to the ground. The smiles they wore told Mori she had to find Duncan again; she had to free him from the prison Dairus had spoken about. Her foot managed to catch a small rock and stopped her for a second so she could watch as they pulled his hands behind his back and put something on them. The rock broke free, and she resumed her unwilling descent back down the crag. The last sight she had of the captain was the raiders pulling him to his feet while they cuffed him and dragged him away. He was shouting something, but Mori couldn't make out what he was saying. There was panic in his voice, and the trepidation on his face was enough to tell her that she needed to find him again, and fast.

Death was an unusual thing sometimes. It could come when you least expected it, or leave you alone when you expected it to cross your path. Sliding down this steep cliff, watching the only friend she had met in this forest being taken away, they were all things that led Mori to believe death was waiting for her. She had no idea what was at the bottom of the crag, but she hoped it wouldn't hurt too much when she finally reached it. Looking up and watching Duncan disappear felt like she was frozen mid-slide. The captain was calling out for her to follow the sapling. She couldn't process what that meant. Her thoughts were filled with a desire to find him and expecting to die soon all at once. Before the young girl knew it, she had reached the bottom, and what felt like the embrace of death finally took hold.

Chapter Five

D*rip.*

Just a little longer, Missy. School can wait. I want to sleep more. My head hurts.

Drip. Drip.

Something was falling on Mori's face, something small and wet. She was lying in the grass at the bottom of the rock face she'd slid down from.

When did it get dark out?

She opened her eyes briefly and noticed the sun had already set. There was no way for her to figure out what time it was or if this world even had the concept of time, but when she opened her eyes fully, she realized she had landed hard enough to knock her out cold.

Sitting up slowly, Mori held her head in her hand for a moment. The splitting headache was making her vision a little blurry just before the actual pain set in. She had landed on a flattened part of very long grass, thankful she didn't break any bones, but her muscles were sore and there were definitely going to be bruises. She forced herself to take deep breaths to calm down before trying to stand and look around. There was no way of knowing where she was, and she was not familiar enough with the forest to make her way back to the oak tree. A rather earthy smell filled her nose while her clothes, covered in semi-dry mud, clung to her body. With the rain starting to pick up, they were not going to dry any faster. Her gray sweater was ripped to shreds, so she pulled it off and tossed it onto the ground. Her pants were just as muddy and torn, but she didn't have a spare pair on her. The gray sweater she had been wearing was completely ruined. She loved that sweater. It was big on her and made her feel like she was being wrapped in a warm hug. She reached for it but stopped, not about to put it in her bag with things that couldn't get wet.

Come to me.

Mori whipped her head around in a panic as she looked frantically for the source of the voice. She couldn't see anyone, but after everything she had been through today, she wasn't taking any chances. Bending down, she picked up a rock from the ground near her feet and was poised to throw it if anyone came too close.

"Show yourself." Her voice trembled, but her hand remained steady.

Look at the cliff you just slid down. There is a cave beside it. It can provide shelter from the rain.

"Who are you? Why can't I see you?" she screamed.

I am a friend. It would be wise to stop yelling unless you want them to find you again.

The voice was deep and had a hint of a growl to it. Mori gasped as she realized that the voice was only in her head.

"Do I have any choice but to trust this?" The rain had picked up significantly in the minutes since Mori had regained consciousness. She wasn't sure she could take much more of the downpour. "How do I know I can trust you?" Mori turned to face the cliff, and sure enough, there was a small cave entrance close to where she'd fallen.

You do not have any other options but to trust me.

Mori's head was spinning once again and her back was killing her from her slide down. It wouldn't take long for her to get to the cave, her legs like Jell-O as she stumbled her way over to the entrance, feeling like they could give out at any moment. They took the impact of every rock and branch on the way down, and she could feel every aching cut and bruise they had received as a result. Even the scabs she'd gotten from her fall had reopened from her movements, and blood trickled out of her pant leg and onto the grass.

Finally, Mori reached the entrance. Stepping inside, she wrapped her arms around herself, her body shivering in a desperate attempt to warm herself back up. At least she was out of the rain and that was what mattered right now, but that was the least of her worries. Cold was one thing, but wet and cold could be very deadly. She desperately needed a fire right now, but that would have to wait.

Deeper, young one. I am further back.

Mori sighed, not liking where this was going. It felt like the start of a horror movie, going into the spooky cave because a mysterious voice said to. It seemed like the fastest way to die, going toward the voice and hoping it didn't belong to the serial killer.

"I have too much stuff to do to be killed right now by whatever you are, so this better be worth it." Mori made her way deeper into the cave, keeping her hand on the wall to guide her through the darkness.

She was surprised to find the cave walls were dry and solid, her fingers dislodging a few small rocks as she walked, until she came to a dead end. The room was a decent size and had no light just like the rest of the tunnel, but in the middle was a pair of glowing red eyes. They stared directly at her, and she did her best not to show how startled she was. Her heart raced as her palms started to sweat again. She had never come face-to-face with something so large and intimidating before.

The eyes were not coming closer or moving, just staring as if peering into her soul. After she released the breath she didn't realize she was holding, she put her hand on the wall to her left to steady herself. She pulled her hand back as the spot she touched let out a green light, and the whole room lit up with torches that lined the walls. *I'm never going to get used to this magic thing,* she thought as she took in the scene before her.

The creature in the center looked like a very large wolf, and chains gripped its legs, neck, torso, and muzzle. Each chain was attached to many parts of the cave's walls, ceiling, and floor, making the animal seem like he was trapped in a massive spider web. A quick glance to the left where her hand rested revealed the glowing green symbol she'd seen on the oak tree. A two-leaf sapling with a ring of circles around it.

Follow the sapling. Is this what Duncan meant? This symbol glows just like when I touched the tree, she thought before turning her gaze back to the wolf.

"Are you the one who has been calling me?"

I am. The wolf's mouth was not moving, yet his voice was loud and clear in her mind.

"How are you talking to me?" she asked as her brow scrunched together.

Telepathy. I can use it with you, but no one else can hear me.

Mori moved closer to the being and started to walk around him. She had to step over many chains to continue. The wolf was watching her intently, his eyes narrowing every time she got within arm's length of his fur. Touching him without knowing how he would react could be deadly. She only needed to see him in order to take note of the many scars his fur tried to hide. There were countless patches of bald spots that must have been from battles long past and injuries that never healed properly.

Does no one here actually know the basics of first aid?

When she was behind him, she noticed the sheer size of the beast in front of her. Mori had seen wolves before when she went camping deep in the woods, but the one before her had to be at least twice their size. "You are too big to be a normal wolf. What are you?"

I am a direwolf. I am much bigger and much stronger than the wolves you might see in the forest.

"Is that why you're chained up?"

No, I was chained up for a very different reason. His voice was heavy with regret and sorrow, almost as if he mourned the reason for his imprisonment. Mori glanced back at the creature's poorly healed wounds, some of them as long as her forearm. What could he have done to deserve those scars? This direwolf didn't belong here and they both knew it.

"I want to hear about it. I want to know why you were chained up." Mori made her way to the front of the wolf, stopping where both of his eyes could see her and within reach of his muzzle. She didn't feel afraid of him. It wasn't because he was chained up, but because something inside her said she could trust him. Hopefully that gut feeling was right.

My story is long, but I will do my best to tell it concisely. I was born a human from another world. I was brought here by mistake and had to make my way in this forest in order to survive. It took many seasons to start my own farm and be fruitful. One night, I found a wolf trying to kill my livestock, so I grabbed my pitchfork and chased it off. He attempted to move closer to her but was unable, and the chains rattled with resistance.

Night after night I would scare off this wolf. Shortly after, a dark-looking fae stumbled upon my farm. He offered me power that would be able to rid my land of the wolves permanently, but in exchange, all my possessions would be surrendered to him when I passed away. I had no children, and my farm was the only thing that was important to me. I could not lose it, and I would not need my possessions after death, so I agreed. He huffed quietly and shook his head a bit. *The strength he gave me was more than enough to keep the wolves at bay. For many moons, I did not see a wolf around my farm. One evening, I saw a wolf larger than any I had seen previously. I assumed that was the alpha of the pack and drove my pitchfork into it, killing it quickly. It was then that the forest king appeared and called out in anger at the loss of his companion. That night, he cursed me to live forever while still being able to die and to be reincarnated into this body. I was condemned to live in the form of his companion for the rest of my life. To ensure my punishment continued after his death, I would forever be forced to serve the royal bloodline. My memories were stripped from me as part of the punishment, except for the ones pertaining to how I came to be like this. He wanted to make sure I never forgot what I had done. The queen who took the place of the king once he passed locked me up in this cave.*

He paused for a moment as he stared intently at her, his body relaxing in the chains as his face and eyes softened. *I could feel the connection to you when you appeared in the forest. I can tell you are destined to be the next queen. The current royal grows weak and will likely pass soon.* His head drooped when he spoke of the queen. The sounds of the stiff chains rattling from his movements echoed inside the cave, his gaze returning to her after a few moments.

May I know the name of my new master?

Mori stared at him in stunned silence. He used to be human, just like her, and was brought here suddenly just as she had been. She knew exactly the kind of confusion he must have felt being thrown into this world and not knowing what was going on. He had to figure out how to survive in an unfamiliar place with no help. Everything he felt, she could feel, not just because of their similar circumstances, but she wondered if she was feeling his emotions through the bond of his curse. Should she trust a creature she just met, a chained-up and cursed one, nonetheless? Not to mention that he still hadn't told her why the queen imprisoned him. Something felt off, but she wasn't sure what it was. She would need to press for more information.

"That was quite the story. I don't even know how to respond to it. I can't blame you for wanting to protect your farm, but to curse you like that is pretty harsh. Especially for an accident. How do I know you're telling the truth?" Mori sighed as she pushed some hair from her face to give herself time to think. "As for your question, my name is Mori. I don't know anything about this 'next forest queen' business, but it's not the first time I've heard of it since arriving here." She looked up at the wolf curiously. "What's your name?"

I cannot remember my name as part of the curse. The only thing I remember is how I was cursed and locked up. Since you are my new master, you can give me a name if you prefer.

"Master? I don't know about that. I don't like how it sounds." She had to admit, the thought of having a wolf, no, a *direwolf* companion did sound really nice, and it was on her list of fantasies she wanted to happen in her real life.

After thinking for a few moments, Mori came up with a name that she felt suited him. It was from a German legend back on Earth of a man who sold his soul to the devil for knowledge and power, which was a pretty similar situation to that story he'd told her.

"Your new name is Faust," she proclaimed proudly.

Faust . . . he mused. *Yes, that name will suit me. Release me, young queen, and I shall serve you faithfully until your last breath.*

That sounded ominous. She raised an eyebrow as she crossed her arms over her chest. "How do I know you won't do something like kill me the moment you're free?" she asked skeptically, eyes narrowing.

I am unable to hurt you as per my curse.

"So, it could be five minutes or five hundred years. It's a roll of the dice," she muttered to herself, trying to calm her nerves with a light-hearted joke meant only for herself. Still, her plan was to play this cautiously.

The king felt I would betray him if I had the ability and has since made it impossible for me to harm any of his lineage.

Guess that will have to be good enough. It's not like I have much of a choice. I can't leave him chained up here for all eternity, she thought.

Mori ran a hand through her long red hair, still unsure of what to do, but her mind went to the sapling that lit up the room a little bit ago. She paused before going to the symbol.

"You told me how you came to be cursed, but not why you were chained. I need to know the truth before I set you free in the forest."

Faust closed his eyes. Whatever the reason, he could not look at her while he admitted it. *The one who cursed me forced me to do unspeakable things. I could not refuse him. The next in line chained me up in this cave as a punishment, and I have been here ever since.*

His eyes opened and seemed to plead with her to believe him.

"That's not fair! The person who forced you to do those things should have been punished, not you." Mori knew what it felt like to be shunned for things that were out of her control. With that statement she knew the bond between Faust and her was sealed. She whipped around and marched to the symbol that was still glowing on the cave wall and placed her hand against it, knowing she was doing the right thing.

The sapling light changed from green to red and the ground beneath her started to vibrate. Mori looked down at her feet, watching some of the smaller rocks start to dance where they lay. The chains rattling made her look back up at Faust just in time to see the metal cuffs around the direwolf's legs and body come loose one by one. Metal clanged to the ground, and the chains from the ceiling hung straight down, lifeless and unmoving. The air was still as the wolf was released and began to stretch and move his stiff joints, the sounds of them popping and cracking echoing off the cave walls. Then the moment he had been waiting centuries for happened. His collar unlocked and crashed to the ground, making everything still. Mori realized she could no longer feel the ground vibrating.

Faust lowered his chest to stretch his front legs before shifting to raise his chest and lower his back end to stretch his back legs. The sounds of his joints cracking filled the cave once again before he stood straight, eyes staring down at the young girl. Slowly, he moved his front paw to take a wobbly step, almost losing his balance. He hadn't moved in so long that his sense of balance was lost on him. Step by wobbly step, he walked over to Mori, his head above her own now that he was much closer. She could feel his breath and smell the stale scent of stomach acid in the air.

"When was the last time you ate?" she asked as she fanned the smell from her face.

I do not know. It has been several centuries since I have left this cave. Faust lowered his head. *Hold out your hand.*

That was very suspicious to Mori, and she wasn't sure she should really trust this wolf. She hesitantly lifted her left hand, figuring if she was going to be hurt, it would be on her nondominant hand. Faust lifted his large paw and attempted to give her a scratch on the hand with his claw, but no matter how hard he tried, he was unable to break the skin. He then bit her with his teeth, startling Mori as she tried to pull her arm free. After only a few seconds, Faust let go to reveal a saliva-covered arm with no marks or blood. She inspected her arm curiously before cleaning it off and looking up at him.

You see? I am unable to hurt you, not even a scratch. I will not be able to kill you, nor would I want to. You are the one who has given me a name and my freedom. I am forever in your debt. The large wolf knelt to bow to her as his eyes closed. As he did so, Mori could see just how skinny the wolf was. He had been starving for so long and was now free to actually live his life, hunt, run, and eat. Any anger she had about him attempting to bite her immediately disappeared.

"OK, well, that settles that. I guess I have a wolf companion now. We should find you something to eat. You're really skinny." Mori laughed nervously before turning to walk back to the entrance of the cave with her new companion in tow.

Thankfully the rain had cleared up by the time they reached the entrance to the cave. Mori breathed in deeply. The whole area smelled like fresh rainfall, and that was a scent she lived for. She stepped out of the cave and turned to look up at the crag she slid down, her face souring. The mark she'd left from sliding down had been washed away. There was no trace of it, and it now looked like the rest of the cliff face. That also meant the footprints from Duncan's captors were likely washed away as well. It would be difficult to track him even if she were an expert at it.

"I slid down this cliff before the rain. It's even more muddy than before," she said sadly.

Is there anything in particular you need from up there? Faust asked as he gazed up at the cliff as well.

"Well, there is an oak tree up there that only I can open and expose as a house. I remember there being drawers and a large bed in there, so hopefully there are some clothes and maybe a way to shower." She looked down at the ground by her feet. "That's also where Duncan was taken." She fidgeted with the muddy hem of her shirt as her body shivered. She was still wet from the rain and covered in mud. Faust walked up to her and pressed his warm fur-covered body against hers in an attempt to warm her up.

Sir Duncan Wynett?

That got Mori's attention quickly as she whipped her head toward the wolf, eyebrows raised and mouth hanging open slightly. "How do you know Duncan?" she asked with a surprised tone.

Duncan is bound to the royal bloodline and was named captain of the royal guard and the personal protector of the ruler by the first king. He was around long before I was cursed and forced into servitude, as well as when I was locked away, Faust explained. Mori was listening to the wolf but was also staring up at the tree line the elf had disappeared through.

"Why would he stand around and let that happen?"

I did not see him much after I was cursed. I do not think the king who cursed me liked him much and had sent him away. The queen after him must have brought him back right before she chained me up in that cave.

Mori wrapped her arms around herself, doing her best not to cry at her predicament. All this time Faust had been alone for so long, constantly starving and being chained up for something he'd had no choice but to do. It reminded her of her own loneliness after coming here. Duncan had been nice to her and she had started to get used to his presence, but now he was gone and she wondered if she would ever see him again. Faust nuzzled against her cheek with his muzzle, making her giggle lightly and pet his head.

"Thanks, Faust. I needed that. I'm not used to being alone. Missy and Jason were very protective and hovered over me a lot."

Who are they? Faust asked. *Those are not the names of the current queen and her mate.*

"They're my adoptive parents. I was born and raised on Earth. My mother wasn't able to keep me and raise me, so I was given to Missy and Jason by her. At least, that's what they told me. Something about her being in danger with some criminals. I don't have the full story. They've always treated me like their own child, though." Mori frowned. She tried many times to get answers from Missy but was never able to. Coming to this forest and reading that letter from her mom had her questioning everything and guessing about the real story of her adoption.

That is quite far from the truth. You were born here. I felt your presence when you were born and knew I wanted to meet you one day. I thought you had died when that connection was severed many, many seasons ago. At least, until recently. You are fae, Mori. You belong here. Faust looked up at Mori and noticed she was still staring up. He followed her gaze to the top of the cliff. *I can get us up there. Climb on and I will see if I can follow your scent back to the tree.*

Mori hadn't expected to hear that. Why would a wolf willingly allow a person to ride them like some sort of steed? Then again, this wolf did say he would serve her. Without a word, she climbed on his back, and Faust easily jumped up the steep cliff as if it were level. Mori hung on tightly to his fur all the way to the top, doing her best not to fall off. As soon as they reached the top of the cliff, he started to sniff around the grass.

There are traces of your scent on the ground, he said after a few moments. *The scent of your companion is faint due to the rain, but I should still be able to track it.*

"That's pretty incredible, especially after the heavy rain."

My sense of smell is stronger than an average wolf's, and I can use my own magic to enhance it, he explained.

"Follow his scent. I want to know where he was taken. We can always prepare ourselves and return to the place to get him if we're outmatched." Mori was thinking a little more rationally now, and looked up and down Faust's skinny frame, knowing there wouldn't be much they could do to save her friend without some sort of magic or weapon. She had yet to figure out the extent of her own magic, and she only managed to do anything out of defensive reflexes.

Faust sniffed the air to get a better sense of direction before taking off running, heading northwest. Mori was deep in thought the whole time they were moving. She couldn't believe how much had happened in the span of a few hours. Her train of thought was leading her down a dangerous rabbit hole. Depression threatened to overwhelm her when she thought she might never see Missy, Jason, or Duncan again. She would be stuck here all alone with a wolf she barely knew, constantly wondering if he would betray her.

Faust's voice in her mind yanked her from her thoughts.

There is blood on the ground, and bodies.

Mori looked up before getting off Faust once he stopped moving. Blood covered the ground quite heavily, and much of the surrounding foliage was cut and trampled on. Even without the bodies scattered around, the forest showed signs of the struggle that had happened here. There were nine bodies in total, none of which belonged to Duncan. She released a sigh and turned to look at Faust.

"He isn't here. We should keep following his trail before it disappears. It's good to know he was fighting back." The girl climbed back onto her companion, and they went off when he got the scent again.

It didn't take as long as it felt to get to where the trail ended. Mori found herself once again at the familiar large oak tree that had the sapling symbol on it.

Faust sniffed around some more and moved in a circle around the tree before finally stopping. *The trail ends here,* he told her, and waited for her to get off him so he could continue to sniff around.

"DUNCAN!" Mori called out, her hands cupped on either side of her mouth. Worry and fear filled her mind when she didn't get a response right away. What if he was really badly hurt? What if he died? Where did he go? "Duncan!" she called out once more before she heard her wolf companion start growling. She whipped around and saw Duncan holding his side and covered in blood.

"I don't recommend shouting like that. They may come back." The elf chuckled a bit before coughing.

"Duncan . . ." Mori ran to him and hugged him, tears flowing down her cheeks as the man put one hand on her head and the other around her.

"It's OK, Mori. There's no need to worry anymore." Duncan patted her head and then glanced over at the wolf, who was now calm and sitting. "Why do you have the cursed wolf with you?" he asked, a brow raised and curiosity filling his tone.

"I found him at the bottom of the cliff in a cave." She looked up at her friend. "He said he serves the royal family and only I would be able to hear him."

"That is actually true." Duncan sounded surprised that the wolf was willing to be truthful with her. "He's cursed to be an immortal direwolf, with conditions. The queen who locked him up told me he will still feel pain and die but will come back to life after some time."

Do not talk about me like I am not here, Faust growled, but only Mori heard his words.

"What did he say?"

"He asked us not to talk about him like he isn't here." Mori let go of her friend and turned to the wolf. "Thank you for finding Duncan. I couldn't have done it without you, Faust." The girl smiled and went to hug her wolf companion, even scratching his head and chin. She watched in surprise as his body shrank to that of a normal wolf size and his tail happily wagged despite his protests.

"Faust?" Duncan asked with a confused tone.

"That's what I named him." Mori smiled. "Who's a good boy?"

Do not treat me like a common dog. I am—Oh, yeah, right there! The wolf lulled his tongue as he started to pant happily and closed his eyes as he enjoyed the head scratches. This made Mori laugh.

"I think you like it because it's me. If it were anyone else, you would bite them."

That is very true. I would have bitten their arm off and chewed on the bone. Duncan groaned in pain and held his side. Faust quickly moved to the right to catch him as he suddenly fell over. *We need to get him somewhere safe and treat his wounds.*

Mori nodded before she went to the tree and placed her hand on the sapling symbol. "Please open your door to let us in."

You only need to touch the tree and it will open. No need for formalities, Faust told her.

"Oh, I didn't know that." Heat rushed to her cheeks as she looked away sheepishly even though she had no reason to think it would work without the spoken words. That was how it had opened before, and she was doing her best to figure things out as she went.

The oak tree formed the door and windows before the trio. After Mori pushed the door open, they all went inside. She moved Duncan onto Faust's back to be carried inside and to the couch where he could lie down while the wolf sat by the door to keep an ear and eye out for raiders. The elf grabbed a first aid kit from under the couch and opened it to get to work on his wound.

"I didn't know there was a first aid kit in here," Mori said as she pulled the desk chair close to assist.

Duncan removed his cut-up jacket and button-up shirt. He was toned and muscular and covered in scars from previous battles. "I have spent a lot of time here with your mother." He took out some gauze to start cleaning himself up. "I need to take you to see the queen. She is eager to meet you," Duncan told Mori as he worked on cleaning himself up.

"My mother wants to see me?" Mori asked hopefully. She wasn't the best with first aid, so she didn't know what to do to help.

"Yes. It's been a rough couple of years, so when your presence was detected in the fae realm, she sent me to find you," Duncan explained before using his teeth to rip the medical tape. Mori inspected the items in the kit. When she looked back up, Duncan was smiling at her. "Your mother was quite fond of your world after she stumbled there. This medical kit was something she brought back with her, and it has been really helpful."

Mori stopped listening to Duncan after he started talking about the medical kit. She was so lost in her thoughts about how she imagined her mother looked and acted. Then the intrusive thoughts wormed their way through her mind. What if she wasn't good enough? What if her mother was disappointed in the person she became? Mori didn't think she could handle being rejected by her mother a second time, especially now that she was old enough to understand what was going on.

"Mori," Duncan called to get her attention, which snapped her out of her thoughts and made her look up at him. "We will start our journey to her in the morning. Get some sleep for now. She is a bit of a distance away, but it shouldn't be too long of a trek if we keep moving. You might want to change clothes before sleeping. There should be some in the drawer on the far side."

After she made her way to the dresser, she opened a few of the drawers and found some clothes. She changed out of her muddy ones and into some clean ones. The green shirt and white pants looked like something one would find at a renaissance faire back in her own world. She was just happy they fit her well. Her hand went to her hair, but she was unable to run it through because of the caked-on mud.

"Is there a place where I can wash my hair and face?" Mori asked.

"There is a river nearby that you can use to wash." Duncan looked the girl up and down after she finished getting dressed. "All the clothes in here are your mother's. You look just like her." The guard captain moved to lie down on the smaller bed once he had unburdened himself of his sword and slipped on a clean shirt from the lower left drawer of the dresser.

Mori nodded and went to the door. "Come on, Faust. I'm gonna need someone to keep an eye out in case those raiders come back. Plus, you need to find some food." She opened the door and the two left.

Thankfully, they were left alone when they went to the river. Mori was able to rinse out her hair and wash all the remaining mud off her body, and Faust caught some small prey to eat for the first time in a very long time. After washing the blood from his mouth, they returned to the tree. Once they were inside, she closed up the tree and climbed into the loft bed. It was huge and had a lot of space. Faust moved to the couch on the first level and lay down. This day had not gone how she'd imagined it. Being kidnapped, knocked out, finding a wolf, and meeting a friend were not on the list of things she thought would happen today. Mori was exhausted, and as soon as her head hit the pillow, she was asleep.

Chapter Six

Mori woke to the sounds of movement and scuffling. Looking down into the main area of the tree, she saw Duncan was already up and had the lights on. She sat up and yawned as she rubbed the sleep from her eyes. It had been a day since she'd gone missing, and she was worried about Missy. How was she holding up? What about Jason? Both of them had to be worried sick about her disappearance. She pulled out her phone to see if she had a signal, but there wasn't one. To conserve the remaining fifty percent of her battery, she completely shut it down. It was all she could do for now until she could find her way back to the human world.

"Morning," the elf said from below when he heard her moving around. "I have breakfast ready, though it's not much."

The girl moved off the bed and sat on the couch next to Faust to eat some cut fruit and nuts for breakfast. The only slice of meat went to Faust, which Mori was fine with. She wasn't going to eat it. The wolf was quite happy to get some food, and she wondered how many times over the centuries he was imprisoned that his body had succumbed to starvation.

How far is the queen? I can faintly sense her, but I am unable to pinpoint her location, the direwolf asked Mori. That had the elf looking over at him with a furrowed brow.

"What's wrong with you this early?" he asked before taking a bite of his own food.

"Faust isn't angry. He was asking a question," Mori explained. "He wants to know how far away my mom is. He can't pinpoint her location." She picked up an interesting-looking dragon fruit and cut it open to eat the insides. As she took a bite, the juices and some seeds ran down her chin. She used her sleeve to clean up, gaining a disgusted look from her elf companion.

"She's holed up in a cave in the Faenor Mountains. We were able to find one hidden there to make a base that would be too tough for the raiders to find." Duncan covered his mouth and shook his head at Mori using her sleeve once again. "You should really learn some manners if you want to be a good queen."

"What's wrong with the way I'm eating? Am I supposed to starve? Is that what ladylike is these days?" Mori asked defensively. She didn't know why he was saying that and didn't know what she was doing wrong, but it felt like a personal attack.

"I'm talking about using your clothes to clean yourself. That's not what they're for. Not to mention that if you do that to *royal* attire, you will be in a lot of trouble with your subjects." He crossed his arms.

"Fine, I will find a napkin." Mori groaned and looked around for one.

"What's a napkin?" Duncan asked.

"It's a square piece of paper or cloth used for cleaning your face and hands or whatever spilled," she explained.

Duncan handed her a clean square of linen from his pocket. It looked like a cloth napkin you would find at a fancy restaurant. "You mean a cleaning cloth?" he asked.

After she wiped her face with it, she smiled. "This is called a napkin where I'm from. You could just call it that."

Duncan looked dumbfounded by the name but just brushed it off when Faust got their attention. Faust moved to where the front door would be and growled, though Mori heard it as he was shouting, "Hey," at them.

"All right, all right, we're coming. Keep your fur on." She laughed as she revealed and opened the door. Duncan groaned behind her, but she didn't really care. Faust went right outside to sniff around a bit, disappearing past a tree. Mori had a good idea of what he was doing and just turned her attention to Duncan when he spoke.

"Sniffing for danger? I didn't think he would be that diligent about keeping you safe." Duncan chuckled lightly.

"Why wouldn't he?" A confused look crossed Mori's face.

"It was rumored that he tried to kill the spouse of the queen who imprisoned him. I don't know if it's true, as I was away on a mission. I returned home and was told he was locked up for attempted murder of a royal." The elf shrugged as he got his gear on so they could head out.

"That doesn't seem like the Faust I know, but then again, I haven't known him for long. He can't hurt me, that has already been proven, but I will still try to be careful." This was all new to her, but after the demonstration he had given her in the cave, she wondered if it was even possible. She had a feeling only Faust and the royals knew he couldn't actually hurt his master. Though that same protection didn't extend to spouses. This was something she would have to talk to her wolf companion about at some point. With a sigh, she waited for the other two to get ready before they all set out for the Faenor Mountains.

The long trip to the mountains started out smoothly, but things took a drastic turn after only a few hours of travel. Mori had been listening to the natural sounds of the forest while learning about the different creatures they came across. Plants were more her specialty, but she wanted to expand her knowledge, especially if she was meant to be queen of this place one day. The hardest part was finding the fae creatures. Duncan told her that since life in the forest had become more dangerous, they did their best to stay out of sight.

She was so engrossed in what she was doing that she almost didn't notice Duncan and Faust slowing their pace. Pausing her stride, she looked at them with confusion, only now realizing things were eerily quiet. Definitely too quiet for a forest in the middle of the daytime. Not even a bird was making a sound, as if most of them had flown away. She saw one take off when she looked up. Something felt off, and that same feeling she got when she was being stalked returned to her. The hair on the back of her neck stood on end, and her whole body was tight with goosebumps, as though something fierce was closing in on them, but she wasn't sure where from. Faust's ears shot up suddenly before he crouched down and bared his teeth, not daring to make a sound, ready for anything that could come.

"What's there?" Mori whispered.

Danger. Something big is nearby, and it smells like blood, he communicated to her using their mental link.

"I don't need a translator to know what he just said. I sense it, too." Duncan drew his sword and had it at the ready. The forest grew stiller for several moments before the sound of heavy footsteps echoed in the trees. Large tree being ripped from the ground and crashing into other trees followed, making Mori take a step closer to her wolf. Faust and Duncan glanced at each other with wide eyes for a split second before the elf put his sword away and ran to a large bush, pulling it open to make a hole for them to fit. At the same time, Faust grabbed Mori's wrist with his teeth and pulled her to the bush and pushed her inside it. Duncan followed the wolf inside, and the three of them ducked down quickly before he placed a hand over the girl's mouth to stop her from speaking.

"Don't make a sound. Nothing," he whispered, the serious look in his eyes telling her she absolutely needed to listen to him, that whatever was out there was out for blood. With wide, scared eyes, she just nodded quickly in understanding so the elf would remove his hand. He wasted no time in using a little bit of magic, but nothing seemed to happen and Mori didn't dare ask what he did.

It was only mere moments later that a deep growl filled the area as the sound of large footsteps thudded closer. She could feel the vibrations in the ground from the heavy footfall. Mori didn't move, and she didn't have to in order to see between the leaves of the bush at whatever it was that made the other two panic and hide. The thing in front of them was at least fifteen feet tall and had a deer skull for a head with large antlers on top. Short black fur moved with the light breeze around its shoulders, down its torso, and over its stomach. The leg fur acted as pants to cover the rest of its body from the hips down, going all the way to its hooved feet. Patches of missing fur that appeared to be pulled tightly over its bone-thin body exposed ash-gray skin. Its fur-covered arms were long enough to drag on the ground beside it with every step. Attached to those arms were long, skinny fingers and sharp, bloodstained claws. The creature had a few arrows sticking out of its chest and back, and the fur was matted from the dried blood.

It looked like it didn't have eyes in its skull, but that was not the case. The right side had nothing in the eye socket, but when it turned its head to sniff around, Mori was able to see a bright red eye in the left socket. It looked like it was trying to find something by scent, but was having a hard time locating it. The beast turned back in the direction it was walking, the same direction *they* had been walking in, to continue tracking its prey.

Faust and Duncan waited several minutes before even attempting to move the slightest bit to see if the creature was gone. When the footsteps from the creature could no longer be heard or felt, they left the bush and helped Mori out and to her feet. Some leaves were stuck in her hair that she had yet to notice.

"What was that thing?" she asked with a terrified tone.

"*That* is Bob. He's some kind of skull-headed spirit that has lived in the forest an insanely long time. Almost as long as I've been around. He is very dangerous and will eat anything that moves," Duncan explained.

"Bob? Really? You expect me to believe that someone named a terrifying monster 'Bob'?" Mori finally noticed the leaves when one hung down in her face. While she listened to Duncan's explanation, she pulled them out of her curls.

"We aren't entirely sure what he is now, but he is a former human who has been consumed by his greed and weakened by extreme conditions, like cold and hunger. Originally, we thought he was highly intelligent, but Bob seems to have an empty skull. He runs on pure instinct and will eat anything that moves. My guess is he was knocked around too much during battles and sustained a lot of head injuries. I don't know if that will affect a spirit creature, but it seems to have made him more brawn than brains." Duncan shivered at the thought of ever being caught by the beast.

The fae folk say Bob stands for "beware of beast," which is very accurate, Faust added, making Mori shiver as well.

She laughed nervously. "A creature that will eat anything and used to be human. That's totally not terrifying *at all*. Complete nightmare fuel, for sure," she muttered under her breath before remembering what she wanted to ask. "Uh, Duncan, what magic did you do in the bush?"

"It was a barrier that would block our scent. Bob follows his nose because his vision isn't currently the greatest, as you could tell by the missing eye. That allowed us to actually hide from him," the elf explained as he looked around again to make sure they were actually alone.

I had a feeling something was following us, but until things got really quiet in the forest, I did not know for sure.

"That is something you should speak up about," Mori informed the wolf as she looked at him, but then turned her gaze to the elf guard. "Same goes for you. If you sense something is wrong, speak up, even if you are not sure."

The guard captain nodded in agreement, and the three started back on their way.

"Before we reach the mountains, there is one place we should stop at on the way. There is something I need to show you," Duncan told Mori.

During their walk, the sounds of birds and fae had returned. That comforted Mori since the last thing she wanted was to run into that human-eating beast again. Especially because *she* was human. Around midday, they reached their first destination. Mori could feel the crunch of the brown and yellow leaves beneath her feet, making her look up to see the sickly and dead trees and plants that lined wherever they were. The wilted plants were hard for Mori to witness, as she loved to see them thrive.

As they continued to walk, they entered a space that looked more like a throne room, but it was in just as bad of condition. The pews facing the front were broken, rotted, and covered in dead vines. The whole place looked like the plants were allowed to grow out of hand because no one took care of them. Then eventually, there was no nutrition left in the soil to make them grow bigger, so they died. Dead vines covered four large pillars in the open room, and at the far end, opposite where they stood, were a few steps that led up to a dark throne with moss covering a lot of its crystal and stone features.

Behind the throne was a massive round picture made of different colors of leaves in various stages of death that were in the shape of a woman who looked similar to Mori. However, she didn't have freckles across her face. They were on the woman's left side in the shape of a small swirl. The picture made the woman look sick and weak as she frowned with her eyes closed. It was heartbreaking to see the state the place was in. Mori was a little startled when her foot stepped on a thick vine, making a loud crunching sound, and it crumbled to dust from the pressure.

"What is this place?" Mori asked as she walked more toward the center, stepping over many stems, and spun around slowly to see everything. The ceiling looked like glass, but it was made of something else that she could not place. It wasn't cracked despite the fallen tree limbs covering it; the glass was just dirty. She looked up at the two side walls that had balconies for people to stand and overlook the throne room, but a few of them were broken to varying degrees. The area was void of fae, no doubt due to the decay and death that consumed it. Mori could feel the desolate aura within the place. It was no wonder the creatures of this realm steered clear for fear they might be next.

"This is the royal throne room. The vegetation here directly reflects the health and status of the current ruler, your mother. She's not doing well, which is why I need to take you to her soon, but I knew you needed to see this first. To help you realize why you're so important to this forest," the elf explained as he watched the girl. "Without the royal magic, the forest will wither and die, just like the throne room. Whether you want to accept it or not, Mori, you need to lead us to peace. Keep the spirits alive." It was hard to believe that she, a young eighteen-year-old girl, was to be the next forest queen. Mori found the idea ludicrous. She had never stepped foot in the forest until two days ago, but it appeared this was her new reality.

"So, my mother is dying and I have to take on her responsibilities?" she asked with a somber tone.

"I'm afraid so."

I have only been able to faintly feel her presence. It has been fading fast as of late. Faust walked over to Mori and nuzzled her arm. She petted him with her hand a few times, realizing the action was keeping her calm.

"And we will, but I wanted to show you this place for one other reason." Duncan walked over to the throne and motioned for her to sit. Mori gave him an odd look before making her way over to the throne. After clearing away some of the dead foliage, she sat down. Surprisingly, a few of the crystals sparked a dim light inside.

"What's happening?" she asked.

"I was confirming something." Duncan moved to stand in front of her. "The crystals are linked to the royal magic. When it's time to choose a successor, they will light up when the person sits on the throne. Even though it's dim, it would have not done anything for anyone else."

Mori stood up and turned to look at the crystals, watching as the light slowly dissipated. "Am I the next ruler simply because of my bloodline? I don't have the royal magic."

It is not much of a reason for someone to rule, but that is how it has always been, Faust communicated as he walked around the throne to sniff it.

"It's hardly a good reason for someone to rule," Duncan repeated, not knowing Faust had already said it, "but that's how it is around here." Mori snickered, but the elf ignored her. "Once the next successor is born, they hold a small piece of the royal magic within them. If you were not meant to be the next ruler and your mother was pregnant, then it wouldn't glow for you. That is not the case, but it has happened before."

Mori nodded in understanding, and Faust nuzzled her again.

We should keep going.

"Let's get back on the path. We have a long way to go."

Mori did her best to stifle another laugh and looked up at Duncan once she calmed herself. "We should get back to walking. I want to meet her while she's still alive."

Duncan side-eyed her curiously and silently before the three of them left the throne room. Mori walked alongside Faust, keeping one hand on him, petting him absentmindedly. The more she learned about being a royal, the more she became lost in her thoughts. Hopefully her mother would have more answers for her.

The dimly lit dusk sky was a sight to behold. The array of colors that it brought to the forest was something Mori felt everyone should experience in their lifetime. Hues of orange, red, pink, and yellow fell over the trees, mixing with their green color. She wished Missy and Jason were here to see it with her, and wondered if she would ever see them again. Duncan and Faust insisted she had magic, but she had yet to figure out how to use it. Her thoughts raced from one thing to another, and before she knew it, she was wondering if time was a concept here in the forest and how it differed from time on Earth.

"The sun is already setting. Are we getting close? I have a bad feeling about being out at night." She checked her surroundings in an attempt to figure out where they were, but to no avail. She simply didn't know enough about the geography of the forest. Her legs were sore from the long walk, and she could smell her own unpleasant scent from the lack of bathing. When she'd washed the mud from her hair in the river, she hadn't thought to fully submerge and bathe, but now she wished she had.

"Yes, we're close. It's just up ahead," Duncan told her as he pulled some bushes to the side so they could leave the forest path. The ground looked as though it had not been walked on for some time, if at all.

"Why are we leaving the path?" Mori asked as she slowly moved toward the bushes. Just past the bushes were more bushes, and she had no way to tell which direction to walk in. She sighed heavily and groaned a bit.

"If the cave was on the path, we would have been discovered a long time ago. This was the only way we could ensure the safety of our queen." Duncan moved past Mori to push away some more bushes that were in the way as he pressed forward. Mori understood immediately why the raiders had never found this place. It looked just like any other dense area in the forest. When she was through, Duncan released the branches. Keeping the bushes intact helped conceal the path to the cave.

This is a good hiding spot. No one would think of going through the foliage to find a cave off the beaten path, Faust communicated to her through their connection.

"The dense plants make it a really good place to hole up when in danger. That's for sure," Mori agreed as they continued on. She looked over the side of the cliff when she got the chance and saw just how high up they were, before turning her head to look up with a small sigh. There was still a much longer way to go to reach the top. She was just glad they weren't so high up that the air was thin. It would make climbing that much harder than it already was.

A high-pitched cry startled Mori out of her thoughts. It filled the air with a wailing sound, one of mourning and despair. All three of them stopped in their tracks and covered their ears with their hands.

"What's that sound?" she asked as her body started to tremble.

"That sounds like the cry of a . . ." Duncan's voice trailed off, and he glanced at Mori.

"The sound of what?"

"A banshee," he answered, worry filling his voice.

"What does that mean?"

Someone nearby is going to die soon. They are able to sense imminent death and are considered a bad omen. We will not be able to see the banshee, but we are hearing her cries of sorrow, Faust explained, making Mori look at him.

"Who is going to die? There are only three of us here? How do we know which one of us is going to die?" She could feel her heart racing in her chest, and a cold sweat started to creep in. Her breathing shallowed as she waited breathlessly for the answers to her questions.

"Quiet your worries, Your Highness," Duncan said with a soft, calming tone, although his face looked pained. "We're here. The queen is just through there." He walked up the cliff and pulled some vines to the side to reveal a cave entrance. Faust had walked up to Mori and nuzzled her side to try to calm her.

"Don't call me that," she bit out as she walked by, hating that no one answered her questions. It was an unsettling feeling, not knowing anything about the world she currently lived in. Hearing that her mother was so close startled her from the uncomfortable thoughts and pulled her back to reality. She glanced at her elf companion before she walked cautiously into the cave behind Duncan.

The smell was the first thing she noticed. It was musty and stale, but still full of moisture. The stone walls were covered with bits of moss growing along the spots where streams of water would flow after heavy rain. Dim torches lit the tunnel, and she noticed the ones further inside the cave barely had enough fuel to keep them ablaze. As they drew closer to where they were going, her never-resting heart pounded in her chest more and her sight started to blur. The rush of blood inside her head made Duncan's words sound muffled. Mori shook her head in an attempt to clear the fog in her mind so she could hear him better.

"What did you say?" she asked, her voice a little unsteady.

"She's right in here. Her Majesty is eager to meet you." Duncan's voice echoed off the walls of the cave as he spoke. At this point, Mori's heart had been beating so fast and for so long that it was actually starting to hurt. She couldn't stop the cold sweat that covered her skin, and her mouth went dry. There wasn't enough saliva to wet her lips, but she still tried. Just the thought of being able to see her mother, *meet* her mother, was very overwhelming, but she had a feeling she was going to love every second of it.

"Bring her here," a woman's raspy voice said right before a coughing fit.

Coughing? Why is she coughing? Mori's thoughts drifted to the decayed throne room once more. *Duncan said she was ill, but surely this won't be the only time I meet her . . . Is this why Duncan seemed to be pushing us to walk faster?* Mori thought as she continued onward.

The moment the elf moved to the side, she saw a woman with the same bushy red hair as her own lying in a makeshift bed. Furs covered her body to keep her warm, and royal-looking attire covered the parts of her body that could still be seen. She had bright green eyes, the same as Mori, but they had different freckle patterns. Hers was the same as the portrait in the throne room. It started at her temple, then came down past her eye and made a small swirl on her cheek. This line of freckles was very unusual and almost seemed as if it were painted on. The only thing that was the same was their color.

"My darling Moriana." The woman sat up in the bed with some help from an attendant. "I have been dreaming about this day for so long." The fragile-looking woman was doing her best to smile.

Mori could tell she had been bedridden for a long time. She lacked muscle mass and was even paler than Mori, who was practically snow white.

Mori was searching her memories for anything on this woman, wondering if there was something from when she was an infant to remind her of what her mother looked like, but nothing surfaced in her mind's eye. She had to be sure this really was her mother instead of just blindly accepting the reality before her, but something seemed familiar. A scent that had made its way to her senses brought buried memories out. Spring roses after a rain shower and the scent of an oak tree filled her nose. Whenever she imagined her mother, this was the scent that came to mind, even if she had not smelled it since she was an infant.

"Mom?" she asked hesitantly, slowly taking a few steps toward her.

"My daughter." Viviana beamed and opened her shaky arms.

Mori ran to her and flung her arms around the woman's shoulders as tears filled her eyes. She had finally found her birth mother. This one simple hug melted away all the hurt, pain, and loneliness she had felt her entire life. While she loved her adopted parents, she felt so different from them, but now she had found the one person she wanted to meet the most in the world.

Mori pulled away after several moments of hugging, tears still falling down her face, knowing there were so many things she wanted to talk to her about. "Mom, I have always wanted to meet you. I imagined this moment for so long."

Viviana used her thumbs to wipe away the girl's tears as her face softened. "I've dreamed of this moment as well. You are even more beautiful than I could have ever imagined."

Mori felt the warmth spread from her torso throughout her body. To hear her mother thought of her, too, brought a sense of calmness and relief. But there was something she needed to know, a burning question in her mind that she knew she needed the answer to.

"I have to know, Mom. Why did you leave me on Earth? Why did you abandon me with Missy and Jason?" Her heart ached to ask such a thing at a time like this, but she knew she would never be able to fully enjoy the moment if she didn't know the reason.

Viviana let out a deep breath and nodded in understanding. "We were in danger. I knew that I could keep you hidden within the oak, but I also knew that was no life for a child. Being raised to never leave the tree or experience everything beautiful about Albright Forest was not what I had in mind for you." She coughed a bit as the attendant brought her some water. Viviana took a few sips before continuing. "I tried to come visit, but the war was devastating the entire forest. I had to protect my realm; that is the duty of a royal. I needed to make this place safe for you when you returned."

Mori could see just how tough it was for her mother to talk about this, but she was glad to hear it. "What about just visiting me so I could get to know you?" she asked, her voice filled with sadness as her fingers fidgeted with the hem of her tunic.

"By the time I felt it was safe enough to leave for a short time, I took an iron bolt to the shoulder." Viviana pulled her clothing down off her shoulder to expose the wound. It was purple and black with veins traveling away from it like she had been severely poisoned. "This happened about five years ago." She pulled the shirt back up. "I might be the queen, but I am still fae, so iron is deadly to me. What I didn't know at the time was that some of the iron had broken off when it hit my bone and had been traveling through my body. I could feel my powers and health slowly slip away from me. It has not been easy to keep up with fighting back the raiders. Before I knew it, I could no longer open a portal to your world. Now, I'm completely bedridden and not strong enough to leave this cave. I knew one day you would make your way to this forest, and the moment I felt your presence, I sent Duncan to find you. I told him not to return without you." The queen coughed a bit after speaking.

"My queen, you must rest," the attendant said. There were horns on the side of her head and a long tail behind her. She quickly moved to Viviana's side and knelt. The woman had long black hair that cascaded around her white horns and down to her waist. Her warrior's uniform was similar to Duncan's, but in black, with her hooved feet exposed from the bottom of the pants. Gear hung from a black leather belt that rested at the bottom of her red underbust corset she had cinched around her waist. Those red eyes complemented her caramel skin, and Mori found herself staring. She was absolutely beautiful, even if Mori had no idea what species she was. Duncan must have seen the confused look on her face, because he moved to kneel beside the princess and spoke in a low voice.

"That is Lorem Epsum. She is a satyress who was rescued from a raider prison a few years back. She has sworn her life to the queen in return. I guess she used to travel with a circus before she was captured." Duncan stood up and took a few steps back when he had finished speaking.

Mori nodded in understanding, not taking her eyes off the cow-like woman. Lorem looked over and flashed a small smile at Mori, and she realized she had been staring a little too long. Heat flooded her face as she looked down at her hands in her lap while she sat on the bed, completely embarrassed.

"I will rest when I finish speaking with my daughter. I have waited a very long time for this." The queen shooed everyone away with her hand, making her attendant leave the room. "That includes you, Duncan."

The elf sighed and stood up as he placed a hand on Mori's shoulder for a moment. He then bowed slightly to Viviana with his right arm across his chest and left the room as well.

"You can wait with everyone else, Faust. I'll be OK." Mori gave her wolf's head a gentle pet before he turned to leave as well. Turning back to her mother, she waited anxiously to hear what she had to say. Her heartbeat had relaxed when they'd been speaking normally, but now it was starting to quicken a bit with nerves. They were alone, just the two of them, mother and daughter for the first time.

"My dear, I'll be honest with you. The iron has taken its toll on me. I'm not strong anymore and I know my time is soon. Once I pass, the magic that makes me the queen of this forest will pass to you. It is an age-old tradition for the firstborn child to receive the magic, but I must tell you something about yourself. Something that has never happened before in our bloodline." Viviana grabbed the glass of water to take a few sips again. When she finished, she put the glass down and looked Mori in the eyes. "You are half-human."

Mori did not know what her mother was saying. She already knew that she was a human. "What do you mean? I'm just a human, always have been."

Viviana shook her head. "You're not fully human. I'm fae and your father is human, which makes you half."

Hearing such a thing was strange, and somehow even stranger the second time. Mori felt her heart quicken as her hands began to tremble in her lap. "Why would that be an issue?"

"The fae have always been untrusting of humans, or anyone from outside their realm." A small smile formed on the queen's lips. "Your father was different and he showed me that, so I brought him here with me. Even though you were born here in the forest, the fae see your bloodline as tainted." Viviana coughed a bit, her complexion growing paler as she spoke a little faster in an attempt to explain everything she needed before they parted ways permanently.

"Is my father still alive? What is his name?" The questions left Mori's lips before she had a chance to decide if they were even important at this moment.

"His name is Renfred Williams. I don't know if he is still alive. He was taken prisoner seven years ago and I . . ." The queen's words trailed off as she looked down sadly at the thought.

"You haven't been able to find him," Mori finished, her words full of sorrow. The whereabouts of her father felt like they were within her grasp, but then were suddenly taken away. She had wanted to meet both her parents and had just assumed her father was dead.

Viviana shook her head. "I spent my remaining years looking for him before I was brought here to live out my final days. He's not fae, so I'm not able to sense his location."

"Your letter mentioned the raider king and the raiders who are trying to take over the forest. It's likely he's with them." Hopelessness filled her mind.

"I forgot I wrote that letter. It was so long ago. Moriana—"

"Mori. Just Mori."

The queen paused for a moment before continuing. "Mori, there is something you must know about the raiders. They are humans from the human realm where you've been living. They're descendants of a group of humans who were brought here as prisoners of war during the first royal's reign. They faced abuse and were forced into slavery by the fae. Then one day, the humans were able to escape. I don't know where they went, and no other royal has been able to find them. I believe they managed to leave this realm. I think this siege on the forest is revenge for generations of violence against their people. The raider king convinced the others to follow him, claiming that he is the rightful heir to the royal magic, though he has not been able to prove it." Viviana grabbed the glass and drank the water inside.

"I haven't been able to find their stronghold and I'm not sure why. But no matter what happens, I need you to stop the raider king and take your rightful place as queen of the fae. Your people may turn their backs on you at first, but you must keep your head held high, just as royalty should. You will win them over with time." Viviana moved some hair from Mori's face to behind her ear. "My precious girl, no matter what happens, I will always be around for you to talk to. All you will have to do is look inward and speak to me just as we are now. I, and many others, will answer your call and come to your aid. I have detailed everything you need to know about being the queen of this forest in my journals inside the large oak you found my letter in. I call it the tree house." She giggled a bit before coughing.

"Don't speak like you're about to die. I'm not ready to be queen yet. I just got you back in my life. I don't want to let you go." Tears streamed down Mori's cheeks as she listened to everything. Her mother told her all this information like it was nothing, and she was not sure if she was up for the task of taking on the raider king.

"Even if you aren't ready now, you will be. Work with Duncan to hone your skills with magic. Remember to follow the sapling. Anything that responds only to royal magic will bear the insignia. It will always point you in the right direction." She smiled as she adjusted herself to lie down on the bed. "There is a poem that has traveled down the royal bloodline that tells of where the Hammer of the Royals is located, but the weapon has been lost since the third royal, our first queen.

'With the saplings as your guide,
find the place where it resides.
Lavender bloom alights the course

to this power's sacred source.
Where it flowers night and day,
regal boon will find your way.'

"Remember this poem and hopefully one day, you will be able to do and find great things." Viviana started coughing up blood and was struggling to stop. This made Lorem come running to her aid. "I love you, my dear Mori," the queen managed to get out.

Mori leaned over and gave her one last hug before standing and taking a few steps away from the bed. "I love you too, Mom."

Duncan walked to Mori and gently guided her out of the cave where Faust was waiting. Tears stained her cheeks even after she wiped them away with her sleeve.

"Do you think she will be OK?" Mori asked with a sniffle.

Duncan shook his head. "I don't think so. I have watched her deteriorate over the last five years. I'm just glad you were able to meet her before her time," he said dejectedly.

I do not want to give false hope, either. Faust stood beside the girl and nuzzled against her hand so she would pet him, and she did.

Mori took the time to walk to the edge of the cliff they were on that overlooked the majority of the forest. It was so beautiful in the twilight. Little fae creatures were scattered around the different groups of tree canopies, all shining different colors. Duncan had called them Deva fae because of their size and habit of lazily hovering around. She was trying to process everything that just happened. As if the last few days hadn't been enough, now she had to wrap her head around becoming the queen of an entire realm of people and creatures she knew nothing about. On top of that, she would become queen because her mother would be dead.

She decided then and there. It didn't matter if she didn't know them; there was no way she was going to let anything bad happen to them or this forest. A spark of determination ignited inside her as a fierce protectiveness flooded her mind and body. Everything she laid her eyes on was worth the fight that was to come.

After a deep breath, she turned to look at the other two. "We should get going. I have a lot to learn before—" Mori's eyes suddenly widened as she stumbled and fell to her knees, her heart now pounding in her ears. She felt like she had just been punched in the gut and chest at the same time.

MORI! Faust called out as he quickly ran to her.

"She will be fine, Faust. It reached out to her," Duncan told him as the wolf looked back at the elf with a confused look.

Mori was trying to find the words to explain what she had just felt, but they were caught in her throat. Looking up, she noticed some sparkling green mist flowing out of the cave and making its way to her before balling itself up right in front of her. Instincts took hold as she lifted her hand to gently touch it before it shot straight into her chest, pushing her body back until she was on the ground.

Duncan frowned but then smiled sadly. "It was time," was all he said before standing up to take a step back. Faust followed his lead and stepped back as well.

Mori was lifted into the air as her body and eyes started to shine bright green.

"She's gaining the forest queen powers," Duncan said.

A massive shockwave burst from Mori's body across the entire forest. Birds scattered from the treetops and flew away. The bright green acted as a beacon to the forest that the next royal had arrived. In only a matter of seconds, she landed back down on her feet and the glow around her body dissipated to nothing, but her eyes continued to gleam. When the world around her stopped spinning and she was able to get her bearings, she looked up at the other two.

"Forest queen powers? Does that mean . . ." She looked back toward the cave, the light in her eyes finally starting to dim as they returned to normal.

"Yes, that means you are now the queen." The elf took a knee to bow to her, and the wolf bowed his head. This freaked Mori out until she remembered what her mother had just told her. Her face paled as her eyes widened.

The new queen quickly ran inside the cave. "MOM!" she cried out, stopping when she entered the room. Lorem had just laid the blankets over the top of Viviana's head. "No . . ." She breathed out and walked over to where her mother's body lay and knelt before taking her mother's hand into her own. There was no holding back the flood of tears that poured out of her. She was not ready to lose her mother. "I will make you so proud, Mom." The tears that made their way to her jaw fell onto their hands. She felt like she had just gotten her mother back and now had to lose her all over again. And this time, she knew there was no way to find their way back together, not a second time.

"I will prepare the body for a royal funeral. We burn the bodies of royals to make sure no one can harm them again," Lorem explained, and wrapped up Viviana more in the blankets before walking outside to give the girl some privacy.

Mori was alone once more, left to grieve the passing of her mother. She needed this time to mourn and process so she could move on and do her duty as the new queen and protect the forest. Though, those were the last things on her mind currently. The only thing she had ever wanted in life was just taken from her once more. She laid her head down on her mother's hand and sobbed uncontrollably, letting all her pain out.

After several minutes of crying and then taking a few more to compose herself, she emerged from the cave to see Duncan, Lorem, and Faust all bowing before her. She wasn't sure she would ever get used to this. Her puffy red eyes looked them over as she sniffled.

"What are your orders, my queen?" Duncan asked.

After a deep breath, she gave her first command as the new queen. "I need to stake my claim to the throne and gather support to go after the raiders. I may have just gotten here, but I won't be forced into submission. This is my home now and my land to protect. I refuse to let it fall into the hands of someone so undeserving." The determined look in her eyes and voice said it all. She was going after the raider king.

Chapter Seven

Mori couldn't believe that it had been two weeks since her mother's passing. The funeral planning had taken an emotional toll on her, and there were days when she couldn't get out of bed. Grief was a cruel thing to have to endure after finding the one person you wanted to meet all your life. Even today, Faust and Duncan had had to physically drag her out of bed. Mori had fought them every step of the way but eventually ran out of energy to keep it up. After that, Lorem had come in to help her get dressed, but Mori was already in the only black attire she could find. They were just regular clothes because she didn't have anything formal.

"I'm sorry, I don't have anything nice to wear for the funeral," Mori said, and turned to see Faust wearing a green bowtie and Lorem in a brightly colored green-and-tan warrior's uniform with her usual red underbust corset.

"Why would you wear black?" the satyress asked with confusion.

"On Earth, it's customary to wear black for a funeral." Mori looked dumbfounded by the strange use of bright colors for something so depressing.

I am told we wear bright colors to funerals because we are celebrating their life, not their death. Faust sat down and let his tongue hang out as he panted happily, his tail wagging behind him.

"I told Faust-y Wowsty here all about the colors he should wear," Lorem said with more of a baby voice, and it made Mori cringe. That was definitely not how one talked to a centuries-old wolf.

It is a weird feeling to be spoken to like I cannot understand what people say. Faust looked up at Lorem and growled. *She talks to me like I'm some kind of dog. I do not like it.*

Mori looked from her wolf to her friend. "OK, that sounds like that needs to be addressed."

Lorem glanced up at Mori with a confused look. "What needs to be addressed?" she asked.

"Lorem, Faust is intelligent and doesn't like to be spoken to like he's an animal. He has our level of intelligence, even if he can speak only to me." She was doing her best to not sound accusatory, but that was difficult. Mori had grown quite protective of her direwolf.

Lorem's face paled as her hand came up to run down the back of her neck nervously. She looked at the wolf, who was looking up at her. "I changed clothes in front of you!" She threw up her hands before turning to face away from them, mumbling about feeling like an idiot for not knowing. Mori laughed and Faust made a noise that was as close to a laugh as a wolf could make.

You might have to talk to her. I did not want her to continue speaking to me like I am a mindless animal. That is all, the wolf informed her, making the queen nod.

"I will talk to her and smooth things over. I'm just glad everyone here speaks English." She chuckled.

"What's English?" Lorem asked.

Mori looked over at her friend, her brows pinched in confusion. "The language you're speaking."

Lorem shook her head. "I'm speaking Fairy. I don't know what English is." She shrugged.

"Then how am I understanding you? I don't know any languages of the fae."

"I think it has to do with the royal magic. I remember Queen Vi saying when she went to the human realm, she could understand everyone. I think it's also a translator."

"That's been convenient. What about Duncan? He spoke to me fine before I received the magic."

Duncan knows English. I hear the two of you speaking it all the time, Faust informed her. Mori looked down at her wolf companion.

"How do you know English?"

My connection with you allows me to speak your native tongue.

"That makes sense. And I remember Duncan saying I had a very small amount of magic before receiving the rest of it. That could explain how I was able to talk to all of you."

"I gotta head out. I hear something going on outside. Finish getting ready, Mori. We need to start." Lorem walked out of the room to tend to the guests outside.

"That was informative and good to know." She let out a breath. "I need to change clothes real quick and then we can go." She laughed a bit. "I don't mind changing in front of you." She smiled and patted his head before getting changed into a brown-and-green warrior's outfit. Then she walked with her wolf out to the lakeside where the service was being held.

The walk out to the shore felt like it was in slow motion. Numerous fae folk had shown up and were murmuring to themselves as she made her way down the two rows of fae. She could feel the cold ground beneath her trembling feet despite wearing her normal boots. Her mind was struggling to piece everything together, the events that had led up to this point. From the death of her birth mother to planning this funeral. She didn't know how funerals in the fae realm were supposed to go and wondered if she was doing anything correctly. The sun was starting to set on the horizon, and the forest began to grow dark. She watched the sun disappear beyond the forest and couldn't help but shed a tear. The red in the sunset was the exact color of her mother's hair. It was almost as if the forest itself was recognizing her. Mori couldn't help but watch the setting sun trying to disappear, just as her mother had when she was not ready to say goodbye.

She stopped on the rocks as the water gently caressed the soles of her boots before she turned to face the crowd, her heart pounding in her chest as a cold sweat covered her body. So many people had come to pay their respects to the former queen. Mori glanced at her mother's body wrapped tightly in leaves and covered in oil to preserve her body long enough for this moment. She lay in a wooden box on top of a large pile of wood that Mori was told would be used to fuel the flames that would cremate the body. A feeling of dread swelled within her, forming a pit in her stomach as tears threatened to fall from her eyes. She had used every birthday wish and every shooting star wish to meet her birth mother, and she barely got twenty minutes with her before she passed. Her vision began to blur and tunnel.

Could she have done anything to save her mother? Why was the royal magic not good enough to keep her from dying? Why was she not able to do anything? While Mori knew the answers, she still hated how helpless she had felt. Iron was deadly to fae, and she had no idea how to dig out the pieces of iron that were inside her mother, broken off from the bolt that eventually took her life. Helplessness was the only thing Mori felt when she thought about her mother's final days, final minutes. They had to have been spent in agony, but the strong woman had fought through the pain so they could talk for the first, and last, time.

Mori, are you all right? Faust asked as he nudged her hand with his muzzle.

The girl looked down at him and then back up at the body. "Yeah, I'm fine." She turned back to the crowd to address them, feeling all their eyes on her. She had no idea what to say. She had barely known the former queen, her mother. What could she say? "Hello." She let out a shaky breath. "I'm Mori Albright, Viviana's daughter. Um . . ." She trailed off as she tried to think of what to say. "I didn't get to know her for very long, but I wish I had gotten to. Everything I know about my mother I learned from all of you. Stories of her heroics, kindness, and adventures around the forest have all reached my ears. I have been told of her bravery in the war we are still fighting against the raider king. I didn't get the chance to learn much about her, but I'm hoping to continue to hear of her tales."

She looked down at Faust once more to search for the courage to keep going. He gave her an approving nod. Mori's eyes made their way to Duncan, who was in the front row, sitting with one leg over the other and trying to hide the handkerchief in his hands. His own eyes were puffy and red, but he was using his hair to try to cover them.

Keep going, he mouthed with a slight smile.

"I don't know much about funerals that happen here, but where I'm from, people usually say nice things about the deceased to try to reminisce. I can't say I have many good memories, only about twenty minutes' worth, but I know she was a good person and a great queen. She helped as many people and fae as she could, never backing down from a fight or turning her back on someone in need." Mori had to take a moment to collect herself. She had heard so many stories about her mother from others that it was like she had lived them herself. Her mother was the kind of queen Mori could only hope to be, and she would spend her reign doing everything she could to make her proud. She could feel her heart breaking at the thought of not living up to her potential, of disappointing her mother, and of letting everyone in the forest down. This funeral was much harder than she'd expected it to be.

"My mother was an amazing woman, and I wish I had gotten to know her better. I do know that she gave her life to keep you safe, and I will do the same." Mori didn't know what else to say or do, and that spoke in her silence. Faust nuzzled her hand a bit.

You are the one who has to light the flame, he communicated to her.

Mori glanced down at him before turning to face her mother's body. Despite everything that had happened and the intense sadness she felt, she knew her mother was finally at peace. She was no longer in pain. Something in the air made her feel like everything was going to be OK, that everything was going to work out in the end. Mori didn't need to be able to see the future to feel the change of energy in the forest around her.

The new queen lifted her hand and summoned fire using the royal magic she'd gained, shooting the ball at the stack of wood underneath the body. It was set ablaze instantly. Soft music came from the crowd as they started to sing. While Mori couldn't understand how the song felt familiar, she could feel the meaning and the love behind the words. It was a beautiful melody that seemed to ring out and fill up the area with a feeling of ease and tranquility.

Before she knew it, Mori was singing along as if she had sung this song many times over the course of her life, even though it was the first time she heard it. Deep down inside, she could feel the royal magic coursing through her body, giving her the knowledge she needed to sing and understand the song's meaning. It cleared up the fog in her mind, and she could feel her own depression and sorrow lift off her body. This song had such a sorrowful melody, but it went much deeper than that. It was a way to lift up hopes for the future even though the one who was gone would never be in their presence again.

Mori lifted her hands with the palms up at her sides as small green balls of energy flowed from them and moved toward the former queen. As they caressed what was once her mother, a swirl of blue energy sprang up to form the swirl that was on her mother's cheek before it changed form to look like Viviana. More tears ran down Mori's eyes at the sight of what happened next. The blue magic started to dance. The way it flowed flawlessly, as if it had danced like this its whole life, was something to behold.

Mori's chest tightened as her jaw clenched. She was fighting back the overwhelming urge to break down as what felt like an endless stream of tears continued to run down her face and drip onto the ground. The only time she'd seen her mother was as a frail, sick woman, but this beautiful soul before her was lively and laughing happily. Her graceful movements flowed effortlessly above the fire as the song continued to make the ambient magic in the air become visible in the now darkness.

Beautiful bright multicolored lights emanated from the attendants to fill the darkness, illuminating the area as they hovered around for a few moments before moving skyward. The blue soul scooped a few lights up and tossed them upward so it could watch them fan out. Mori couldn't help but sob at the beautiful sight, and the words to the song slipped away from her.

"Bright-colored clothes were the way to go. They look so much better in the light from the magic!" she exclaimed to Faust as she continued to watch the scene before her.

As the lights floated out of their view over the forest and the fire fizzled out, the soul bowed to the audience before it walked down an invisible set of stairs and right up to Mori. Her breath hitched as she looked right into the eyes of her own mother's soul. It smiled happily at her before she heard a symphony of voices speaking directly to her in her mind alongside her mother.

We pass on to you, Moriana.

Mori couldn't help but stare at the soul before her, tears still running down her cheeks. "I love you, Mom," was all she could get out before the soul started to ascend above the trees as it waved goodbye.

With the magic gone and darkness returning, the young girl wiped her eyes on her sleeves as she sniffled and smiled at Faust before patting his head.

Duncan stood up and turned to address the crowd. "The queen has passed on and a new reign begins. Thank you for being here to witness Queen Viviana's soul pass on to the afterlife," he said before he walked over to Mori and gave her a hug before the attendees made their way back to their homes.

As Mori hugged her friend, she noticed something red and glowing in the distance among the trees. She couldn't tell what it was, but just as fast as she'd seen it, it was gone. Duncan released her from the hug and noticed her staring.

"What are you looking at?" he asked, following her gaze over his shoulder.

"I thought I saw something . . . interesting." Her voice trailed off a bit before the final word, but she shook it from her thoughts and looked up at the elf. "Thank you for being here. It was tough to get through, but I'm glad to have done it and been part of it."

"It was only right that you do it. You're the new queen, which means it's time I teach you our customs and culture so you will be prepared for what's to come."

"I would like that, but right now, I'm very tired and would like to just sleep." She peered back at the tree line and saw the red glow again, squinting to figure out what it was. Without thinking, she went as far as to take a few steps toward it before stopping. She knew she shouldn't get closer without knowing what it was.

What is it, Mori? What do you see? Faust asked as he walked up next to her.

"Do you see that red light over there?"

I do, but I do not know what it is. Would you like me to investigate?

As soon as Faust asked, the light was gone for a second time.

"No, I have a bad feeling about it. I think we should just leave it for now and move on." Mori shook her head as she turned to rejoin her friends so they could head out.

The funeral was tougher mentally on Mori than she'd expected. They'd gotten back to the tree house a few hours ago, but she was unable to fall asleep. Duncan was passed out on the small bed on the first level, while Mori sat next to her sleeping wolf on the loft bed. She was using a small candle to read over the royal journals to learn as much as she could about the next steps she should take as the new forest queen. Duncan told her that the coronation would be tomorrow, but Mori knew she wasn't ready for it. Just the thought of being in charge of a whole realm filled her with anxiety and made her want to hide in the tree house forever. That was no life for her, as her mother had pointed out in her letter. She just didn't understand why the coronation had to be right after the most heart-wrenching day of her life.

As she continued to read through the journals, she came across a section on how to manipulate trees and vines to use as weapons and shields.

That explains how I was able to move those trees back in the park. It was a reflex to being in danger, she thought as she read about how the magic worked. Acceleration of growth and moving the plant were the key factors. The more she read about her plant powers, the more she wanted to learn as much as possible. So far she found that the seeds had to be present for her powers to make them grow, and that she could actually make the nutrients inside the plant return to the soil to essentially make the plant shrink again. It was all fascinating information and had Mori up well into the night.

Are you going to sleep soon? Faust asked with one eye open as he looked at her. Mori had gotten quite the shock when he'd suddenly shrunk down to a smaller size when they'd gotten back to the oak tree. He'd sauntered into their safehouse and lain on a pile of blankets and pillows. She'd kept adding them on top of her furry companion until he was completely covered, and he ended up falling asleep in her makeshift pillow fort.

"Soon," she whispered to him as she reached through the small hole where his face was to pet his head. "This part is really good. I promise, just one more chapter," she added with a smile.

You will need your rest for tomorrow. A lot can happen at the coronations, from what I have learned. People like to talk around me like I cannot understand them.

"That makes sense, but it's also good for intel." She blew out the candle and adjusted her position so she could lie down. "Fine, I will sleep now," she continued to whisper, wanting to make sure she didn't disturb Duncan. Faust carefully reached a paw out so he wouldn't disturb the blankets and pillows on himself and touched Mori's hand. She held it in her hand with a light giggle. Even though their friendship had been short, it was the best one she had ever had. Now that she was comfortable, sleep was able to take hold of her for the rest of the night.

Chapter Eight

I t's time! It's time!" a gnome told his friends as they all gathered with the other fae creatures of the realm. Now that the royal magic had passed to Mori, the throne room was vibrant with living plants, beautifully colored flowers, and living creatures once more. Even the foliage portrait behind the throne had changed to depict a healthy-looking Moriana Albright looking over the crowd with her unique line of freckles stretching from cheek to cheek. The room was buzzing with everyone excited to meet the new queen.

Mori peeked through the large doors into the main gathering area through a small opening. She closed them and turned to face the others in the room. "Are you sure this is a good idea?" she asked her companions as some forest fairies struggled to get her hair ready while she walked across the room to the mirrors to look at herself. The new queen was being put into a long green dress that had leaves and purple flowers cascading down and ending on the train. She couldn't help but feel like she was wearing a wedding dress between the long train and the tulle dropped shoulder sleeves. Her normal clothes consisted of sweatshirts and jeans, so wearing long sleeves that flowed down her arms to loop around her middle finger like delicate decorations was more than a little uncomfortable.

She stood with her attendants in a back room that connected to the throne room, trying to get ready for her coronation as the new forest queen. Her hair was pulled up into a bun and adorned with an assortment of flowers and gold chains. She expected the queen to wear some sort of crown, so the odd head decorations were rather strange in her mind. It wasn't that she hated just the headpiece; she hated *all* of it. She hadn't worn a dress at home since she was young and Missy forced her into them for the holidays, and while she loved flowers for making tea, having them cover her body and outfit felt uncomfortable.

I think you look really good. Just like a queen should, Faust said as he moved to sit beside her chair.

"I think I look like a plant," she said, exasperated. Her body was tense as her heart raced in her chest from nerves and her breathing quickened.

Here, that is a good thing. We, as fae, value plants and everything they bring. A lot of us live our lives the way we want and enjoy being around nature. That is what I learned from my short time with the king. The direwolf looked up at the mirror and then turned to Mori while she returned his gaze. *Go out there and show them you are here to be the queen they need to save the forest. You will not have to be alone through this whole thing. I will be by your side the entire time.* Faust panted a bit, which made him look more like a dog and brought some comfort to his queen.

Her shoulders relaxed as her breathing calmed. "Thanks, Faust. You have been a really good friend and companion. I couldn't have asked for better." Mori petted his head with her hand before taking one last look in the mirror at herself and turning toward Duncan, who appeared in the doorway to get her.

Duncan stopped dead in his tracks when he saw her. "Wow! You look incredible!" the elf exclaimed, and offered his arm as Mori let out a nervous laugh. "I can take you to the aisle, but that is as far as I can go with you. It will be up to you to convince everyone you belong here and that you should be queen. Not only is it your birthright, but the magic chose you," he explained as she took his arm. He patted her hand gently with his free hand and gave her a reassuring smile as he began to escort her out of the dressing room.

"Wait, the magic could have *not* picked me?" she asked with a horrified look on her face.

"Technically, yes, but it knew you were worthy and chose you. That's what matters. Come on, your subjects await."

Duncan led Mori to just before the doors and pulled his arm away slowly. "You will do great. Hold your head high and walk with purpose, just as we practiced." He then bowed to her before turning to walk with Faust down the aisle and stand to the left of the throne.

Guess there is no turning back now. I have to just take one step at a time and make sure I present myself as royalty. Not too hard to do, right? she thought to herself before taking a deep breath and letting it out slowly.

Her first step was shaky as her body trembled with trepidation. The large courtyard throne room full of fae was much more intimidating than she'd expected. Her heart was racing from the nerves, and when she looked at her hands, she was sure that her skin was paler than usual. So many people and creatures had come to see her, yet she felt like she was going to mess everything up. By the time she took her third step into the room, her entire body was stiff and she could feel a cold sweat taking over.

The little whispers Mori heard from the audience around her didn't help her overwhelmed nerves, even though the ones she could make out were compliments on her appearance. However, she knew in the back of her mind that being "pretty" didn't make her a good queen. She kept her eyes forward as she continued to walk, her back painfully stiff from the corset under her dress.

Halfway there.

That thought didn't help ease her mind at all. The room started to spin as dizziness clouded her mind.

Am I really going through with this? How can I be the queen of people I have never met, in an unfamiliar place?

She knew she had no qualifications to be one, but she had to try, if for nothing else than because it was what her mother wanted.

Relief filled her body when she reached the front of the room at the bottom of the steps. Mori stopped and turned to face the fae who had gathered in her royal court. They were all still whispering among each other, and it was making Mori more nervous, but she did her best not to show it.

Duncan took a step forward to address the audience. "Two weeks ago, we mourned the death of Forest Queen Viviana Albright, and yesterday we guided her soul back to the forest from which we all came. Today, we celebrate the arrival of Forest Queen Moriana Albright. She has been deemed worthy by the royal magic and will take her rightful place as—"

"We don't want a halfling in charge of our home!" shouted someone from the crowd, sparking an uproar of many people shouting in anger at the same time.

"She never even grew up here! For all we know, she was sent by the raider king to kill us all!" a woman shouted louder than the rest of the crowd.

Mori's breath seemed to catch in her throat, taken aback by the comments that continued to be shouted and the angry arguments that floated around the throne room. She was able to make out some of what was said, but not all of it.

Duncan lifted his hands in a gesture to try to get everyone to calm down. "Everyone, please listen to me! Mori has the power in her. We all know the magic will pick the rightful heir to the throne. We saw it with the fourteenth royal. She was the second-born. The magic knows who is worthy." He was trying to reason with the crowd, but it was not working. It was just making them angrier.

"Please, settle down!" Mori called weakly, but it didn't work. The crowd of fae were too riled up.

It's now or never to prove I belong here. "I SAID STOP!" she bellowed, her magic amplifying her voice and sending a soundwave across the room, silencing everyone instantly. After a deep breath to regain her composure, Mori spoke with confidence. "I know I did not grow up here, but that was not my choice. My mother, Queen Viviana, removed me from the forest to make sure I was safe, to make sure the forest was safe for *all* of you. She knew if something happened to her, the magic would find its way to me, and it did. I am here now and have been learning everything I can in order to stop the raider king. I may not have been raised here, but this forest is my home. Albright Forest is *our* home, and I will protect it for all of us." She thought her speech was really good, but silence hung in the air.

It took a minute, but someone finally spoke up. "We don't want you here, half-breed! You're not fae and we don't trust your kind!" The crowd started their uproar once more, and something sailed past her, inches away from her head. Duncan and Faust did their best to cover Mori as they quickly moved her out of the room and back to safety. Lorem moved to the front of the room to try to control the crowd and convince them to calm down.

Mori wasted no time falling apart. Everything had gone exactly as she'd feared. They didn't want her. She was too different from the fae folk, and they rejected her. She covered her face with her trembling hands as she fell to her knees, unable to deny the tightness in her chest. The rejection of everyone was soul crushing. "They hate me!" she cried. "I'm trying to protect them and they hate me for no reason!" Her sobbing filled the room as Faust moved to rub up against her and sit down.

"They don't hate you, Mori. They're just not used to you." Duncan was trying to be comforting, but this was not his strong suit.

"I'm half-human, a halfling just like they said. My mother warned me that they may turn their backs on me. I just didn't know they would hate me that much. I know they're afraid of humans, but I don't know how to show them I'm not someone they should fear. That I can protect the forest."

There is one way to force them to recognize you as their queen, Faust told her.

After a few moments, Mori calmed down enough that she was only sniffling through silent tears. She looked up at him, moving her hands from her face just enough to peer at the other, her heart still pounding painfully in her chest. "What would that be?"

The royal weapon. I have heard about it from the king who turned me into a direwolf. He had gone looking for it but was unable to find it. It's believed that only a true royal is able to wield the mighty weapon.

Mori sniffled a bit more and wiped her eyes with a cloth that the elf handed her. "I don't know where it is. I just know the poem my mom gave me before she died."

The wolf shook his head, signaling that he also didn't know where it was.

Duncan sighed and put his hands on his hips. "I guess we will have to go looking for whatever it is the two of you are talking about. Would you mind clueing me in?" he asked.

Mori looked up at Duncan. "The royal weapon my mother told me about. It's been lost since the third royal and no one has been able to find it. I doubt I will be able to. I don't know this forest at all," she explained with a defeated tone, her eyes turning toward the floor as her fingers played with one of the leaves on her bodice.

There was a knock on the door after she finished speaking, and a dryad woman came in. She had short black hair covered in orange leaves and was wearing a minimal amount of clothing like most of the fairies did. Mori quickly wiped her red eyes and stood up, almost stumbling over the long dress. The smile that crossed her lips never made it to her eyes.

"Pardon me, my queen." The woman closed the door behind her and took a few steps forward. "My name is Pettil. I was Queen Viviana's royal advisor." Her words sounded like she was bored and was there against her better judgment. She rolled her eyes before limply placing her arm across her chest and bowed slightly toward Mori.

"Hello, what can I do for you?" Mori's voice shook when she spoke.

Pettil shook her head. "While I do not see you as my queen, nor do I accept you as such, you are my queen's daughter, so I must work for you as your advisor." She was so snarky and direct that the young queen was taken aback, but she knew she shouldn't be surprised.

Mori knew she shouldn't be surprised, especially after what just happened minutes before in the throne room. She was just glad the woman wasn't throwing anything at her. A red fruit resembling a tomato fell out of her food-covered hair and splattered on the floor.

It seemed no one other than her two companions would accept her as the rightful queen. She decided that would be the last time someone would tell her who to be or criticize her for something out of her control.

As her brows pulled together, she glared at the woman. "No." She shook her head and the room fell silent. "I don't want someone who doesn't believe in me working for me. If you don't think I deserve to be queen, then you don't deserve to be my advisor. An advisor is someone who helps guide, and there is no way I'm letting someone who rejects me to advise me on anything. You're dismissed." Heat swelled inside her chest and spread through her body. She had finally stood up for herself and her queenship, and she felt so proud of herself for doing so.

The fae woman furrowed her brow with confusion or shock. Mori didn't care which. "Pardon?"

"You heard me. You're dismissed. Until you can accept me as your queen, I have no need of your advice." Mori crossed her arms.

"As you wish," Pettil said before spinning on her heels and leaving the room.

Mori let out the breath, relieved to have the whole confrontation over. If she was being honest, she was glad the entire coronation was over. She knew what the first step to acceptance by her new subjects needed to be, but the next part was going to be the hard one. After pushing some loose strands of hair out of her face, she faced her two companions.

"I'm going to find the raider king and put a stop to him. I can't expect everyone to accept me as their queen if I don't show them who I really am. I can manipulate plants, I know how to heal and fight, and I *am* going to save this forest." Mori had a new fire lit under her as she spoke, and a determined look graced her face. Turning toward Duncan, she walked up to him. "Get me my clothes. We're going to the tree house to find any information on the hammer and the raider stronghold."

After Mori changed clothes, the three of them made it back to the tree house. The day's events plagued her mind the whole way. The looks on everyone's faces haunted her and made her stomach clench. How was she supposed to be a good queen if no one wanted her there? Then again, it wasn't like she had much choice in the matter. The royal magic picked her to be the next forest queen, and she couldn't just give it away to someone she thought was worthier.

Arriving at the tree house, Mori looked up at it and was about to open it up when she heard a voice.

"There she is! The new queen of the forest." The voice sounded like it was mocking her. Faust growled while Duncan drew his sword, and Mori looked around to find the source of the voice.

A large black cat was sitting on a tree branch, laughing like the Cheshire cat from *Alice in Wonderland*. Upon closer inspection, Mori noticed this cat had bright red eyes and a white spot on its chest.

The cat was the size of a Maine Coon, something Mori noticed when it jumped down from the tree branch it was on. She watched as the feline strolled over toward the three, making Faust start to growl again.

"Oh, hush now, puppy. No need to bare your fangs at me," the cat said as it walked by Faust, flicked his chin with its tail, and then stood in front of Mori. "You are the new forest queen, descendent of Queen Viviana. She was a magnificent queen, but I believe it was her time."

Duncan moved between the cat and Mori with his sword still in his hand. "You should leave, Cait Sidhe." He scowled.

"That's not the way to speak to an ancient fae such as myself. You could learn a thing or two from me." The cat sneered before turning around to go up to the oak tree. "I have heard that there is an oak tree in the forest the previous queen would spend a lot of time in. I'm guessing it's this one." The cat put a paw on top of one of the circles on the trunk. "It has that symbol that the royals seemed to be drawn to."

"Who are you?" Mori finally asked.

The cat looked at her with a smile. "I'm Eclipsativa, but you can call me Eclipse. As your elf friend here said, I am a cait sidhe."

"She is a soul-sucking witch who takes the souls of the dead before they can cross over," Duncan said. "I heard you tried to take Viviana's soul the night she died. Lorem caught you and refused to leave the queen's side after that."

Eclipse took a few steps away from the guard captain and snickered. "Caught me red-pawed, but I guess that is to be expected. That satyress has a keen eye for danger. I never could underestimate her." The cat moved to a spot where she could see all three of them. "It seems you have it all handled, being the new queen and gathering the affection of your people." Eclipse did a backflip onto the branch she had originally been lying on and giggled once more. "I could teach you how to make the fae folk like you."

Mori resisted the urge to quirk her eyebrow. While interested, the way Duncan was speaking about the cat had her questioning her trustworthiness. "Why do you think I need help?" She crossed her arms and glared at Eclipse.

"Right, because that coronation back there went *so* well," she said before licking her paw a few times. "Our new queen clearly has everything under control and has the full support of the forest. I guess you really *don't* need me after all." The sarcasm was like venom to Mori, but she refused to let it affect her.

Duncan sighed and turned toward Mori and spoke in a low tone. "She may be some sort of witch in cat form, but that doesn't make her wrong. Even I have to admit, that coronation was the worst I have seen." He shrugged.

"Um, excuse me! I can still hear you!" the cat called, and sighed. "I'm not a witch, for your information." Eclipse put her paw on her chest as if to clutch her pearls. "I am just a humble cait sidhe who does my job well."

Duncan shot the cat a look. "We don't need you! Get lost!" he bellowed. Eclipse giggled before she jumped a little and disappeared into thin air. Mori sucked in a sharp breath as her eyes bulged. That the cat left so quickly, and without a fight, but had little time to ponder it before Duncan was speaking again.

The elf sighed before looking back to Mori. "I think traveling to each of the fae territories would be a good idea. Fae don't tend to trust me because I'm supposed to do anything to help the current royal. And no one but you can hear Faust, so I'm not sure how to get around that."

"That sounds like a good plan. I will just have to try my best to communicate that I'm here to do good, not harm." Mori shrugged, though she knew that was easier said than done.

That is true. While I do not like the idea of traveling to unknown territories, I do not see any other choice, Faust communicated to Mori, who nodded and looked to Duncan to translate the growls he heard.

"We can leave tomorrow for the closest village. I have to find a way to convince people that this forest is my home now, too, and I *will* protect it." The new queen sounded confident, but her mask fell away instantly as a frown took hold of her lips. Sounding confident and being confident were two different things.

That night, Mori could not sleep. She was sitting on the desk chair by the window, looking out at the night sky, lost in her thoughts. The confidence she had hoped to have by now was simply not there. Her mind was racing as she thought of the day's events. She must have run every scenario in her head about how to convince the villagers tomorrow that she could be the queen of a forest she had only been in for two weeks.

Unable to sleep? Faust asked. He was lying on the couch beside Mori's chair. She looked over at him and gave him a small smile.

"Nothing gets past you," she teased with a whispered voice before glancing over at Duncan as he stirred in his sleep. The last thing she wanted was to wake up the elf.

Not when it comes to you. Think of me as your familiar. I can feel what you feel and can communicate through a mental link. It goes both ways. Try to intentionally share your thoughts with me.

Mori could feel her heart start to pound hard in her chest at the thought of trying to make the link work. She had no idea she could use it like this. Her first attempt didn't go as planned, and neither did the second. She was not the type to give up, but after a few more tries, she had to take a mental break.

Calm your mind. That might help with the connection.

Mori nodded before closing her eyes and taking a deep breath, letting it out slowly so she could calm her frustration and racing heart.

I guess this would be better for speaking while Duncan is sleeping. I would hate to wake him up, Mori managed to communicate before she looked back at Faust with an excited smile. *I did it!*

You did very well, Mori. Now tell me what is on your mind, Faust said back as Mori moved to the couch to sit so her wolf could lie down against her side and legs, his paws lying on her lap. Her smile fell as she looked out the window and let out a deep sigh.

It's hard to believe I rule all of this forest, in a sense anyway. Being a royal, a queen, and being able to make a difference in so many people's lives is quite the intimidating thought. Now I have to go convince others I'm worthy of being their queen. I just . . . She shook her head. *I just don't feel like I have it in me to do this whole ruling-over-a-forest thing.* Mori could feel the tension ease from her shoulders as she spoke, not realizing until now how much she needed someone to talk to. While Duncan was her first friend from when she arrived, she felt more of a connection with Faust. Whether that was because he used a mental link to communicate with her or because he had always been very protective of her, she was not sure. He had been a loyal companion to her since they'd met in the cave, and she was thankful for that.

I do not think the hardest part will be convincing them. I think the hardest part will be convincing yourself. He cocked his head to the side as his eyebrows pinched together. *You seem to have high expectations for yourself, and since you are new to having powers, you have yet to achieve that goal. It has been two weeks since receiving the magic from your mother. You must give yourself some time. As we travel, Duncan will train you, so there is no need to worry yet.*

Mori looked over at him with a soft smile. *You're right. I keep thinking I can automatically control this magic overnight, but I can't. I need to be more realistic, well, as realistic as I can be while living in the fae realm after eighteen years in the human realm.* She laughed silently. *Talking like this is fun. I hope we can do it more.*

There will be plenty of time. You should get some sleep. We begin our long journey tomorrow. Faust moved off Mori's lap so she could climb up onto the loft bed.

Get up here. You're my body pillow tonight. She chuckled lightly as her wolf jumped onto the loft bed and lay beside her. She fell asleep with her arm wrapped around her new best friend.

The sounds of shouting woke all three of them up in the early dawn. It took a few dazed moments for Mori to realize someone was calling for help. Without thinking, she grabbed the sword Duncan had given her to train, threw on her boots, opened the tree house, and ran out toward the sounds of growling and yelling. A man dressed in green was trying to fight off a pack of wolves with a stick. The smell of blood hung in the air, and what was left of his clothing was rapidly turning crimson from his wounds. More than likely he had been fending them off for a while.

Mori's heart was pounding hard in her chest as she held her sword firmly in her hands in front of her, doing her best not to let sweat make it slip from her grasp. "I get it, you're looking for food to feed yourselves, but you need to stick to other animals." She tried to reason with the wolves, but they didn't seem to understand.

Of course they don't understand me. They're normal wolves.

She turned her gaze to the man just as Duncan and Faust appeared behind her. "You need to run!" she shouted as she lifted her sword to block the lunging wolf's claws. Her training with Duncan was helping. She was not the fastest with her sword, but it was effective enough. Faust snarled behind her for a moment before charging to attack the wolf who had tried to hurt his queen. Duncan used this time to make his way toward the wolves' former prey, but his path was quickly cut off by the other pack members. Mori ran to the side to try going around them but was quickly blocked as well.

"There're too many of them. Mori, use your magic," Duncan said before lifting his arm to block an attack, claws ripping his flesh open. The dark-red blood spilled from the wound as he pulled his arm close and grunted from the pain. "We can't hold them off forever. We need—Hey!" The elf cut off his sentence when he saw the other man take off running now that the wolves were focused on them. "Wait!"

You need to restrain them. Faust lept to the side to avoid another wolf that tried to jump on him. The pack adjusted their stance to the offensive.

Mori pushed the wolf she was fighting away from her and held out her hand. At first, nothing happened. "Come on, work!" she yelled out in frustration before forcing herself to calm her nerves and focus on finding the roots in the soil beneath them. As soon as she located them, she whispered, "Grow." The ground started to quake beneath them as tree roots surfaced and lifted the wolves into the air. Their teeth ripped the roots that were beginning to hold them while allowing them their freedom.

"Don't play with them, just restrain them," Duncan shouted.

"I'm not trying to play with them!" Mori yelled back with a shaky voice as she waved her arms in an attempt to make her magic listen to her, but that only made the roots wiggle around in the air like they were dancing.

It might be best to change strategies. Pull down to trap them instead of pushing up, Faust said.

"I'll give it a try." Mori closed her eyes, and instead of focusing on all the roots that were now flying around them, she located three in her mind. She followed their energy to the ends and coerced them to obey her. The roots managed to dance their way around some of the pack members, and instead of going up, they pulled each one down to the ground, even wrapping smaller roots around their muzzles to keep them from freeing themselves again. However, the wolves that managed to evade capture took off running after their original prey.

"Good! Now let's finish these wolves off and catch up with our mystery man." Duncan and Faust moved closer to the wolves before Mori's shout stopped them.

"No!" The two turned back to her. "I know they attacked us, but I will not let you kill them for simply being the predatory animals they are. We need to let them go." There was no changing her mind.

"What do you expect us to do with them? They're dangerous. We can't handle them like they're dogs. Besides, if we waste time on them, we won't be able to follow the rest of the pack." Duncan was clearly exasperated with his queen, but she stood firm.

"Don't worry, I know what to do." She disappeared into the tree house and came back with one of the many vials from the shelves. Taking aim, she threw it against the tree above the wolves' heads. The contents shattered and covered the wolves. One by one, they fell asleep beneath the roots that covered them.

"There. They will sleep for hours." Duncan and Faust looked at her, amazed, but Mori simply shrugged. "Poppy powder. I found it among my mother's things and thought it might come in handy at some point. Now we can go after the others and relocate these three to a more remote part of the forest."

"How did you know poppy powder would work?" Duncan finally asked with the shock wore off.

"I studied plants all my life. I know a lot of different potions. We need to go if we want a chance to catch up!"

Duncan wasted no time running in the direction the man had gone, with Mori and Faust following behind. The smile that formed on the queen's lips turned into a big grin when she realized she had actually used her magic intentionally rather than reactively. This was a big moment for her, and she didn't even have time to enjoy the feel of her magic flowing through her body.

Upon reaching the clearing where the wolves had caught up to the man, Mori watched as he was used as a tug-of-war rope between the remaining three wolves. She wanted to try using that magic again now that she had some practice. Her arms moved around her body as green energy danced through the air. Tree roots rapidly grew from the soil beneath the wolves' paws to wrap around their bodies and pull them away from their victim. With the predators away from their prey, Mori sprinted to his side and knelt, her hands applying pressure to his wounds in a futile attempt to stop the bleeding.

"Hold still. I'll try to heal you." The queen channeled the magic flow through her body to her hands, a soft green glow shining from underneath her pale skin, but the wounds remained open instead of sealing shut as they would on her own body. A pained look filled her features as her lips tightened into a frown just before she let out an exasperated breath. "Why isn't it working?" The glow from her hands had stopped, but she kept trying to heal his wounds, to no avail.

"Mori, I don't think he's fae." Duncan put his hand on her shoulder and gently pulled her away from the man.

"What do you mean?" Mori snapped, frustration still in her voice.

"I mean, he's a raider. He's not from this land, so your healing magic won't work on him." Duncan sighed a bit.

Color drained from her face as she glanced up at Duncan before looking back at the man who lay before her. She was trying to save a raider? The group of people she'd promised to defeat to protect the forest and fae folk? She stood up on shaky legs and took two steps back, her gaze never leaving the dying man.

"I'm sorry," the man breathed out with a strained voice. "I was a raider, but I don't believe in the destruction they're doing to the forest, so I left." He coughed up some blood into his hand and glanced at it with a frown before his tear-filled eyes trailed back up to Mori with a small smile and sadness. "Thank you for trying to save me."

Mori felt tears on her cheeks and wiped them away with a sniffle. "I'm sorry I wasn't faster and that I couldn't heal you. I failed you."

The man shook his head. "No, my queen, you did not fail me. I should never have joined them or sought you out to join you when I left. I'm sor—" His sentence was cut short as he succumbed to his injuries.

Duncan gently pulled Mori into an embrace as her tears fell from her eyes and landed on the ground at her feet. "You did everything you could. I think we should bury him here to lay him to rest."

Mori nodded and glanced down, blinking in surprise at the new glowing flowers at her feet. "What the . . .?" Her sentence trailed off as Duncan and Faust also looked down.

"Those are princess flowers. They sprout when a royal cries from intense emotions," Duncan explained, and knelt to inspect them. "They're glowing a soft blue." His eyes found their way up to hers. "Mori, there is no reason for the sadness in your tears. This man helped keep a war going. He doesn't deserve your tears or your flowers." The elf stood up once more.

Mori shook her head. "A life is still a life, and a life lost is still a tragedy. He may have been with our enemy, but that doesn't mean his life was not worth living." The ground under the former raider's body moved to the side as the roots below gently lowered him down before covering him with the soil. Grass grew over the mound as gladiolus flowers bloomed around it.

Gladiolus? Why those? Faust asked as he sat down.

"They mean integrity and strength. It takes a lot of both to stop doing something bad and stand up for what's right. I want him to be remembered that way." Mori wiped her eyes again with her sleeve.

"We lay this man to rest so he may return to the forest." Duncan clapped his hands together once in front of his chest while he closed his eyes. Mori sucked in a breath before imitating the elf. Faust sat back on his hind legs and put his front paws together in an attempt to copy the other two. "Please accept this child back to you so he may continue into the afterlife and live with those he loves. When we're born, the forest gives us life. When we die, we must give it back. Thus is the circle of life," Duncan finished, and opened his eyes as his hands fell to his sides.

"May he rest in peace," Mori said softly, and looked at Duncan, her eyes still sad and now a little puffy from crying. "Why did my magic not work on him?"

"I suspect it's because he's not from the fae realm. Since the royal magic is connected to Albright Forest, it will only allow you to heal creatures who are from here," he explained as his hands settled on his hips. "It's also believed that the royal magic has a consciousness of its own. It will pick and choose who to heal, but there is yet to be any proof of that."

Mori nodded in understanding before going still, her eyes fixed on the blood running down the elf's sleeve. She grabbed his wrist and pushed the cloth up to expose the claw marks the wolves had left. Duncan winced from the sudden touch as she used her healing magic to close the wound. "It works on you just fine. I guess that will be how I can tell if they are fae or a raider." Mori sighed heavily. This was going to be difficult if any more of the raiders were roaming the forest without their signature brown clothing.

"Everything will be fine. We can save our own. That's what's important," Duncan said. She knew he was trying to comfort her and help her feel better, but it was futile.

"Yeah . . . Right . . ." Mori mumbled as she walked back to the tree house so they could prepare to leave for the village.

Chapter Nine

They ate breakfast in silence. Mori was lost in thought over the events of the last few days. Her deep thinking had her eating her food slowly while she stared at nothing in particular.

"Are you OK?" Duncan asked as his eyebrows furrowed.

"Yeah, I'm fine," she lied after looking up at him. She shook her head a bit before giving a weak smile. "Where are we going first?"

"The pixie territory. They're the closest to us, and once we pass through, we can make our way to the coast where the water nymphs are," Duncan explained as they cleaned up their mess. Mori grabbed her bag and slung it over her shoulder while the guard captain looped his sword through his belt and secured it.

We should be careful. Bob is normally seen near the pixie territory, Faust said as he stood up from the couch and made his way to Mori.

"Oh, great . . ." She sighed as her shoulders slumped. "We might run into *him*. I hope not. I would rather not know how strong he really is, or how hungry." Mori shivered at the thought.

"Who?" the elf asked.

"Bob. Faust said he hangs around the pixie territory." She paused for a moment, her face scrunching and the corner of her upper lip lifting a little. "Wait, *territory*? Like, a massive piece of land they call their own?"

Duncan shook his head. "Not quite. While it's called a territory, it's more like a town or village. It's where a large number of them gather in one spot—at least, the ones who don't live in solitude. There are some fae who don't have their own territory, but merely wander around," he explained.

"What about when you're talking about the entire area of land they own?"

"That is called a province. I think the humans' word for a larger city is a kingdom, but fae don't like to use any words that could potentially suggest a royal owns it directly. Even if you actually do." He shrugged. "Just make sure to remember those words. It can send fae into a frenzy if you mix them up or call their territory a village or kingdom." Duncan chuckled. Mori got the impression that he had experience with mixing words up and the consequences that followed.

As they approached the pixie territory, Mori began to hear a soft purr coming from somewhere nearby. She stopped and looked up to see Eclipsativa on a nearby tree branch. The other two stopped as well to follow her gaze up to the cat. It was surprising that neither of the more experienced travelers had heard the cat before she did.

"Where are you three going in a hurry?" she asked with a smirk.

"Wouldn't you like to know?" Duncan crossed his arms, his tone filled with venom.

"Mmm, maybe. I heard something *big* was coming this way." The cait sidhe stood up and stretched out her front paws. "I'm just trying to be nice and give a friendly warning."

"Nothing you say is friendly, Cait Sidhe," Duncan growled.

"Oh, don't be like that, Duncy. I'm on your side, after all." The cat jumped down from her branch, causing Faust to growl the closer she got to Mori. "Hush, puppy. No need to get your tail in a twist."

I do not like this cat, Mori. We should leave. She is a bad omen.

"Faust, I don't think she is a bad omen, but I agree we should move on." Mori looked from her wolf to Eclipse. "Please stop following us. We're making it just fine without your help." She started to walk again with her two companions in tow.

"Are you certain you know what you're doing?"

Mori stopped with a groan and spun on her heels to face the black cat, some of her red hair flying into her face. She quickly wiped the hair away with her hand, trying to blow it out of her mouth before regaining her composure. "We're figuring it out, so don't worry about us."

"I'm not worried. I just think it's pretty funny how you three wander aimlessly around the forest, looking for helpless fae to protect." She laughed as her tail swished behind her.

"That's not what we're doing. We're protecting them and will help them however we can," Duncan interjected before Mori could speak. "Come on, we need to leave now. Before that *thing* can get inside your head."

"Suit yourself." Eclipse shrugged before she ran off and disappeared.

Mori stared in the direction the cat fled and wondered if what they were doing was really considered "protecting" fae. Going from place to place to see if any of them needed help to gain favor seemed like a selfish thing to do.

Maybe she is right. There must be a better way to do this. Lost in her thoughts again, the young queen followed behind her two companions.

Mori was surprised by how much energy she had by the time they were close to the pixie territory. It felt like a shorter walk to her than the one from the coronation to the oak tree, not that she was complaining. Looking up, she took notice of the large tree canopy they were traveling under. Their path was dark from the shade, but still light enough for them to see, reminding her of walking under the night sky illuminated by stars and the moon. As they approached where the pixie town was established, she noticed tiny signs of life starting to appear. She couldn't help but stop and kneel to look at something in a bush that caught her eye. It looked like a little birdhouse with a working door and little windows. As she surveyed the rest of the bushes around her, she saw several more birdhouse-looking structures of different colors, but this one in front of her was green and seemed to camouflage itself with the leaves around it.

"What are these?" Mori asked.

"They're pixie houses. Pixies usually live in little fairy houses or make their own inside trees. They prefer the shade and flowers around this area." Duncan pointed over toward a flower-filled spot. "When they want to go be around flowers and more nature, they go over there. Just keep your belongings close. They are known for being"—he flung his hands around his head as a blue light flew past—"mischievous . . ." He snarled and made sure his bag was sealed tightly.

Mori slowly stood up as she turned and watched a rainbow of colors light up and float around them. Upon closer inspection of one of the nearby lights, she saw a small humanoid pixie with two pairs of fluttering wings, a leaf wrapped around their body like clothing. They looked like something out of a fae book back on Earth and were only about four inches tall.

"Wow, they're so pretty," she said with a smile.

When they aren't trying to take things from you or pull pranks. Faust bucked one away that tried to land on his back and ride him like a steed. *These pranksters are not the type of fae you want around.*

"Is there a leader we could talk to? Someone who is in charge of this territory?" Mori asked.

"They once answered to Titania, but she was a past royal. One of the ones who lived the longest, but she was four royals before you." Duncan groaned. "I'm having second thoughts about this visit."

"Then who runs things while the royal is away?"

"That would be me." An older-looking pixie who was close to a foot tall flew over to them. She had long salt-and-pepper hair and dark eyes and was wearing an orange dress to match her orange wings. "I am Astalla. I'm in charge of the pixies in the absence of Queen Titania."

"I am Queen Moriana, but you can call me Mori. I'm traveling to the different territories of the forest to offer my help and support for whatever issues you may have." Mori smiled, hoping that rehearsed greeting would allow her the chance to help.

"Help?" The pixie scoffed. "You think the pixies need help?" Astalla laughed, and so did the pixies around them. The sound echoed off the trees and was loud enough that Mori and Duncan had to cover their ears while Faust did his best to cover his own with his paws. Just as quickly as the laughter had started, it stopped, silence filling the air. The pixie woman leaned in close with an eyebrow raised. "Why would we want *your* help? You are not Queen Titania, and so we do not need you," she said with disdain before turning to start flying away, the rest of the pixies following after.

"Queen Titania is dead," Duncan shouted at them, making all of them stop and turn to look at him. "She died a long time ago, four royals before Mori. Your beloved Titania is right here, inside her, and she wants to help." It was nice that Duncan was trying to stand up for her, though it brought an uneasy feeling. There was no way these creatures would believe what he'd said, and she was right.

All the pixies glared at him. "LIES!" Astalla yelled, and the swarm of angry pixies charged at them, buzzing like bees while they bit and scratched the elf and queen. Faust swatted at them the best he could to try to protect his queen, but there were too many. Mori's arms flailed around her, trying to knock away the ones that were going for her face and pulling her hair.

"OW! Knock it off! We aren't the enemies here!" she shouted, but they refused to stop. The three had no choice but to run until the pixies stopped following them. Mori glanced over her shoulder when they were several yards away just in time to see the swarm scatter for an unknown reason, at least for a few moments. Bob came charging from the side, mouth wide open, and snapped it shut around a few of the stragglers who had yet to leave.

Mori ducked behind a bush, her hands quickly covering her mouth as her eyes widened. She hoped he wouldn't be able to hear her panting breaths, and her hands had to muffle a scream that threatened to escape her throat. Sweat was already running down her temples from running, but that didn't stop her heart from pounding in her ears with trepidation. With a quick glance, she saw Faust beside her while Duncan hid behind a tree.

Good, they're safe.

The sound of the creature's maw snapping shut echoed in the queen's head each time, the horrors of what he was doing flashing in her mind.

Then things went still and quiet. Not even the sounds of the forest could be heard. Slowly and carefully, Mori turned her head to see what had made the beast stop his feast, only to be met with the sight of Bob clapping the pixies between his massive hands, squishing and killing them easily. It took all her willpower not to shout at him, tell him to stop. The fact that he looked like he was enjoying watching their crushed bodies fall to the ground sent a chilling shiver down her spine. There was no way he was truly enjoying this massacre, right?

"He isn't eating them?" Duncan's brow furrowed. "Rumors said he enjoyed eating them, but he is actually *playing* with them, like some toy he can squish and throw away."

That is wrong. Faust winced when another pixie was killed with his hands. The scream that rang out from the creature made the wolf lower his ears.

Mori couldn't handle watching anymore. She crouched down and covered her ears with her hands and clenched her eyes shut tightly. Her only focus now was tuning out the cries that echoed off the trees, their pleas for life falling on deaf ears. Bob was merciless in his hunt for entertainment. Mori was startled by Faust's sudden touch, her eyes shooting open in alarm and looking at him. The sigh of relief that passed her lips was enough to make the wolf move closer to her.

We will not let him find you. I know you are worried about being eaten because you are half-human. I would never let that happen, he told her through their link, which made the queen give a small, shaky smile. Tears ran down her cheeks, the consternation of their situation setting in as her body trembled against her companion's body.

The sound of the pixies swarming the skull-headed beast hummed in the air as they tried to get him to stop, but he was unfazed. They couldn't hurt him with their own teeth and nails, so he just kept clapping them and stepping on them. As he moved around to reach more of the creatures, he stepped on their cloaked houses without a care. He ripped out a tree, broke it in half, and dropped it onto more pixies as their cries continued. It seemed the survivors finally got the hint and fled their homes for safety.

"I think it's time we run too. His *toys* ran away," the elf said with a panicked tone as he took a step out from the tree to make sure the beast was looking in another direction. The two agreed silently, but only Duncan and Faust took off running away from the massive homicidal creature. It didn't take long for Faust to notice Mori was not beside him. He stopped and turned to look at her, quickly returning to her with haste. Mori's body continued to shake, her knees pulled to her chest as she continued to cry. She was petrified, and her mind was hyperfocused on the thudding footsteps in the direction of Bob. He was on the move, and she was not.

We need to run, Mori, Faust told her, and motioned for her to follow, but she didn't budge. Her body was glued to the ground as fear paralyzed her. The wolf moved behind her to push her onto her knees before using his head to force her butt up to get her on her feet. Panic made Mori stumble as he continued to push her body, forcing her legs to walk. *Let us get out of here.* After a few more shaky steps, her feet unglued themselves and her legs started to pick up speed before running on their own, the two catching up with their friend quickly.

The three of them kept going until they could no longer hear the beast, and the natural sounds of the forest returned, wanting to make sure they were not being followed. Mori leaned against a tree as she panted hard, trying to catch her breath with her burning lungs. Faust lay on the grass as his tongue hung out of his mouth, short-breathed. Duncan looked like he was going to fall over while gasping for air. After a few moments, he ran a hand over his silver hair to push the loose strands out of his face.

That could have gone better, Faust communicated. *It seems pixies will not be on our side, especially after we stood by and watched them be killed by Bob.* He got up and sat beside Mori so she could lean on him instead of the tree.

"You're right, Faust. I don't think the pixies will join us, but it's not like we could have done anything to stop Bob. He is much stronger than all of us combined." Mori leaned against her wolf and stared down at the grass as they all took a break. She was doing her best to appear strong and not let Faust feel her quivering body. Memories of the events played through her mind, and she felt embarrassed and angry that it had taken Faust pushing her to her feet to get her to run with them. It did not escape her notice that she was powerless to help the pixies in their time of need.

"I just wanted to help with whatever problems they have, but I couldn't save them from that beast," she said, her voice wavering. "It's not about being queen for me; it's about making sure the fae of the forest are taken care of, protected, and happy."

"That sounds like something a true queen would say." Duncan choked out a laugh and leaned against the tree behind him for a moment. "We should keep moving. The leprechauns are not far from here. We can pass through their territory next. They are generally on the royal's side and easy to get along with if you can drink."

"I have never had alcohol before. In my world, you have to be twenty-one to drink."

"That could be a problem." The elf stood up and helped Mori to her feet. "We should still try, though."

It took a day's journey to get to the next territory. When they reached the town, Mori gasped as she clasped her hands over her mouth, her eyes going wide moments before tears started to form. The entire territory was razed to the ground from a conflagration, leaving nothing unscorched, and it was not recent. Burned skeletal bodies were scattered everywhere and had been dirtied by the weather, partially covered in soil. The few buildings that were left were only charred frameworks and soot-covered fabric that managed to escape the inferno. Smoke had long been gone, and the blackened wood was starting to look worn from the rain.

As the scene before her processed in her mind, she froze as a memory from deep in her subconscious surfaced and played in her mind's eye. A flash of a memory that was only a moment for the others, but Mori relived it for much longer.

The territory was vibrant, and everyone was going about their lives as the kids played. The memory played through someone else's eyes as they sat by a group of young leprechauns in what looked like a tavern. There were tables and chairs filled with mostly shorter fae, but also some she couldn't identify. Behind the bar were several barrels, just like you would see in a Western movie back on Earth. They were talking among themselves and laughing while drinking from their steins. When a short man handed a cup of liquid to the person, Mori could see small callused hands reaching for it before bringing it to their lips for a drink.

"Please, enjoy yer stay wit' us," the leprechaun said with an Irish accent.

"Thank ye kindly, Sir Seamus. I enjoy e'ery moment I'm 'ere," the woman responded with an Irish accent of her own as she raised the glass again and then took a drink. Mori could taste the alcohol and hops on her tongue. Beer? "That hit the spot!"

"Stay as long as ye like, Elissa. We enjoy havin' ya 'ere." The leprechaun waved goodbye before walking off to talk with others. The woman, Elissa, looked down at her half-finished beer and released a deep sigh. Mori could feel the sadness that filled that breath, the weight of which she knew all too well.

The memory ended there, and Mori was brought back to the present, still staring in stunned silence. What was that just now? A memory of some sort? But it wasn't her memory; it belonged to some woman named Elissa. And then it dawned on her.

Elissa must be a past royal. One who spent her time with the leprechauns. That sigh at the end is the same weight-filled one I let out from time to time, she thought to herself, blinking her eyes back into focus in time to see Duncan gently kick a piece of wood with his boot while Faust sniffed around. Neither of them had noticed how spaced out she had been. That was a good thing.

With a slight shake of her head to clear the rest of the brain fog, she finally asked her question. "What happened here?" Mori's voice was shaky as her hands slowly dropped to her sides.

"It seems we arrived much too late." The elf looked around for any clues, but there were no footprints after the amount of time that had passed, nothing to suggest who had done this. "My estimate is this happened at least a month ago, before Mori took the throne and magic. More than likely before she got here. There was nothing that could have been done to prevent this." He crossed his arms and shook his head somberly.

Noticing the queen's silence, Faust went to nuzzle her hand with his muzzle. Mori looked down at her wolf, her face a little scrunched up before she fell to her knees and threw her arms around him and sobbed. Faust wrapped one of his front legs around her to keep her close.

This was brutal. This goes beyond what the raiders would do. The direwolf glanced over at the elf when he started speaking.

"This looks like the work of Dairus." Duncan surveyed the area, looking for any signs of life.

"You said that name before, but who's Dairus exactly?" Mori asked now that she was a little calmer but was still holding on to her furry companion.

"He's a pyromaniac and a very dangerous man who only wants to watch the forest burn. He's been known to return to the scene of his crime to breathe in the smell of death. At least, that's what the rumors say. He loves everything related to death and destruction."

Duncan shook his head. "We should keep moving. I can't imagine he would stay away from this place. It's completely ruined."

You can ride on my back if you cannot walk, Faust told his queen. Mori let go and stood up as he grew in size to accommodate her body. She was about to climb on him when she stopped suddenly.

"Wait, there's something I must do." The queen took a few steps toward a blackened part of the territory and knelt to place her hand on the ground. Her heart thumped in her chest as she took slow, shaky breaths. Closing her eyes, she channeled her magic through her body, commanding it to regrow the grass that had been destroyed. That grass then pulled the bodies underground for burial where they lay and brought the flowers back to life. She wanted to create shelters for those who passed through, so she commanded some tree roots and vines to climb up the burned structures and sprout large leaves as a makeshift roof. The vines and tree roots wrapped around the support beams to reinforce them and make walls to shield those seeking shelter from the elements. By the time everything stopped moving, the place looked like a naturalist's paradise.

She stood up and inspected her work, releasing a breath of relief that her magic had done what she'd wanted it to. "This was home to the leprechauns, and I do hope they can return one day, but in case they don't, this will provide shelter for another fae who needs it."

"That was really kind of you," Duncan told her.

Mori nodded a bit while climbing onto her wolf's back, lying down as best she could. Then the memory she had viewed before popped back into her mind.

"Hey, Duncan, who was Elissa?" Mori asked.

"She was a past royal. She spent a lot of time with the leprechauns and even took on their accent. Loved their whiskey too. She was the forty-second royal. Why do you ask?" the elf asked her with a curious look.

"No reason. I read her name in a book and was curious. So, where to now?" She wasn't sure why she didn't tell Duncan the truth about the memory, but decided for now it would be a secret she kept to herself.

"We need to cross the river to head toward the fairy territory," Duncan said.

"Sounds good to me." Mori pondered the memory flash she'd had, glad to know who the woman was. She wondered if there was a way to use these memories to her advantage with the fae in the forest.

Chapter Ten

The walk toward the river was silent. Mori was still replaying the memory she'd witnessed, trying to decipher what it meant and why it was shown to her. Was there a reason she needed to know who Elissa was? Maybe there was something she was supposed to do with this knowledge, like help the leprechauns rebuild. She was pulled from her spiraling thoughts when her wolf's voice popped into her head.

Do you hear that? He stopped walking as his ears focused on the sounds around them. Mori listened closely as well, hearing distant wailing and screams of fear.

"Yeah, I hear that. Let's go see what's happening." She turned her head in the direction the cries were coming from.

Hold on, Faust told her. Mori gripped his fur tightly to hang on just before he dashed off, Duncan following close behind. When it came to speed, the two were evenly matched.

The scene they came upon made Mori gasp. Raiders were attacking a group of naiad women and dragging their flailing bodies to large caged carriages. A few of the raiders were punching the women to make them stop screaming and crying, but it just made them do it more. Children were crying for their mothers while being carried by strangers to be locked up in the cages. Most of the women who were dressed as warriors were on the ground in a pool of blood, some with their eyes still open, their corpses filleted open by sharp weapons the raiders used.

Mori sprung into action without thinking, her arms moving up the sides of her body in a lifting motion as she jumped off her wolf, making tree roots sprout up from the earth and grabbing raiders to pin them down to the ground. Tree trunks were diving underground and popping up under the raiders' feet to launch them into the air, away from the group. She turned in time to watch Faust lunge at an enemy attempting to sneak up on the queen and ripped his throat out viciously, letting out a guttural growl.

The queen nodded to him in appreciation before reaching toward the ground with her arms at her sides. Long blades of grass grew rapidly to wrap around her hands and create a handle for her to grip on to while the long blades broke from their roots to make a sharp tip. With a smirk at the flinching men before her, she charged at them, grass swords at the ready. The first strike against a battle axe broke the handle in half while slicing the man's chest. With a quick outward motion of her other hand, her blade clashed with another sword. Her free hand moved from above her head down toward the ground as a large boulder came down on this man's head. Mori ducked under a swinging hammer before shoving her sword through the raider's stomach.

"She's just a girl! Kill her!" a raider shouted, making Mori spin around. A whole group of raiders were charging her way.

"If you want me, you gotta get through my plants!" she yelled back as she reached into the pouches of her belt and tossed several small seeds at the approaching men. As she raised her arms with a smirk, the ground beneath their feet began to rumble and split as gigantic leaves appeared. Some of the men fell into the ground as more of the plants emerged. The swallowed prey yelled and screamed as the pitcher plants digested their bodies in the acidic juices within their bulbs. The rest of the men in the charging group were grabbed by huge dual leaves with spikes to trap them, their screams of terror muffled as the venus flytraps consumed their flesh for nourishment. There was no escaping either of these deadly carnivorous plants. Mori was glad she had stocked her bag with seeds and vials from the tree house before leaving to explore the forest.

Duncan ran to her and smiled. "Nicely done. The rest saw these and took off."

"We aren't done yet. We need to rescue the ones they captured." Mori dashed off after the fleeing raiders, catching up quickly. Faust was already working on killing raiders while making his way to one of the cages. The naiad women were quieter now as they huddled together in the middle of the cage the best they could.

"Release them!" Duncan shouted, and raised his sword.

"Over our dead bodies!" one of the raiders shouted back.

"That can be arranged." He lunged at the men, blocking an incoming attack with his sword before jabbing his foot into his attacker's stomach. While he was hunched over, the elf kneed him in the face, breaking his front teeth and nose. With a quick spin, he slashed down the chest and stomach of another raider who was coming at him from behind, before turning once more to stab a third through the throat. Without warning, two men jumped on Duncan at the same time, clinging to him like their lives depended on it.

"Faust, I could use some help!" he called out, not having to wait long for backup. The direwolf grabbed the man on the elf's back and pulled him off, throwing him to the ground. With a fierce bite to the throat, the raider's life ended. Duncan pushed the man on his front off him, and in one swift movement, his sword stabbed through the heart of the enemy.

While the two took care of the main group of raiders, Mori made her way to the final one, who was guarding the caged naiads. Her grass blades dripped with blood as she approached the trembling man.

"You won't be able to break the bars with those," the man said with a shaky voice before falling backward onto his butt.

"I'm not going to break your steel bars. I'm just going to take the key around your neck." She walked right up to him and pressed the tip of her sword to his chest but didn't put it in. Instead, she reached down and yanked the key off his neck, breaking the leather strap that was tied around it. "You better run and hope my wolf doesn't catch you." Her piercing green eyes dared the man to try to escape, and he took that dare. He scrambled to his feet as he tried to run, but Faust got to him first. The screams of pain followed by drowning in blood behind her were unpleasant but unavoidable.

The queen made her way to the door of the cage and unlocked it before forcing it open. She and Duncan helped the women out of the cage, making sure they didn't injure themselves. Faust was on the lookout for any more straggling raiders, taking his guard dog duties very seriously.

While the naiads were being taken care of, Mori felt a twinge of pain in her arm. She pushed up her sleeve to reveal a bleeding wound, but just as quickly as the pain had come, it was gone, and the wound sealed itself up as if it had never happened. The royal magic was healing her, and she wondered if she could heal the naiads. She decided to try it after she escorted them back to their home

With everyone returned safely, Mori used her magic to pull the bodies of the raiders underground and out of sight. She would do the same for the naiads if they asked, but she wanted to respect their culture for now, so she left their warriors alone.

As she walked among the women back to their home by the river, she noticed their skin appeared flawless and smooth and their hair was long, both of which were a different color for each woman. Their pointed ears reminded her of elves, and most of them wore small dresses made of varying colors of plant fibers. One woman looked very pale and struggled to breathe due to a deep wound across her bare chest. The queen knelt and gently hovered her hand over the gash, allowing the green energy to flow from her hand to the naiad. The skin pulled together to heal completely, leaving no trace of it ever being there.

"I didn't know your magic could heal us," one girl said to Mori.

"It seems to only work on fae or myself. I'm not able to heal someone who is not connected to this forest," she explained, giving a small smile to reassure the girl of her abilities.

"That's really cool! Thank you for saving my mommy." The naiad girl hugged her mother, who was regaining her ability to breathe, and color started returning to her body.

"It seems you came at a good time, Queen Moriana," a womanly voice said behind her. When Mori turned around, she was met with an older woman, around her late fifties by human aging standards, who was wearing a bright-blue strapless dress that went down to her knees. The woman had graying hair and dull-blue eyes.

"Just Mori is fine. No need to be so formal. I'm glad we showed up when we did. It looks like we were able to prevent anyone from being taken." She peered over at the dead naiad women who were now lined up along the tree line close to the river. "I just wish I had come soon enough to save them. My powers allow me to heal, but sadly I cannot bring the dead back to life." Her gaze turned back to the woman.

"Yes, today was a sad day for our numbers. We lost a lot of great women, but we were not captured to be tortured in the raiders' camp. That is what's truly important." The woman nodded in agreement with herself. "I am the naiad territory queen, Adairria. I thank you from the bottom of our hearts for helping us." Adairria and several other naiads, who had gathered around Mori, Duncan, and Faust, put their hands together in front of their chests before pushing them outward with their fingers pointing toward the queen and then opening their arms as if to move through water, doing this one time before their arms rested at their sides. Mori recognized it as a human swimming technique called the breaststroke, with a little flare to it. She beamed at the realization that this was their way to show respect, the same way some humans bow or shake hands.

"I'm glad we were able to help," Duncan told the leader.

"Please, stay and join us for a feast after the memorial. It's almost sundown, and you all must be hungry. We will celebrate your queenship with a feast and dancing!" Adairria seemed very excited by this, and Mori looked at Duncan with pleading eyes.

"I don't see why not," the elf said with a shrug as three nymphs started rubbing their hands all over him. Mori had heard nymphs were very kind, especially toward men. At least the ones who were not trying to harm them.

"All right, we will stay for the night." Mori laughed and followed her companions. Faust's tail wagged happily as he stayed by his queen's side.

The feast mostly consisted of fruit, nuts, and some venison. It seemed the naiads stayed away from seafood, as they saw underwater animals as part of their home and sacred. Mori had noticed how water-based the decorations of their houses were. Many of the shelters were covered in sea plants, such as reeds, seaweed, and algae, and different things that had washed up onto their shores. The wood that was used for their huts had worn holes and reminded Mori of driftwood. Each hut looked like a vacation beach house she'd seen on Earth when going to the ocean with Missy and Jason. Mori sighed fondly at the thought of the two who raised her. She knew they had to be worried about her by now, but she had no idea how to return to them or even contact them.

Even through the music and dancing, Mori was lost in her thoughts while staring blankly at nothing in particular. She thought about all that she still had to do, the worries that filled her mind about if she would be a good queen or not, and how she was going to defeat the raiders and their king. As if he could read her mind, Faust walked over to her and lay behind her so she could lean against him. She was sitting on a cushion on the ground, so there was no backing to lean against. The wolf was his usual size now, so she found him perfect for leaning against and did so.

Try to push your worries aside for a while. They are not worth focusing on right now. We may have had a rough start, but there was a victory today. The river nymphs are safe from the raiders, and we are getting a rest. We must celebrate the small victories while we can. The wolf looked up at his queen, his red eyes reflecting the dancing flames.

Mori petted his head a bit and sighed heavily. "You really are in tune with my feelings." She chuckled. "It's annoying at times, but also nice. I don't always have to say how I'm feeling out loud when it's too hard to put it into words." She shook her head to clear her thoughts enough to string her sentences together so she could convey what she was thinking. "I guess I'm just worried that next time, we will be too late, just like with the leprechauns. I don't want anyone else to get hurt, but it seems I'm already too late to save most of the fae folk in the forest."

That is not true. Your mother was injured badly, and you did not know this place existed until recently. You have no need to assume the blame for what happened. It has been going on much longer than you have been alive.

Faust's wise words resonated with Mori, finding them—and him—a big comfort. He had been her best friend since they'd met, and she felt a special bond with him. She felt she could trust everything he said to be true, without any doubt. She nodded before speaking again. "You're right. This has been going on longer than I have been alive, but that's why it's so important that I stop it. This may not have been my original destiny, but it's the task I will take upon myself for the better of everyone in Albright Forest." Mori thought for a moment before looking at her wolf. "Where do you think the raider stronghold is? I haven't heard anything about its location."

"The stronghold?" a woman's voice asked beside them. "I don't know why you would want to go there, but it's kinda far from here." The naiad woman eyed them curiously.

"Do you know where it is? I need to know so I can stop the raider king." Mori and Faust both stared wide-eyed at this woman with piqued interest.

"Well, I don't know the exact location. It's pretty well hidden, but I heard it was by the Ursamong Peninsula." The woman shrugged. "I overheard a few raiders talking about it."

That is on the other side of the forest. It would take at least three weeks to reach it on foot, if not longer, Faust informed Mori, which brought an incredulous look to her face.

"Why is your wolf growling?" the naiad asked.

"He is speaking, but only I can hear him. He was saying it would take at least three weeks to reach the Ursamong Peninsula."

The naiad thought for a moment before nodding. "Yeah, that sounds about right. It's pretty far away from here, but that's if it actually is there. No one really knows for certain." She was going to say more, but another nymph pulled the woman to her feet so they could go dance.

Mori leaned back against Faust and snuggled into him. "I guess we have a location to check first when the time comes." The wolf nodded in agreement.

Mori and Faust looked over at Duncan in time to watch a few naiad women pull him to his feet. The elf smiled happily as he followed them toward the fire. The women placed shell necklaces and cloth over his head and neck before they started to dance. Their bodies were fluid as they moved, reminding Mori of swimming in the water. The firelight reflected off their skin and scales, emitting a radiance of beautiful colors. Mori had no idea what the dance was called, but it was beautiful and worth the sight. This was truly a once in a lifetime chance to witness.

Queen Adairria made her way over to Mori and sat down beside her. "How are you enjoying the festival?" she asked, a smile stretching her features as she looked out at the dancers.

"It's wonderful. The dances are elegant and fun to watch. I wish I could dance myself, but I have two left feet." Mori laughed, shaking her head a bit.

"Even with only one foot, one can dance. You just have to let the rhythm move your body." The naiad queen wiggled her arms and swayed with the beat. "You can dance while sitting or standing. Dancing is not just an action; it's a feeling that comes from within."

"There are a lot of things I want to feel from within, but I'm not sure that's going to be possible for me." Mori's green eyes found the grass she was playing with between her stretched-out legs, her fingers running over the blades.

"What troubles you, Mori?"

She looked up to see Adairria watching her curiously. Was it really OK to ask the things she wanted to ask? Surely the naiad queen would know a thing or two about being a leader.

"I don't know how to be a queen," she admitted, her eyes returning to her fingers. "I know I'm supposed to do great things, but I feel useless. I can barely heal anyone, and I certainly can't save them."

"You saved us," Adairria pointed out.

"I had help."

"We all help each other, but that doesn't diminish your contribution. You still took the initiative to save my people, and we are forever grateful for that." A webbed hand rubbed Mori's back, not helping with her nerves, but it was at least a comfort.

"I have never been good at being a leader. Anytime I made friends, I followed them everywhere like a lost puppy. Where I'm from, having a line of freckles and red hair is considered bad." The forest queen looked up at the woman, her eyes on the verge of spilling tears. "I want to be a good leader, but I don't know what to do."

"My dear Mori, you are doing everything you can right now. You didn't grow up here, so I can only imagine how hard it's been to acclimate to our ways. Personally, I think you're doing fine. You just need to hold your chin up and make sure the whole forest knows you're here to be the queen they need, even if it's not the queen they want."

Damn, that's some sound advice.

"I don't know if that's something I can do. I would rather be in the back pretending I don't exist. Being alone is all I'm good at, so interacting with others has been hard. I can't connect with anyone here." Mori sighed heavily, wiping the tears that managed to escape her eyes.

"I know it will be hard, but do little bits at a time. Being queen means sacrifices, but that doesn't mean you have to sacrifice everything all at once. Growing into the role is a much better way to learn, just like how our children grow into their adult selves. They grow up learning what they need to take on everything life has to offer. So maybe being small and unnoticeable is not such a bad thing."

Was that really true for someone who had to make themselves seen? The "being small and unnoticeable" part aside, Adairria was right. She would grow into the role of queen. As long as she did her best, she would learn from every mistake she made. In her mind, that was the best kind of royalty. Someone who could learn.

143

Chapter Eleven

When morning arrived, Mori felt refreshed. During the night, someone had put a blanket over her since she had fallen asleep against her wolf companion. Faust was still sleeping peacefully when Duncan walked up to her with a wooden plate of different fruits and nuts, none of which she knew the name of, but by the looks of them, they were good. He seemed in good spirits after his night there. Considering the fact Mori had watched some of the nymphs escort him to a house, she had a pretty good idea as to *why* he was so happy, but didn't want to think about it too much.

"I feel refreshed. Those nymphs really know how to pamper an elf." Duncan chuckled as he rested his hands on his hips.

"I'm glad you do. It's been nice to relax, even if it was for a night." Mori watched as a few of the nymphs went about their morning chores while she ate her breakfast. Duncan sat beside her with his own food. A naiad walked over with a bowl of meat for Faust. The wolf's movement startled Mori, and she turned to look at him. "Morning." She smiled.

He dipped his head so she could pet him before he started to eat.

After they ate and packed up, they said farewell to the naiads before continuing their journey through the forest. Their next destination would be further away than she'd realized. One of the naiad women explained it would take at least a few days to get to the fairy territory. It was one of the biggest settlements because the location was the ideal place for many different kinds of fairies of different elements to coexist, at least, according to Duncan.

"How have they been there for so long with raiders trying to take over?" Mori asked.

"They're very good at fighting. They have dedicated trained warriors who are stronger than the raiders, and they have magic. Nothing as strong as yours, but still it's enough to protect them," Duncan explained as they walked along the river.

"So, do we just follow this river to get there?"

"Mostly. Once we reach the base of the mountains, we head west. I have been there before many times. They're usually very kind to the royals, so we shouldn't have any issues once we're there." Duncan kicked a rock into the water, a bored expression plastered on his face.

They were making great time until it started to get late into the afternoon, bringing an early twilight. Mori stopped, sighing deeply with relief as she sat down by the water's edge, exhaustion taking over her whole body as it sagged.

"My legs hurt from all the walking. We should stop here and get something to eat. I'm hungry." She leaned back on her hands, her fingers almost touching the water as her palms lay on the very edge of the riverbank.

"I guess that leaves you and me to hunt," Duncan said to Faust, who nodded in agreement. "I think there were some sturdy branches back there that we can use for fishing rods." Duncan hooked a thumb over his shoulders at the scattered branches that littered the ground.

"I think that would be a good—" Mori's words were cut short by the scream she let out as something pulled her into the river.

"MORI!" the other two called at the same time before Duncan ran and jumped into the water after her.

Mori opened her eyes and looked around to try to get her bearings, only to see a black horse in front of her with a mane that extended from its neck to wrap around her. She struggled to get the hair off her, tugging at the strands that gripped her body, legs, and left arm. Heat rushed through her body as panic started to set in, until she watched a dark figure cut the hair, allowing her to swim up to the surface.

Bursting up with a gasp of air, the queen sucked in some much-needed oxygen before she could find her cracked voice as the elf came up as well. "What is that thing?"

"Kelpie!" Duncan shouted so the other two would hear. He swam over to Mori to get her out of the water quickly. He pushed her up while Faust grabbed her arm and pulled her out of the water.

"What's a kelpie?" Mori's voice quavered as she asked.

That. Faust growled at the other kelpie on the shore, and Mori looked over at it, finally noticing Duncan was no longer behind her. She frantically searched for her friend before her eyes settled on a disappearing dark figure in the water behind her. *It will lure and drag people to bodies of water to eat them. We need to get Duncan out of the water and leave this area.*

Mori stood up and shook off the scared feeling threatening to take over her body. Hands at the ready, she tapped into the royal magic that coursed through her body, and with an upward movement of her arms, plants in the deepest parts of the river water started to grow at her command. It took a few moments for the algae and water weeds to push most of the rocks and fish out of the water. Among the flopping fish were Duncan and the kelpie tangled in a mass of foliage. He was gasping for air and breathing heavily while the horse fae struggled to break free of the newly grown plants. It used its teeth to rip the water weeds that ensnared its body.

"I don't think so." Mori closed her outstretched hand to make a fist. The kelpie shrieked with pain as the plants tightened their grip, constricting the fae's movement. With her other hand, she opened her fist, commanding the plants around Duncan to release him onto dry land beside her. The kelpie who had confronted Faust jumped into the water and swam away, leaving a trail of blood in its wake. "Don't come near us again!" The plants pulled back into the water, dragging the horse along with it before Mori gasped and fell to her knees, panting hard.

Sweat plastered her face and hands as her heart pounded painfully in her chest. During her training, she had grasped the ability to control plants the way she wanted, but she was still weak when it came to using magic. Growing that many plants at once was very difficult, and she had underestimated how many plants would be at the bottom of the river. When she looked up, both her companions sucked in a breath as their eyes widened.

"Are you OK, Duncan?" she asked once she finally caught her breath, though their expressions made her brows furrow.

"Am I OK? I should be asking you that!" He knelt beside her as he took out his handkerchief. Warm liquid dripped from her nose onto the ground, making her look down. Blood. Mori hesitantly took the cloth and pressed it to her nostrils before pulling back to look at the red blood that stained its white color.

"Oh, I guess I overdid it again." She let out a humorless chuckle before looking over in the direction the kelpie had taken off. The water was calm and all was clear. "I don't think we should stay here. They may come back and try again. I don't think I can handle using my magic like that for a while." Mori tried to stand but stumbled and held her head in her hand.

Get on me. I will carry you, Faust said as he moved closer so she could climb onto his back. They followed the river a little more so they could find somewhere safe to camp for the night.

"Are we there yet?" Mori complained. It had been two days since they were attacked by kelpies and left the naiad territory. The kelpie attack was not their only setback. A massive thunderstorm had come from nowhere, forcing them to seek shelter for half a day and lose valuable time. She knew that every step of their journey would be worth it, but she was exhausted.

"Almost. It should be just up here." Duncan pulled back a tree branch filled with leaves to reveal a village full of life and laughter.

Mori gasped excitedly as she took several steps forward. From what she could tell, the village was split into sections. There was a large gathering area with luscious grass and a lot of room to run around. Many different-colored fairies sat in small groups, chatting away with each other and enjoying the sunshine. She smiled when she saw them having a picnic while the children played on overgrown toadstools and tree stumps with blooming flowers.

A long stream flowed through the middle, and she noticed small intricate bridges allowing the fairies to cross from one side to the other. In the distance were mushrooms the size of a small two-story townhouse, with doors and windows, each decorated uniquely depending on what the fairies who inhabited it liked. She took several more steps in and observed the farmers tending to their large plants that hung plump ripe fruit. One fairy was kneeling and pulling purple carrots out of the ground and putting them in a wicker basket that lay beside him. Mori could feel the strong ambient magic in the air, and it filled her with a euphoria of calmness and serenity. It was everything she had imagined it would be from what she'd seen in books in the human realm.

"Welcome to the fairy territory," Duncan said to his queen before he walked past her, wearing a smile on his lips that split into a laugh. "Are you OK? You're crying. I hope those are happy tears."

Mori reached up and gently wiped away the single tear from her right cheek with her fingers before nodding. "They are. This is such a beautiful place. Makes the whole journey here worth it, even dealing with the kelpies." She laughed, her hands over her stomach as she started to walk and quickly glanced over her shoulder before stopping suddenly and spinning on her heels. Faust had not moved from the tree line and continued to hide in the shadows of the branches. Her brows frowned as she moved a little closer to him and motioned with her hand for him to follow, but when he didn't, her smile faded and was replaced with worry. "What's wrong?"

Fairies do not like me. They will attack me on sight. I do not have a good history with them, he explained, making Mori raise an eyebrow.

She crossed her arms and stiffened her posture. "If any of them try to say anything bad or hurt you, I will keep you safe." She gave him a reassuring smile before dropping her arms and motioning for him to follow. Faust took a hesitant step out into the sun, followed by another slow, cautious one as two children ran past Mori. She didn't move until her wolf was by her side, right where he belonged. His tail was tucked between his legs and his ears were pinned back as he kept his head low. Seeing him scared like this made Mori's heart hurt, but she knew she would ensure his safety, just like he had been keeping her safe this whole time.

As she walked with Faust more into the open area, the sounds of conversation and playing halted when the fairies noticed the three of them. They heard whispers as they walked and a few fairies flew away.

This is more uncomfortable than I thought. What did you do to them that was so bad? Mori asked Faust, a nervous smile forming on her lips as her heart started to race. She suddenly wondered if he had been right to want to wait at the tree line. Before he could answer, an elder fairy flew to them and landed in front to block their path, making the three of them stop in their tracks.

"I am Fairy Queen Sophie," she introduced before moving some of her long pink hair to the side so it was out of her face. Mori studied the elegant fairy woman, taking notice of the regal green dress with pink peony flowers that adorned the left side of the bodice down to the main skirt. Her hair was braided in the back, and wisps of hair that had come undone framed her slightly wrinkled face. A tiara sat upon her head and shone in the sunlight. "We welcome our new forest queen, Moriana, to our territory." Sophie turned her gaze from the queen to the wolf behind her, a scowl taking over her once soft features. "*He*, on the other hand, is not welcome here. We will not allow that *thing* to walk among us." Her tone was filled with venom that made Faust flinch. Mori stepped protectively in front of her wolf, her brows furrowed and a stern look gripping her usually kind face. Her eyes glanced back at Faust in time to see him look down at the ground with a soft whimper before her eyes returned to the fairy before her.

"Faust is with me. He is my loyal companion now. If he's not welcome, then neither am I. Are you sure that's how you want to greet your new queen? Hostility toward her protector and trusted advisor?" Mori spoke with authority, something she had been practicing while they'd walked. However, she was only masking. She was not very good at backing up those words with confidence, as she was still new to her powers and this world.

Sophie shook her head. "We mean no disrespect to you, Your Majesty. We simply don't want this mass murderer of our kind to be here." She took a hesitant step back, as if worried she would be smited by the queen for speaking so freely.

Mori's face fell as the stern look she'd once held shattered and was replaced by shock and indignation. Mass murderer? What was she talking about? She turned to look at Faust for a moment, watching as he nervously pawed at the ground. His eyes shifted up to her for a split second before darting back to the grass. This wasn't right, accusing him without proof. She turned and knelt, gently petting his head with her hand to let him know she wasn't mad at him. "Stay at the edge of the forest. I will get this sorted out and come find you."

Are you sure you can? he asked. *She is accusing me of something I had no control over.*

"I'm sure," she told him. *If I can't convince them to let you stay, then we will all leave. I don't need their help if they can't accept you,* she added through their connection before she stood up and turned her gaze to her guard captain. "Come with me." Mori turned back to Queen Sophie as Faust scurried back to the tree line to hide. "Let's go somewhere we can speak privately. I would like to know what you mean by those harsh words. That was quite the accusation." Her own voice was unwavering as she struggled to keep the anger out of it, only managing to succeed a little. After everything Faust and Duncan had done for her, how they protected her and kept her safe, this was the least she could do. The fairy queen nodded once before turning to walk toward one of the largest houses in the area.

As they walked, a memory flashed in Mori's mind. It was so sudden and powerful in her mind that she knew someone was trying to convey something to her, something she needed to know before the talk she had with Sophie.

The memory was of Faust running through war-ridden chaos in the fairy territory. The mushroom houses behind the wolf were on fire, and the grass was nothing but blackened ash. He was biting and scratching the fairies he could catch, ripping off their wings and tearing out their throats to end their lives. His eyes glowed a solid red, and he looked like a feral beast with blood matted in his fur. When Faust looked over his shoulder, Mori got the sense she was in the first-person view of a previous royal, the man who had made Faust a direwolf, because he was looking right at her, or him in this case.

The man glanced down at his blood-covered hands and then back up at his wolf, who had just killed a fairy. Her gaze drifted from Faust up to the hundreds of bodies that lay throughout the same courtyard Mori was standing in now. She wanted to look around more, but she was not in control of anything in this memory, nor was she in control of how long the memory flashed. Just as quickly as the memory had come, it was gone and she was back in the courtyard with Duncan and Sophie, still being stared at by the fairies who had remained to witness the interaction.

"Are you OK?" Duncan whispered as they walked.

Mori jerked a nod before giving a weak smile. "Yeah, just a little nervous is all."

Sophie motioned for the two to follow her to her home. It was a large beige mushroom decorated with little festive lights and was surrounded by hundreds of smaller decorative mushrooms. She opened the door and allowed her guests inside before following and closing the door behind her. The inside was beautifully decorated, with many peonies, daffodils, tulips, and orchids growing in their pots, and canvas paintings of small animals lined the walls of the main room. Mori was amazed by the details in the paintings. Her favorites were the mice, a pair of squirrels, and a cat curled up in the sun.

In what Mori considered the living room was a two-seater couch and an armchair facing a central coffee table. Beside it in the dining room was a small table with two chairs. She turned her gaze up to see a loft with no ladder. She assumed that was the bedroom, but she couldn't see what was up there from down below. The kitchen was small compared to the other rooms, consisting of a small fire pit with a grill for cooking, a countertop, a sink basin, and a few storage cabinets. Mori was so impressed by the nature within the house that she wished she was the one living in the cozy home.

"Please, sit and make yourself at home." Sophie went to the kitchen to make some tea while Mori and Duncan sat on the couch. When the tea was ready, the fairy made her way to the living room with a tray with three cups and set it down on the coffee table before handing her two guests their cups and sitting in the armchair with her own.

"Sophie, can you please tell me what happened from your point of view? Faust is my trusted companion, and while I have some knowledge, I would like to hear from you," Mori said, not taking a sip of her tea yet. She was very wary of it, noticing a hint of something that she felt shouldn't be in an herbal tea, but unable to place what it was.

"As I'm sure you're aware, we are one of the strongest fae here in the forest, but we are no match for a royal. There have been fifty-eight royals in the line so far, you being number fifty-nine. It was number thirteen, Asani. I am part of a lineage of fairies who managed to survive the attack." Sophie took a sip of her tea before continuing. "The one you call Faust was cursed by that royal and committed mass genocide on our provences. He went from territory to territory in an attempt to kill as many fairies as possible. He refused to accept the outcome of the war that had happened a few royals before him."

"War?" Mori asked, and lifted her cup to her lips, only pretending to take a sip. She didn't trust it just yet.

"The four main fairy factions took sides and fought each other. I don't know what stopped it. I was on a diplomatic mission when, all of a sudden, there was a treaty being signed. I couldn't find the ruling royal at the time. He disappeared, so I went to his son to keep him safe while he grew up," Duncan explained, also not drinking the tea, but not pretending to drink it either.

"The war devastated us, and we were in the process of replenishing our population when Asani appeared to kill us." Sophie took another sip of her tea. "It has taken a long time to recover our numbers and build peace after he finally left us alone." She shook her head. "I simply cannot allow Faust to be here after what he's done."

That explained the memory Mori had witnessed, and the way Faust was acting. She had already determined the person in the memory was a male royal, but until now, she hadn't known which one. But after hearing Sophie's story, she knew that must have been a memory of the thirteenth royal. She still wasn't sure how she was able to witness the previous royal's memories. Was it because of the royal magic or because she was part fae? She pushed the thought from her mind, knowing she needed to focus on the fairy queen before her. These memories would have to wait to be explored.

"We are so sorry your people suffered. I tried to stop it, but I was locked up for disobeying an order. He wanted me to kill fairies as well, but I refused. I believe he was seeking revenge for what happened to his father, but I was never given the chance to ask. I was imprisoned for most of his reign," Duncan explained, and hung his head in shame. "I can't apologize enough for not being able to stop it." The elf looked back up at her when she shifted in her seat.

The fairy queen held up her hand to silence him. "You defied orders and tried to stop it; that is good enough for me. I'm a reasonable leader, but I can't turn my back on history and let that wolf in here. I can't trust him."

Mori nodded, understanding where the woman was coming from. She wouldn't trust someone who had tried to kill her, either. She took a deep breath as he put her teacup down on the tray before turning her gaze to Sophie. "While I won't invalidate what you have been through, I do have my suspicions about the whole ordeal. I don't think Faust had any control over himself. I remember reading something in a book back at my tree house, and I want to confirm something." She stared intently at Sophie, searching for any hint of deception as she asked her question. "Did his eyes glow a solid bright red?" She was mostly asking to know for sure if what she'd seen was a memory or if her mind had created a false memory. Though she had to admit to herself, it felt more real than any dream ever did.

"Yes, they were glowing solid red, and he always had blood around his mouth, fairy blood."

Mori exhaled, realizing her suspicions were unfortunately true. "As you seem to be aware, Asani had the ability to curse people. Faust told me the story of his being cursed. It happened because of a mistake, and he was forced to do horrible things he never wanted to do. I believe Asani put a spell on Faust to control him so he could never disobey."

"Controlled? That sounds like a rumor. Rumors have no authority here," Sophie said as her eyes narrowed.

Mori's heart started to race as nerves took hold, but she needed to do this for her best friend. "I am certain of it. I read about how our royal powers allow us to learn curses and blessings as we age and study. If we curse someone, we can control them, and they might or might not actually be aware of what they're doing. From the feelings and thoughts I have shared with Faust through that connection, I know he is aware of what he did and actively fought against the curse, to no avail. He was not in control of his actions."

Mori moved to the edge of the couch cushion she occupied. "That being said, I will not make excuses for what has happened to your people. Wounds like that do not heal and go away with time; they simply leave a visible scar for all to see. This scar was a particularly nasty one from how traumatic of an event it was, especially after a war." She moved off the couch and onto her knees before the fairy queen, her palms sweaty and her heart pounding in her chest. "I apologize on behalf of my predecessor. I know that can't bring anyone back from the dead, but my goal as the current forest queen is to right the wrongs of the past and help everyone living in Albright Forest live their best, happiest, and safest lives." She bowed her head briefly and lifted it back up. "My plan is to stop the raider king and take back our forest. However, to do that, I must be able to go into battle with an army. The raiders are strong and I am one person. I won't be able to do this alone. I need your help, but I also need Faust." It was time Mori put her diplomatic skills to use—at least, the ones she had been practicing with Duncan since getting the forest magic.

Sophie's eyes narrowed until they were little slits and put her teacup down on the tray. "You bring a murderer here and expect us to back you up in a war?" she snapped, her back straightening in her chair as she sat upright.

"I will take full responsibility for Faust for anything he does while we're here. I will help your territory however I can, even after the war is over." Mori hoped this would be an acceptable compromise for Sophie. She stared intently at the older woman, watching as her eyes shifted to the side as if in deep thought.

"I will help as well. I'm strong, and Faust will be put to work too. He's good at carrying things and people. He carries Mori all the time. He's not the wolf he used to be, and we are just asking for a chance for him to prove it. There will be no slacking for any of us while we are in your territory," Duncan explained.

Sophie thought about it more before shifting her eyes to the queen and nodding. "All right, but if he does *anything* out of place or that could be seen as hostile, all of you will be punished harshly and banished from every fairy providence, including you, Queen Moriana."

"Understood, Queen Sophie. And please, just call me Mori." She stood up, her heart painfully pounding against her rib cage as relief flooded her mind and body. Her last comment got her a glare from the fairy. "If there is nothing else, I will go see what work needs to be done to earn our stay and your trust." Mori stood up, and so did Duncan. "If there is something specifically you wish for us to do, please let me know now and I will see to it personally."

Sophie exhaled an audible breath through her nose. "You can help in the medical ward. Some of the kids fell in the river this morning and got hurt. Then some plants have been dying in the fields and need tending to. Ask around if you need more work, but this will give you a start. As for the army for the war, we will see what you do with your time over the next few weeks." She showed them to the door so they could leave.

Once outside the house, Mori turned to Duncan and winced. "Was that bad? How bad was it? I know I'm not good at being diplomatic, but I tried." Her words were quick and shaking.

Duncan shook his head. "You did fine. It wasn't bad. You didn't let her walk all over you, and that's a good thing."

Mori nodded before she noticed in the corner of her eye someone staring right at her. She turned to see Lorem leaning against the wall of the mushroom, but she stood up straight when she saw the girl.

"So it's true, you are here," the satyress said with a smile, and gave a light bow.

"Lorem! I'm glad to see you again, but what are you doing here?" The queen beamed.

"I came here after Queen Vi passed away. I wanted to do some good for the forest by joining the fight once more. I just needed to hone my skills more with my longsword." She hooked a thumb over her shoulder at the highly decorated black handle of her sword strapped to her back.

"I'm glad to have you back in the fight. I hope I can count on you when we take on the raiders. We were talking to Queen Sophie about gathering an army to stop the raiders. We could really use your talents in the upcoming war."

"You can count on me, Queenie." Lorem beamed, the smile reaching her eyes as her hands rested on her hips. Mori loved how committed the satyress was.

"I appreciate it. I hope I can train more alongside you during our stay." Mori held out her hand to the satyress, and they shook.

"It would be my pleasure to whoop your butt in a sword fight to help you improve." She chuckled before walking off when she heard a fairy warrior call for her. Mori just laughed a bit and shook her head before she went to the tree line to meet up with Faust.

Now it was time for a more serious conversation that she knew she needed to do. While she walked to her wolf, she tried to summon the words to say and think of how best to string them in a way that made sense and conveyed what she wanted. Upon reaching her best friend, she knelt in front of him. "I'm sorry for making you do something you were uncomfortable with and embarrassing you. I should never have made you do anything you didn't want to do."

Faust shook his head. *I do not want you to worry about me, and I accept your apology. I know you did not mean any ill intent.*

Mori hugged her wolf for a few moments before sitting back and explaining to him what was talked about and that the wolf had to be on his best behavior. She didn't want to actually get in trouble because he stepped out of line after she'd vouched for him, not that she had any reason to worry. He had been kind to everyone who was deserving the entire time they had been together. When she finished her explanation, she stood up and led him away to their first assignment.

Her first stop was in the medical hut. There were a few fairies with burns and cuts from doing chores and not being careful. The worst injury the queen saw was a broken wing, which was fixed pretty easily by her magic. With everyone healed up and on their way, she wiped pretend sweat from her brow with the back of her hand.

"All in a day's work." Her lips curved up as she placed her hands on her hips, feeling confident in her abilities after using them over and over.

"You barely lifted a finger," the nurse fairy teased as she helped clean up the used dressings.

"It was still work. I'm not the greatest at using magic. Besides, I did good here and I'm glad I could help." Mori walked off to clean up her mess and get everything put back. Even though she had used magic the majority of the time, she still used some things to clean up blood and dirt so she could get a better look at what needed mending. This whole experience made her relieved that she'd paid attention in anatomy and biology classes in school. "I'm gonna go talk to Sophie about us staying here so I can train and continue to help." With that, Mori walked off to talk to the fairy queen.

Chapter Twelve

That night, the fairies decided to hold a feast to celebrate the arrival of Queen Mori. She felt uncomfortable having these festivals held in her honor, because she didn't feel like she deserved them, especially after being rejected at her coronation, unable to save the pixies, and having done nothing to dispatch the raiders from the forest. So far she had done nothing noteworthy for the royal journals.

She leaned against Faust while they sat in front of the fire with Duncan and a few other fairies. They were talking about something, but she was not paying attention. Mori was lost in her thoughts, going over the memory that had flashed in her mind hours before. This was the first chance she'd had to really think about it. To see her best friend like that, covered in blood he didn't wish to be covered in. Doing the bidding of another against his will broke her heart. That was no way to live. Faust's movements startled her back to reality as she looked over her shoulder.

You should listen to what they are saying, he told her, and motioned toward the two fairies on the other side of the small fire. The woman had long black hair and was adorned with different kinds of plant jewelry over her blue dress. The man had short blond hair and wore just a green kilt-like cloth around his waist. They were arguing now.

"I'm telling you, I saw it!" the man said to his companion.

"I doubt it. There's no way you saw it. It's too far away. You would never venture that close." The woman crossed her arms over her chest as her brows pinched in disbelief.

"What are you two talking about?" Mori finally asked, her head cocked to the side a bit.

"Yu'telle says he saw the ghost ship, but I think he's lying. He would never go near the island," the woman explained.

"Shut up, Yasha. I have been there. I went with the last scouting party. Everyone was asleep and that's when I saw it." Yu'telle rolled his eyes.

"Uhh, what is this about a ghost ship?" Mori asked.

"Haven't you heard about the ghost ship of Scuttle Island? It's famous throughout the whole forest." Yasha leaned forward with interest as Mori shook her head. "It's a story every fae is told as a way to keep us from going to the island. Long ago, the fairies were split into two factions. The earth and water fairies against the fire and air fairies. The water fairies were really good at building ships and would come in by the sea and river in an ambush attempt." Yasha used her arms to show a winding river while she spoke. "One day, the water fairies discovered the fire fairies had built a ship of their own and were heading straight to their ship to take back their prisoners of war and capture the ship. However, the water fairy captain, known as Captain Avarisha, was told he couldn't be captured for any reason. Mostly because if he was tried, he would have to spill the secrets of their cruel ways." Yasha's hands slapped down on her knees, making Mori flinch a bit. "He was using the prisoners as slaves to build and maintain his ships. That's a capital crime in the forest, always has been."

"So what did he do when he learned about the approaching enemy?" Mori asked.

"He scuttled the ship in the dead of night," Yu'telle told her. Mori's confused expression made the two fairies laugh.

"To scuttle a ship means to sink it purposely. Captain Avarisha sank his whole ship and killed everyone while they slept, including himself." Yasha shook her hands in the air, doing what Mori knew in the human world was "jazz hands." It was weird to see here in the forest.

"What happened after that?" she asked as she leaned forward, invested in this story.

"No one really knows for sure. Shortly after the ship sank near Scuttle Island, the war between the fairies ended peacefully. But there are rumors of the ship still guarding the treasure on the island. Some unconfirmed rumors say he hid his treasure on the island to keep it safe, but no one has been able to find it." Yasha shrugged.

"The ones who try always come scuttling back with their tails between their legs." Yu'telle laughed. "I think it's funny how the island name has a double meaning, but the bloodshed it has caused is not funny at all."

"Shut up, Yu'telle. It's a ghost story, not the punchline to one of your lame jokes. It doesn't need a funny name." Yasha rolled her eyes.

I want to see this island now. Maybe I can sniff out the treasure. Faust nudged Mori, making the queen chuckle.

"I'm not sure I want to go. Horror has never been my thing. I don't enjoy getting scared." She petted her wolf's head.

"Yasha, Yu'telle, dinner is ready," a woman behind them called out, the two turning to look over their shoulders.

"Great," Yu'telle groaned. "Mom's calling us." The two fairies stood up.

"Wait, did you really see the ghost ship, Yu'telle?" Mori asked quickly.

He nodded. "Yup. It was really brief, but it was definitely a ghost ship. It will stop anyone from getting to the island." The two fairies ran off to catch up with their mother.

"Those two fight like siblings. I think they are." Mori chuckled.

I think they are siblings too. They smell similar. Faust looked up at her. *You should get some sleep. Your training starts tomorrow.*

She nodded and snuggled up against her wolf so they could sleep.

"That was brutal," Mori said as she plopped down on the grass, sweat glistening in the sun as her heart pounded in her chest and she took quick, shallow breaths.

"You're doing well in your training," Orian said. The fairy military general had been tasked with training her in sword fighting alongside Lorem and Duncan. When she wasn't learning the way of the sword, she was learning how to control her powers better from Sophie. Mori lifted her sword and looked it over. "It still looks new and shiny. It's like I never hit anything with it." She sighed.

Orian walked over to her and knelt, his long black hair still neat and tight in its long ponytail. His dark-brown eyes looked into Mori's green ones as a smile formed on his lips. "You will get better with time. You can't expect to become a master with the sword in a fortnight." He laughed and held out his arm to help the queen to her feet.

"I know that. It's just . . ." She paused as she looked at the sword she held in her hand. "It doesn't feel right for me. The sword is lightweight and fast, but I have to be conscious that I don't end up hitting the enemy with the flat side, like I keep doing during training. I can't help but wonder if a different weapon would be better for me."

"It's normal to feel this way about a weapon you have never used before. I'm sure with more practice and time, you will get it down. But you *have* to give yourself time and patience to learn." Orian sheathed his sword. "We should end training for today. You look really exhausted. More so than usual."

Mori chuckled lightly. "There was a cooking disaster this morning, and I had to use my magic more than I have been. Sophie is a great teacher, but my body is still not used to having magic."

"I think that comes from your human side. Just like with the sword, you should keep in mind that mastering magic when you had none before will take time."

"Now you're starting to sound like Sophie." Mori laughed.

"Who do you think I learned it from?" he asked rhetorically as he flashed a smile. "I will see you tomorrow to continue your training. Get some rest for now." Orian walked off, leaving Mori with her thoughts. So much had happened since arriving in the forest. So many new people had come into her life, most of which were good. She sighed as she thought about how much she missed Missy and Jason, hoping they weren't too worried about her with how long she'd been gone.

Mori, let us go! Faust called to her, snapping her out of her thoughts. He was standing outside the guest mushroom house, his tail wagging and his tongue hanging out. He looked happy, and some of the fairies were willing to interact with him now that he had shown he was not a threat to any of them. The two had been going for runs in the forest since the area was much safer. Mori learned that Bob stayed away from the fairies, and so did most of the other dangerous fae creatures, such as kelpies. The fairies were very well established as being at the top of the food chain.

"I'm coming! Keep your tail on!" The queen laughed as she made her way over to him. Her light-blue tunic was accented with her usual brown belt full of pouches she'd grabbed from the tree house. Her once-white pants looked decorated with brown and green stains from being on the forest floor. They were tucked into her mid-calf brown boots that she always wore because she was so comfortable in them. Her curly red hair was pulled back into a high ponytail with a thick scrunchie in an unsuccessful attempt to keep it out of her eyes. "I'm ready. Race ya to the big tree!"

Mori took off running through the trees, Faust quickly on her heels. Due to her training, she had to stay in top shape to keep up with the others, especially her speed, stamina, and agility. As the two raced, Mori jumped over a downed tree before quickly jumping off a rock to avoid the small stream. Faust was able to jump over both in one leap. Mori was jealous of that ability, but she would never admit that to anyone, especially him. The two were neck and neck during their race. Her motivation for making sure she could run fast lay with the skull-headed beast and her intense, paralyzing fear of being eaten by him.

Seems you are as fast as me now, Faust commented as he ran beside her. Mori panted hard, but she was keeping up with the four-legged beast.

"One day, I'm going to outrun you completely." She laughed a bit. Unfortunately, today was not the day for her to win the race. Her foot caught on a strong stem, causing her to trip and fall just before their finish line. The wolf crossed between two trees, each with a red scarf wrapped around it to signify the end of their challenge. Faust quickly turned around and ran back to her, helping her to her feet. Mori noticed he'd barely broken a sweat by the lack of panting, while she, on the other hand, looked like she was about to keel over. She decided the grass was a much better place to be than standing up on shaky legs, and lay down. Her lungs still felt like they were on fire, but not nearly as bad as they had been when she'd first started training. Sweat glistened her exposed skin as she did her best to suck in lungfuls of air.

Faust moved to stand over her and look down before cocking his head to the side. *You will beat me one day, but not today. You should work on your stamina.*

Mori snorted. "I know. I just want to get better at sword fighting and magic first. For whatever reason, I can't get the hang of a sword. It just doesn't feel right in my hand," she explained as she stared up at her wolf. "It feels too light and takes too many specific movements to do any real damage."

Sounds like you need something you can just swing around that will do damage no matter where on the weapon it hits.

"Exactly!" Mori exclaimed, and let out a breathy laugh.

You told me what your mother said when you met her. There was a poem about a weapon that the royals use. It was a hammer of some kind. Do you think a hammer would be a better weapon for you? he asked curiously.

Mori thought about it for a moment. "Maybe. That does sound more like my style. Being able to swing a mighty hammer around and not have to worry about what direction the sharp end is facing. It always smashes." She laughed.

Have you put any thought into finding the hammer?

"I have, but I don't know the forest well enough to know where to start. I have a feeling it won't be easy to get to." She shrugged and looked up at the sky when Faust moved to lie beside her on his back, his paws in the air above him. Lying in the grass was so peaceful, but that peace was short-lived. The smell of burning wood filled her nose, making her bolt upright, her gaze turning toward the direction of the fairy territory. "Faust . . ." she breathed, her voice trailing off. The wolf looked at her to follow her gaze.

We need to head back.

"Agreed." Both of them scrambled to their feet before taking off running. As her wolf grew in size, Mori jumped onto his back so they could get there faster.

When they finally came within the boundaries of the territory, her heart sank as she let out an audible gasp and her eyes widened. The whole place was swarming with raiders, their swords striking down innocent fae or clashing with steel. Mori slid off her wolf companion and took a few shaky steps forward, just to be pulled back by her hood, avoiding being run over by a large red bull that was *on fire*. But that wasn't the only one. The beasts were everywhere, swarming the fairy territory. Every red bull that she could see had intense flames emitting from their bodies. Most of them were in a heated battle with two or more fairy warriors, while others were chasing after civilians. Everything they touched was set ablaze, the fire eating away whatever it could get ahold of.

When she regained herself, she ran after the bull that had almost hit her as it made its way toward a young woman. As the creature brushed against her wings, they were burned up in an instant. The woman fell to the ground in agony, her screams joining the many others around them. After the creature passed her, it headed straight for a row of houses.

Mori did her best to catch up to the rampaging bull, but lost it behind several mushroom houses, all of which went up in flames not too long after. This felt like a lost cause, as she couldn't put out that much fire, so she turned on her heels to see who she could help, only to be met with even more horror. Flashes of the pixie massacre played out in front of her, making her heart pound painfully in her chest as she gasped for the shallow bits of air she managed to pull into her lungs.

An overwhelming drowning feeling swept over her. Her legs threatened to give out and pull her down, but before they could, she felt a sudden warmth pressed to her side and an arm braced her to keep her on her feet. The familiar scent of an oak tree filled her nose, slowing her racing heart so it wouldn't pound in her ears and bringing her back to reality.

"What are those things?" Mori asked frantically, not looking up at Duncan so she could keep her eyes on the civilians before her. All the affrighted fairies were doing their best to fly to safety so the fighters could take on the threat without fear of friendly fire.

"Those are aatxe, or red bulls. They're usually controlled by Mari of the Seelie Court, so I'm not sure why they're here," Duncan answered. "Are you OK? You were standing here instead of fighting like you usually do."

"I don't think I am, but I don't have time to be miserable and traumatized. I need to help." A bull roared out before charging at one of the taller fairies. "Those things are huge!" Mori knew that particular fairy was six and a half feet tall and estimated the bulls had to be at least nine feet.

"Those are more like calves. The adults are much bigger." Duncan slipped his arm from around Mori's back before he grabbed her arm and pulled her to the side, out of the way of a charging bull. "They're on fire, so plants will burn up quickly. We need to use swords to stop them."

"Wait, why are you surprised they're here? And what is the Seelie Court?" Mori dodged an arrow and used some vines to send a raider flying.

"Now is not the time for explaining. Now is the time for fighting." Duncan blocked a swing from a raider's sword before rejoining the fight fully.

We need to get the fairy folk to safety, Faust told her as he ran up beside her, some of his fur singed from the intense heat.

Mori nodded in agreement. "Do what you can to get them away from here. I will try to provide cover." With renewed confidence and her sword out, she dashed away toward the nearest raider and bull to take them head-on so Faust could get the trapped fairies out of their hiding places and to safety. Mori created massive stone walls to protect the civilians while they made a hasty escape whenever an aatxe charged toward them. Walls were a specialty of hers in more ways than one.

During the entire battle, only one bull had been taken down, with many others restrained with chains or magic. Mori had done her best to help, but most of her magic could grow very flammable plants, so she was of no real help in that regard. Many of the fairy warriors were either exhausted to the point of making mistakes, or dead. As she was kicking away one of the last raiders, a voice she didn't recognize spoke behind her.

"You really think you can stop my aatxe? They're quite useful for burning things to the ground. Worked wonders against the leprechauns a few months back." The man laughed and motioned for two flaming red bulls to join him on either side.

Mori didn't recognize him at first, but then the memory of Duncan being cuffed and taken away at the top of the crag filled her mind's eye. It was the man who had sneered down at him when he had been captured. Dairus. She gripped her sword tightly in front of her, her knuckles bleaching, as she glared daggers at the man who had been a destructive force against the fae folk.

"You really think I will let you get away with this?"

"*Let* me?" He howled with laughter. "Do you really think I need *your* permission to pave the way for my king's arrival? You are not *my* queen, foolish girl. You are simply an obstacle standing in the way of the rightful king's power. A *pretender*." Dairus took a step forward and held out his hand. "You don't deserve what you have been so carelessly given. So give it to me and I will let the rest of the little fairies here live." His lip curled up into a wicked smirk. "At least, the ones who will fall in line," he spat, scrutinizing her with malice as he looked her over, the weight of his words bearing down on her and threatening to pull her under.

Truth be told, he was very intimidating with those dark, soulless eyes and strong build. Considering her options, she looked over his dark-brown leather trench coat that covered his white dress shirt and part of his black pants that were tucked into dark-brown boots. His own sword was strapped to his waist with a belt, and it looked untouched and clean, as if he had never used it at all. His words choked the air.

Give up her power? It wasn't like she knew if that were even possible, and even if it were, she would never want to give him anything, let alone the only precious gift she'd received from her mother. But the fairies were losing this battle, and their deaths were the last thing she wanted to continue.

"Even if I knew how, I would never give it to the likes of you!" she shouted, her voice wavering more than she wanted it to.

Dairus shrugged nonchalantly. "I guess you really don't care for your subjects after all." His smirk spread into a fiendish grin as he snapped his fingers, and the two aatxe on either side of him snorted as their flames kicked into high gear. Mori could feel the intense heat from several feet away, making her take a step back and throw up her arm to shield her face.

When the heat was no longer burning her front side, she lowered her arm, her mouth hanging open as her eyes widened. Trepidation flared up her spine as she watched the bulls charge at several unsuspecting civilians to set them on fire. She watched as the flames behind them spread to the nearby trees in an attempt to set the forest ablaze.

"NO! STOP THIS!" Mori cried out as she watched the two flaming bulls turn more homes to ash and ground even more fairy warriors by burning up their wings. Helplessness shot through her like a sword through the heart, sweat trickling down the sides of her face, and not just from the heat. Everything was falling apart around her, just as she was starting to feel comfortable in her new role.

She turned back to Dairus and screamed, "You're insane! All this pointless destruction will get you nothing!"

Dairus let out a hearty laugh. "Nothing, you say? My dear girl, this 'pointless destruction' is not just for fun. I have you exactly where I want you." He sneered and started to walk away, but a wall of vines shot up from the ground to block his path.

"I won't allow this to continue!" Mori gritted her teeth as her eyes started glowing a solid green and a light glow formed around her body. The wind around her whipped into a small storm, throwing around branches and leaves. She spoke again, but this time, it didn't sound like just Mori's voice. It sounded like a womanly voice overlayed her own as if something ancient had taken over. "You shall learn that your actions have consequences."

Her arms moved behind her on one side before arcing over her head to the front of her body, leaving a trail of green light that dissipated quickly. Water from the river rose to form a massive wall with her movements and came crashing down in a deluge over the territory, instantly putting out the roaring flames and extinguishing the bulls. She then stomped a foot down on the ground as vines and tree roots came up to grab the raiders, bulls, and even Dairus. This was a new power, unlike anything Mori had ever experienced. It was raw, hungry, and filled with untapped potential.

She felt herself slipping away, giving in to the surges of elemental power that seemed to come from deep within, and although she could see what was being done, it was as if her body was acting under someone else's command. She felt like she had been locked up inside her own mind.

The sound of flint and steel striking together echoed in the sudden quiet. Steam started to pour from some of the bulls as they thrashed about violently against their restraints, eventually thickening and giving way to smoke. Flames erupted from their bodies but no longer had an impact on their surroundings. The warriors, emboldened by her show of power, charged back in, desperately trying to aid in the situation.

"Why are the aatxe rampaging? They are bringers of peace and justice! Why have they turned on us?" A warrior grunted as the restraint was almost ripped from their hands. The fae were trying not to kill the aatxe but instead bind them until they could figure out what was really going on.

"Let me go, you wretched girl!" Dairus bellowed as he struggled to break free. It wasn't until another raider cut the man free that he was able to move again, shaking off the bits and pieces of foliage from his coat. "You really need to learn your place. This forest doesn't belong to you and I won't let you have it," he added as he glared at Mori.

Suddenly, her world froze. All she could see was the man in front of her, newly freed and giving her a wicked smile that sent chills to her very bones, but her body refused to submit. Before she could register what was happening, the air around her was filled with agonizing shrieks of pain as Dairus snapped his fingers and, one by one, the bulls fell to the earth, reduced to nothing more than piles of ash.

"NO!" Mori roared, but Dairus and the raiders around him were gone.

The queen twirled into the air as a patch of earth rose from the ground so she could land on it and take in the scene around her. Fairies were running around, gathering survivors, pulling some of them from the wreckage of their homes. The bodies of their enemies were scattered alongside the bodies of their allies. This was not the scene Mori had been hoping for. Using her magic, she summoned tree roots to wrap around the deceased raiders and pulled them underground, where they would become fertilizer for the new plants when this territory was rebuilt.

Faust and Duncan hurried to the base of the platform and looked up.

"I don't think she will hear me if I shout. See if you can get through to her," Duncan told the wolf.

Faust nodded. *Are you all right?* he asked, but Mori blocked their communication. The last thing she wanted was for her best friend to feel the extent of her fury. No one here would understand why it was directed solely at herself. The platform she was standing on slowly rescinded back into the earth, her body lowering with it. Her glowing gaze fixed on the elf as she realized the cage that held her magic prisoner had been ripped apart and she was now set free.

"How could this have happened?" The words came out hoarse and with her own voice this time, her anger tangible in the air.

"I don't know." Duncan dropped to a knee to bow and kept his head low as he answered her. "The aatxe should not have been here. There was no reason for them to be away from their posts. I don't know what madness took hold of them."

Mori sighed with indignation, knowing that Duncan had no control over the events that had transpired that day. She did her best to regain her composure before speaking again. "What do we know?"

"The bulls were young. None of them were fully mature—"

"He was controlling them," Mori interrupted. It wasn't a question; she knew it was true. She had seen the evidence with her own eyes when they'd simultaneously dropped dead at the snap of a finger.

Duncan nodded, seeming to ponder what his queen was telling him. "We may not know for sure, but I can tell you they would never align themselves with the likes of Dairus without outside forces at work. Right now, however, we have more pressing matters to attend to." He motioned to the devastation around him. Countless fae lay dead, and the ones Faust had managed to keep away from the fighting were trickling back, lamenting over their lost loved ones and the destruction of their homes. The anguished cries that filled the silence broke something in Mori, and she knew she couldn't sit back and do nothing while more of her people suffered.

Mori took one last deep breath before stiffening her stance and holding her head high. As she spoke, a different voice overlaid her own. "Duncan, how many are dead?"

"Eighty-seven, my queen."

"Tell them to bring the bodies to the trees, the injured as well." She could no longer feel in control of her body, only a passenger as she watched through her own eyes as someone else took over again.

The elf nodded once before standing to go inform the remaining warriors of what to do with the bodies of their fallen comrades and the injured.

Do you have a plan? She didn't remember letting Faust back into her mind, but she supposed at some point her anger calmed enough for her to think clearly.

"I hope so," she said. Faust didn't question her further but kept a watchful eye as she walked over to the crescent-shaped ring of trees that surrounded the territory.

When all the fairies had been placed at the base of the burnt trees, Mori could feel the surge of power from deep within once again, power from the royals before her. She could only watch as the magic flowed from her hands toward the bodies. As the green light encompassed the dead and injured, their wounds began to knit themselves back together. It took mere moments for the breath of life to return to those who had lost it. Not only did life return to the fae, but it returned to the land beneath them and the charred trees behind them. Blackened bark fell away and was replaced with new. Leaves rapidly grew on the branches, filling with luscious vegetation that shined in the sun. Cheers rang out as the fairies moved in to hug their once-dead loved ones, tears of joy staining their cheeks. These were tears Mori could handle.

That was incredible! How did you do that? Faust asked as he nuzzled her hand gently.

"Honestly, I don't know. It's like the past royals were helping me somehow. That shouldn't have worked. Magic isn't supposed to bring people back to life. Whoever was helping me, I'm thankful. This could have been a great tragedy." Mori smiled, relief washing over her. As the fairies rejoiced at the miracle, she turned to look at the still-destroyed territory before shaking her head and clicking her tongue. "This won't do," she said with an airy and lighthearted voice.

Her hands rose from her thighs as if she were lifting something heavy, even though nothing was there. The grass began to sprout from the ash-filled soil as flower beds regrew their flowers. The mushrooms that were still standing shed their charred exteriors and plumped back up with life. Mori swept her hands to the side, making the water flow down through the territory in its usual riverbed. As the magic continued to spread through the ground, it reached the trees on the other side, bringing them back to life again. With new life in their branches, the trees began to sway with the breeze that picked up. Everything was now as it had been before the attack. The only thing left were the piles of ash that used to be the aatxe.

Mori tried several times to bring the young bulls back, but in the end, she collapsed to her knees, fingers digging into the newly grown grass. Exhaustion filled every fiber of her body as the driving force inside her was pushed back, unable to continue their hold over her any longer. The glow around her body dissipated as she panted hard, trying to suck in air as sweat covered her whole body. As the world around her darkened, she could hear the familiar voice of Duncan saying something to Faust.

"We should take her to the birch tree. She will be able to rest there."

Then the world went dark.

Chapter Thirteen

Mori groaned as the sounds around her started to come into focus. The heat beside her moved, making her face scrunch up as her arm reached for that warmth. The bed moved more before becoming very still, and the sound of nails clicking on hard floors echoed slightly as it got further away. Her eyelids felt heavy as she attempted to open them, but as soon as she managed to, she realized she didn't recognize the ceiling above her.

"What the . . .?" Her hoarse voice trailed off as her eyes opened more to take in the green tulle canopy above her. Every muscle and joint in her body ached, but she pushed through it to prop herself up on her elbows to look around the room. The room itself was massive and held more furniture than Missy and Jason had in their entire house. Bookshelves full of books lined the walls around a sitting area with a wooden coffee table, a white three-seater couch, and two white armchairs. The table had a candle that had not seen a flame for some time. Her eyes drifted to the bed she lay in. Tall wooden posts held up a green tulle canopy that was tied to them. The sheets that covered her body looked extravagant, with their green color with gold accents in the shape of the royal insignia, the sapling.

"You're awake!" Duncan's voice echoed in the large room as he hurried over to the bed with Faust right behind him. Mori looked over his new clothes, a puffy dress shirt and brown pants. They were his lounge clothes he would wear when relaxing inside the tree house rather than his adventuring attire.

"Where am I?" she rasped, finally sitting up fully as her hand gently touched her sore throat.

"Relax, Mori. Your body is exhausted after the amount of magic you used. It's not used to that kind of strain." Duncan sat down on the edge of the bed as Faust jumped up to lie down beside her, the familiar warmth from minutes ago returning. So her wolf was the one who'd kept her warm. "You've been asleep for three days. We brought you here so you could rest."

"That doesn't answer my question." She crossed her arms over her chest as her gaze narrowed. "What aren't you telling me?"

You are in the royal palace. Mori turned to look at Faust as he spoke. *Every royal needs their palace. This is yours. You are lying in the royal bed in your bedchamber.*

She looked around the room again, a puzzled look dancing across her features.

"You're in the royal palace. Every royal needs one," Duncan repeated, not knowing Faust had already said that. "This is birch. We're inside a large birch tree near the fairy territory. This is where the royals typically live."

"That's what Faust said. At least the first part." Mori chuckled lightly as her gaze trailed around the room more. "What happened to me? I felt like I was the backseat passenger in a car and had no control over what happened while watching everything."

"That is what we call the Royal Transcendence. The royal magic holds a small piece of every previous royal to ever possess it. When in times of extreme danger, it will call upon a previous royal's specialty to aid you. Usually you're in full control and it gives you the knowledge to use their power. I have never heard of a previous royal taking control of someone."

"Who took control of me? I couldn't tell."

"Well, the first voice sounded like Queen Viviana. My guess is she didn't want to see her daughter in danger and stepped up." He crossed his arms as he thought for a moment, his brows pinching together. "The second voice sounded like Queen Titania, queen of the pixies. She was known for her incredible healing abilities."

That would explain how everyone was brought back to life. She had a special ability that kept all newly deceased souls linked to their bodies so she could resurrect them with the soul intact, Faust explained.

Mori's brows shot up to her hairline as her mouth fell open, staring at her wolf companion. "Woah, linking souls to their bodies? That's a pretty cool ability." She smiled excitedly. "Am I able to do that?"

"I'm afraid not. Until you hone your skills and focus on one area to advance in, you will have the basic magic abilities. Every royal picks a specialty, most opting to improve their sword skills to fend off intruders in the forest." Duncan stood up and turned to face her. "Do you want to see the rest of the castle?"

"I have so many questions, though." Mori pleaded with her eyes.

"We will answer them in time. Come, take a tour of your palace." Duncan held out his hand, to which she promptly took and stood up from the bed. Her calmness lasted moments before she rushed to the door with an excited squeal and pulled it wide open to sprint down the hallway. Paintings of different fae lined the hallways, but her fast running made them all a blur. Arriving in the living room, she saw the many couches and chairs all spread out into smaller groups where many people could sit among their friends to chat without disturbing others. Faust ran up beside her as he looked around as well.

This is the gathering hall, he said, his tail wagging happily behind him.

"This is my kind of palace." Mori laughed as she walked through the room to check out the rest of the tree castle. It had your standard guest rooms, bathrooms, large kitchen, and large open ballroom. Mori couldn't see herself hosting lavish balls and wondered if she could repurpose the space into a training area. She was about to voice the question when they turned the corner and Duncan opened the door in front of them.

The room was quite large, though smaller than the ballroom, and was lined with training dummies, swords, shields, and mats. As she slowly made her way around the training room, she inspected everything. The sapling symbol was imbued on the end of every handle of every sword. It adorned the shields' front, the green standing out brightly against the black background. Mori ran her hands over the marking, feeling the ridges of the lines of paint that covered the incredible smithing of the raised insignia.

"The sapling must be really important for it to be on everything," she commented before glancing over her shoulder at her two friends.

"The sapling was created by the first royal as a symbol of new beginnings. Like how a tree starts as a small seed and grows into a mighty tree. At first, he believed everyone deserved a new start in life."

"At first?" Mori asked as she looked up above the equipment. The drapes that adorned the walls all had what looked like star constellations, but when she noticed one that looked like the swirl from her mother's cheek, she started to see the pattern. They were all marks of the past royals. Hers was the only one missing, which made sense. Her time as queen had just begun, and no one accepted her yet. She couldn't reach the royal-blue fabric to touch the white circles, but she imagined they felt soft and the fabric would feel like a soft blanket.

Duncan nodded. "He changed several years into his reign. I think it was the death of his wife. Some humans had made their way into the fae realm and tried to take her when she was on a solo mission of peace with the fairies. She fought hard, but they killed her as a message." The elf sighed heavily. "Something changed in him for the worse. He hungered for the power to bring her back and take his revenge."

Mori's eyes drifted from one drape to the next, still listening to what her friend was saying. "That had to be tough." Her words echoed slightly in the large room before her eyes landed on the drape that had started it all. It was a circle with a line through the bottom, similar to the power symbol used on video game consoles in her own world. She stopped in front of it, looking over the design. "Do you know what this symbol means?" She looked at Duncan with a blank expression.

"I know it's the royal marking of the first royal of Albright."

Mori let out a humorless chuckle. "In my world, it means power. It's used on electronics as a power button to turn them off and on. It doesn't have a deep meaning or anything as we're used to seeing it, but here I imagine it showed the forest the kind of king he was. One who sought out power to command others."

Duncan brought his fingers to his chin as he stared off, thinking deeply about her words.

That makes sense to me. I was not around when the first royal was alive, but I heard many stories about him. Most of them being about his thirst for power. I did not know the reason until now. Faust walked a little more into the room so he could look up at the symbol himself.

"I can understand his pain. He lost his wife, the love of his life. I, too, would be tempted to take my revenge on those who harmed my loved ones." Mori shrugged with one shoulder. She looked back over the different drapes before her eyes trailed to the weapons lining the room one last time before turning back to her friends and smiling. "Let's get some food. I'm hungry."

The kitchen Mori walked into looked similar to a restaurant kitchen setup. There were lots of counters for preparing food, a large pantry in the wall, and several pots and pans hanging from a rack attached to the ceiling. Everything was covered in a fine layer of dust.

"Did my mom use this kitchen at all?" she asked, running her fingers over the counter as she walked slowly. When she pulled them away, her fingers were covered in dirt and left streaks in the many layers on the counter.

"She did, but it's been many years." Duncan walked over to the biggest wooden cabinet and pulled it open before faltering back and slamming the door shut. Mori didn't understand his reaction until the stench of rotting meat and vegetables assaulted her sinuses.

"What is that smell?" She quickly covered her nose and mouth while her other hand fanned the smell away.

"This is a cooling unit. Magic is used to preserve food for longer. It seems the magic ran out a long time ago," Duncan explained as he quickly moved to what looked like a sink and started dry heaving.

"A fridge? That's pretty neat considering the lack of technology here."

"I don't know what a fridge is. Is that something from your world?" Duncan looked sickly green as he slumped over the sink, his head resting on his arm.

"It's an electric device that keeps food cold to preserve it longer. It doesn't use magic, but it still needs a power source to work." With the smell finally gone, Mori dropped her hands to her sides. "I hope we can find someone else to clean that out. I don't think my stomach will be able to handle the smell either. Especially from up close. I only got a whiff and I feel a little nauseous."

"I know the feeling." Duncan groaned as his knees quaked, struggling to keep himself up.

Mori walked to the pantry to try to find something to eat, but there wasn't much there that wasn't rotten. *Hunting and foraging it is.*

Faust was sent out to hunt for something they could eat while Duncan lay on the couch in another room to try to settle his stomach. After Mori returned from getting some fresh fruit, she walked between rooms to learn the layout. The rooms were massive and beautiful, but it was too much for her. The sheer size of the palace was more than she wanted to deal with. She had always been a cozy-cabin-in-the-woods kind of girl, so the tree house was more than capable of keeping her happy.

When her wolf companion returned, Duncan cleaned the deer he'd brought back to make food for them, and smoked the rest of the meat in the smoker that was part of the kitchen. It even had a chimney for the smoke to escape to the outside. It was definitely more convenient than smoking the meat over a fire like at the tree house. Mori didn't particularly like the smell of meat and declined to taste it, but she knew Faust couldn't survive on a vegetarian diet, and his needs came before her personal choice of food.

Morning brought many different shades of pinks, blues, and oranges as the sun rose above the horizon. Mori was returning to her room after having breakfast when she found Faust lying on the nook under the large window. The sadness she could feel through their connection moved her legs toward her best friend.

"Faust," she said softly as she sat beside him. "Is everything all right?" Concern filled her features, her hand making its way over to pet his head.

No, everything is not, the direwolf said as his eyes pulled away from the window to look at her. Mori felt herself swimming in the sadness that pooled behind his red eyes.

Her lips curled into a small smile as she moved closer and guided his head to her lap, gently petting his head with one hand and his back with the other. "Would you like to tell me what troubles you?"

I would like that very much, Mori, he said, his voice a little shaky in her mind. *A lot has happened in my life. Most of my time was spent locked up in that cave. I had hoped that by being released, I could start anew with you and Duncan, but that does not seem to be the case. My past will continue to catch up to me, and I fear I may have to leave your side so that you may face the raider king without backlash from my company.* He paused as his eyes looked up at her. *I would prefer to be there when you defeat him. I would prefer to* help *you defeat him.*

Mori let out a breath through her nose. "I would prefer that too. I want you by my side. I *need* it. I can't change your past, but I can try to change their minds about the future. Every queen needs their best friend beside them, and you're mine." Her smile grew in size before she leaned down to kiss his head. "No matter what happens, it's you and me against the world and whatever it decides to throw at us."

Even if the world throws the whole forest against me?

"*Us.* It would have to take us both on. I am certain of that," Mori said, her voice level and confident. "We watch each other's backs and keep each other safe, even from ourselves."

That is a big promise. The wolf looked out the window with the same uneasy look he'd had the whole time.

"Faust, what's really on your mind?" Mori asked with a gentle voice.

The wolf let out a huff. *Nothing gets past you,* he tried to joke, but Mori shot him a look that said to get to the point. *After the battle in the fairy territory, when you were passed out, the fae were thanking Lorem and Duncan for their part in saving all of them.*

Mori arched a brow. "You didn't get credit? It's not like you to care about getting credit."

Faust lifted his head to glance at her before turning his gaze out the window once more, a look of longing taking over his features. *I do not care about the credit, as I did not save them to receive such a thing. I saved them because they needed saving from Dairus.* Mori looked out the window, trying to figure out what he was looking at. A family of fairies was playing in the garden, the two children helping their parents do some weeding and planting new flowers. *While you were passed out, several of the civilians I had protected from raiders threw rocks at me once the threat had been neutralized. I do not know what brought it on after what I had done for them. It seemed as if they were seeking revenge for something they did not directly experience.*

"What?" Mori's head snapped to Faust's face as he slowly turned his head to set his gaze upon her. "That's not OK. I will have a talk with—"

No, he interrupted. *I do not wish to cause further trouble with the fairies than I already have.*

"But you aren't that person anymore, Faust. They need to realize that sooner rather than later."

Do you plan to force them to do such a thing? he asked, his logic drowning out her own rage. *Mori, I do not have the ability to make anyone forgive me for what I have done in the past, willing or unwilling, but I want to show them that I'm not the same wolf they remember. I have grown a lot in my short time with you. I do not want you to force anyone to accept me, but a part of me wants them to keep an open mind.* He shook his head. *That is not something anyone, even the queen, can force upon another.*

He was right. Mori didn't have the authority over another creature's mind. It was up to them to decide how to feel.

"What would you like for me to do?" she asked, sadness staining her voice as she spoke, still petting his back with her hand. The wolf lifted the corners of his mouth in an attempt to smile.

If it is alright with you, I would like to stay by your side for as long as you will have me. I have been alone longer than anyone can imagine. He leaned up and licked her cheek. *You have saved me from a fate worse than death and I am forever grateful, but the thought of you eventually leaving me to be accepted by the fairies has me scared of being left behind.*

Mori shook her head. "That's never happening, Faust. It's you and me, always. I would rather turn my back on the entire forest than not have you by my side. You have become invaluable to me." She petted his head some more. "I promise that no matter what I will always come back to you."

I promise to always return to you, too, Mori.

"Besides, you're my first real friend. I refuse to be the type of person who turns her back on her friends." Mori let out a light giggle.

Your first?

She leaned back against the window and nodded, her smile waning as she recalled her harsh social life. "I didn't have any friends growing up. I was always the strange girl with bushy red hair and weird freckles. Some of the other kids thought I had something contagious because my freckles didn't look the same as anyone else's. They weren't all over my face or on my body, just across my nose from cheek to cheek. For humans, anything different is considered bad. I was bullied, picked on, used for target practice when throwing food." She laughed. "You name it, it was done to me. In fact, two days before I was kidnapped, one of the football players threw pudding at my head. I had to wash it out in the bathroom sink. It was not a fun day." She pulled her leg up to rest her arm on her knee. "It may sound pretty bad to say, but I'm glad I was kidnapped by those incompetent raiders. It meant I got to meet you and Duncan. I got to see the forest and meet my mother and Lorem. I never felt like I belonged in the human world, but here feels like home." She raised her arms to gesture all around them. "This palace is amazing, but I prefer our little tree house." Her arms relaxed in her lap as she grinned. "This place has become home to me."

Do you miss your parents? Faust asked as he cocked his head to the side.

"Missy and Jason? Yeah, I miss them a lot. I would love to see them again, let them know I'm OK so they don't keep worrying." She shrugged. "I don't know. Their place was always my safe place. No matter what happened, I could always go there and be safe from the world. I'll be honest, I have been practicing opening the portal. Just to tell them where I've been. I haven't had much luck, but I got close once."

I would be very sad if you left. Faust moved to sit beside her and leaned his body against her arm, his ears pinned back. *I do not want to be alone again.*

"Don't worry, buddy. If I manage to get the portal open, just remember that I will always come back. I can't save the forest without my crime-fighting wolf, right?" Mori laughed as Faust cocked his head to the other side.

Crime-fighting wolf?

"It's a joke. There are numerous TV shows back on Earth where the main character has a dog companion that helps them fight crime and take down the bad guys."

What is a TV show? Is it something I can lick? he asked as his tongue escaped his mouth and hung loosely, his tail thumping the cushion behind him excitedly.

"I'm afraid not, but I know what you can lick." Mori smirked just before Faust licked at her cheek, making her laugh. "And you say you're not a dog." Her teasing voice had Faust barking a single time in protest, but he rubbed up against her nonetheless. The two played for a while before she had to put a stop to it.

"Hold on, Faust. I need to write in my journal before I forget what happened during the battle. I was going to write it when I woke up, but I needed some rest after everything that happened."

All right, but be sure not to take too long. Lorem is coming to train with you and see the palace. You will be more tired afterward. His panting breaths filled the large room where they had just been wrestling.

"I remember Duncan telling me that this morning at breakfast. I will get ready soon, don't you worry your fuzzy head." With one last pet to his head, Mori stood up and went to the nightstand to get the royal journal so she could record what she knew about the battle. Maybe one day her own child would read it.

Chapter Fourteen

The month that followed the fairy territory attack was brutal. Mori traveled nonstop with her friends between the birch tree castle and the fairy territory to help them rebuild their homes. Mostly her job consisted of using her magic to grow the mushrooms rapidly so the builders could hollow them out. She was just happy she could be of service; the guilt of being the reason for the attack weighed heavily on her shoulders. Even though her friends and Queen Sophie tried to tell her it wasn't her fault, the burden didn't lessen at all. She knew if she wanted to prevent this from happening again, she would need to get stronger.

With no real choice but to continue her training with the swords, she trained with Lorem, Duncan, and Orian whenever she wasn't helping the fairies. Magic training with Queen Sophie was going well, and she was getting the hang of it quickly. As she trained, resentment toward the lack of damage she could do with the swords continued to build inside her, and she found herself dwelling on the poem her mother had told her before she died. The Hammer of the Royals seemed impossible to find, but it plagued her thoughts every night. There was so much ground to cover in the forest, and she hadn't even seen a quarter of everything this realm had to offer.

After a while she took a break from training and spent a few days at the oak tree house. She wanted to go over the journals to see if she could find anything that would give her a lead, anything at all that she could use to start her search for the weapon of old. She sighed as she lay in bed with yet another royal journal that was no help in her search. In between the journals, she would read books about plants. Sophie told her that the magic could only work if she knew *how* it worked. You couldn't grow a flower from soil; it must have a seed. The books were very interesting and detailed a lot about how the plants grew, what conditions they needed to thrive, and if there was anything that could be beneficial about them.

Mori was lost in her thoughts when the ground shook, making her bolt upright and swing her legs off the bed. She jumped down from the loft bed and made her way to Faust, who was sitting on the couch. "What was that?"

I smell something bad. We need to close the tree, he said, and stood up just as Duncan burst through the door and slammed it shut, putting his back against it to keep it closed.

"It's Bob!" the elf panicked, panting hard. He took a few steps toward the queen and drew his sword, holding it at the ready.

Mori quickly used her powers to close up the tree house so it would look like an ordinary oak tree on the outside. At the same time, Duncan switched off the lights, as if that would somehow affect whether they could be seen. Another tremor shook the tree, and a deep, guttural growl came from somewhere nearby. Mori held her breath as Faust moved beside her to a more protective position.

Soon, things grew eerily quiet for a few moments. Mori wondered if Bob had decided to move on and left after not finding anything. Duncan was about to speak when a loud roar echoed just outside the tree, making it shake from the force. Faust quickly grabbed Mori by the arm and pulled her down at the same time Duncan put an arm around her shoulders and pulled her toward the floor. A massive claw ripped through the tree, destroying the upper half of the room. If it hadn't been for their quick thinking to duck, all of them would be dead. She looked up just in time to see that claw take the devastating swipe, destroying the home she'd known for the last month and a half. It was gone in an instant. The force from the creature pushed Mori onto her butt. Landing with a hard thump, she knew she would bruise later.

"We gotta go!" Duncan shouted as he grabbed Mori's wrist and pulled her to her feet. The three of them jumped over the remains of the tree house as Bob let out another roar behind them.

The skull-headed beast ripped through the rest of the tree house just as they landed on the other side of its trunk and took off running. Chunks of wood were flying everywhere, barely missing Mori's arm as she fled. The creature took off running after them, his glowing red eye locked on the half-human queen as he closed the distance that separated him from his prey. His footsteps shook the ground, the loud thumping echoing off the trees.

"We must protect Mori at all costs! We can't lose her!" Duncan shouted as they ran, glancing over his shoulder at Bob before he pulled Mori close to him and lifted her up and onto Faust. "Get her to safety! I will try to hold him off the best I can!" The guard captain skidded to a halt as his body turned to face the approaching creature, his sword in hand. Faust's speed never faltered as the queen turned to watch her friend take on the beast, trepidation filling her wide gaze.

"DUNCAN!" Tears stained her cheeks, and her hand reached out toward him for a few moments before pulling it back to stabilize herself on her wolf as she faced forward again. "We have to go back for him!" she shouted at Faust to make sure he could hear her, her voice strained and a little shaky.

That is not happening. We need to get you to safety. If you die, we lose our queen and the royal magic. None of us know what will happen if you die before an heir is born, Faust explained.

There was no denying that her wolf was right. If she died, the entire forest would lose everything and could very well die completely, not that she knew for sure. The magic could fade into the ambient magic of the forest or go to someone completely undeserving who would use it to control the fae. That was a risk she knew she couldn't take, and her two best friends weren't willing to take that risk either. Even though the urge to go back for Duncan was strong, she knew she was the important one, the one who had to survive.

A roar rang out behind them, pulling Mori from her thoughts. She thought she heard shouting, but if there was any, it was drowned out by another roar that sounded a lot closer than it should have. With a glance over her shoulder, the color drained from her face as she saw Bob approaching at a rapid pace, gaining on them as his massive claws tore up the ground beneath him with every step.

Mori let out a scream as Faust dodged a swipe from the creature, its claws missing them by mere inches. The hot breath of the monster chasing them brushed her skin and filled her nose with the stench of rotting meat and probably a rotting tooth. That was too close for her comfort. Using her magic, she transferred it to her wolf to give him extra strength and a much-needed speed boost to put some distance between them and the hungry beast.

Hang on! The wolf darted between trees and lept over bushes, taking advantage of whatever the forest had to use as an obstacle to slow the beast down. Mori threw whatever her power could get its hands on at Bob in an attempt to disorient him. Every time he was hit, Bob would roar at them before trying to swipe at the queen and her wolf. Even with the speed boost and the obstacles, they were not able to put much distance between them.

"Keep us going straight. I have an idea." Mori looked over her shoulder before waving her arm. A wall of oak trees sprang up behind them, but the creature burst through them easily. "Fine, Bob, let's dance." Mori smirked as she called for a vine to cut and tie around her thighs and under Faust so she wouldn't fall off. Next, the queen waved her arms around to create a massive wall of the strong trees, much thicker and taller than before, and wrapped vines around them to add strength. A loud crash rang out behind them as Bob crashed into it and got about halfway through the wall before it completely stopped him. He bellowed out a roar of rage as he struggled to keep pushing through the vine-wrapped trees before switching tactics. Now he was trying to pull out. Trapped by the vines, his claws did their best to tear up the trees to escape.

"That did it!" she cheered, and turned to face forward.

Nice job, Mori, Faust complimented.

"Thanks. Let's get back to the tree house. We have to find Duncan."

Mori and Faust thought they were in the clear before the ground beneath them rumbled and split apart, large fissures opening around them to expose tree roots. Faust tripped on the rising earth, and they were both sent tumbling to the ground. She flipped a few times before a root stopped her momentum. There was no time to groan; she knew the beast had done this, which meant only one thing. Her eyes trailed up and were met with Bob running straight at her. Seeing the hunger in his eye and the drool dripping from his mouth sent a shock of fear through her spine. Her heart had already been beating fast inside her chest, but now it felt like it was trying to burst out to make a run for it. That fear petrified her body as the creature made quick work of the distance between them. His mouth opened wide like he was coming in for a bite of the most delicious taste of food. More drool leaked from his maw as he was almost within reach of her. Mori was glued to the ground, her shoulders hunched up and her whole body filled with trepidation of its impending consumption. The only thing she could do was watch as she was about to be eaten alive.

MORI! Faust yelped out in agony, pulling her from the deep pit of her mind. She watched her wolf companion hang from Bob's jaws, blood dripping down his fangs and matting the wolf's fur. The direwolf had jumped in front of the beast and wound up in his mouth, Bob's teeth wrapped around his torso. The creature bit down harder, making Faust cry out more before his body dropped on the ground with a sickening thud. A massive chunk of his chest and stomach was missing, and his intestines spilled out onto the grass. Blood pooled underneath him as Mori saw more of his organs and bones, including his spine.

"FAUST!" she cried out as a waterfall of tears poured down her cheeks and dropped below her. Her best friend, the one who had comforted her when she was sad, had been her warm bed and pillow when she was cold and tired, and had been there for her when she needed someone the most. This best friend of hers was lying in a pool of blood and saliva, his insides exposed to the world, and dying a very painful death. Mori's instinct was to get to him and heal him, but Bob roared at her, halting her in place.

Mori, run . . . His words were breathy at the end, and the connection she felt with him died along with him. It was completely gone, just as he was. Mori stood up and used her magic to encapsulate the skull-headed beast in dirt and pulled him down underground, hoping his new prison would last long enough for her to escape.

She ran to her wolf, sliding to a kneeling position beside him, and gently touched his head. "I couldn't save you." Her voice cracked as she spoke, coming out as more of a whisper. "I'm a pathetic excuse for a queen. I don't deserve you." Her voice shook more as she leaned down to put her head to his, tears dropping into his fur as she sobbed. His lifeless body lay motionless beneath her as her hands dug into his fur, gripping it tightly as if he were going to suddenly disappear. "I will find a way to bring you back," she gritted out between clenched teeth before standing up with new determination. Magic pulled dirt over Faust's body to mark his grave before she wiped her tears away with the back of her hand and turned to go find her other friend.

When she reached the tree house, she saw her friend leaning against a nearby tree. The trunk of her former home was in splinters and thrown all over the ground. Making her way to the elf, she knelt and held out her hand to heal him with magic. Several deep cuts, bruising, and a broken arm were the extent of it. *It could have been a lot worse. I'm glad he's still alive.*

"I did the best I could to give you time to get away, but he's very strong, fast, and hungry. I imagine it's been a long time since he last ate a human." The elf winced from the pain of the bone in his arm shifting back into place so it could be mended.

Healing these wounds was the easy part for Mori; it was what came after that needed addressing that had her breaking completely. With Duncan's wounds healed, she stood up and surveyed the debris all around them. Shards of wood were littered around the area, papers had been thrown every which way, and their furniture was broken beyond repair. The only place she knew as her home in this forest was gone. She'd lost so much in such a short amount of time, and she knew she would regret not trying to fix this. Holding out her hands in front of her, she closed her eyes to focus her magic, the green swirls of energy appearing in front of her palms, but nothing happened. The tree house remained broken, the journals remained ruined, and all her clothes and blankets were still ripped up.

Mori tried several more times before collapsing to her knees, gasping and panting hard as sweat beaded down the sides of her face. "No," she whispered. "No." She grabbed fistfuls of grass, her fingers digging into the soil. "NO!" she wailed, while endless streams of tears fell from her eyes onto the ground and her hands, her sobbing ringing out around them. Nothing was working and her home was gone. The one connection she had left to her birth mother was destroyed by a creature who wanted to eat her. She wasn't strong enough to bring Faust back, bring her mother back, or even fix a damn tree! Nothing was good enough; *she* wasn't good enough. Everything she did resulted in people dying and getting hurt. Everything she did was *wrong*. She couldn't save anyone, let alone this forest. She couldn't even save her best friend because she'd frozen. She'd *frozen* when she'd needed to act, and that was the reason for—

"Where is Faust?" Duncan asked Mori, breaking her from her racing thoughts.

After a few moments to gather herself, she spoke, her voice full of indignation. "Dead. He jumped in front of that *thing* and was eaten. He died to save me."

The elf gasped at those words before his features softened. "He will be back. He always comes back. We just need to give his body time to repair itself." Duncan's words sounded assuring, but Mori was too far gone in her grief.

"NO!" she bellowed as her fists raised and slammed back down on the ground at the same time as her word, before she glared up at her friend. "I watched his entire chest and stomach be eaten by that *thing*!" she screamed. "There is no coming back from that! There is nothing coming back! Not even the tree house is coming back!" Tears continued to fall. "That was the last connection to my mother! All her journals, her research, everything is all gone! I can't get any of that back!" Her tears of sorrow had turned into anger, the warmth of rage spreading through her body like a warm blanket. It was a comfort right now. A way for her to feel anything other than grief at the loss of everything she held dear. She remained silent for a few more seconds as she struggled to get her breathing under control and her racing heart to stop hurting. "I shouldn't have stayed here. I'm not a queen and I never should have tried to be one. This was all a mistake."

Mori stood up and wiped her face before holding her hands out using her magic. Several blades of grass came out of the ground to pack a bag of what she could see was still good, mostly books, before it came to her. After swinging the bag onto her shoulder, she turned toward a nearby tree and allowed her eyes to flash a glowing green as she opened a portal. That same blue, green, and purple one that she had traveled through before. Her eyes returned to normal now that it was open, her thoughts focused on the human world, where Missy and Jason were waiting for her. Her real home.

"Mori! No! If you return to the human world, we will be left without a queen! We won't be able to reach you until you come back! The time difference could mean literal decades before we see you again!" Duncan shouted as he forced himself to his feet to go after her. "We can get through this together! We can rebuild the tree house and wait for Faust to come back. Don't leave everything we have worked so hard for behind!"

Mori glanced at him from over her shoulder, her eyes glossed over as she gave a small smile. "Goodbye." With that, she turned back to the portal and went through it just as Duncan reached out to grab her, but his hand missed. As she stepped through, she could faintly hear the elf calling her name. His voice was so full of anguish, but there was nothing left for her in Albright Forest.

The colors were much prettier this time now that she wasn't dazed. Her mind was focused on going back to the human world, back to Missy and Jason, back to where she saw her real home.

Chapter Fifteen

The portal opened up, allowing Mori to step out of it before it closed behind her. She was across the street from her childhood home, Missy and Jason's home. Euphoria washed over her now that she was back after everything that had happened. It felt odd to be back in the world with her mother's clothes on, and she knew she stuck out like a sore thumb. Even though it was the middle of the day, the front room light was on. Both of them worked, so it was odd to see both cars in the driveway. At this point, she had no idea how long she'd been gone. There was a time difference between the two realms, but the ratio was never explained to her.

Mori took a deep, calming breath with her eyes closed to give herself the mental time she needed before opening them and walking up to the door. She was glad she had kept her key to the house around her neck, because she would never have found it in the wreckage of the tree. Slowly, she slid the piece of metal into the keyhole and turned it before the door pushed open with the same slight creak it always had. The sound of chairs skidding across linoleum flooring rang through the hallway before Missy and Jason appeared in the opening to the kitchen. Their eyes were wide and their mouths hung open for a few seconds, as if they couldn't believe what they were seeing.

"Mori!" Missy called out, and moved quickly to the entryway to hug her tightly, crying as her husband came in for a hug as well. Mori let out a breath of relief as her arms tightened around her adoptive parents. She had never been happier to see them in her life. When the hug broke apart a full minute later, both parents looked at their daughter.

"Where have you been? We've been worried sick about you!" Jason asked before eyeing her attire. "And what are you wearing?"

"I was kidnapped from the mall by two guys on my birthday and taken to the fae realm through a portal after being hit by a car. I'm OK, so don't worry about that." She chuckled nervously. "I'm sorry, I know I've been gone for a month and a half, but I wasn't sure how to get back until now," she explained. The two parents furrowed their brows in confusion.

"A month and a half? It's been three weeks since you disappeared. We called the police, friends, everyone. I was so scared when I saw them take you that day!" Missy paled as she moved to the living room to sit down, Jason and Mori following behind her. Jason sat on the couch next to his wife and wrapped an arm around her. "Start at the beginning. What happened to you?"

Mori sat down in the armchair across from them and started at the beginning. From the kidnapping at the mall, to meeting Duncan and Faust and her mother, to even the failed coronation. The hardest part was the fairy territory attack and how she almost lost that battle. What broke her was losing Faust to the skull-headed monster, but she managed to get the words out to tell the story. She apologized for not having made it home sooner.

When her story finished, Missy sighed while Jason ran his fingers through his hair.

"That is a long story. So much has happened in such a short amount of time," Missy said, and leaned back to look at the ceiling. Mori could almost see the swirling thoughts in her mind by her indignant expression.

"Are you going to go back?" Jason asked.

"I still feel the magic in me, so I'm sure it's possible. I just don't think I *want* to go back. I was almost eaten and everyone hated me. It was too much. I just want to stay here and be normal." Mori looked down at her fidgeting hands, a mournful expression lining her features as she thought about Faust and everything she'd given up to come back. Was coming here really what she wanted to do? Was staying an option? Or was she running from her problems like she always did?

Missy turned her gaze to Mori and let out a breath. "I think we should take a pause. This is a lot to process. We should give this time to sink in while you get comfortable. If you're hungry, I can make you something."

Mori shook her head. "I'm not hungry. Just glad to be home." The girl got up and walked upstairs to her room. First thing she did was take a shower, allowing the hot water to warm her up while everything that had happened the past month played over and over in her head. It took a while for her to feel clean again after so long of bathing in a river. She changed into her normal clothes once she was dry. A graphic T-shirt, jeans, and ankle socks. When she sat on her bed to put her socks on, she noticed all her plants around her room were half-dead or completely dead. She walked over to the pots to inspect the soil, seeing that they were being watered regularly, but because they had been sick, water was not enough to keep them alive. She let out an amused laugh.

"Glad to see Missy was watering my plants while I was gone." She smiled and lifted her hand to wave it a little. The magic inside her enveloped the browning plants and brought them back to a happy, lively green state. "You all look much better now. Don't worry, I will make sure you stay well."

Sleep weighed heavily on her eyes as her tired body finally started to relax. After everything that had happened, she was beyond exhausted. She slipped under the covers of her bed and pulled them tight just as sleep was taking hold of her. *A nap sounds good.*

Missy came in later that evening with a plate of food. "I figured you would be hungry."

Mori had just woken up from a nap a few minutes prior, so she was still rubbing the sleep from her eyes, the comforter falling to around her waist as she sat up and yawned. "Yeah, starving. It was strange eating the food there. It's like nothing we have here." She took the plate and ate a few bites as Missy sat down on the bed.

"Mori, I think it's time we have a talk," she said as the girl looked up at her foster mother. "I need to tell you about your birth mother, Viviana."

That news made Mori almost spit out her food, but she swallowed it quickly to speak. "What? How?"

"Your mother stumbled into this world a few years before you were born. I saw her come through the portal. We were both shocked and afraid at the time, but we became friends," Missy explained.

"Fae are very distrusting of humans. How did you two become friends?" Mori asked.

"I saved her from being hit by a car. She came out in the middle of the road in front of a speeding car. I was able to get her out of the way. Like I said, shocked and afraid." Missy laughed. "She met Jason, who was just my boyfriend at the time. I taught her about this world and showed her many different things. She was here for about a year, learning English and everything else I could teach her in that time. She even went to school for the year to learn more. She really loved spending time in the library.

"During her time at school, she met your father, Renfred. He was originally from England, but he was here in the States for research. Surprisingly enough, he had been researching fae and was chasing down stories of sightings. He showed up in your mother's life, and they became inseparable. Originally, I thought it was because he'd found out she was fae, but after seeing those two interact, it was pretty clear they were in love." Missy smiled fondly at the memory. "Eventually, she told all three of us about the war in the fae realm and how she had to go back. I haven't seen her since then. Then one day, you appeared on my doorstep late at night in a basket."

"How did you know it was me?"

"Vi left a note explaining that it was too dangerous for you to be in the forest, and she knew you would be safe with us. I knew your mother would never give you up unless she absolutely had to. She spoke fondly of how she'd waited so long to be a mother, but because she was royalty, she had to wait till much later in her life to have a child. I was told royals live a very long time, so having an heir much later in life was better than early in life. It's only once the current royal dies that the magic transfers to the heir." Missy sighed heavily before taking Mori's hand and giving it a gentle squeeze. "I'm sad Vi is dead, but I'm glad she had you first. You have been a blessing for both of us, and I'm very happy you had a chance to meet before her passing." The gentleness in her smile comforted Mori. All this new information had left the girl speechless for several seconds.

"I didn't know any of this." She looked up at her foster mother. "Thank you for telling me." The two hugged before Missy stood up.

"You will always be welcome here, no matter what. Whether you choose to stay here or return to the forest, we will support you. If you want to go back to Albright Forest, we will be sad and miss you dearly, but still support you. No matter what, you are our daughter and we love you," Missy said, her voice cracking a little.

"Thanks, Missy. I haven't figured out what I want to do, but I do know I don't want to go back to that school. I'm tired of rinsing pudding out of my hair." She chuckled.

"I don't blame you." Missy sighed a little. "After you had been gone for a week, we assumed Vi found you after you were kidnapped and there was no time to tell us what was happening or at least let us know you were safe. I guess we were wrong. But if you do return to the forest, please let us know so we aren't worried that something bad happened."

"I will." Mori laughed before returning to her plate of food. Missy got up and left, leaving the girl with her thoughts, which were plagued with the image of Faust being killed. She finally had two best friends, and one of them ended up dying. She would never be able to unsee or unhear that. The echoes of the sounds it had made filled her nightmares that night after she went to bed. How his nearly lifeless body squelched when it hit the ground.

Over the next two weeks, the night terrors grew more intense. Missy and Jason would take turns staying up with her while she cried, trying to bring her comfort. Some nights Mori wouldn't sleep at all. She couldn't sleep; it was too terrifying. Everything she saw involved Bob eating one of her friends, or herself. The trepidation of being eaten alive had filled her whole body and consumed her mind since learning about him and being pursued by him that first time. She could have gone her whole life without knowing about him, but that wouldn't have prepared her for what he had done to her beloved Faust.

Chapter Sixteen

"*Moooriii*," an ethereal womanly voice called out. It sounded familiar, her eyes darting around her still bedroom. The moonlight from the window was the only thing illuminating the room. It was the middle of the night, so she knew it wasn't her parents. Missy was asleep and Jason had the night shift at work. Besides, Missy would never just call out to her all creepy like that, especially after knowing everything she had just gone through.

"Hello?" Still sitting on her bed, she tried to locate the source as a chill ran down her spine.

"*Moooriii*," it called out again, making the girl almost jump out of her skin. Her body shot up as she stood, panic setting in quickly.

"Who are you? What do you want?" Mori's voice trembled, but before she could take a step, she was suddenly standing in the forest right next to the destroyed tree house. It looked the same as when she had left two weeks ago. The splinters of wood scattered all over the ground, blood spattered nearby from Duncan's injuries from the fight against Bob. It was as if no time had passed since leaving that day. *This has to be a dream. It has to be. That's the only explanation for this.*

The forest around her grew darker as twilight set in, the vibrant pink and orange hues filling the sky as the sun was slowly setting behind the Faenor mountains in the distance. Mori's eyes scanned around her, and when they returned to the destroyed tree house stump, her face paled quickly as her mouth fell open and her eyes widened. But it wasn't at the demolished home; it was at the ghostly white figure that now stood inside the broken pieces. Her pale features didn't take away from the beauty that resembled Viviana, her mother. The cascading curly hair, the swirl of freckles on her left cheek, and the long dress she wore the day she died were exactly how Mori remembered her. The ghost smiled as she walked over toward Mori, stopping a few feet in front of her.

"Mom?" Mori's eyes narrowed as the left corner of her lip was tugged up, her brows pinching in confusion. Surely this wasn't *actually* her mother. She was a ghost, and her mother had died a while ago.

"Mori, I'm glad you're doing well, even if it meant going back to Missy and Jason," Viviana said, her voice the same as Mori remembered in the cave. There was no ethereal overtone, just purely her mother. "You and I really do look a lot alike." She giggled lightly before she glanced to the side, then back to her daughter. "I am here because you are not safe in the human world. You must go back to Albright Forest."

Mori raised an eyebrow. "Why would I do that? People were *dying* all around me, and there was nothing I could do to stop it. Faust *died* protecting me from Bob. How could I—"

"Mori," her mother cut in, "you must listen to me. The raider king knows who you are and has sent people to find you. They are going to the different territories, hurting the fae creatures, and threatening to kill anyone who doesn't give up your location. We need you to go back and help them."

"*We?* Who is this *we*? I'm on my own. And in case you didn't see, they all *hate* me. Every single one of the fae hates me and wishes I were dead." Heat filled her chest and spread through her body, her face flushed as rage fueled her words further. "They would prefer to have the royal bloodline end with you rather than have a half-human rule over them, or even a quarter human." Mori started pacing, arms flying all around as she grumbled to herself. There was too much going through her mind, too much anger she shoved down to appease *them*. Finally, she stopped pacing and turned back to the image of her mother.

"Besides, why *should* I help them? They hurt Faust, taunted Duncan, and rejected me. Why should I help *any* of them?" Mori bellowed, her words filled with venom as the hurt of betrayal flooded every vein in her body. Her best friend was dead, her guard friend was injured, and no one had helped them. None of the fae could bring Faust back, and they never lifted a finger to help her. So why should she put her life on the line for them? She shook her head, her tense shoulders relaxing as she came to a decision. "They don't want my help, so I'm staying here. I want to stay with my parents."

Viviana sighed softly and stepped closer to her daughter. Mori felt a chill wash over her as her mother's ghost came closer. "My darling baby girl, your friends do not hate you. They are worried about you. And don't forget, Faust will come back to life. He is immortal as part of his curse," she explained as Mori crossed her arm over her chest. "I can't force you to go back, but just know that you are never alone." The former queen stood up and took a step back. Behind her were more ghosts. Mori's mouth fell open as her arms fell to her sides. The anger left her body, replaced by shock. There were so many of them, and they were all staring at her.

"Who are all of you?" she asked.

"We are your past," a man standing to Viviana's right said. Mori didn't recognize him at all, but noticed the line of freckles that flowed along his jawline.

"We are the previous royals who reside within the magic you now possess. You can call on our strength and guidance whenever you need." A woman with long black hair stepped forward as she spoke. Her line of freckles was on the right side of her neck in the shape of a single pixie wing. Mori felt like she knew the woman from somewhere, her brows pinching as she thought for several long moments.

"Titania?"

The woman smiled and nodded. "I am Titania, queen of the pixies, better known as The Wing. My specialties are thievery, mischief, and healing."

"I was known as The River, King Remus," the man said as he motioned toward his line of freckles. "I swam with the merfolk and kelpies. I could swim faster than anyone and was a man of the water."

Another woman behind Remus stepped forward. Mori recognized her as Elissa from the flash of memory she'd had back at the leprechaun territory. "I am Elissa, The Sword." Her shirt had a V neckline to show off the downward-pointed sword made of freckles that was on her sternum and upper chest. "My ability to fight with a sword was legendary, as was my ability to drink anyone under the table and hold my liquor. I won many battles during my time as queen, both on and off the battlefield." She let out a hearty laugh.

"Mori, you are never alone," Viviana told her. "All of us are with you and will lend our skills and wisdom whenever you call to us."

"Is that what happened during the battle in the fairy territory? Did I somehow call for help?"

"I took control of your body because I could see that my daughter was in danger. I couldn't sit idly by and allow you to be hurt. I was known for my innate magical abilities, so I stepped in to lend you a hand." Viviana smiled fondly. "It felt good to get back in the fight after so long of being bedridden or ill."

"Mom, did you heal all the fairies too? Bring them back to life?" Mori asked, a pleading tone to her voice as she pried for answers.

"That honor belongs to me." Titania stepped forward and waved a hand. "My pixies are small creatures and would get hurt often, so I devoted my practice to healing magic to keep them safe. I learned how to return the soul to the body so the pixies' numbers would not dwindle to nothing." The former queen took a few steps back to return to her place in the lineup.

Mori's eyes swept over all the royals who had come before her, noticing a few in the back of the group were blurred out and one was just a shadow. "Who are the people back there?"

Viviana looked over her shoulder at the blurred images before turning her gaze back to her daughter. "The ones who do not wish to interact will not come to you when called. What you see now are merely the shadows their souls cast. I wouldn't recommend attempting to contact them," she warned.

"I think one of them did come to me, or at least, I saw a memory of his." Viviana raised a curious eyebrow as Mori spoke. "I was looking through his eyes and was with Faust in the fairy territory. He was killing so many people, and I saw blood all over Faust. There was a lot of senseless violence. Who was that?" Mori asked as her eyes met her mother's gaze.

"That sounds like The Cursed, King Asani. He's the one who cursed Faust and went on a rampage through the forest. He believed the forest belonged solely to him, and everyone else should not be allowed to live in it." Viviana shook her head with a deep sigh. "It's no wonder so many fae have lost their faith in the royals. We have not been the best leaders. Many of us believed we deserved everything because we were raised to believe it. That the forest belonged to us and we could do whatever we wanted with it and its inhabitants. We were tyrants, including The First."

"The First?"

"He was the first royal of the forest and the creator of the royal warhammer. Humans had managed to find their way into the forest and destroyed many things. He created the hammer and went to the human world to wipe them out, though was quickly overrun, but not before he took a few of the humans as prisoners. The fairies he'd taken with him fled after returning to Albright Forest because they didn't believe in their king's ways." Viviana's hand rested upon her own cheek as she glanced off to the side with a troubled look on her face. "I believe the raiders who are attacking now are descendants of those humans who were captured. They fled the forest, but none of us knew where they went. I couldn't figure out the truth while I was still alive." Her hand fell as she looked back at Mori. "Either way, you must go back and protect the forest. It is your duty as the forest queen to keep them safe."

Mori still couldn't believe all this was happening. The idea that flashbacks of memories that weren't hers could arise at any time was stressful, to say the least. Knowing the past royals were always with her was comforting to a degree, but hearing that so many had failed in their leadership of the forest broke her heart. She looked down as her fingers fidgeted with the hem of her shirt, and her teeth found her bottom lip to chew on it.

"I just need to know one thing, Mom." Mori looked up at the ghost of her mother with a gaze filled with sadness and searching. She needed a reason, even a small one. "Why should I protect them? They have all turned their backs on me, taken everything I held dear to me away, and made me an outcast because of something I have no control over. So *why* should I help them?" Her cold voice lingered on her lips, daring to say more, to ask why over and over.

Why should she care about anyone who tortured her and made her feel less than? Why did she even try to begin with? Why was destiny the only answer anyone ever gave her? Why didn't anyone care about what *she* wanted? Mori wanted a simple life, and even that had been taken from her.

Viviana moved closer to Mori, her brows frowning as her shoulders released tension. "Our bloodline has only ever been raised in the forest," she said in a low tone. "During the time we're learning who we are, we're learning about the people around us. We make friends with the other fae while we're learning what it means to be a royal." She placed a hand on Mori's shoulder, the cold touch sending a shiver down her spine. "You did not get that chance and didn't make those bonds and friendships. If you are anything like me, then telling you it's your destiny will do nothing to persuade you."

"Got that right." Mori rolled her eyes.

"I will say this. During your time there, was there anyone you felt a connection with? A connection you had never felt with anyone before?"

Mori stared blankly forward, as if looking through her mother's body instead of at it. A connection she had never felt before? Growing up in the human world with weird freckles and being adopted meant she didn't make many friends. No one wanted her around, even Jessica, who claimed to be her friend, only tolerated her. When she'd gotten to the forest after being kidnapped, she'd learned Duncan only wanted her because the queen was dying and he needed to train Mori to be a warrior, to fight a battle she was not part of.

Images of Faust flashed in her mind. How he kept her warm at night when she was cold, how he let her tell him anything and kept all her secrets. He had not wanted anything but freedom from the prison forced on him by another. Freeing him started their bond, and it had been growing ever since. He had become her therapist, best friend, blanket to snuggle with, mentor, safe space. If it weren't for her direwolf, she would not have stayed in the forest as long as she had.

A chance meeting after sliding down a crag had given her the one thing she truly wanted, a best friend. He had been there for her when she'd needed him most, but when he'd needed her the most, she'd run away. *I'm a coward.* There was nothing she could do to make up for what she'd done, leaving him there to suffer a horrific and painful death.

Viviana interrupted her thoughts, a smile on her lips. "It seems you have someone in mind."

"Faust." Mori exhaled. "He wanted nothing from me other than to release him from his prison. Even though there was no reason for him to stay by my side once he was free, he *chose* to and fought for me. He let me ride him when I was tired and let me tell him all my worries when I was stressed or scared. Kept me warm when I shivered. He cared more about me than he did himself, enough to sacrifice his life to Bob." She let out a shaky breath as tears ran down her cheeks. "He knows that creature is the one major fear I have in the forest. It's not the raider king, not the new environment, not the fae who wanted to do me harm. None of that scared me. It was only Bob; the fear of being eaten by that *thing* is what terrified me the most." Mori looked at all the past royals who were now holding a small image of their best friends from their own lives. Each cloud of magic formed an image of the one they connected with the most. Many had a fairy they held dear, but others had different species. Titania's cloud displayed a young-looking Queen Astalla of the pixies. Even Viviana had a small cloud of magic showing the image of Lorem.

The same cloud everyone else had appeared in front of Mori, her eyes darting down at it as her eyes widened, and her hands cupped it gently like it was something precious. Faust appeared, and she smiled fondly at the image. He truly had touched her heart in a way no one else had. A wave of warmth flooded her body at the memories of the two of them together. Dogs might be a man's best friend, but wolves were a woman's best friend. She stifled a laugh at her own thought.

"I would not be the woman I am today without Lorem. I had no idea she would become so important to me when I stumbled upon her in the forest while she trained with her sword. She had been traveling with a circus that took her in after she was shipwrecked when she was a young girl. A sword dancer was teaching her how to fight during her travels. We became instant best friends and have been together ever since." The image of the satyress disappeared along with the cloud. "If you can't find a reason to do it for yourself, do it for him. Do it for Faust. He's the only reason you need to fight this battle." Viviana's hands moved in a circle in front of her to create a ring of green magic, the inside filling once the circle was complete. Faust was sitting by the tree Mori had disappeared through, pawing at the ground with his ears lowered. He looked a lot skinnier than he had when he was killed. Duncan was nearby, going through the tree house wreckage and picking up anything that wasn't completely destroyed. "They are waiting for you. Faust returned to life a week ago by human world standards. It's been over a month since you ran away, according to the fae realm's time difference." Viviana let the magic continue to show the wolf so Mori could stare at him.

She couldn't pull her eyes away from her best friend. Even with a curse, how could he come back after so much of his body had been eaten? That was just not possible. Then again, being the queen of an entire forest and having magic felt impossible. Her eyes fell to the ground as her thoughts continued to run a marathon in her mind. There was one thing she couldn't deny despite all the chaos. Faust was alive. And Viviana was right—she needed to protect the forest for him. After all, they'd promised back at the birch tree to never leave each other. She promised that if she ever found a way to get home, she would let her parents know she was OK and then return to him. What kind of person would she be if she broke her promise to the one person who didn't make her feel so alone? She stifled a small laugh as she looked back up at her mother.

"This feels like a highly manipulative way to make me go back," the girl pointed out.

"Maybe a little." The previous queen laughed a bit and gave a small shrug. "Am I wrong?"

Mori shook her head. "No. Even if I don't have a connection with any of the other fae or with the forest, I should still do it for Faust and Duncan."

"Even if your bond with Duncan is not strong, that doesn't mean it can't grow. He will be by your side for a long time, just as the rest of us will be, too. Even a garden doesn't grow without work and tending to it." She gave her daughter a smile. "If you ever need a helping hand, just call us. There is a list of all the past royals and their specialties in one of the books. It's a green leather journal with our symbol on it, the sapling. That was chosen because everything has a beginning. Only a royal will be able to open it. When you discover what your power is and who you are, you will need to write it down in that journal." Viviana closed the view of the wolf and let her hands fall to her sides. "Build the bonds with the forest and fae, show them you deserve to be the forest queen. You will make friends wherever you go."

"How am I supposed to stop the raiders? I can barely hold a sword!"

"Remember the poem I told you before I died.
> 'With the saplings as your guide,
> find the place where it resides.
> Lavender bloom alights the course
> to this power's sacred source.
> Where it flowers night and day,
> regal boon will find your way.'

"I do not know what awaits you when you find the place, but I know you will be ready. Arm yourself with magic and friends and you will be able to get the Royal Hammer."

"What makes you so sure I will be the one to find it?" Mori asked as her brows pinched together in confusion.

"I have faith in you, Mori. You take after me in more ways than you might think." Viviana took a few steps back to join the other royals before they all disappeared.

Mori woke up with a jolt that morning after the dream ended, sitting upright and panting hard. She held her head in her hand for a moment before looking around her room. Everything was still as it had been. Nothing was out of place. Was that really a dream? It felt very real to her, including the pain of seeing her best friends waiting for her. After getting up and getting changed into the forest clothes she had gone home wearing, she went downstairs to say goodbye to her parents.

Missy grew teary as soon as she saw her in the clothes. "You're going back." It was not a question. Mori nodded slightly.

"Thank you for letting me stay here these last couple weeks, but I have to go back. The forest needs me." Mori smiled and gave both of them a hug.

"Do what you need to do. We will worry less now that we know where you are. Just promise us you will be safe," Jason said as he returned the hug.

"You will always have a home here with us. Please make sure to visit from time to time so we know you're well. Eat properly out there and don't do anything too reckless." Missy chuckled.

"I will visit when I can. I have to go defend my home and take my rightful place on the throne."

"We're so proud of you, Mori. We love you." Missy gave her daughter one last hug before letting go, tears running down the cheeks of all three of them.

Mori waved as she walked out the door and locked it behind her. She had to return to the forest and keep everyone safe. The fae were waiting for her. She was glad she'd gotten to spend time with Missy and Jason, and she had no idea if or when she would see them again. But at least now they knew where she was and that she was safe enough.

It was quiet that morning when she stepped outside, which was perfect for doing magic. With one last look at the house she'd grown up in, she turned back to the grass, opened the portal, and jumped inside.

Chapter Seventeen

The euphoria of stepping onto the grass of Albright Forest filled Mori completely. The bright sun and all the greenery around her made her feel like she was home. She inhaled deeply as she opened her arms, taking in the earthy scents she missed so much as the sun caressed her skin. After taking a moment to look around, she realized she was not anywhere near where she had made her first portal. The destroyed tree house was nowhere in sight, but there was something familiar about where she'd appeared. She was next to the river where the kelpies had dragged her into the water. Thankfully, the creatures didn't seem to be in the area.

Before she had a chance to take a single step, she was yanked from behind and a rope was thrown around her, tightly pinning her arms to her sides. Mori struggled against her restraints, but she couldn't use her magic without her hands. In fact, she was having a hard time feeling the magic inside her.

"Let me go!" she shouted as she looked over her shoulder to try to see who had bound her.

"What do we have here? It seems the queen is away from her bodyguards." The throaty, ominous voice of Dairus filled her ears as he walked around to face her. Raiders surrounded her, all with spears and swords at the ready in case she tried to run, a futile thought considering her predicament. "There's no getting out of that rope. It's laced with pure iron, your weakness." A sinister smile curled his lips. "You should be falling to your knees any minute now, girl."

Mori stood up taller to defy his words. Physically, she felt fine, other than being tied up. Magically? That was a different story. The feeling of magic flowing through her body was growing dimmer with every passing second the rope was in contact with her body. "I should have known you were waiting for me to show up. As you can see, I'm not affected by your iron rope." If only looks could kill, Dairus would be dead instead of moving some of his black hair behind his ear to keep it out of his face. It had really grown out in the time since they'd last seen each other, however long ago that was. "So now what? Are you going to kill me and take my body back to your master?"

Dairus let out a hearty laugh. "Not in the slightest. In order for your powers to go to my boss, he needs to kill you himself. We will be taking you to our prison to await his return." He motioned toward her with his head. Two men stepped forward and encased her hands in iron so she couldn't use magic at all. The moment the iron clamped shut, the feeling of magic inside her ceased completely. Mori attempted to resist, dread filling her as she was forced down to her knees and restrained by enough men to keep her from moving a single inch. Heat rose through her body as anger took over her mind. This was not how she'd planned on seeing Dairus again. When she'd seen their meeting in her mind, there was a lot more death on his end.

With the new anti-magic cuffs in place, the raiders pulled her to her feet so they could start walking. Each one who wasn't restraining her physically and keeping her on the path had a trained weapon pointed in her direction. They were taking no chances in her being able to run.

The walk took three days as they were marched to the western part of the forest where a large building was located. It was only one story tall and looked like a mini log cabin mansion complete with windows, doors, and benches on either side of the entrance. Mori overheard some of the men talking about the prison camp they were heading to and how they couldn't wait to return to the main base. Mori tucked that information in the back of her mind for later.

As they passed by the tall wooden walls made of solid logs and went through the iron gate, she remembered that iron could actually hurt the fae, like it did her mother. The iron bolt head lodged in her mother's shoulder had been slowly killing her, making her physically and magically weak. Mori had no idea if the same would happen to her, but after three days, she noticed her strength had yet to waver. It was just the connection with her magic that she'd lost.

"Keep moving, prisoner," one of the guards shouted as he pushed Mori forward, making her stumble.

"Don't touch me, you brute." She glared up at none other than Tom, one of the guys who had kidnapped her and brought her to the forest. Tom pushed her again, making her fall to her knees with a hard thud, and a grunt of pain escaped her throat. Another raider ran over to help Tom pull her back up to her feet. "Stop manhandling me!"

"Shut it!" Tom growled between clenched teeth before hitting her with the handle of his sword. Blood trickled from her fresh temple wound. "I guess I was able to capture you after all. Tim and I got a real good scolding after you ran away."

She narrowed her eyes up at him as she snarled, "Good. I'm glad you both got in trouble for what you did. Kidnapping is a serious crime." She grinned, earning herself a punch in the face by Tom. She panted a bit as she spat a mixture of blood and saliva on the ground next to Tom's boot. Without her magic, she wasn't healing like she would have, so the dizziness from the hits was taking hold.

Through bleary eyes, she managed to look around the compound. Several fae were being herded into large iron cages with wooden floors. Most of the young ones looked like they had lost all their strength instantly, while the adults took a little more time before their skin and faces took on a more ill-looking color and expression. One even threw up at the edge of the cage after a failed attempt to get it outside their prison. He had grabbed the iron bar to brace himself, and smoke lifted away from his burning flesh. He quickly pulled his hand away, and a woman tried to tend to the new injuries. Mori hated it here but also knew this was good intel. She now knew where the base was and would be able to find it again if needed, unless she burned the whole place to the ground after setting the fae people free.

She was pushed from behind to force her to walk before being led inside the wooden building. It was an unremarkable building with very few things inside. A few tables with chairs, a desk on the far wall, and a staircase that led to a basement. She could instantly feel it was reinforced with iron.

The guards took her and a few other fae folk down a set of stairs to a large room full of iron cages. Her heart sank when she saw the fae people, *her* people, imprisoned within them. One of them reached through his cage to try to take something off a guard but got burned too badly and had to pull away. That was not a smart move, but Mori could not fault the man for it.

"It's pure iron." Tom knocked on the bars with his sword to demonstrate. "You aren't going to be able to do anything down here." He smirked and pushed Mori into a cell, making her stumble and fall against the bars on the other side. She didn't burn from it, but she knew it would leave a bruise from the impact. "I can't wait to see what the king does to you." He laughed as he removed the cuffs and rope from her hands and body before he locked up the door and walked away toward the other guards who were finishing caging their prey.

Mori groaned from the pain as she sat on the bed, holding her head with her hand as her blurry vision started to return to normal. A noise from a neighboring cell made her tilt her head to look up. So many fae were in tiny cells similar to her own, many of which were doubled and tripled up. The whole place was cramped and smelled like mildew from a leak where rainwater must have found its way in. Each fae creature looked bored, hopeless, and defeated, as if the will to escape had fled with the closing of the door. She shook her head and stood up.

"That won't be me . . ." she mumbled to herself before leaning against the bars beside her bed.

"Vi?" a man's voice said behind her, and she turned to look at him. A hopeful look filled his brown eyes as he stared at her, his hands gripping the bars tightly. There was a cell between them, but that didn't stop him from calling her.

"No, sorry." She shook her head. "Try not to worry. I'm working on getting us out of here." The man's face fell as hope fled his gaze. She was not the person he was looking for, that was for sure. Mori finally noticed she wasn't alone in the cell. A fairy woman was sitting on another bed, cut up and bruised badly with a large gash on her arm that was hastily bandaged up. Mori wished desperately that she could feel at least a little magic, but while inside the cell, the connection was gone. Not being able to help at all was killing her inside while she sat on the bed with her knees pulled to her chest.

"Hey," the man called again.

Mori barely lifted her head to eye him suspiciously. "Yeah?"

"Do you know Queen Viviana?"

Mori paused for a moment as the suspicious look faltered but didn't completely go away. It was a strange thing to be asking while locked up in a prison cell. She took a moment to look over his messy brown hair that looked like it hadn't been washed for weeks, long and tangled as it draped over his shoulders. Those dark-brown eyes that held only a spark of hope that was slowly fading with each passing silent moment. Her eyes trailed down to the clothes he wore. A dirty pair of black slacks that had seen better days and a gray polo shirt covered in mud and something black where it wasn't torn up. *Wait* . . . Mori narrowed her eyes before standing and turning to face him fully.

"Wait a minute, that's a polo shirt. No one here wears polo shirts. Where did you get that?" she asked, recognizing the human world's clothing.

"I'm not from here," the man started with a slight shake of his head. "I'm from the human world." His shoulders relaxed as he continued to speak. "You look so much like my wife that I thought you were her. She is the queen of this forest. My sweet Vi." He smiled fondly for a few moments before that smile faded and he sat down on the cot.

Mori's eyes widened at his words. "Is your name Renfred Williams, by chance?"

His gaze slowly moved to look at her again as his mouth hung open and his eyes grew wide. "Yes, it is." His brows furrowed. "Why do you ask?"

"Queen Viviana was my mother." Mori couldn't believe it. She had actually found her father.

Renfred's blank expression stared at Mori while the pieces of the puzzle were put into place. Mori saw a spark of realization flash in his eyes just before a smile spread from cheek to cheek and some pep was added to his tone. "Moriana?"

She chuckled lightly. "I go by Mori, but yes, that's me." She had to blink away the tears that threatened to blur her vision. "You're my dad," she said, her voice cracking as she took a step closer to the bars.

Renfred went to the cell wall and grabbed the bars, tears streaming down his own cheeks. "My sweet daughter. I never got the chance to meet you. Vi gave birth while I was with the fairies. I didn't receive the message that you were born until after you had gone to the human world." He fell to his knees, his voice growing hoarser. "I tried to find my way back to the human world, but without your mother's powers, I was never able to." Renfred had to wipe away tears just so he could see Mori. "Where is Vi? I hope she wasn't captured as well."

Words failed her, but the grim expression that replaced Mori's smile explained it all. The returning heartache she'd felt the day she'd met and lost her mother took hold of her entire chest, making it tough to speak. She swallowed back the lump in her throat as her eyes averted him in favor of the dirty floor. "S-she died a couple months ago. I was able to t-talk to her for a few minutes, and she told me a little about you. I learned some from Duncan as well," she said, stumbling over her words as she tried not to show how depressed she was about the whole thing. She was still grieving the loss as if it had just happened an hour ago.

"Oh . . ." His voice trailed off as his bottom lip trembled, his eyes closing as he took a deep breath. "I'm glad Duncan is still alive. I was worried. When I was captured, he was with me and I didn't know if he made it out or not."

"He did." She wiped her tear-stained face with her hands. "I'm the queen now, but my magic is not responding. I lost the connection when I was tied up with that rope and had the cuffs put on me. I think it's from the iron."

Renfred wiped his eyes as well, sniffing the mucus back up his nose as he did his best to regain his composure. "Fae are affected by iron. It makes them weak and blocks magic, so I'm not surprised. Is the iron affecting you physically?"

Mori shook her head. "My body feels fine. It's just my magic that's weak. My guess is it's because I'm half-human." She assessed the room and finally realized that everyone who was conscious was staring at them.

"It's all fine and dandy that you found your father, but we're all sufferin' here, *Queen*. How about rescuing us?" a gnome man called to her mockingly, the large room suddenly filling with the echoes of agreement from the other fae.

"All right, all right, settle down." Mori let out a breath of annoyance before searching for anything that could help. "Does anyone have anything in their pockets? Maybe there's something I can use to get us out of here." One by one, the fae dug into their pockets, and those who had something inside would pass it to the next cell as it made its way to Mori. After gathering a lot of twigs, leaves, and rocks, the queen sighed and sat down on the bed. Nothing useful here.

"I have a bobby pin. I picked it out in the hopes I would be able to put it in your hair one day. I think this is more important," her father explained as he passed the pink bobby pin with a little flower on it over to the cell between them, where a leprechaun handed it over to Mori.

"I will try not to break it." She smiled gently before setting to work on picking the lock, but she didn't get much of a chance before she had to quickly hide it. The door above had opened and the sounds of heavy footsteps down the stairs rang out in the large room. The fae around Mori started to cower in fear at the possibility that they might be the unlucky one being taken away for who knew what.

Dairus came down the stairs, along with some guards, and walked right up to Mori's cell. She stared daggers at the man who'd imprisoned her and made her life a living hell. "You can glare at me all you want, but it doesn't mean it will do you any good," he sneered. "The king returned earlier than expected. You are going to be tried before him."

One of the guards stepped forward to open the cage. Before Mori had a chance to push them away, iron cuffs were put on her wrists and she was quickly overpowered. The queen was recalcitrant, doing everything she could to get out of the cuffs and fight off her captors.

"Leave her alone!" Renfred shouted, earning a death glare from Dairus before he was promptly ignored.

"I will kill you one day, Dairus! That's not a threat, that's a *promise*!" she bellowed when she was forced to start walking.

"Mori!" Renfred called, trying to reach out to her with his hand, but it was futile.

The queen was forced up the stairs. The guards all but carried her up as she continued to put up a fight.

"The raider king is *dying* to meet you." Dairus snickered. "We better not keep him waiting."

Chapter Eighteen

Outside the building stood the raider king with a battle axe resting on his shoulder. His piercing dark-blue eyes watched Mori carefully as she was brought before him. She was watching him closely back, taking notice of his royal-looking red jacket that hung over slightly dirty white pants. Brown boots protected his feet and ankles from the rough forest foliage. What she couldn't stand was his greasy-looking black hair that had been slicked back to keep it out of his face while his sweaty body odor assaulted her nose. She estimated he hadn't properly bathed in well over a month.

Before she could say anything, her captors stomped on the back of her knees, forcing her down to the ground with a thud in a small dust cloud, a grunt releasing from her throat.

"There she is! The queen of the forest, Moriana Albright. I have been *dying* to meet you." The false king walked to her, making sure to stay out of her reach.

He's lucky I can't reach him or use my magic. I'd gut him like the fish Duncan catches.

"I am King Yorn. You will have to forgive me for not taking your hand like a proper gentleman, seeing as you're bound with iron to keep you from using your magic on me. The same magic that *belongs* to me."

"What makes you think it belongs to you?" she spat with indignation.

"It's really quite simple. I'm a descendant of the royal family. It was supposed to go to my ancestor, as he was the firstborn, but the magic went to his younger sister," Yorn explained as he paced a bit, barely looking at her.

That didn't make any sense. Why would the magic go to the second-born? Unless . . . Mori thought hard for a moment before remembering what Duncan had said. "You're a descendant of the fourteenth royal's older brother. I was told the magic went to the second-born and—"

"Exactly!" Yorn interjected. "That magic was supposed to go to the *firstborn* child of the royal, which was my ancestor Jerro. Instead, it went to his younger sister when their father passed away. Silvana was believed to be everything a royal should be. She was kind, helpful, and never had to fight to maintain the peace. It's all lies!" His words were filled with venom from generations of hatred and resentment. He even mocked the previous queen's good qualities as if they were something disgusting and unbecoming of a royal. "She used that magic to control the fae and force them to do things they didn't want to do," he spewed, his breaths quick and shallow.

"The magic chooses who is better suited for the title of royal. If Jerro didn't get it, then it must have been for a good reason."

Yorn backhanded her across the face. "Shut your mouth, you insolent girl! How dare you suggest something like that in my presence! Jerro was brave and strong and knew how to fight to protect this forest. You wouldn't know what that is like."

Mori spat out blood, the slap having reopened her busted lip, before looking up at the man. "I'm here, aren't I?" she retorted with a smirk.

Yorn's face turned red as he started to grind his teeth. "You wouldn't understand anything. You weren't even born here!" His voice carried in the open air of the forest, a slight echo bouncing off the many trees that surrounded the compound walls.

"Actually, I *was* born here, but I was not raised here. I won't try to pretend that I was, but that doesn't mean I don't see *my* forest as my home now." Something shiny caught Mori's eye below her head, but she didn't dare look at it. "Are you really so pathetic that my ascension to the throne threatens you? That just tells me how incompetent you—"

Yorn slapped her once more, allowing her to look down at what was shining as she spit out blood. Little lines of magic appeared around the parts of her wrists that were exposed around the cuffs. But how was this possible? She hadn't felt her magic this entire time. Even though she was seeing the magic around her wrists, she knew it wasn't coming from her. If she had to guess, it was coming out of the ground. A simple, small movement confirmed that suspicion. The flow of magic was connected to the dirt below her. The pressure from the magic inside the cuffs around her hands was building up, and it started to make her wrists hurt.

"You need to keep your mouth shut. I don't want to hear anything more out of you." Yorn turned to another raider and spoke to him, but Mori wasn't paying attention. She was instead looking down with just her eyes at the green magic that snaked its way up her arms. She had to wait just a little bit longer, and then she would be free. Pain radiated from her wrists up her arms from the immense pressure, and when it was finally time, she made her move.

Mori quickly stood up and swung her hands at Yorn, aiming for his face with all her might. The raider king was faster, grabbing her hands with one of his large ones to block the attack. By the time he noticed the iron cuffs expanding and ready to burst, it was too late. The magic exploded through the cuffs, turning the iron into shrapnel right next to his face. Iron pieces lodged themselves into his face, neck, and shoulder, causing him to cry out in pain as his hand let go of Mori's fists so he could press them both to his face.

Mori fell backward from the force of the mini bomb that had just gone off. Fear filled her mind at what may be left of her hands, yet she felt no pain. Her eyes flicked to her hands, inspecting the lack of damage. Somehow she only had minor burns on her wrists from the friction of the cuffs, but that was it. Had the magic protected her? How was she even able to use it while touching iron? More questions than she had time for swirled around in her mind, but she didn't have the luxury of mulling them over. She had to move while Yorn was distracted.

While the raiders were distracted with helping their king get the pieces of metal out of his body, Mori snatched the cell key from one of the guards and sprinted back to the compound and down the stairs, almost tripping in her haste to reach the fae. She could feel the connection with her magic once more, but it died down once she was around the iron cells.

"See, I told you she would leave us. She doesn't care . . ." The voice she recognized as the gnome's died away as she rounded the corner. One by one, she used the key to open every cell. When she reached the gnome, a smile curled her lips as she opened the door.

"You should try having more faith in me as your queen. I would never leave anyone behind." The gnome stepped out, a sheepish look on his features.

"Apologies, Your Majesty. And thank you," he said before following the others out of his cell.

Upon reaching Renfred's cell, she opened it and hugged him tightly. She couldn't describe the feeling of finally meeting both of her parents face-to-face and being able to hold them, hug them. Her father was the one no one knew about. No one knew where he was or what happened to him. Tears flowed from her eyes, and she sniffled before pulling back to look at him.

"I'm gonna need your help getting everyone out safely. I still have to deal with Yorn. Can I trust you to take care of the fae?"

Renfred nodded. "You can count on me, Mori. And after this is over, I want to know everything about you." With one last hug, she reluctantly let him go to finish getting the rest of the cells open. "I will meet you back in the fairy territory," he called to her before helping the fae who were too scared to move leave their cell.

"We gotta run! Go!" she shouted as she watched some of the fae creatures barely move at all. "Come on, we have to leave now." Why was no one instantly running away? After a quick look around the room, she realized not a single person had gone up the stairs to freedom. Her brows pinched together as she looked between all of them.

"The raiders will just torture us if we leave," one of the captives said.

"I will fight them off. Go with Renfred. He will do what he can to keep you safe while I fight off the incoming raiders, but we have to leave now." Still, no one left their cells.

Let me take over.

What was that? No, more like *who* was that? The womanly voice came from inside her, just as she heard the other royals speaking from time to time. Instead of speaking to the voice out loud, she closed her eyes and spoke within her mind. *Please help them.* Permission was given, even if she didn't know which royal it was who had called out to her, but her gut told her to allow this to happen. When her eyes opened once more, they were glowing solid green.

"All is well, my little ones. We must leave so I can get you back to your loved ones. All will be fine." This voice overlapped Mori's own voice, just as it had during the attack at the fairy territory. Even Mori felt a sense of calm wash over her as she watched through her own eyes the effect this royal had over the fae.

As if a spell and bravery had taken over their bodies, each person in the room started walking—or flying—to the stairs, climbing its height to freedom. Renfred watched with amazement and confusion at the sudden change but decided to go along with it. He moved quickly up the stairs past everyone who had already started their ascent and pushed back the awaiting raiders with the help of a few stronger fae folk.

Mori followed behind him once every cell had been opened, helping to push back those who threatened their escape. Now that she was out of the cells, away from the iron, the connection and flow of her magic returned. Her strength increased, allowing her to push the raiders away from the door with a blast of force, making all of them fly backward several feet and land on their backs. The floorboards of the building wrapped around the raiders before they had a chance to get back up. The former prisoners wasted no time making a run for the exit.

"Stay inside the compound walls and out of the way if you're injured. You will be tended to shortly." Without a single word of complaint, the fae stopped in their tracks and stayed inside the building, huddled together as they stared blankly ahead.

"What is going on with them?" Renfred asked with a confused tone.

"Fae listen to their queen, as they should," the royal in control said. Mori still had no idea who it was, but she could make an educated guess if she had to.

The doors to the building were pushed open with magic as Mori stepped outside, Renfred following behind.

"You despicable girl! Those are my loyal subjects you're taking!" Yorn shouted, the left side of his face now covered with cloth. It was already soaked with blood from the injury he'd received from her.

"They are not your subjects, they are your prisoners. I have come to release them." Mori reached her hands toward the ground. Grass grew rapidly below her until they wrapped around her hands and wrists, both of which had healed along with the wounds on her head and lip. The blades of grass turned into swords that she now held at the ready.

"Wait, that voice. I know that voice! Silvana." Yorn growled out her name before drawing his own sword. More raiders had gathered, trying to surround her. With a simple movement of her hands, the grass under the raiders' feet grabbed their ankles and pulled them down into the ground to their shoulders.

"It's nice to meet a descendant of my brother's. Though I must say, I'm disappointed by the way you turned out." She let out a small giggle. "My brother was just as arrogant and stupid as you, a tyrant who was never fit to be king. My parents knew this the moment he was born. There was no connection between him and the royal magic. So they tried again. A defect for a firstborn child was unheard of, and they became the only royal in our long bloodline to have a second child. I was deserving, and still am." Mori smirked as she took a few steps closer.

"You're wrong! That magic belonged to Jerro. He was the firstborn. You should never have existed!" Yorn rushed toward Mori, sword by his side to give him the power he needed for a deadly slash.

I'm not much of a fighter. This part is up to you, Mori.

Her eyes stopped glowing as Mori returned to the driver's seat of her own body. "Thank you for the assist, Silvana." As she raised her grass swords, the plant-and-metal weapons clashed together. The two were evenly matched in sword skills, so she was a mere distraction while Renfred led the fae toward the gates. After making Yorn stumble, Mori reached her hand out toward the trees just past the iron gates. Their branches came to life and pulled until it was forced open, allowing her people to escape.

Mori was able to get the key to her father so he could tend to the prisoners who were locked up in cages outside. She paid for this moment of distraction when Yorn cut her arm with the tip of his sword. She cried out in pain before blocking the next attack with her own sword while the wound healed almost instantly. She needed backup, and only one person came to mind when she needed help.

Faust? Are you there? she called out in her mind as she fought off the king. The connection between them had been growing stronger since her return, and now it was time to reach out to him. She needed his help desperately. She needed her wolf.

Mori! Yes, I am here! Where are you? We have been waiting for you to return! he called back to her eagerly.

Faust, get to the fairy territory. I returned to the forest and rescued several fae prisoners from the raiders. There are injured people, and I'm going to need help with all of them. Send some soldiers to my current location. I found the raider king and he's trying to kill me.

We will be right there shortly, Faust called back.

"Stupid girl! You took everything that should have been mine!" Yorn shouted indignantly, bringing her back to the fight.

Mori shook her head. "This power was never yours to begin with, Yorn. Silvana was the rightful heir and accomplished many good things in her time as queen, while your ancestor was only good for destroying and killing. There would have been no peace with him as king." Mori stopped talking as her eyes glowed green once more and Silvana's voice spoke overtop Mori's own voice.

"Do not interfere with my descendant's destiny. The Seer has seen it all. Mori will be your downfall."

"I don't believe you, Silvana. She is a mere child who barely has a grasp on *my* magic. You know nothing about Jerro's suffering! He was an outcast when the royal magic didn't choose him!" Yorn's face scrunched in anger, with a snarl showing off his grinding teeth.

"Then you were misled. He was by my side my entire reign. We did everything together. He was my best friend." Mori could see flashes of Silvana with Jerro in her mind's eye. The two were just as inseparable as she was with Faust. "Jerro did the things I was not strong enough to do. He was a valuable member of my family and my royal court."

"Stop lying!" Yorn charged at Mori, barely giving her enough time to raise her swords in defense after Silvana disappeared, her eyes no longer glowing. The former royal's presence was no longer in the forefront.

Mori and Yorn exchanged several blows from their swords, trying to end each other. The raider king took out a throwing knife, and with as much force as he could, he sent it flying toward the queen, but she was able to dodge it. A grunting sound of pain met her ears rather than metal hitting wood. Mori spun around and saw Renfred behind her, the knife lodged in his stomach and his hand clutching it. Her eyes went so wide they looked like they would pop right out of the sockets. Blood rushed away from her face, making her as pale as paper as flashes of losing her mother came to life inside her mind. No, there was no time for a panic attack, or PTSD, or whatever this feeling was going to manifest into.

"Don't pull it out," Mori said quickly before running to her father just in time to catch him, dropping her weapons so they wouldn't harm him. "We gotta get you to the fairies. They will be able to help."

"What about Yorn?" Renfred asked as he looked over. Mori followed his gaze to the approaching false king.

"He's not my concern right now. You are." Using the strength her magic provided, she lifted her father and ran toward the open gate, only to be greeted by a few raiders who had managed to escape their earthly prisons. She stopped in her tracks and gritted her teeth. Trapped.

Just then, Faust came flying in from behind a raider and tackled him to the ground, ripping out his throat so he couldn't scream.

"Faust!" Mori had never been happier to see her best friend alive and well.

"I brought reinforcements." The wolf's tongue hung out as he panted happily, his tail wagging behind him.

"Good boy, Faust. Hold off the raiders and Yorn. I need to get Renfred to the fairies." As if on cue, several fairy warriors came rushing in to take on the raiders, Orian going straight for Yorn. "That was fast." Mori's brows shot up to her hairline as she rapidly blinked a few times.

"We were already close by when Faust came running right for us," Orian called over his shoulder at the queen before blocking another attack from the furious raider king.

"I'm glad you were. Thanks for the help." While the raiders were distracted, Mori carried her father over to Faust, placed him on the wolf's back, and climbed on so they could get out of the compound and head toward the fairy territory.

They made it to the fairies within an hour due to Faust's size and the enhanced speed that came from Mori feeding his body magic the whole way there. In no time, the three of them came barreling into the fairy territory, stopping just short of the small creek that ran through the middle. The fairy queen and several healers were there to greet them. While the healers worked on getting Renfred off Faust, Mori hopped down and went straight for the fairy queen.

"Queen Sophie, this one is human. My magic won't work on him," Mori explained with a panicked tone, her chest tightening, making it harder for her to suck in enough air to speak.

"A human? Why would you want to heal him?" Sophie asked.

"He's my father. Please, save him."

Renfred had grown paler since they'd left the prison. Mori had done all she could by immobilizing the blade and putting pressure on the wound to keep it from ripping open again.

"We will do everything we can, Mori. Take him inside," Sophie commanded. The healers went straight to work carrying him to the healing mushroom to get started. Mori was panting hard, trying to catch her breath and failing. Her stomach dropped as Renfred disappeared from her sight, her heart trying desperately to jump right out of her rib cage to follow after.

Faust walked up to her and rubbed his body against her, his tail wagging behind him. Mori fisted his fur, holding on as if her life depended on it.

Everything will be OK. The healers know what they are doing, he said with that soothing tone he always had when calming her.

"I hope you're right, Faust." The queen fell to her knees as exhaustion started to settle in from the intense amount of magic she'd used and the iron that had severed the connection. It felt like heavy weights were back on her shoulders, similar to when she had first received the magic. "I already lost my mother. I can't lose my father, too."

"I'm surprised you were able to find him at all. He's been missing for seven years." Sophie let out a relieved sigh and looked over her shoulder at the healer's door before looking back toward Mori. "I didn't know he was still alive. How did you find him?"

"I was ambushed by the raiders and captured. The iron they used blocked my connection to my magic. I met him in the jail they have under their compound. I didn't know who he was at first, but he mistook me for my mother," Mori explained as she leaned against her now-sitting wolf, mindlessly petting his fur.

"You do look exactly like Queen Viviana. A mirror image except for the royal freckles." The fairy queen knelt and put a hand on her shoulder. "You look exhausted. We should get you inside to rest."

Mori shook her head. "No, I need to help the others. My magic is still strong, and I can't rest until they're healed." The redheaded girl struggled to get to her feet and managed to stand on her shaky legs. The fight with Yorn had taken a massive toll on her body. Faust helped Mori to the medical mushroom to help.

As she walked up to it, the gnome from before made his way to her. "You're not bad for a human," he said before walking off. That comment made her smile and gave her the strength she needed to continue on, feeling like she was finally winning over some of the fae.

Mori set to work healing who she could, starting with the worst ones and working her way to the minor scratches and iron burns. She got the chance to heal the arm of the fairy she'd shared a cell with, Marion. By the time the healer mushroom was empty of patients, Mori was sweaty and tired, and her eyelids felt very heavy. Her father was the only one left, but there was nothing she could do for him.

"You have done enough for one day. Let our healers take care of Renfred," Sophie said as she tried to get Mori to at least sit down.

"No, I need to help somehow." Mori attempted to stand up, but the fairy queen pushed her back down on the bed.

"You may be the queen of this forest, but you are a guest in my territory. This was not a request. You need your rest so you can fight another day." Mori stared at Sophie for a few moments before moving to lie down.

"I want to be woken up the moment he's awake," she said before looking over at Faust, who was standing beside the bed. She did her best to move over enough for him to join her for a snooze, but she passed out the moment her head hit the pillow.

Chapter Nineteen

Mori was woken up by voices in the room. Someone was talking, a woman. Instead of making it known that she was awake, she kept her breathing steady and her eyes closed.

"Is she still sleeping?" the woman asked. Mori recognized the voice as Queen Sophie. "Good, I was hoping to speak to you, Faust." The wolf adjusted his position against the pretend-sleeping queen and lifted his head. "I want to apologize for how you were treated when you first came here. We still held a grudge for something you did that we now understand was not the case. You were forced, and we need to let the past stay in the past if we want to move forward." The sound of a chair being dragged across the floor echoed slightly in the empty room.

I know you are awake, Mori. Stay still, Faust said through their link, but Mori knew everyone else heard only growling.

"Can I take that as you forgive us?" Mori felt a slight movement from her wolf.

He's probably nodding.

"Thank you, Faust. I hope you continue to support Mori while she learns what it means to be queen." More small movements from Faust. The chair skidded a small distance on the floor, probably from Sophie standing up. "Give her my best when she wakes up. I must attend to Renfred. Oh, and let her know he is resting right now and his condition is stable." Her small footsteps grew distant as she left the mushroom.

Mori opened her eyes and propped herself up on her elbow. "You knew I was awake the moment I was conscious, didn't you?" she teased.

Yes, but I did not want Sophie to know. She may not have been so open if she had known you were awake. I knew she wanted to tell me something yesterday, but before she had a chance, I ran toward you. He licked her cheek a couple times. *I have missed you, Mori.*

"I missed you too, buddy." She wrapped her arms around him and hugged him tightly. "Now, you gotta tell me what happened. I thought Bob killed you!"

He did, but I did not stay dead. Immortal does not always mean invincible. I can die, but I will always come back with some time, he explained. *What made you decide to come back?*

"My mother. She visited me in my dream and told me about the royals. After two weeks in the human world, I realized I don't belong there. I actually never belonged there. My place is here with you and Duncan, and I can't just run away because things get tough. I need to stand and fight for the fae, my people, so they can live a happy life. That is the duty of a royal." She reached out and petted her wolf's head with her hand.

"You're awake. That's a relief," Duncan said as he walked up to the bed. "I'm glad to see you conscious. After you passed out, we weren't sure when you would wake up. You used a lot of magic." He sat down on the chair Sophie had pulled over.

"I'm just hoping I wasn't out for days again." Mori chuckled.

"Not this time. Just overnight, which is a good thing. It means your body is getting better at handling the royal magic." He pulled the chair a little closer. "Can you tell me what happened?"

That is something I would like to know as well, Faust commented.

"Alright, I will tell you." Mori briefly recounted going to the human world before moving on to the dream featuring most of the past royals, and then to being captured and her time in the prison, as short as that was. By the time she'd finished, Duncan's mouth might as well have been on the floor with how low it was hanging.

"Wow, that's a lot to go through. All the royals?" he asked.

"Well, there were shadows of some of them, but for the most part, it looked like there were fifty-eight." Mori shrugged, now sitting up.

"So, the man you brought back with you is . . ."

"My father," the queen finished, and closed her eyes for a few moments while taking a few deep breaths. "He was taken prisoner by the raiders and kept in their jail under their base. He was not affected by the iron bars, unlike the others, but was unable to escape." She opened her eyes to look at her elf companion.

"Were you affected by them?"

Mori shook her head a bit. "Not to the extent everyone else was. I'm half-human, so physically, I was fine, but I felt cut off from my magic." She looked down at her hands, noticing that they looked fine. The magic had protected her and healed all her wounds once she'd had the connection again. "Duncan, I need to ask you something."

"Sure. What is it?" he asked.

"While my magic was cut off from me due to the iron cuffs, there was magic seeping up from the ground that had collected under the cuffs until they exploded. Why did that happen? I couldn't control any magic. So what did?" She looked back up at him, worry tugging at her features.

"I see. It seems the magic really does have a mind of its own." Duncan pondered. "It's believed the royal magic has a consciousness, but it's also connected directly to the forest. With the connection to it cut off, the forest reached out to try getting to you. It knows iron blocks magic and harms fae, so it was more than likely instinctual to go straight for the cuffs." He shrugged. "That's the theory I have, anyway. Nothing was really proven, until now."

"That actually makes a lot of sense to me." Mori leaned against her wolf.

"Was there anything you learned while at the prison that could help us defeat the raiders?"

Mori nodded. "The raider king, Yorn, is a descendant of Jerro."

The elf's eyes widened. "The older brother to Queen Silvana? I guess jealousy about his ancestor not getting the royal magic has made him do crazy things. I'm just surprised someone this far down the family tree would still care." He ran a hand through his long hair that was not in its usual ponytail.

"Yorn was saying Silvana was a liar and was actually an evil person. She was the one who took over my body earlier. After she did, the fae listened to me when I spoke. Well, *her*, but they didn't move when I told them to. They were too afraid." Mori was not sure what to think at this point.

Silvana is known as The Compassion. She was also the one who imprisoned me. I do not know how she was able to, but I remember her telling me to walk into the cave and I did. I was not in control of my own body, and she locked me up, Faust explained as Mori turned her gaze to him.

"She imprisoned you?"

I was under the control of King Asani and forced to do bad things. I knew them both and learned that they both had similar powers of manipulation and control over the fae. I watched them use it, but Asani was not using it for peace, but to destroy the territories around the forest.

Mori translated for Duncan before commenting on what was said. "I think that's what Yorn meant by she was a liar. From what I read in the journals, Silvana was known for being kind and compassionate. She was really good at dissolving feuds between fairies and brought peace. I wonder if she was using the royal magic to control the fae and forcing people to let things go or making them forget their anger."

"Or making them forget the incident ever happened."

"Exactly. Wait . . ." Her brows pinched together. "Can magic actually manipulate memories and the mind?"

"I believe so," Duncan said. "She was the only one I saw who was able to do it fully. Jerro was able to change how someone feels and put them in a trance, but that was about it. His magic wasn't as strong as Silvana's."

"I think there is a lot more to this story. I will try to talk to Silvana when I have the chance. For now, I would like to see Renfred." Mori swung her legs off the bed and stood up. After fixing her clothes and smoothing them out, she smiled at the two of them. "Don't worry, I will be OK."

As she left the healer mushroom, she couldn't help but notice how lively the fairy territory was. Several of the former prisoners were sitting on blankets in the grass with fairies and chatting. She walked by a group of fae weaving baskets. One of the fairies had invited Mori to join them, but she declined politely. She entered the guest mushroom where her father was being housed. When she opened the door, he was sitting up in bed, reading a book.

"Mori." He smiled as he looked up at her. Renfred was covered in bandages and had food on the side table that he hadn't touched.

"Renfred," Mori said as she got closer.

"Just Ren is fine."

"I'm glad you're OK. I was worried." She moved to sit on the chair by the bed.

"No need to worry about me. I'm a tough old man, but enough about me, I want to know about you. About my daughter." He got comfortable before Mori started to explain about her life. Living in the human world, how she'd come to the fae realm, and how she had been faring in this new place. When she finished, Ren ran a hand through his graying hair.

"Wow, that's a lot. Kidnapped and brought here? I'm surprised you aren't traumatized by that," he said, his hand rubbing the back of his neck.

Mori looked down at her fidgeting hands in her lap that were playing with the hem of her shirt. She'd suffered silently this whole time. People trying to kill her, a beast trying to eat her, fae who hated her, and her mother dying shortly after meeting. Who wouldn't be traumatized by that?

"I have nightmares about all of it, and a little voice in the back of my mind keeps telling me I will never be a fit queen. That everything I'm working so hard for is for nothing and I would be better off with Missy and Jason." Her fists tightened around her clothing and wrinkled her shirt. "I found it best to just keep looking forward. I have too much going on and too many people relying on me. I can't deal with the past before I save the future. I will have time to grieve my losses and deal with my trauma after the raider king is dead."

"You do know he isn't the one pulling the strings, right?" Ren asked.

Mori's head snapped up to look at him, her eyes wide. "What do you mean?"

"I'm talking about Dairus."

She shook her head. "He follows the raider king's orders."

Ren shook his head. "No, he is biding his time and waiting for Yorn to fall. Why put in the work to gather an army to take over the forest when you can have someone else do it? In case you haven't noticed, Dairus isn't the most persuasive person. He lacks the kind of personality that draws people to his cause. All he cares about is power, and no one will follow him when they know they will receive nothing in return." Ren fidgeted with the blanket covering his lap. "You need to do what you feel is right for you regarding everything you have been through. I will be here to support you the best I can." He gave her a gentle smile.

"Thank you, Ren. I will take this knowledge and do what needs to be done. Once Yorn and Dairus are taken care of, we will be sure to catch up and learn all about each other."

"It will take some time for me to get my strength back, so go do what you need. It seems you have very good companions beside you." He reached out a hand to gently take hers. "I will be here for guidance should you need it. This forest has been my home since your mother brought me here. I wish I had the chance to see her again, but I know she is with you. She will be there whenever you need her."

"Thank you, Ren. I would like to get to know you, not just as Ren, but as my dad." She leaned over and hugged him, getting a weak hug in return from his frail body. "Focus on getting better. I will need all the support I can get while I come up with a plan to take on Yorn and Dairus."

The three had decided to take a break on the beach close to the stronghold. Some fairies were taking care of the newly freed prisoners to make sure they got the care they needed and were sent home, while others were overseeing the compound being turned into a military base for the fairies. Mori had done her part in freeing them, and Orian assured her that they didn't need her help and that she needed rest. As if that was something Mori could do at a time like this.

"The water is rather calm today," Duncan said as he lifted his hand to his forehead to shield his eyes from the sun.

"Is that not normal?" Mori chuckled.

"Not usually. Scuttle Island is just over there." He pointed off into the distance at some trees. "The waves hit its rocky cliffs and return this way with the wind in full force."

"Wait, Scuttle Island?" She looked at Faust.

From the ghost story we heard.

"Yeah, it is. Why?" the elf asked curiously.

"The first night we were with the fairies, some younger ones were telling us the legend of Scuttle Island. How a ship captain sank his own ship to prevent capture. Now it's believed that the same ship stops anyone from approaching to claim his treasure," she explained, and looked back at the strip of land. "The island isn't that far. Is there anything actually on it?"

I do not think there is, but I do not know. Faust stood beside his queen and looked out at the water.

"Some believe it to be cursed, others believe it to be sacred. Either way, it's off-limits by fae law," Duncan said, and dropped his hand as he looked over at Mori. She was staring intensely at the island with her eyes wide and her mouth slack-jawed. "I don't know if the treasure rumor is true, but I know it's unlawful. It was the twelfth royal who made that law and said it was dangerous to be there, but he never said why."

"I wanna go there," she finally said after several seconds of staring.

"We aren't allowed to go there under penalty of—"

"I'm the queen and I make the laws," Mori snapped as she glowered at Duncan, but flinched at the way she spoke. "Sorry, I didn't mean . . ." She sighed and looked back at the trees. "Something is calling to me over there. I need to see what it is. Surely the fae can't be mad their queen is going to such a sacred—or cursed—place. Royalty makes the laws, so I'm the one who gets to choose the punishment for breaking them." She looked over at the guard captain with a small smile. "Which means I choose the three of us will receive no punishment for going over there." Her smile grew until she was beaming at Duncan.

The elf just nodded, a shocked expression on his face. "I will secure us a boat."

Chapter Twenty

It took a few days for Duncan to procure a boat so they could travel to Scuttle Island. Whether it was called that because of the ghost ship or because people turned tail and ran away didn't matter to Mori. They were just rumors, though she didn't believe them at first, considering how many people in the fairy territory happened to know someone who knew someone who was friends with someone who went to the island. The story was told so many times that it had probably lost a lot of its original details.

With the boat on the shore and the waters calm, Mori climbed inside with Faust and Duncan before the elf pushed the boat with his oar to get it going. Thankfully with the calm water and strong elf, it was not hard to start sailing. Mori was telling the two about some of the things she'd learned while in the fairy territory with the prisoners. Just stories of the prisoners' lives before they were captured. It definitely helped pass the time while waiting for fairy guards to escort manageable groups to their homes.

"Then Ren told me . . ." Her sentence trailed off as she noticed the daunting sight of thick fog. It surrounded them suddenly and was so dense she could no longer see the island. "This feels like something straight out of a horror movie."

"Stay close, Mori." Duncan put down his oar, gripped his sword—ready to draw it—and stood up slowly so as to not capsize the small boat.

The air was still and silent; not even the sound of birds overhead could be heard, even though they were there just moments before. Mori moved closer to Faust, who was growling at something out in the distance.

Something is here, he told her, his ears flattening against his head as he bared his teeth.

None of them saw the large ship until it was almost on top of them. Mori quickly pulled rocks up from underwater to push their small boat out of the way so they wouldn't capsize. The jerking motion made Duncan lose his balance and fall back down into the boat.

"Hold on!" she called out as she moved her arms in circles in front of her, swirling the water below them to create a waterspout to lift their boat up. She had no idea what to expect, but it was definitely not what she saw. The deck of the larger ship was bare and eerily quiet. Most of the planks of wood were rotting away, and holes had broken them into splinters.

"Where did this come from?" Duncan asked as he jumped from their smaller boat onto the ship, aiming for a part of the deck that looked the strongest. Mori jumped toward the guard captain when he was ready to catch her. Faust was right behind her and started sniffing around as soon as he landed. The sound of their rowboat falling into the water behind them echoed in the silence.

"I don't know, but this is really scary." She gripped the elf's sleeve, staying partly behind him as they started to walk.

I do not smell anything alive, but I do think there is something here. Mori flinched at Faust's words. *I can hear something below deck.*

"What did he say?" Duncan asked in a hushed voice.

"Something is below the deck, but it's not alive," she whispered.

"What could possibly be alive on *this*?" A floorboard creaked under the elf's foot, making Mori jump out of her skin.

"I don't wanna be here!" she shrieked, grabbing his arm and trying to hide behind him.

"We should keep our voices down. We don't know what's out there," Duncan hissed.

You can stay close to us, Mori. There is no reason for you to put yourself in danger. That is our job. Faust sniffed around some more, seeming to follow a scent.

Mori couldn't understand how he could follow any smells around here. The whole place smelled like seawater and death. The smell was like something you would imagine when told about a drowned corpse being left out in the sun. A sharp chill ran up her spine as she shivered from the sudden cold, her arms clutching Duncan's tighter. He flinched from how firm her grip was, making it difficult to draw his sword when he heard a faint sound in front of them. Each of them could see their breath as it released from their mouths.

Faust suddenly halted in front of them, ears pinned back and a low growl slipping past his bared teeth. The mist cleared just enough to show the silhouette of a man. He was decently tall and had what looked like a sword strapped to his belt.

"Who goes there?" a booming voice rang out, making Mori hide more behind Duncan.

"Be strong. We won't let anything hurt you," he whispered to her over his shoulder before standing tall with his shoulders back. "I am Sir Duncan Wynett of the royal fae court. Your vessel almost ran into ours, so we came to investigate," he called back, his voice unwavering and full of confidence. Something Mori lacked at the moment.

"We?" the mysterious voice called back.

"I have Queen Mori and her direwolf, Faust, accompanying me."

"Queen?" the voice let out a ghostly laugh. "It seems we have *royalty* in our midst, boys. Perhaps we should show her a proper royal welcome."

Mori sucked in a shaky breath as more silhouettes appeared, surrounding them. Faust barked a warning a few times before moving behind his queen so no one could sneak up on her. Several rotted planks squeaked as the figures started coming into view. Each one was severely discolored to a sickly green, with many of them missing chunks of flesh from their bodies. The ones who had eyes were even worse to look at, as they were clouded and sunken, their blank expressions appearing to look right through them, but also at nothing at all. A pungent stench of decay assaulted Mori's nose, her hand covering the lower half of her face to try to keep from gagging. She could feel the bile starting to rise from her stomach with defiance.

"You won't get far, girly." The first man took several steps forward, coming into view. The captain was not what Mori had expected. His wings were damaged behind him, and his hair was a mangy mess of tangles from long months of never brushing it. Those same clouded eyes the rest of the crew had bore a hole right through the queen when she peeked out from behind the elf, her body trembling violently. The dirty, ripped captain's clothing that looked two sizes too big for the man swayed in the new breeze that pushed the mist away, revealing the entire crew and ship deck. Every member of the crew took two more steps forward.

"Stop! Don't come any closer!" Duncan shouted his warning, shrugging off Mori's grip so he could ready his sword. The captain grinned as the planks below the three were broken by two hands that grabbed the queen's ankles and pulled her down into the shadows.

"Help!" she screamed out as she reached for her companions too late.

Mori! Faust jumped down the hole after her, his red eyes glowing in the darkness.

As she disappeared, she saw Duncan fighting off the crew, who had started to attack. Hope of surviving was fleeing her body as she plummeted into darkness.

A deep growl stirred Mori in her unconscious state. Her vision was blurry as she opened her eyes, trying to blink her view back into focus so she could see what was going on. She tried to sit up, but her wolf was weighing her down. She had no idea why he was on top of her.

"Faust?" she gasped out, shallow breaths fighting their way inside her lungs as she struggled to breathe.

Stay still, Mori. We are not alone. Another growl escaped him as she moved him off her so she could sit up. There was a man on the other side of the cage in front of them, staring at the two.

"Can you call off your wolf?" he asked, bringing his knees to his chest. The man looked just as ghostly as the rest of the crew and smelled just as bad, but he wasn't violent. He just sat in the corner with tattered clothes and a chunk of his cheek missing that showed his teeth on one side.

"Faust, if he isn't attacking, then there's no reason to growl," Mori told her companion so he would get off her and stop the noise. "Why are you here and who are you?" she asked the man when she sat up completely.

"I'm the captain of this ship, or at least I was." The man looked between the two. "I'm Captain Avarisha Albright."

Mori gasped at the name and glanced at Faust before her eyes trailed back to the captain before speaking. "Albright? You're a royal?"

"*Was* a royal. As you can see, I'm dead now. I was the twelfth royal of the forest, The Sailor." Avarisha lowered his knees and turned to face the two. Sewn to the front of his jacket was a ship sail made with little dots, similar to the royal freckles that lined each royal's body.

"What happened to you?" she asked, her fear leaving her body as Faust moved closer to her so she could lean against him.

"It was during the war between fairy factions. I was helping the water and earth fairies defend their territory from the fire and air fairies. They were on a quest to conquer the forest and take everything for themselves. When they learned I was helping their enemies, they sent their most powerful warriors after us to kill me and my loyal crew." He sighed heavily. The weight of what he'd gone through hung in the air. "I knew I couldn't let them take us alive, but I was too late. The ship had found us much quicker than we'd anticipated and I was captured. As a message to the rest of my crew"—he pointed to his right cheek, the side that was missing—"they cut off my cheek that displayed my ship sail freckles that marked me as a royal. They then tied me up and threw me in my own brig before convincing my crew that I was a false king."

Mori put a hand over her mouth as tears welled up in her eyes. She couldn't imagine the amount of pain and humiliation he'd felt when that happened. The freckles were always a sign of royalty in this forest, and to have that removed was the ultimate sign of being dethroned.

"My son was a few weeks old when this happened, so I knew the bloodline would continue. I freed myself and sank my own ship. It was the only way to keep the fire and air fairies from getting its technology and using it against us. My entire crew was asleep, except for my first mate, Marshall. He saw what I was doing and tried to stop me, so I killed him."

"Why would you do that to your first mate?" Mori asked, her eyes wide at the admission.

"I had no choice. He threatened to go to the enemies and help them take over. I couldn't allow that." Avarisha sighed even heavier this time as his body went limp in a hunched-over sitting position. "He was my best friend. It was the hardest thing I had to do, but the forest was *my* responsibility. I had to protect it."

Mori understood the burden that came with the crown more than anyone alive right now. It was tough to have to pick between your own happiness and the well-being of the realm. "Was that your first mate that greeted us on the deck?"

The ghost nodded. "He convinced the crew a mutiny was in order because I killed them all, even though they have no idea the real reason why."

Some scuffling above them made all three of them look up briefly before returning to their conversation. "Sounds to me like we need to set the record straight." She smiled devilishly, that confidence she'd lacked returning to her body, but the man shook his head.

"I don't care for them to know the truth. That's not important. What is important is getting you to that island."

Mori's smile fell as her eyebrows frowned. "Why the island?"

"It's not the island itself, but what's *on* it. I'm sure you felt the pull toward it." Avarisha chuckled as Mori nodded again. "Just as I did when I was alive. I could never figure out why, and I'm not allowed to leave this ship without threat of my soul's destruction by the crew, so I will never know the reason."

"Then I guess we need to get out of here so we can find what's telling me to come to it." She stood up and walked over to inspect the bars that kept them caged in, running her fingers over the cold metal. Something about them felt off, and as she looked around the brig, an idea popped into her head. Gripping two of the bars, she channeled her magic into her strength, making her muscles stronger as she pulled the metal outward. It took only a moment for the metal to creak before it gave in and bent just under her hands.

"How are you doing that?" Avarisha asked as he stumbled to his feet, his eyes never leaving the young girl.

With the bars out of the way, Mori let go and looked over her shoulder. "The entire ship has been underwater for an incredibly long time. If the wood is rotted, then the metal bars are rusted, and I was right." A smirk formed on her lips as the spark in her eye lit a fire within her. "Let's go get your ship back."

They made it topside just in time to see Marshall using a sword to poke at Duncan to walk off a piece of wood that was hanging off the edge of the ship. The crew was cheering and whistling while the scared elf tried not to allow his trembling body to show any form of fear, but Mori could easily see it.

"Let him go!" she shouted as Faust moved in front of his queen and bared his fangs. The dead crew turned toward her with Marshall grinning.

"Looks like the puppies were able to get out. Lock them back up!"

Faust wasted no time letting out a guttural growl as a warning at the approaching ghost crew who were advancing on Mori to capture her. There was no way she was going to let them get anywhere near her. Putting two of her fingers in her mouth, she let out a loud, high-pitched whistle, halting the crew in their place as they stared at her with confused looks crossing their ghostly features.

"HEY! UGLY!" she called, mocking the rebellious first mate. "I think it's time we officially meet. I'm Queen Mori Albright, fifty-ninth royal of the forest. And you are?" She bowed slightly with her hand out toward the false captain, gesturing that it was his turn to speak.

"Captain Marshall of the *R.M.S. Yulie*." The man managed a small bow of his own but quickly stood up straight. Mori glanced over her shoulder at Avarisha. "*R.M.S. Yulie*?" she asked with a raised brow.

"*Royal Military Ship Yulie*. My wife wanted a ship named after her," he said sheepishly.

She let out a breath of understanding before turning back to Marshall. "So, you started a mutiny against your captain and thought what? That you would be able to get away with it in death? I don't think so. Even though your body is at the bottom of the sea doesn't mean you are any less under my reign. As the current royal of the forest, I sentence you to . . . uh . . ." She paused before turning back to Faust and Avarisha. "Can spirits be exorcised here? Punished somehow that I can actually enforce?" she inquired with a nervous smile.

"Your magic can touch spirits, even if your body physically can't." Avarisha shrugged. "That's what I assume, anyway. Never had the chance to try it out. Spirits hide from fae. We're different."

Mori let out an exasperated sigh, her back straightening as she turned back to Marshall. "I guess now is as good as ever to try it out." Her arms moved in a circle beside her as a spark of fire ignited, a fireball growing between her hands. "I've always wanted to try this." She smirked as she pushed the fire toward the ghosts. Most of them were able to dodge it, but several were still hit to some degree by the fire. However, nothing happened. The fire passed straight through them. "That's not good," she said as her smile fell faster than a rock in a pond.

We need a new plan, Faust called to her before barking at the few ghosts who took several steps forward.

"Give me a minute! I need to think!"

"We don't have a minute!" Avarisha grabbed a plank of wood that was close by and held it up as a weapon.

Mori looked around, unsure of what to do as she drew her sword. The ghosts were closing the distance, making her hands clammy around the handle. Before she had a chance to think of something—anything—her sword was in the air to block an incoming swipe.

"Can't a girl have a minute of peace before you attempt to murder her?" Metal clanged against metal as a four-against-a-very-large-and-vague-number fight broke out. Duncan had managed to get free from his rope bindings and retrieved his sword when no one was watching.

Avarisha darted to the side of Faust and held up his wood, just for it to be sliced in half by the ghost man's sword. "Mori, a plan would be very good right about now!" he called over his shoulder as Mori lifted her foot to kick another ghost away from her, still surprised they could even make contact.

"I'm working on it! Just give me a minute!" Mori looked around the ship in between fighting off the hordes of ghostly crew mates trying to get to her. Duncan and Faust were slowly being pinned closer to her as they started to become overwhelmed.

"I suggest we jump ship. It's the only way we're getting out of here," Duncan suggested right before punching a ghost in the face. The elf shook out the pain of the impact before backing up into Avarisha.

"Agreed. We can take your boat to shore and regroup." The old captain turned toward the edge and jumped over, the sound of splashing water echoing a few seconds later.

"I do not like this idea," Faust said as he followed after the ship captain. There was no splash that time, making Mori run to the edge and look over. Below her was the rowboat with Avarisha and Faust inside.

"Let's go, Duncan!" Mori called over her shoulder before swinging her legs over the railing and landing in the boat with a thud. The elf was mere seconds behind her.

The ghost captain started to row the boat away from the ship so they could gain some distance. "That didn't go well." He sighed heavily.

"We got you out and we survived. That's the best we can hope for." Mori rested her chin on her hands and her elbows on her knees after sitting down. This would have been so much easier if she were more knowledgeable about spirits. It reminded her of her favorite TV show. Eyes widening and face lighting up, Mori lifted her head and laughed. "I got it!" She laughed again. "Avarisha, where is the ship located?"

"It's behind us, where it will stay." The captain's brows pinched as the left corner of his mouth pulled up. "Why would you ask something you already know the answer to?"

Mori shook her head. "No, not the ghost ship, the real ship. The one you sank with all your crew on board."

"That's a strange request, and irrelevant at this point."

"Answer the queen's question. If she has an idea, we need to follow it," Duncan said, glaring down at the captain who'd dared to deny the queen an answer.

"Save your glares for the real enemies, Duncan." Avarisha turned his gaze from the elf to the queen before letting out a breath and motioning off to his left. "Over there, closer to Scuttle Island."

"Take us to it."

"Aye aye, Captain," the ghost mocked as he rolled his eyes and turned their boat to head in the direction of his sunken ship. They heard shouting behind them from the ghost ship, making Mori's leg bounce anxiously as she stared down at the sword in her hands. It was a simple and plain sword with brown leather wrapped around the handle and the sapling symbol on the circle end. She had taken it from the Birch Palace when they'd visited. Thankfully it was one of the things she had brought with her when returning to the human world.

The boat knocked into a long piece of wood that stuck out of the water. "We're here," Avarisha said as he pointed to the crow's nest of a ship. That was what they had run into.

Mori stood up slowly so as to not rock the boat too much. "Keep us steady. I can't promise this will work, but I'm optimistic." With her hands by her waist, she closed her eyes to focus on the water around them. The new waves crashed into the sides of their little rowboat as they started to move out of the way of something much bigger.

Slowly but surely, the large vessel rose out of the water, fish jumping away to safety. Coral and barnacles covered the water-swollen wood, and the entire ship looked like it could fall apart at any moment from how rotted and eaten the wood looked. Several planks ended with jagged edges that had allowed fish to enter for millennia.

"I have to hold it up just to make sure it doesn't crash into the water and sink again. Get in there, find as much salt as you can, and lay it out everywhere you see a body," Mori commanded, earning several horrified and confused looks from the other three.

"Are you sure about this?" Duncan asked, a disgusted look on his face as he looked up at the ship. "It smells really bad in there." Faust placed a paw over his own nose. "Very bad."

"Shush, all of you. I can't hold this for much longer, so get a move on. That's an order!"

Duncan and Faust made their way to a hole in the side and carefully climbed in. Avarisha was about to do the same, when he stopped and turned his head to look at Mori.

"If this looney concoction you call a plan works, what will happen to me?" he asked, trepidation filling his voice, the weight of which was not unnoticed by the queen.

"If your body is on the ship and we salt and burn it, then you'll . . ." Her sentence trailed off.

"I will cease to exist, even as a spirit."

Mori nodded. "Is part of your soul inside the royal magic?"

"Aye, just like every other royal's soul."

She gave him a reassuring smile. "Then you will always be with me, Avarisha. I hope I can call upon that piece of you to have a long talk about your adventures as king." Those comforting words made the ghostly captain smile before he turned to enter the *Yulie* without another word.

It was several minutes before the three of them came back through the hole. Mori was perspiring profusely from having to use so much magic to keep the vessel afloat.

"We found a lot of salt and sprinkled it everywhere. There were mostly just fragments of bones. I think the fish ate the soft tissue over the few thousand years it's been down there." Duncan looked down at his clothes and groaned. He was covered in a few different types of sea plants and smelled like sea water. "I hope the smell comes off my skin and hair. So gross."

"I'm sure it will," Avarisha told him.

"I'm surprised you found any bones at all. They decay very quickly underwater, especially when it's been a thousand years." Mori tried not to show her dislike of the extra salty smell that hung in the air.

"Everything here decays differently. It takes much longer due to the ambient magic," Duncan clarified.

What happens now, Mori? Faust sat beside her and looked up at the worn-out ship.

"Now for the really hard part." She summoned as much magic as she could, making her body glow green and her hair float into the air weightlessly. The whole ship started to steam, growing in volume as the seconds ticked by. Beads of sweat ran down the sides of Mori's face before falling to the wooden boat beneath her. Faust, Duncan, and Avarisha all watched with stunned silence as the entire ship heated up to expel all the water before going up in flames. It was sudden and made the three of them flinch while Mori held her position. Grunts of pain escaped her lips as her teeth ground together.

"Be careful, Mori!" Duncan called. She could barely hear his words over the roar of the fire before them. "How did you know that would work?"

She shrugged. "I didn't know for sure, but salt and fire have been used for a long time to fend off spirits. I figured it was worth a shot."

"You didn't know it would work?" Duncan sat down and buried his face in his hands, covering the dumbfounded look that took over his features. "Where did you even learn such a thing?"

"A TV show about two brothers who hunt monsters and spirits. It's one of my favorite shows." She beamed.

"Do I even want to know what a TV show is? Know what? Yeah, no, I don't want to know." Duncan ran his hands over his hair as he took a deep, calming breath. "We should get out of here before that ship cooks us."

Mori nodded in agreement as she lowered what remained of the ship down toward the water and let it slip under. It was nothing more than a few smoldering boards as it sank into the water. A noise to her left shifted her focus from the ship to the former king. His body was starting to burn away, just as the ship had.

"Thank you for setting us free." He did his best to smile with only half a mouth as he faded away with the breeze. Mori could feel the gratitude in the air from the former captain.

"Rest in peace, Captain Avarisha."

Chapter Twenty-One

"What do you think we'll find here?" Mori asked as she took Duncan's hand to get help getting out of the boat. She heard Faust jump out behind her and shift some of the rocks under his paws as he walked.

I am not sure what is here, but we should be careful. The wolf caught up to her to stay close while Duncan took the lead. *Do you still feel the pull?*

Mori nodded. "I do, in more ways than one." She surveyed her new surroundings on the island.

The trees were much taller than the ones on the mainland, with lower branches on the sides due to getting more sun and nutrients from the soil. The grass was much greener and taller and swayed with the light breeze, standing at about two feet tall, by Mori's estimate. It was definitely a species of grass that didn't grow too tall. It had never been stepped on or cut before—at least, not for a thousand years.

Above her, she could still hear the normal sounds of birds and animals running around as she took a few more steps forward on the grass. The queen gaped as her body started to shake with exhilaration before she let out a belly laugh.

"What's so funny?" Duncan asked, his eyebrow raised and his hands on his hips.

It took a minute for Mori to calm down enough to answer the guard's question. "This is so exciting! We are on a literal island that no one has been to in who knows how long!" She then squealed before running toward the trees, dancing around the trunks as she laughed.

Faust and Duncan exchanged confused looks before the wolf ran over to her. *Is everything OK, Mori?* he questioned. Mori finally calmed down enough to speak, panting from the exertion. After running a hand over her hair to pull it away from her face, she beamed.

"I'm not sure. I felt a sudden rush of energy and excitement. There's so much of it, and it feels like it's going to burst out of me if I don't find an outlet." She looked from Faust to the approaching Duncan.

"That can't be good, but I don't have any experience with the sort of feeling you're describing. I have never been here myself. I wasn't sure what to expect." His arms crossed over his chest.

"Let's go explore!" Mori turned to stare toward a nearby cliff, her eyes widening with curiosity. Something inside her was telling her to go toward it, like the royal magic was being pulled to a piece of itself that had been missing its whole life. She could feel that missing piece close by, and the desire to feel whole moved her legs toward it.

"Where should we go first?" Duncan asked as he glanced up at the queen before quickly following after her. "I guess we need to follow her."

Mori? Faust nudged her hand, pulling her from her trance.

"Huh? Um, the base of that cliff." She jerked her head toward the direction she could feel the pull. "Something is telling me to go that way. Like it has a lasso around my waist and is pulling me."

Maybe the royal magic is directing you toward something. Maybe we should go, the wolf told her.

"It could be the royal magic reacting to something here." Duncan took a few cautious steps toward the cliff. Mori would never get used to Duncan repeating what Faust said in her mind.

It was funny most of the time, but right now was not one of those times. It just made her roll her eyes.

With careful steps, they made their way over to the cliff, a floral smell hanging in the air. The familiar smell of an herb she'd used a lot when she'd made teas for her online shop. Definitely a smell she could recognize anywhere, but she was surprised it was in the fae realm, where most of the plants were different from how they looked in the human realm.

"Lavender?" Mori asked no one in particular as they approached the rocky cliffside surrounded by lavender flowers. The light breeze swayed the flowers, moving the scent—and a few petals—through the air. They were in full bloom, just as they always were no matter the time of day or season in a year.

"This looks very promising. Doesn't the poem mention purple flowers?" Duncan asked as he knelt to gently caress one of the small flowers.

"It does. Maybe there's something around here." Mori inspected her surroundings intensely, looking for any sign that this was the place. Her gaze landed on an oak tree that had the sapling insignia carved into it.

"With the saplings as your guide"—she paused for a moment to remember the next part—"find the place where it resides." She smiled, walking up to the tree and placing her hand on the symbol. Green light sprouted from her hand and filled the engraving of the symbol with the magic, making the lavender flowers light up, forming a trail toward the cliff. Stepping close to inspect the flowers, Mori saw some of them were halfway inside the cliff, as if the wall was simply not there. "Lavender bloom alights the course to this power's sacred source." Mori walked toward the cliff and reached out to touch it, but her hand went right through the rock face. Her brows shot up to her hairline and her jaw hit the ground, sharply sucking in air to make an audible gasp. She quickly pulled her hand back as if she were going to lose it if it stayed inside the wall any longer than mere moments.

"That's new." Duncan walked up to the cliff and tried to do the same thing, but his hand touched the solid rock form. "Seems Faust and I will have to stay out here."

"I think you're right. Wait here and I will see what I can find. Hopefully this is the place we've been looking for."

Good luck, Faust communicated to her.

With a deep breath, she stepped through the illusion and into a cave. The small area was lit by the purple glow of the lavender, making it difficult to see. Still, Mori pressed on, allowing her curiosity to drive her wherever it wanted. "Where it flowers night and day." In the center of the large cavern was a dim green crystal with the sapling insignia on it. The queen just stared at it in confusion, but something inside her mind told her to keep going and touch it, so she did.

Swirls of magic shot out of the spot she touched, lighting up the area much brighter now, almost blinding her. The crystal lit up a bright teal color that reminded her of a clear river. The colors flowed together with the white edges, showing off its cracks and age. It had aged well for something kept in the dark for so long.

Before she had a chance to adjust to the new lighting, the crystal flashed a bright white light, forcing Mori to close her eyes tightly. Through her eyelids, she could see the light dimming quickly, and knew when to open them by how dark everything had gotten. That was when she realized she was no longer inside the cave. Instead, she was inside what she could only describe as a sacred grove.

The glade was surrounded by tall trees and moss-covered rocks that acted as a wall. Vines hung from the branches and lay on the grass. Opposite Mori were three statues of people standing at the far side of the circle area. The one to her left was a man with a warhammer in front of him, the handle up and his hands resting on top of the end. Freckles in the shape of a hammer were on his cracked left shoulder. To her right stood a woman who held out her right hand, palm up, with what looked like a magic ball. On the front of her neck were freckles that looked like an exploding firework. Directly in front of Mori was a very large man's statue. Most of his face was completely broken, but the circle of freckles with a line through the bottom dotted his forehead. His right arm lay on the ground after breaking off, and the statue looked completely run down, with cracks in many places as if someone had punched it. All the statues were covered in moss and dirt from age.

In the center of the three statues was stairs in the shape of a circle with a round platform landing. A moss-covered crystal sat at the top, weathered from the elements and had long ago lost its light. It was smaller than Mori had expected compared to the crystal inside the cave, and it didn't have the sapling on it. Nothing about this place said regality, but at the same time, all three of the statues looked very familiar to her, like she had seen the people before.

Looking between the three statues, the girl released the breath she was holding to steady her nerves. "Regal boon will find your way. I sure hope so. I could use a boon. Just hope these statues don't suddenly wake up and attack me," she said out loud with a nervous laugh. "I have watched way too many movies."

As she stepped closer to the center, a voice to her right stopped her in her tracks.

"Who are you, young girl? How did you find this place?" a womanly voice asked. Mori nearly jumped out of her skin and ran for the hills, but instead, she regained her composure and turned to look at the statue of the woman right in her now-glowing green eyes.

"Oh crap!" Her arms flew up protectively in front of her body, like something straight out of a cartoon or anime. "Uh … My name is Moriana Albright." She put her arms down and stood straight. "I'm the current queen of this forest, and I was drawn to the fake cliffside that housed the crystal that brought me here," she said, figuring honesty would probably get her further here since the sapling logo had led her to this place.

The statue was silent for a few moments before speaking again. "Confirmed. Magic within is royalty. Activating spell." The statue's eyes stopped glowing, making Mori take a step back. She was not sure what to expect, but she knew to be on her guard, just as Duncan had taught her to be.

Above the crystal in the center of the glade's landing stood a woman. She looked solid, like she was actually there. The lavender warrior attire she wore reminded Mori of an older version of the green uniform Duncan always wore, all the way down to her brown boots, but instead of leaves, her clothing was covered in lavender flower petals. Her bright green eyes stared at Mori, and her shoulder-length curly red hair hung in ringlets, but that was not what made her flinch. It was the firework-looking freckles on her neck, just like the statue. With a quick glance at the statue, she noticed the ball of magic in the statue's hand now glowed purple.

"Who are you?" Mori asked.

"I am the third royal, The Caster, Vedia Albright," the woman said, and took a few steps closer to the current queen. She stood at the top of the short stairs on the landing, hands on her hips and a scowl on her face.

"I'm Moriana, but you can call me Mori. How are you here? I thought you died a super long time ago."

"I'm not here. I was known as The Caster royal due to my strong magical abilities. I knew one day someone would come for this weapon, and I had to make sure that the royal was worthy to wield such power." Vedia walked down the steps and around Mori, her eyes scanning the young queen's body. She then stopped in front of her once more. "What royal are you?"

"Uh." She thought for a moment. "I don't really have a title yet. I'm just the current queen." Mori shrugged with a nervous smile.

Vedia sighed heavily before rephrasing her question. "What number are you?"

"Oh, uh, number fifty-nine."

Vedia nodded in understanding. "It's been that long." She turned to walk back up the steps to the crystal and stood beside it as she held her hand over it. A purple glow emitted from Vedia's hand, making what looked like a handle start to form up from the crystal until it met her hand. It looked just like the one the statue on the left had under his hands. "Do you know what this is?"

"The royal boon," she breathed out before speaking up. "The Hammer of the Royals. My mother told me the poem, and I was thinking about it when I teleported." Vedia's eyes narrowed as a smile pulled at the corner of her lips with intrigue.

"Teleport? No one has teleported in or out of the forest since my time. I was the last one when I sealed away the weapon." Her face soured, losing her smile instantly, and her eyes glossed over. That was a look Mori was all too familiar with. A bad memory had crossed her mind's eye. Vedia shook it away before continuing. "Did your mother teach you anything about our history?"

Mori shook her head. "I met her for a few minutes. We didn't have much time to talk. The forest has been taken over by the raider king, and he is trying to claim it for himself. She managed to teleport to the human world, where she left me to be raised. I don't know much about the royals except from what I have been able to read and learn during my short time here." She paused for a moment. "At least, before the tree house was destroyed."

"The tree house? I didn't know it could be destroyed. It's massive."

"Not birch, oak. The oak tree house. I don't know who created it, but I like it. It's small and cozy. Or at least, it was."

"A new tree house was made? That takes some intense magic to pull off. Who made it?"

Mori shrugged. "It was there before my mother was born, so I'm not sure."

Vedia let the magic handle disappear before moving to sit on the steps leading up to the crystal and letting out a deep sigh. "It seems you know nothing about us." A hand ran through her medium-length hair to push it out of her face before she spoke once more. "Allow me to fill you in on what you just stumbled upon." When she raised her hands, the magic in the air became visible. Several strands of rainbow colors moved like rivers through the glade. Mori spun around with a smile, admiring the beauty the magic held. Several of the magic moved suddenly to change where they were standing, or at least, put up an illusion of another area. It blanketed the area to show the sacred grove in its beginning, before plants took it over and damage was done to the statues. The crystal was no longer on the small platform.

"Long ago, a man obtained an immense power, with which he used to keep the forest safe and eventually named the land after himself. All was peaceful for many decades, until humans found their way into our world." The scenery shifted to show a forest with a portal, humans charging out of it with primitive weapons. Several pixies and animals fled in fear as these weapons were thrown at them and their blood spilled from their injuries.

"He created the Hammer of the Royals, Fae'ohtan, to fight back against the invaders." The magic shifted to show a man hammering away at a piece of metal against an anvil with a large, glowing teal crystal beside him. Its jagged edges looked sharp, like it could cut you just by gazing upon it. "He managed to fight them back using the magic he possessed and Fae'ohtan." The magic in the air changed again to show a man from behind with long red hair overlooking the forest from a cliff. In front of him was Albright Forest on fire. Smoke clouded the sky, and many birds flew away to safety.

"He concentrated a large amount of magic into the weapon that he would use against the humans after fighting them off, forcing them to return to their own world. As revenge, he gathered up an army of fae warriors to go after them." The visual changed to one of an army of different fae all ready for battle with their weapons at the ready. "After taking up arms, they went through the portal to kill off the humans, but they proved to be too strong and the humans outnumbered the fae." The next picture appeared with the fae army going back through a portal, many dead in their wake as the survivors fled. "The royal chanted 'blood for blood' as he slaughtered as many humans as he could." The magic faded away and the glade returned to its normal weathered look.

"All of that was done by the first royal?" Mori asked.

Vedia nodded. "He was my grandfather. He died before he could get his revenge, and my father, the second royal, was not able to open a portal to continue his father's plan. Instead, he turned on the fae of the forest, claiming they didn't try hard enough to kill the humans. Burning down trees and territories and drying up rivers were just the start. The fae rebelled against him until I was able to steal the hammer." She let out a breath through her nose. "My father was executed for his crimes against the inhabitants of this forest, and I laid his body to rest under his statue." Mori followed Vedia's gaze over to the statue of the man on the left side of the room. She had already deduced the one in the middle was the first royal. "I built this place to lock away the hammer so no one would ever be able to use it to destroy the forest again or try to exact their revenge on humans." Vedia looked at Mori. "My body lies under my statue, but I do not know where my grandfather was laid to rest. My father, King Alder, would never tell me. He was known as The Hammer because of the way he could easily wield the warhammer while he burned down our home."

Mori sat down on a nearby boulder and ran a hand through her long red hair, her thoughts running marathons inside her mind. Her bloodline had more than just their bright green eyes and red hair that passed down to each generation. It was also the magic and the destruction it could bring when used improperly. That was not something she wanted to deal with—if she could ever do any real good without completely destroying the forest in the process of learning to control something she'd had for two months.

"So, I just need the hammer to stop the raider king. It took a long time to realize it, but this forest is my home. I've lived with humans my whole life, but I felt like I didn't belong with them." She looked up at Vedia, who was now standing in front of her.

That bit of information had Vedia raising an eyebrow. "What are you, exactly, Mori?"

Mori was hesitant to say it, but she knew she couldn't lie to this woman. "I'm half-human, half-fae. I don't know what kind of fae the royals are, though."

Vedia shrugged her shoulders. "Never learned. Only The First knows what we are, and he took that information to his grave."

That wasn't very helpful.

It wasn't like there was much she could do about it, so she stood up and smiled. "So, can I get the hammer to stop the raider king?" she finally asked after a moment of silence.

"No." The response came sharply and without hesitation.

"What do you mean no?"

"You have to do something first. You must go find The Seer. She is my daughter, Leana, and the fourth royal. You will be able to find her in the royal throne room. Concentrate your magic on the throne, and it will move to reveal stairs. She will see into the future and give you your royal name. Once you have it, come back to me. Only then will I *consider* allowing you the chance to wield Fae'ohtan." The corner of Vedia's lips curled upward as her eyes narrowed slightly and she crossed her arms over her chest. "Good luck." In the blink of an eye, she disappeared.

"Damn, didn't even get to ask if that was her soul or just an imprint of herself. Next time. Next time." Mori mentally kicked herself for not having the chance to ask since she got caught up in the conversation—and history lesson—but there would be another time. Looking at the crystal one last time, she turned to walk back the way she'd come and touch the large green one that had brought her there.

When Mori emerged from the fake cave, she knew she would need to share with her friends what happened.

Chapter Twenty-Two

"Tell us what happened." Duncan shot up from the rock the moment Mori appeared from the fake cliff.

"I need to find The Seer and get my royal name. Then Vedia will allow me to have the hammer. I was able to find the lost Hammer of the Royals, Fae'ohtan." Mori smiled proudly.

I'm impressed, Mori. I did not think anyone would be able to find the hammer. Faust walked over to her, his tail wagging happily behind him.

"The Seer? You mean Leana? No one has seen her since Viviana got her royal name. She tried to go back to Leana to talk to her, and she was gone." Duncan shrugged.

"I still have to try. Maybe I can find her like I did the hammer." Mori gestured to the cliff. The lavender flowers had stopped glowing, and everything was back to normal.

Where is Leana? Faust asked.

"Well, I think only royals can get in there, I'm not really sure how it works, but I spoke to Vedia, or at least an imprint of her. I'm not really sure. I didn't get to ask." Mori shrugged, which made Duncan pinch the bridge of his nose.

"I guess we are going on, uh, what do humans call it? A wild duck run?" Duncan asked, his hand moving in a circle at the wrist while he thought about what the words he wanted were.

"A wild goose chase," Mori corrected.

"Yeah, that, a wild goose chase." Duncan turned around to start walking with a groan. "The throne room is a several days' journey."

"Actually." Mori walked up to him. "I figured out how to make a portal. Think we can travel that way?"

Duncan looked dumbfounded by her comment. "I don't see why you can't give it a try."

The queen turned to a tree and held out her hands, focusing her magic on creating a portal to the throne room. A circle of magic formed against the tree until the image of the throne room appeared within.

Well done, Mori, Faust said.

"Thanks, buddy. Let's get to that throne room."

Duncan went through the portal first, followed by Faust and then Mori. It closed behind her a few seconds after her feet touched the grass.

The moment Mori was back inside the throne room, negative memories flooded her mind. Her heart hammered inside her chest, attempting to escape its cage as her breathing became labored. The throne room spun as her head began to hurt. Did this place always feel so depressing? Or was it the looming fear of rejection that hung in the air since her failed coronation. How so many people were angry that she became the queen. Even with the failed ceremony, she was still queen, even if no one respected her enough to acknowledge her title.

"Mori?" The words were slow and distorted, her vision doubling and spinning in circles. "Mori?" the voice drawled on, a ringing echoing in her ears.

Mori! Faust called, snapping the queen back to reality, her vision returning to normal and the ringing gone.

"Huh? What?"

What do you need to do here? Where is The Seer?

"Oh, right. Sorry." Mori pushed some hair out of her face with her clammy hand before she walked up to the throne. Her eyes trailed over the dimly lit crystal throne before continuing up to her portrait made of various plants. The plants were alive and healthy; bright colors filled out the picture. Her gaze wandered around the entire room, taking in its new look. While the plants were green, they were still dull in color, like the magic and life inside had been pulled out and left the color behind.

A tight knot formed in the pit of her stomach at the magicless throne room, that same knot from when she'd been there the second time when she'd failed her own destiny.

"What are you supposed to do?" Duncan asked, yanking Mori back to the present, leaving the past as haunting memories once more.

"I need to give the throne magic." She turned to face the throne once more, holding out her hands with her palms facing the throne. After she closed her eyes, she focused all her magic into the throne to bring it to life. The crystals grew brighter and livelier as the power filled each rock with the waves of green light that formed in front of her hands and connected her to the throne. With enough power, the throne's crystals swirled with boundless magic before the ground started to shake under their feet as it moved backward, revealing stairs.

"I did it!" Mori exclaimed, her eyes wide as she peered over at her friends.

Great job, Mori! Faust was wagging his tail so hard his butt was shaking.

"Only the royal is allowed down there. You will be on your own until you come back up here. We will wait for you to finish," Duncan explained before taking a seat on the top step. Mori nodded and turned back to the stairs.

Hopefully disappointment isn't waiting for me at the bottom like it was when I walked to the throne.

After a deep breath to—unsuccessfully—settle her nerves, she walked down to see what was inside. The spiral stone staircase seemed to go on for a long time, and the shift in magical energy made her nauseous. Swallowing back the bile that threatened to escape, she continued on until she finally reached the bottom. The place was dimly lit by crystals acting as torches, just as they had along the stairs. It was certainly an odd way to barely light an entire dungeon staircase to who knew what.

The bottom of the staircase was just a small circular room with stone bricks for walls and the floor. There was a little more light now, but it was still pretty dark. There were no windows, no fire to light the area, nothing. It was hard for Mori to see anything, but she could see *who* was there. In the center of the room sat a cloaked figure in purple. Mori couldn't tell who it was, but assumed it was Leana, The Seer. She moved to stand in front of the person before sitting down on the cold stone.

"I have waited a long time for you," the person said with an old woman's voice. She lifted her head to show a young-looking face beneath the hood of her cloak. She had long, curly white hair and bright green eyes with no wrinkles in sight. Mori thought she sounded like an old grandma, even though she looked like a young woman.

"You were waiting for me?"

"Yes," she breathed, "you are the one who will do the most good for the fae realm. I have already seen it."

"So you must be Leana, the fourth royal and The Seer. I'm here for—"

"Yes, yes, I know why you are here," Leana interrupted. "I have seen the past, present, and future of the entire forest." She cocked her head to the right. "You have not been accepted as queen yet. This I have seen."

"Well, yeah. You live right under the throne room. It was pretty obvious I wasn't wanted by the fae." Mori sighed in frustration, her sarcasm not lost on the woman.

"You joke, but no one is laughing." Leana leaned closer to the girl. "You are here for your royal name. Normally I wait until you have taken the throne fully, but I know what will happen if I don't give it to you now." The woman cracked a smile that told Mori she knew something the queen didn't.

"Without the royal name, I can't get the royal hammer. Without the royal hammer, I have no hope of defeating the raider king and Dairus. So yes, I am here to get the name." She paused for a moment. "Also, I want to know why my mother couldn't talk to you a second time. She tried, but you weren't here," Mori added, speaking fast, as though The Seer might interrupt her if she weren't quick enough. She learned from her mistake of not asking the questions on her mind while she had the chance. Fingers fidgeted with the hem of her shirt as her eyes darted down to them. There was no way Leana had deliberately avoided her mother. Right?

"I may only be seen when I am needed. I know exactly when to appear. Your mother did not need me because she was never the one to save the forest. The Swirl was merely a beginning to the war, but never meant to be the end." Leana pointed at Mori, a smirk crossing her young-looking face. "*You* are the one who stops the raider king and Dairus." Leana turned both her hands toward each other to concentrate her magic. Ribbons of blue light swirled around between them, taking the shape of Mori's freckle line. More lines added to the shape until it looked like a bridge you would cross over water. "Ah, yes, that makes the most sense."

"What does that mean?" Mori asked as she stared at the bridge with her brows pinched together.

"It is your royal name. You are The Bridge."

Heat rose within Mori, her face turning red as her teeth clenched and her eyes darted straight up to look Leana in the face. The Bridge? Really? That was the best she could get? Nothing cool like The Caster or The Hero? Nothing that actually told future royals about the kind of person she was? In the faes' minds, she was just the one who fixed everyone else's problems and ended a war she didn't start. Bridging the gap between divided fae was all she was good for. But what happened when the war was over? Would they still need her? Still want her?

Glad to know where I stand in all this.

It seemed so stupid to her. In her mind, this had to be how her mother felt when she got her royal name of The Swirl. That didn't have much meaning, as being good at magic seemed to be a common theme with the past royals. Nothing set her apart from the others. She blended in with the other royals where magic was their weapon of choice.

Leana quirked an eyebrow. "Do you doubt me?"

Mori shook her head, trying very hard to be grateful while also not showing how disappointed she was. "I-I wouldn't say I doubt you, but I thought my name would be . . ." She shrugged. "I don't know . . . Cooler?" She looked down again at her hands, the heat starting to subside. There was no point in being angry. It wasn't like she could change anything.

"You may not like it now, but it is more important than you can imagine. Being a halfling means you can become the bridge between the humans and the fae. I wouldn't take that fate lightly." Leana gave a small smile.

"Wait, what do you mean *can* become the bridge? I thought you knew all the answers?" Humans and fae? She thought it would be between the fae alone. Why would she need to fix anything between humans and fae?

"I do, but you do not. If I told you that you would die tomorrow, you would do what you could to change that. The future's not set in stone and can be altered if one so chooses. I have seen many possible outcomes to what will happen, but there is only one way you can win." Leana lowered her hands to let the magic fade away.

"Only one? How am I supposed to do that?" Mori asked desperately, her body leaning closer to Leana as she held her breath in anticipation.

The Seer laughed. "I cannot give you all the answers, my dear, but do understand this.

'When the winds carry the cries of panic,

and frightful sounds make you frantic,

be not afraid and go near,

for your strongest ally is also your greatest fear.'"

Mori blinked as her mouth went slack-jawed.

WHAT?

"Why would I want to go toward my fear? That doesn't make any sense!" She threw up her arms, her tone filled with confusion and anger as she questioned the older woman.

"I will call you shall I need to speak with you again. Until then, you will not be able to find me. Now go. You are The Bridge, the one to connect our worlds." The Seer cackled. "Watch your step going back up," she said before she faded away and disappeared.

"Wait! Leana!" Mori called out, and sank to the ground with a sigh. "Damn, now I have to figure out what that means. Why can't anything be easy? Why must it all be cryptic and hard?" Mori groaned before she stood up and dusted herself off. "Even in movies, everything has to be a riddle and hard. Such a stupid thing. Just tell me what I need to do." She walked back up the stairs as she grumbled to herself. She didn't know what her greatest fear was; she had a few different fears that she would never want to confront.

When she made it to the top, the throne moved back into place.

"What happened?" Duncan asked as he stood up and turned to her. "Did you get your royal name?"

"I did. I'm called The Bridge. Sounds dumb to me, but that is what she said." Mori crossed her arms over her chest and pouted. "I wanted something cool, like The Master or The Warrior." She huffed.

"We already have a royal called The Warrior. He was the twenty-fourth. Very skilled man when it came to the whip." Duncan looked to the side as his hand rubbed the back of his neck, not wanting to meet Mori's glare.

"Fine, guess I'm stuck with this name." She turned and looked up at the plant portrait of herself. "I don't really understand what she was getting at. She told me I'm supposed to be the bridge between humans and fae. That I'm the one who should reunite them or something like that." Mori shook her head. "That's a lot of pressure on a new queen. Just protecting this forest is going to be hard. Then she gave me some cryptic message I don't understand." Mori sighed heavily and turned back to her friends. "Whatever, let's just head back to Vedia through the portal. I want to get the hammer and start practicing with it. See if I'm better at it than the sword."

After returning to the fake cliff where the entrance to the sacred grove was, Mori put her hand on the tree with the sapling, lighting it up to allow passage. The lavender flowers started to glow once more to lead the way.

I may need to come here to relax every now and then. The flower lights are beautiful.

"We will wait out here. We can't follow you," Duncan said, and sat on a rock so he could work on sharpening his sword. Faust lowered his ears as he sat down, not wanting to be separated from Mori again.

The queen walked up to him and patted his head. "I will try to be quick. There is no reason to worry. I know my place is here, and I plan to stay here forever. No more running away," she explained as she shook her head a bit to reaffirm she wasn't going anywhere. Faust perked up at the reassurance.

Hurry back. You have a lot of head scratches and belly rubs to make up after your disappearing act.

Mori laughed. "Sure thing, buddy." She turned to walk back to the cliffside and went inside. Once again, she touched the green crystal sticking out of the ground and was teleported to the sacred grove.

"Vedia?" she called out, walking to the base of the stairs. The ball in the statue's hand lit up purple once more, and the image of Vedia showed up, standing on the platform in the center.

"It's about time. Did you get your name from Leana?" the woman asked.

Mori nodded. "I did. I will be known as The Bridge from now on."

Vedia took a moment to think it over. "Makes sense. Being half-human, you could be the answer we're looking for." She gave a half-shrug. "The fairies hate humans so much for something they didn't actually do. The First was the one who started the war on humans and attacked them. Humans retaliated. That's war in a nutshell. It's unfortunate that it's up to you to fix his mistake all these years later." Vedia's voice was nonchalant as she spoke, as if the thought of war meant nothing to her. That made Mori sick to her stomach. How was war ever a good thing or something to shrug your shoulders at? People died in war.

Vedia smiled confidently, continuing on as if she had talked about the weather instead of mass genocide. "I know you will treat this weapon with respect and with the best interest of the forest in mind." The Caster stepped to the side and motioned toward the crystal with her hand. "Your magic will activate it."

Mori looked from the other woman to the crystal and then back to her. "I just have one question before I do, before you disappear again. How are you here? And what are you?"

Vedia flinched from the question, but it still made her laugh. "I placed my soul in the statue over there. In order to seal away the hammer, I had to pull my father and grandfather from the royal magic along with myself to seal them away. You won't be able to call the three of us through the royal magic because we're not there. Our souls are not a part of it. So if you need me, you can return here and call me. I will do my best to help you with whatever I can," she explained, and lowered her arm. "Take the crystal. You have a war to win." She smirked with a little wave before disappearing.

Mori huffed out a breath of amusement and shook her head in disbelief. Even the third royal was pushing her toward a destiny she hadn't asked for. She ascended the steps to the crystal and held her hand over it, infusing her magic in the crystal. The teal crystal lit up as the moss that covered it dissolved away. A gold crescent moon plate with a white gem in the center appeared on both sides of the rectangular crystal as a long, pink wooden handle formed with a teal teardrop crystal at the end. Gold wrapped around the handle near the crystal before hanging freely like a snake wrapped around a tree branch. With a nervous smile, Mori grabbed the handle once the warhammer was fully formed, praying to whatever magical deity was listening to let her lift such a heavy-looking thing.

Slowly, she grabbed the handle and yanked the hammer as hard as she could. Instead of barely lifting it, it flew up over her head, pulling her backward until she was on the ground with a hard thud.

The swift movement reminded her of her childhood cartoons. Her wrist had twisted from the sudden motion but was healed instantly as she rubbed her lower back with that hand. Wasn't this supposed to be really heavy?

"Let's try this again," she said to no one in particular as she stood up and looked down at Fae'ohtan with a determined fire in her eyes. "It's weird how light you actually are. No heavier than the sword I was forced to train with." Reaching down, she picked up the weapon and swung it in circles on either side of her like windmills as a way to test her ability to wield it. It was very light and felt natural in her hands, but it was the power that flowed through it that made her realize exactly why Vedia had sealed it away. This warhammer could destroy entire worlds and maybe even destroy the forest. That power couldn't fall into the wrong hands . . . Again.

"This feels so much better than a sword." Mori laughed before something caught her eye. Lifting up the large teal crystal hammer head, she noticed something appear in the gold. There were circular indents in three places on both sides of the crystal and between them were some words. She didn't recognize them as any language she knew, but somehow she could still read them.

"'Swing once to topple an empire,
swing twice to build one.'

That's pretty interesting. I hope I get to learn what that means one day soon." Mori inspected the weapon once more, noticing something rather interesting. In one of the circular indents in the gold plate was a red ball. It was solid and glowed now that there was power. She wasn't sure what it was, but decided to just leave it for now. Going down the steps, she headed toward the exit crystal before stopping and turning back to the statue of the third royal. "Thanks, Vedia. Fae'ohtan is in good hands with me. I will only use its magic for good."

Chapter Twenty-Three

Over the next three months, Mori trained tirelessly. She learned just how good she was with the warhammer, more so than the sword. Her movements were more fluid and her aim was much better. Plus, her magic had improved as well through focus and Fae'ohtan's ability to amplify the energy. Though nothing she did brought the tree house back, making every night inside the birch tree house that much more depressing. She liked the smaller oak tree house better. It was cozy and had everything she needed to learn about, and it felt like a cabin in the woods, and that was always her dream. Instead, the three of them were going back and forth between the birch tree house and the fairy territory so Mori and Duncan could train more and so Mori could be close to her father. When it came to training, Lorem was giving the queen a run for her berries in hand-to-hand as well as weapon fighting, but having an enchanted warhammer did have a lot of benefits. She had learned that she could take out anything thrown at her with one swing, so she was careful about where she would swing it.

"You are getting a lot better," Duncan told her with a proud smile.

"I agree. You're anticipating my swings a lot more. Orian is having issues keeping up with you as well, Queenie." Lorem snickered. "It really puts him in his place."

"This hammer is a lot easier for me. One hit and my enemies will go down. Took care of those kelpies quite easily last week." Mori laughed before Faust nuzzled her.

Do you feel ready to take on the raiders?

"I feel more confident about it, but I don't know if I'm fully ready. I still have a lot to work on," she said as she swung the hammer like it weighed nothing.

"I would say you may be more ready than you think. I helped train a few of the past guards for Queen Vi. I know a skilled warrior when I see one." The satyress put her longsword in its sheath. "I have some things to attend to, but I will meet up with you when it's time to go over the war plans," Lorem said, before she waved and walked away.

Mori examined the hammer again, still amazed by its power and beauty. The crystal might have looked like it had some chips in it, but she could tell that was just from how it was formed rather than how it was used.

"Can I try lifting it?" the elf asked with a confident smile. Mori shrugged and handed over the warhammer to her guard captain. The weight of the hammer instantly made him fall forward as it hit the ground right before he face-planted into the grass. Mori and Faust burst out laughing once they saw he was OK. "How is this so heavy and how are you lifting it? It feels like it weighs more than ten large trees." Duncan stood up and tried several times to lift it, but to no avail. Eventually, he threw his hands in the air and gave up.

Mori grabbed the handle and lifted it as if it were as light as a feather. "I think my magic allows me to pick it up. It's definitely not Mjolnir, that's for sure," she joked.

"What's that?" Duncan asked in confusion.

"It's the name of the hammer used by Thor. He is a Norse god back in the human world who was then used in a few movies." She shook her head as if to stop herself from rambling on. "Anyway, the hammer can only be lifted by someone who is worthy to lift it and has the power of lightning and thunder. My hammer doesn't have those kinds of powers. I think it just reacts to the royal magic inside me."

Sounds right to me. Faust lay down next to a tree and stretched out lazily.

"Sounds like a children's story. A hammer controlling lightning and thunder. Ridiculous," the elf said incredulously as he rolled his eyes and crossed his arms.

"I love having a hammer instead of a sword. It feels more natural to me and made me realize why I didn't do the best in fencing class." She laughed.

"Personally, I think you're ready to take on the raiders. We have the fairies on our side for the fight, so I think we should meet with them to come up with a game plan. Sophie seems to be itching for payback." The captain put his sword in his sheath before sitting down in the grass to lean against a tree. "I think we should head out to see her and the leaders of their army to come up with a plan to take on the raiders. They are still doing a lot of damage to the forest and the inhabitants."

Mori pondered this for a minute. She knew he was right, but was she really ready? Was it really the time to take on the raiders and their king? Mori still felt like she needed more training, but after so much of it, she felt her powers and abilities were at their strongest. At least, for the amount of time she'd had her powers and warhammer. With a sigh, she nodded and looked up at Duncan.

"You're right. I have been shrugging off my duties as the queen. I need to step up and protect this forest and everyone in it. Let's prepare to leave."

Faust and Duncan both stood up, ready to get started on making a plan.

Mori looked over her hammer with bewilderment. "This thing is awesome, but it's really bulky. I wonder if there's a way to—" Her words were cut off by the hammer shrinking and falling into her hand, causing her to flinch and almost drop it. It looked like a tiny version of Fae'ohtan with a little ring around the end. The queen blinked a few times, her eyebrows reaching her hairline, before attaching it to her bracelet. "That fixed that. I can pull this bracelet off really easily without breaking it. This will definitely make transporting it and hiding it much easier." A smile curled her lips as she looked up at her friends. "It's rather convenient."

That is really cool. Just make sure no one is able to pull it off your wrist, Faust commented.

"Don't worry, buddy, I'll be careful." She laughed. "Now go get fitted for your armor. I hear they have something new for you to try on."

Faust nodded before walking off. Mori turned to leave in the opposite direction and ran into Orian, the fairy general.

"I'm sorry, I didn't mean to run into you." She chuckled nervously and took a small step back. He was three years older than Mori and had already been made general. That was really impressive and definitely nothing to sneeze at.

"No worries, Mori. I'm glad I found you," he said as he moved some of his long black hair from his face, allowing the sunlight to hit it just enough to give it a bit of a blue shine.

"You were looking for me?" she asked as her eyes met his own.

"Yes. We're getting ready for the war meeting. Your presence is necessary."

Mori gestured toward the direction of the meeting mushroom with her hand. "Lead the way."

It took a week for a plan to form, mostly because no one could agree on a plan of approach. Lorem wanted to bust down the doors and take them on with brute force, while Duncan and Orian felt an aerial assault would be better. In the end, they went with Mori's stealth idea that would lead into brute force, a surprise ambush on their compound. The one problem they had was none of the rumors of the raider base were proven true, until Renfred mentioned hearing some of the guards talking about the Ursamong Peninsula. It was on the opposite side of the forest and on the other side of the mountains from the birch tree house and most of the provinces. It was believed to be the home of the most dangerous fae, ones that couldn't get along with others well, or their main source of food was fellow fae creatures.

Duncan explained a war that had raged on a very long time ago where the more "evil" fae were forced over the Faenor Mountains and were to remain on that side. The perfect hiding place for a raider camp. Somewhere no one else dared to go, even Viviana. Now that they had a general area of search, which was later confirmed by scouts as to its exact location, a real plan was formed.

During preparation, Faust had been fitted and equipped with his own armor that included a handle on his back for Mori to ride him. The straps around his body were stretchy so he would be able to grow and shrink his size as he saw fit. For now, he was at his biggest, towering over Mori and Duncan at an impressive nine feet tall. Lorem was dressed in plate armor she had from her sword training days, while Duncan had what armor the fairies had on hand.

Mori's armor was custom made to her size, bearing the sapling insignia on her green chest plate.

"Are you sure we're ready for this?" Duncan asked Mori as they stepped through the large portal she had created. Most of the army had already gone through and were staying out of sight in case any beasts awaited them.

Mori let out a breath. "I hope so. We went over the details of the plan pretty thoroughly. I'm still not sure why Lorem thinks we can just bash our way through the front door and take them by surprise." She rolled her eyes. "It's as if stealth isn't a thing here."

"Lorem always says stealth is not as fun as bashing heads together. She's all brawn and no brain sometimes." Duncan shook his head and then surveyed the area once they were completely through. Unfortunately, Lorem heard him and punched him lightly in the arm, still making the elf wince.

"According to your father's recollection of the compound and the scouts' report, the raiders leave the iron walls and gate unguarded. I'm assuming they think the fae are completely terrified to the point they won't do anything." Lorem grinned. "They should be scared. We were always going to stand up for this forest."

We must stand up for our home, Faust communicated, making Mori look at him and nod.

"I agree. This forest is our home, and we refuse to let anyone have it. *I* refuse to let anyone take it from me." As they walked, Mori had to adjust the green plate armor on her chest and pulled the bracers on her arms so they rested better against her hands so as to not inhibit her movement. The symbol of the royals was etched into the armor, and she had decided to paint it a brighter green so it stood out. Last thing she wanted was for the raiders to not know who was about to take them out.

"Hey, Duncan, maybe you should wear that armor more often. Suits you better," Mori teased.

The elf adjusted the jacket that was over his own armor and made sure the arm and leg bracers were in place. "I think I look quite stunning in them, but they are a little too bulky for me to use every day." He adjusted his ponytail so it was a little tighter. "I could get used to it with time, but I would rather not."

As they reached their meeting area, they stopped. The iron gate of the raider camp was now in view. Its high iron walls made it impossible to see inside, and the gate only had a few holes to look through. Smoke rose from the center of the compound from a building that Mori could barely see the top of. All was quiet in the darkest parts of the forest, but the sun still gave enough light for them to see. It felt like dusk despite being high noon. From the reports of the scouts, the building in the middle was massive and the grounds were always busy with movement. Raiders shuffled different fae creatures they'd captured into cages, where they were tortured and starved into complete submission and obedience.

Mori and Duncan crouched behind some bushes, along with Orian and Lorem.

"We just need to bust open the gates and take them by surprise," Lorem said as she punched her own fist and looked around. There were no guards, which seemed strange to her.

"No, we need to stick to the plan. Have everyone move into position. The east and west fairies should fly over the wall and find places to hide before we take the gates on the north and south sides. Attack from all fronts." Mori glanced over her shoulder and held up two fingers and pointed to her right, and then four fingers and pointed to the left. Two groups of fairy soldiers silently moved out so they could make sure the area was clear before flying over the walls to hide behind supplies.

When they were over the wall, Mori held up three fingers and pointed straight forward. Another group of fairy soldiers, led by Lorem, went around the camp silently to the south side, sticking to the trees to remain unseen. After pulling the bracelet off her wrist and enlarging the hammer with her magic, she waited for Lorem's group to be in position before she stood up and charged toward the front gates. Duncan, Faust, and the remaining group of fairies charged behind her. Using her mighty hammer, she broke down the entire gate with one swing, allowing the soldiers to rush in. While the raiders' attention was on the front and back gates as they were breached, they were picked off by the hidden troops who had snuck in minutes before the assault.

Mori effortlessly swung her hammer to take out the enemies, her movements resembling someone dancing with the fluidity and grace of a professional dancer. A true natural fighter shown in her even steps. Lifting her hand, she used magic to pull tree roots out of the ground to grab the red bulls that were now charging toward them. Water seeped out of these roots and put out their fires quickly while the handlers tried to free them. It was no use; the water could replenish itself faster than the fire could evaporate it. Aaxte cried out as their bodies were squeezed and their flames were extinguished.

"Take the compound!" Mori ordered before jumping on top of Faust. The direwolf was still at his max size and had blood all around his mouth and paws from biting and scratching the enemy forces.

They are not that tough to kill. Victory is near. The wolf ran toward the building, but was rammed from the side by something big, sending the two of them several feet to the side. Mori and Faust both looked up and saw a much larger aaxte that was on fire. Faust was the first to his feet, with Mori not long after him, climbing back on.

"Are you hurt?"

No. I can still fight. A guttural growl released from the wolf's throat, a warning for the bull, who did not heed it. The moment the aaxte charged at Faust, he did the same, but he jumped on top of it moments before they collided and bit its neck over and over to kill it. Mori used her magic to keep pulling water droplets from the air to put the fires out quickly. This method seemed to weaken them exponentially.

"Faust, we need to get off it. The air is too dry for me to keep pulling water." Mori let go of the armor's handle to grip her hammer with both hands, but before she could swing, the bull bucked them both off its back, sending them flying. Mori hit the ground with a hard thud and a groan, but when she looked up, her eyes widened and an audible gasp escaped her throat. While in the air, the bull had impaled Faust with its horn right through the stomach. The wolf shrieked in agony as the bull flung him to the side, his body landing hard on the ground. Hard enough for the sound of breaking bones to fill Mori's ears.

"Faust!" she yelled out, watching as the beast readied itself for another attack. There was no time to tend to her best friend; the bull turned its sights on her and charged with a roar. She dodged the incoming attack, rolling to the side and steadying her footing before swinging her hammer into its side to send it into the nearby wall. The beast grunted from the impact, stunning it long enough for Mori to sprint to Faust and slide to a stop beside him, using her magic to heal his wound. The puncture was bleeding profusely as the magic created new strands of skin and muscle to stitch itself back together. It was painful, but Faust held strong through the pain all the way until his fur grew back.

Thank you, Mori. I feel a lot better. Let us get back to the fight. Faust stood up, his legs shaking from using the new, tender core muscles, and turned his head to growl at someone approaching them. Mori followed his gaze toward none other than Dairus. Gritting her teeth, she stood up and readied her hammer, holding it like a baseball bat.

Of course he would be here. There's no way Yorn could lead an elaborate plan like this.

"You really think you can win with *that*, little girl?" Dairus sneered.

Wait, did Dairus not know who created Fae'ohtan? Or what it was and represented? He couldn't have been in the forest since the beginning if he never knew about the Hammer of the Royals.

Mori's confusion turned into a smirk as her advantage dawned on her. Dairus had no idea *what* he was up against.

"You think we'll lose? How naive of you, Dairus. Look around! We are taking your compound as we speak!"

Dairus let out a boisterous laugh. "Are you?" He motioned over his shoulder with his head, a devious smile curling the corners of his lips.

Mori looked past him with a sharp inhale at the soldiers being forced out of the building by something much larger than she had seen before. The creatures had the body of a dark fur dog and a humanoid-looking face that sent chills down her spine as sweat built up on the handle of her hammer from her palms. They all growled like dogs at the fairy warriors, nipping at any who didn't move fast enough. When the group of fairies was out of the building, they lunged at them, biting their arms, legs, and torsos as the men and women screamed out. The ones who were able to get away took to the skies to fight back with their arrows and spears.

"What are those things?" Panic swept through her body as she moved the hammer in front of her.

"Those are yeth hounds. I found them wandering aimlessly on this side of the mountain and gave them a purpose and home." Dairus snickered. "You can make this all stop. Just give me the forest powers."

"Giving you the magic would be the same as surrendering, and I'm not the type of queen to give up." Mori charged at the man, her hammer glowing as she channeled magic into it. Just as she was about to bring Fae'ohtan down, she was suddenly forced backward, landing on her feet and skidding to a stop with her weapon behind her to stabilize herself. Glancing up, she saw nothing—no residual magic, no creature, no weapon. An unusually strong breeze swept her hair from her face as realization hit and missing pieces fell into place. Dairus was able to control the winds and used that power to push her away from him. "It seems you got a new power." Mori stood up, her chest puffed out as confidence filled her stance.

Dairus shrugged. "What can I say? I'm favored by the courts." Wind picked up around the two of them, forcing Mori to cover her face the best she could with her arms so dirt wouldn't blind her. Suddenly, her feet left the ground as she was thrust right out of the busted gate she'd come through and into the bushes.

Mori groaned from the impact before rolling onto her side in an attempt to get up. Everything hurt, her arms, legs, back, and head. Dizziness was setting in, but her magic mended her aching body quickly. This battle was not going in the direction she was hoping. They were losing quickly from sheer numbers and were outmatched due to the large yeth hounds. What could she do? She was one person and had twice the army up against her. Panting hard, she managed to get to her hands and knees, sweat dripping down her face and splashing onto the grass below. Was there really no winning?

With great strain and effort, she managed to stand up once more and turn toward the compound and bloody battle that still ensued. So many fairies had been slain. Blood coated the ground, and cries of pain and suffering filled the once-silent forest. They were losing, which would result in losing everything. The forest, the fae, and everything she held dear to her would be killed or destroyed.

Dairus still had the wind blowing out the gate as if to keep her out, amplifying the cries of her people. There was no way she could give up, but she had no ace up her sleeve, no backup plan in place for when they were inevitably defeated. Then something else rang out from behind her in the distance, an all too familiar roar. Color drained from Mori's face as her sweat turned cold. She dropped to her knees, trepidation threatening to paralyze her once more, just as it did the first time she heard that sound. But something pulled her away from her nightmare-ish thoughts. The red ball on her hammer was shining brightly. A white line shot out from it several inches, as if to point her in the direction she dared not tread.

As she picked up the hammer, the white light moved, keeping its point in the direction it wanted her to go.

"A compass? No, a locator." After a glance over her shoulder to see how the battle was going, another loud roar rang out, scattering birds overhead. "'When the winds carry the cries of panic.'" The fairies were still fighting, but it was only a matter of time before they lost. "'And frightful sounds make you frantic.'" Another loud roar behind her made her turn and look once more. "'Be not afraid and go near.'" The queen stood up, ready to face the beast making that sound. "Leana better be right about this." Channeling her magic into her legs, she took off running, knowing what she needed to do and what she had in her possession.

Faust, I have an idea. Do your best to keep the fairies alive. I will be right back, hopefully with help, she mentally said to her wolf. He sent a quick confirmation and wished her luck.

Chapter Twenty-Four

Mori stopped just before reaching the clearing where the skull-headed beast known as Bob was standing. He was feasting on a deer he had caught when he turned toward her direction, no doubt smelling her scent. She was panting hard but determined to do what needed to be done, despite her fear.

"'For your strongest ally is also your greatest fear,'" she whispered to herself. "Didn't know my greatest fear was some *thing* named Bob." She chuckled lightly to herself before resting her hammer against her shoulder and walking to stand several yards in front of the beast. "Hey, Bob, I think it's about time we have a talk," she called out to him.

Bob's one red eye peered down his skull at Mori before his large mouth opened and he roared at her, growling some as he started walking toward her. Drool and blood mixed together before falling to the ground. Just when she thought he wouldn't stop walking, he flinched and ceased his movements, even taking a step back. Pulling the hammer from her shoulder, she noticed the red glow was pointing toward the beast and shining much brighter than it had before.

"Oh, so you know what this is?" She held it up, making him take another step back after another flinch. Vibrations traveled through the handle of the hammer, making her glance at it. Mori had a pretty good idea of what it was, but it wasn't completely clear until she looked right into Bob's hollow eye socket. "This is your eye, isn't it . . .?" With some effort, she pulled the red ball from the hammer and turned it over in her hand. It was hard instead of squishy, the opposite of what she had been expecting. Thankfully, it wasn't slimy or wet. It felt more like a rock in her hand with a smooth surface that was molded by water for thousands of years. "I think it's about time we have that long overdue talk and make ourselves a deal." She smirked, tossing the eye in the air and catching it.

Bob stayed where he was and just nodded once in understanding.

"I'm glad you're smart enough to understand me. That will make this a lot easier." She held up the red ball. "So, I'm guessing you want your eye back?"

Bob nodded once more.

"I will give you your eye back in exchange for your help. I know you've been killing and eating raiders." As she spoke, the beast's mouth opened to let his tongue hang out, along with some more drool. "And right now, we're fighting the raiders. I will give you back your eye *and* allow you to eat as many raiders as you want. All you have to do is go in that direction." She pointed toward the way she had come. "And go destroy their camp and kill as many of them as you can. You will get a feast no matter what, but you will only get your eye back if we're successful in defeating them." She twirled it in her hand with a confident smile. "Do we have a deal?"

Bob growled at her and attempted to get close with his arms outstretched, reaching for her hungrily. Mori froze for only a moment before she pointed the hammer at him, making him stop once more and back away a few feet as his hands fell to his sides. Now that she knew he was intelligent, he seemed less frightening, as if his nightmare fuel effect on her was rendered powerless.

"It seems you're definitely afraid of this hammer. Must have been one of the first three royals who took your eye, but you also know this power can kill you. Don't think for a second I won't use it against you if you kill any fae. If they die by your hands, you die by mine." She rested the hammer on her shoulder and stood tall, all traces of fear melting from her body. "I'm not afraid of you anymore, and I never will be again." She narrowed her eyes at the beast. "So, do we have a deal or not?"

The creature stood still for a few moments before nodding his deer skull head.

"Good, let's go. Your feast, and eye, are this way." Mori motioned for the creature to follow her, and he did.

Guess he isn't as instinctual as everyone thinks he is, she thought to herself before reaching out to Faust.

I have our plan B. Make sure the north gates are clear of fairies. I don't want them becoming a snack.

A snack to what? came the reply before Mori ran through the gates and quickly rolled out of the way. The ground quaked as Bob ran straight through the broken gate into the raider camp, a thunderous roar releasing into the camp that would terrify even the strongest warriors. The massive fifteen-foot-tall beast scanned the area for a few moments before charging at a group of raiders. New screams echoed off the trees as Bob bit and slashed all who got in his way, taking chunks of their flesh to eat. Mori looked up when movement caught her eye. Fairies were flying in the air out of the creature's range, some holding prisoners they managed to rescue.

"What is that thing?" a raider shouted, the sword in his hands shaking violently as he watched in horror as his fellow comrades were eaten. None of their weapons were piercing Bob's skin; they just bounced off or broke, causing dread to fill their faces and bodies.

Faust and Duncan reached Mori once she was up and watching the slaughter. "Are you OK?" Duncan asked, his own face and clothes covered in blood. The metallic smell punched Mori in the face like an outhouse that needed to be cleaned six months ago.

Holding out her hand, she healed Duncan of the wounds he'd sustained and fanned the air with her hand.

"I'm OK, don't worry about me," she responded. "Elf blood has quite a strong smell." Duncan shrugged at her comment.

It is kind of hard to not worry about you. How did you convince Bob to fight for you? Faust asked as he watched the skull-headed beast continue to kill the raiders while the fairy warriors broke open the cages to rescue their fellow fae. The ones who had strength fought back the yeth hounds who were closing in. Fierce growling and barking were mere attempts at making themselves look more intimidating than they had become.

Holding up the hammer for her friends to see, Mori showed off the glowing red orb attached to the gold plate. "This red ball that we thought was a gem is actually his missing eye. One of the first three royals ripped it out of its socket and combined it with the hammer. He seems to be terrified of Fae'ohtan." She inspected the hammer once more, feeling the power enhancements it gave her. "Probably because of the pain it caused him. I was finally able to look him over and noticed some ribs were not healed properly. I'm guessing it's from a good few whacks with this," she explained, and looked over at the beast. "A feast and his eye in exchange for his help." Bob made what could only be described as an attempt at laughter as he bit down on a raider's head, the crunching sound of breaking bones sending a chill down Mori's spine. "Despite what you may think, he's very smart. Understood everything I said and responded in his own way. I think he has human-level intelligence but doesn't want to talk to anyone." She glanced back over at Bob, watching as he picked up the yeth hounds one after another and threw them against the building. Their yelps made him laugh more as raiders stayed out of his reach.

"I think it's about time we wrap this up." Duncan drew his sword and Faust readied himself.

"I got this." Mori smirked and walked toward the battle, lazily spinning Fae'ohtan in one hand beside her. With all the raiders focused on Bob, she walked right up to Dairus, who was shouting at the raiders to stop the skull-headed beast. When he heard footsteps, he whirled around and glared daggers at her, grinding his teeth together as he seethed. "You have no power over me."

"We will see about that, girl." Dairus lifted his hands and activated his wind powers, but Mori lifted her hammer and stabbed the handle into the ground, making sure she couldn't go anywhere. Locks of red curls slipped off her face as her eyes closed to keep them safe from dust. She hoped he couldn't keep his powers going indefinitely, or she could be in for a lot of trouble. Just as she was about to call for help, Faust ran right up to him from the side, with Duncan on his back, and tackled Dairus to the mud. The man groaned and tried to use his magic again to defend himself.

"Oh no you don't!" she shouted, removing the hammer from the ground and running at him, her hammer raised above her head before she swung it downward where his head was. Just before making contact, Dairus disappeared, making Fae'ohtan hit the ground, breaking it apart as an earthquake rumbled beneath everyone's feet. Magic surged through her body from the impact, making her arms tremble and almost making her lose her grip. He was gone in a puff of smoke. She had not been expecting that. After yanking her weapon from the small crater she'd made, she turned toward the snarling she heard behind her. Dairus was red faced as his knuckles turned white from clenching his fists too tightly.

"Don't think for one second that this battle is over!" Dairus bellowed.

"I wouldn't dream of ending our fight this early." She let out a war cry as she charged at him once more, her hammer held to the side, ready to smash. Once he was within range, Mori swung Fae'ohtan with all her strength, anticipating an impact, but the man managed to duck out of the way at the last moment. Keeping the kinetic energy going, she looped the hammerhead up over her head and brought it back down. Once more, Dairus jumped to the side and out of the way. Fae'ohtan connected with the dirt, creating another mini crater and another earthquake.

"You'll have to do better than that to get me," Dairus mocked.

"You ain't seen nothing yet." Tree roots sprang up to grab him, but the man knew all her tricks. With one swift movement of his hand, air blades sliced the roots into pieces. Each piece made a small thud as it hit the compact dirt.

"Your signature move? Really? Predictable." He laughed.

"Good thing I have new ones up my sleeves." Long blades of grass wrapped around Dairus's legs, snaking around his body to pin his arms to his sides and his feet to the ground. He struggled to break free, but the grass was infused with magic and much stronger than ordinary grass.

"I learned some new magic. You won't win against me this time." She dashed toward Dairus and punched him hard in the stomach, ripping the grass from the ground, but not from the rest of him. Landing a few feet back, Dairus was able to recover fast enough to roll out of the way of Mori's hammer. It once again broke up the earth beneath it on impact.

Dairus was able to break free from the grass restraints and stand up, dusting himself off.

"I see you brought someone else out to fight your battles for you. Typical of a royal." Dairus scoffed.

Mori growled as she gritted her teeth, finally noticing Duncan and Faust coming to her aid. "I don't need their help to defeat you, but I'll accept it if it means doing it faster." She lunged at him again as he finally drew his sword to block the hammer, the steel hitting the upper part of the handle with a loud clunk. Wind whipped up around her before sending her flying backward and right into

Duncan, making them both fall backward before Faust jumped over them and bit Dairus's arm. That gave Mori and Duncan the chance to get up and charge at him, but he snapped his fingers and disappeared into smoke.

"This has been swell, but I have more important things to attend to." Dairus's voice echoed around them. He was gone.

"Coward! Come back here and fight me!" she called into the open air. Her screams of rage filled the silent air, leaving her panting hard by the end. "He must have realized he couldn't win against all of us." Mori breathed hard through her clenched teeth, holding back more screams with every ounce of willpower she possessed. With Dairus gone, it was time to end things once and for all.

With her hammer in hand, she made her way over to the building and swung her weapon with all her strength, channeling magic into her attack to hit it as hard as she could. The impact shook the ground violently as the entire structure caved in on itself, crushing all who were inside.

Mori was blown back by the force of the impact, but she recovered quickly and was able to land on her feet. A wall of stone shot up from the ground the moment her feet touched the earth to protect herself from the debris and smoke. She only needed to cough a few times. When the dust cleared, she peeked out at the destruction. The compound was now a pile of wood, iron, and bodies. Blood seeped out from under the rubble as random limbs and body parts lay between the pieces of wood and stone. She couldn't imagine how much that had to hurt and was still hurting if the raiders inside were still alive. While she didn't like killing, she knew it would be the only way to stop them, a time and place for such things.

I hope this isn't the beginning of my downfall as queen. I refuse to be this merciless all the time.

Her thoughts were interrupted by a deep, loud howl behind her. Spinning around on her heels, she watched as Bob's massive form fell to the ground. The raiders had managed to overpower him and bring him down, where they tied him up with rope and iron. He yowled as they made every attempt to cut his flesh with their weapons.

"Save Bob! He came to help us! Now it's time to help him!" Mori commanded. Warrior fairies swooped down to tackle the ones tying down the skull-headed beast. Fresh blood spilled from his body as the raiders' weapons finally pierced his skin.

"No!" Mori shouted, charging at the raiders and striking most of them with her hammer, instantly sending them flying and killing them. As she tried to get to him to free him, she was stopped by yeth hounds as more raiders seemed to show up out of nowhere. "Hang on, Bob! I'm gonna get you out!"

Without warning, Mori was yanked backward from behind, making her drop her hammer. Duncan and Faust stopped ripping the ropes and reached for her, but they were soon grabbed by the reinforcements. She was overpowered by the men and forced toward the center of the base. In front of her stood none other than Yorn, the raider king. He glared down at her disdainfully, his teeth clenched and his hand gripping his sword handle so hard it could break.

Uh oh, not good.

Chapter Twenty-Five

"How dare you!" Yorn bellowed as he drew his sword, his voice carrying throughout the base. Leaves and twigs littered his clothing from his long walk back through the denser parts of the forest. Mori knew all too well from traveling a lot by foot that there was no way to avoid just how dirty a person got trudging through the forest.

"I was wondering where you were. Glad to see I get another shot at kicking your butt." Mori's smile made no apologies.

"I was busy elsewhere. You just had to wait until I left to attack my men," Yorn said sarcastically as he took a few steps toward the queen.

"You mean, it's as if we *planned* to attack while you were away so we could take out your forces so you would be easier to deal with." Mori fake-gasped and rolled her eyes. "Sounds like blasphemy to me." She scoffed.

"You'll pay for your insolence!" Yorn bellowed in rage.

This was getting old, and Mori was getting bored. Without moving her arms, the two men restraining her were swallowed up by the dirt below them, allowing Mori to take a few steps toward the raider king.

"How about we make this quick? I have things to do that don't involve staring at your ugly mug." Mori held out her hand to allow Fae'ohtan to be caught when it came to her. Duncan held up his sword and Faust bared his teeth, but Mori put out her free hand to stop them. "No, guys, this is my fight. I will deal with Yorn. You two go free Bob. He deserves our help." Walking forward with a determined spark in her eyes and confidence in her step, she rested her hammer against her shoulder. The middle of the yard cleared to make way for the two. "It's just you and me, Yorn. It was always meant to be you versus me." Lifting her weapon off her shoulder, she glared at him as she held it up like a baseball bat. "Let's settle this once and for all!" the queen shouted as she stormed the raider king.

"Let's." Yorn rushed at Mori at the same time until their weapons clashed, his sword hitting the haft of her hammer and pushing both of them back. Grass grew all around him to restrain his movements, but Yorn sliced through them like melted butter. The raider king pulled something small out of his pocket and threw it in the queen's direction, but she was able to evade it. With a quick glance to see what was thrown, she noticed three small throwing knives stuck in the wall behind her. One of them had grazed her shoulder, and a small red stain formed on her sleeve. Instead of letting her magic heal it, she pulled the blood from her wound and morphed it into something she'd seen back on Earth—shuriken. She used to practice throwing them in the backyard when she was bored, so she had a pretty good throwing arm. That combined with the royal magic meant she had a deadly projectile at her disposal.

After making three more, she flung the newly formed weapons toward her enemy. All three sliced through his flesh before dissolving away so he couldn't use them against her. While he was distracted, the queen rushed him.

"You little—" Mori interrupted his sentence by swinging her hammer sideways to hit him, but was blocked by his sword once more, always clashing with the handle of Fae'ohtan. The raider king quickly pushed her back and brandished his sword, but Mori backflipped out of his range.

"Hold still so I can kill you!" Another swing, another miss.

"Even if I stood still, you wouldn't be able to hit me. You remind me of a stormtrooper," Mori mocked, and jumped to the side to dodge another incoming attack from his sword.

"What is a stormtrooper? Is that an insult?"

"It means you can't hit anything." She laughed. "You really don't know how to use that thing, do you?" She did a backflip again to avoid another attack. "You should try *actually* hitting me. It might get you further." The queen shrank her hammer before she slid between his spread legs and punched him as hard as she could in the stomach, but he didn't even wince. As she came out on the other side, she quickly stood up, enlarged her hammer, and blocked a downward swipe from Yorn.

"You're quite the cocky girl, aren't you? It looks like I will have to put an end to that mouth of yours, permanently." Yorn struck with a lightning-fast jab to the side of her breast plate, making it also slice the inner part of her arm. Mori groaned from the pain as her magic quickly healed the wound just in time for her to duck under Yorn's swinging sword and get Fae'ohtan up to block the pummeling the false king was bringing down on her weapon.

"And you're too full of yourself when you have nothing to back up your ego." Mori pushed back with the last swing to force him off-balance, but it was no use. Yorn wasn't angry enough yet to make a mistake. She knew deep down inside that she wouldn't be able to win this fight on her own, but she was ready to die trying. Standing tall after they'd broken apart from the last clash of steel against steel, Mori shifted tactics.

"You really think you scare me? I faced a skull-headed beast that eats everything that moves, and *survived*!" She yelled the last word as she raised Fae'ohtan above her head and brought it down onto the sword, shattering the blade as the crystal finally made contact with the metal. Yorn stumbled backward and held up the handle that still had some sharp pieces of metal attached to it. "You came here with the intention of hurting my people." She swung her hammer once more and hit the handle out of his hand. "I can never let someone who manipulates others for evil live in my forest!" She stepped closer to Yorn, making him stumble backward until he fell onto the ground. "No one gets to rule over *my* forest but me."

With one final fluid motion, Mori lifted Fae'ohtan above her head. "For Albright Forest!" she screamed as she brought her hammer down, bashing the fake king's chest plate, shattering the armor completely. Pieces of it fell to his sides, indignation making his nostrils flare as his face turned red.

"You haven't won yet, little girl!" Yorn growled out.

"You may be bigger than me, and older, but that doesn't mean you're fit to rule. I am Moriana Albright and I am the rightful ruler of Albright Forest, and I will protect it and my people!" Mori spun her weapon in her hand. "This is where your reign ends and mine begins." She swung Fae'ohtan upward before bringing it down onto the false king's chest, breaking his sternum and all of his ribs. The break of each bone reverberated around them as blood pooled around his torso, staining his clothes and the dirt beneath him.

Yorn gasped for air before coughing up blood, making Mori take a step back as she watched his body finally go limp. Using some of her magic, she felt for a pulse from a distance. Her face paled as her mouth fell open and her stomach twisted in nausea. There was nothing left to keep him alive. All his organs had been crushed from the impact and were liquified inside his body.

Lorem, Orian, Duncan, and Faust all walked up to Mori, prepared to defend their queen if Yorn was not dead.

"Is he . . .?" Lorem asked, and Mori nodded.

"The false king is dead!" Orian shouted, before everyone else started to whoop and celebrate.

Cheers erupted all around them as Mori finally took in the outcome of the raiders. During her battle with the raider king, the rest of her army was able to free Bob, capture or kill all the raiders, and rescue the remaining prisoners. Letting out a relieved sigh, she felt the fatigue of her long battle finally take over as she collapsed onto the awaiting direwolf.

Mori, are you OK? Faust asked, concern filling his tone.

"I'm OK, just tired." With the help of Duncan, Mori climbed onto Faust as her hammer shrank down to become a bracelet once more.

With Bob free and the reinforcements of fairies there to help, they were easily able to restrain the living raiders and heal the injured fae. Mori was covered in blood, and her bracers were cut up badly.

Damn, I liked this armor.

With a little bit of magic, the blood was removed and left on the ground to nurture the soil.

"I'm glad that's done. I could use a bath and a week-long nap." Mori chuckled.

"Not quite yet. There is still a lot that needs to be done, including rounding up the raiders that ran away during the battle," Duncan told her, his hands resting on his hips.

Mori glanced around at everyone being tended to, but she focused on the raiders being loaded up into their own iron cages. She quirked an eyebrow at the sight. "What will happen to the raiders we captured?"

Duncan followed her eyes to the cages. "You're the queen. You will get to decide what happens to them."

That was more power than she was expecting, but it made sense. She was the queen after all. She had to think about what to do for a minute, not sure what kind of punishment they deserved, but a thought crossed her mind.

"They hurt the forest, so now the forest will hurt them." She shrugged her shoulders. "Leave them near the kelpies and other meat-eating beast provinces and let the forest decide what happens to them." She turned her focus from the cages to her elf guard. Duncan had paled a ghostly white just as a shadow moved across his face. It was an easily recognizable shadow from the antlers on top. Spinning on her heels, she came face-to-stomach with Bob. He was so close to her that she could smell his rancid breath as he looked down at her, taking steady breaths through his slightly open mouth. Slowly, her eyes trailed up his bloody form as she lifted her head to peer at his skull face.

"Eye," he breathed out, his voice deep and guttural as if he had been eating rocks for decades.

"I?" Mori raised a brow before the other shot up as well. "Oh, you mean your eye." She enlarged the hammer and pulled the red sphere from it. "Kneel down."

Bob didn't move, just continued to stare down at her. Mori waited a few seconds before she sighed and grew the grass beneath her feet to lift her up to his height. "Wow, I don't think I've been up this high before." Laughter erupted from her, reaching her eyes for the first time in months. With Yorn gone and being back with her friends—and now helping her greatest fear—her future no longer looked so bleak.

The skull-headed beast cocked his head at the sound of her laughing. Mori just shook her head before reaching up and placing the eye against the empty socket. A green flash of light burst out from under her hands before she removed them to reveal his red eye safely in its rightful place. Bob moved it around to check its functionality before turning his gaze back to the queen.

"There, back to normal." This whole experience had shifted her view of the beast, but she wasn't sure if it was for the better or not. A deal was a deal, and she would honor her end just as he did.

She knew in the past she had used his blindness as a means to stay hidden, but she didn't really need that anymore, now that she knew he was terrified of Fae'ohtan.

Bob watched as she lowered herself back down to the ground and adjusted his focus to Duncan before turning it back to Mori. "Not a bad queen. Inexperienced," he growled out with that husky voice of his.

"Then I guess I need to get better. Thank you for your help, Bob. I hope I can count on you again when the forest is in danger."

The beast nodded once before his long legs carried him toward the tree line, grabbing a stray raider and biting his head off on his way out as if to take a snack with him.

Duncan let out a sigh of relief as his body relaxed. "That was completely terrifying. He just stood there and growled."

Mori's brows pinched together as her hands went to her hips. "Growled? I mean, his voice is really deep, but he was speaking just fine for whatever kind of creature he is."

Now it was Duncan's turn to be confused. "What are you talking about? Did he say something to you?" His eyes narrowed. "Is this another Faust thing where only you could hear him? That gets real old real fast."

Mori shrugged. "Possibly. He told me I'm not a bad queen, just inexperienced." She smiled softly as she turned her gaze toward the gate as the last of Bob's figure disappeared past the trees. "He really is much smarter than we give him credit for. I think he's actually of our own intelligence level, if not more. He has been around a very long time."

Mori didn't get a chance to speak before Lorem came over and put her arm around the queen's shoulders as the satyress grinned. "You did it, Queenie!" she exclaimed excitedly.

"*We* did it, Lorem. It was a group effort." Mori laughed before she was tackled from behind by Faust, almost knocking her down, but she caught herself. His front legs hung over her shoulders as his head appeared beside her head. Lorem heard him coming and moved out of the way in time.

Are we done here? Can we go home? the wolf asked as his tongue hung out of his blood-covered mouth and his tail whipped back and forth excitedly.

"Not quite. We need to give you a bath. You'll scare everyone looking like that." She shrank her hammer down and put the bracelet back around her wrist before she sighed heavily. With her friends gathered around, she figured this moment was as good as any to remind them of what was to come. "The war is not over yet. We need to hunt down the runners and bring them to justice for the atrocities they committed against our people. We can't allow any of them to go unpunished," Mori declared, a determined look in her eyes. "We also need to rest up, heal, and go after Dairus. If we don't stop him permanently, this whole war will start over. I intend to put an end to it completely."

"We've got your back, Queenie. Whatever you need, you have my sword at your disposal." Lorem hooked a thumb at herself as she beamed.

"You have my sword and army as well, Mori." Orian placed his arm across his chest and bowed slightly. "The fairies support you."

"All hail Queen Mori!" Duncan called before kneeling. Faust bowed his head as well while Orian and Lorem followed suit.

"All hail Queen Mori!" the remaining fae shouted, and everyone, with the exception of the imprisoned raiders, gathered around her and knelt before her. Mori's eyes grew wide as she saw everyone bow to her, something she never thought would happen. Her body refused to move, and it was hard to breathe around the lump in her throat.

You should address your army, Mori, Faust communicated to her, snapping her out of her trance. She swallowed that lump and stood up straight with authority she didn't know she had in her. Determined and confident, she addressed her subjects.

"This battle may have been won, but the war still rages on. I, as your queen, will not rest until the remaining traitors are brought to justice and pay for their crimes. I will not rest until every fae creature has a place to call home. I will not rest until Dairus is slain for his crimes." She took a moment to breathe. Her voice was very commanding, something she had thought was snuffed out a long time ago. "This war has gone on for far too long and it's about time we all live in safety and live our best lives. For Albright Forest!" She shot her fist into the air with the last three words.

"For Albright Forest!" the army shouted in unison as their arms shot into the air as well, everyone now on their feet.

"Let us begin our healing journey, starting with the fae who are here. Any who have passed on will need to be returned to their home so their loved ones may claim their body and return them to the forest. The living who need immediate medical attention before the journey to the fairy territory should come see me first. The rest will start their walk there, and then we will send escorts to return them home once they are able to do so." She looked around once more at all the nodding heads.

"Lorem, help the injured that can't travel come to me for healing." Lorem nodded and ran off to start helping the injured gather in one place. "Orian, I want you to gather the remaining soldiers and help the fae ready to travel to the fairy territory through my portal. Keep them from freaking out and doing something reckless."

"Shall we wait for you and the injured to be ready?"

Mori shook her head. "No. Once the fae folk are through, go. I will make a new portal when the rest of us are ready."

"We will see to it, Your Highness," he said, and bowed again with his arm across his chest before walking off.

"Duncan, Faust, get the remaining raiders ready for transport. Those cages are on wheels, so take them south of here and release them to fend for themselves. The forest will dish out justice for the harm they caused. Then return back here where I will need your help to carry some of the injured through the portal." Holding out her hand, Mori opened a portal on a nearby tree so the uninjured could make their way to safety.

Both of the guys nodded before setting off to do their job.

Mori sighed with relief, finally having some breathing room. Exhaustion filled every aching muscle in her body, but she was snapped back to reality when she heard a rock move to her right. Quickly enlarging her hammer, she took her stance, ready to strike.

"Please don't hurt us," a familiar voice said. The last two people Mori ever expected to see again were hiding poorly behind a small pile of rocks. Tim and Tom. "We wanted to know if we could join you?" Tom asked her.

"We never wanted to be raiders, and to be frank, we suck at it." Tim cowered, his hands hovering above his head in a piss-poor way of protecting it. "We just needed a place to stay. We never did anything but scout out areas. We aren't fighters."

"You're forgetting one bad thing you two did." Mori placed the crystal of her hammer on the ground and crossed her arms.

"W-what was that?" Tim stammered out.

"You two kidnapped me!" She glared at them, making them shrink.

"We're sorry for that. We didn't want to do it in the first place, but the boss said if we didn't, then he'd kill us," Tom said with a quivering voice as both raiders trembled, their legs looking like they could give out at any minute. It was rather pathetic in Mori's eyes, but they might actually prove useful to her.

After some thought, she sighed. "Fine, the two of you can join me, but no more bad things, and you will be supervised every moment before I deem it no longer needed." Mori waved a stern finger at the two. "If either of you step so much as a *toe* out of line, you will meet a similar fate as the rest of the raiders. Do I make myself clear?"

Both men nodded frantically. "We are excellent servants and scouts! We won't let you down!" Tim was way too eager to serve. It was a little off-putting for Mori.

"Good. Your first task will be to change out of those raider clothes so you don't look threatening to the fae folk, and then assist with helping your victims through the portal. If someone needs to be carried, you carry them. The portal is not only one way, so get back here and continue to help." She placed her hands on her hips, feeling proud to finally have two lackeys to boss around.

"You got it, Boss!" Tom said, before the two saluted awkwardly and turned to walk away.

Are you sure it is wise to trust them? Faust asked as he walked up to the three of them and growled at the two raiders. *I hope you know what you're doing.* Both former raiders sheepishly took a step back with their heads down.

"I'm sure it'll be fine. From what I saw, the worst they did was taunt some prisoners and kidnap me. I saw them cowering during the battle." She shrugged. "We need to finish our tasks so we can get back to the fairy territory."

Faust nodded once. *Duncan is taking the prisoners into the forest. I will wait here for him before we make the journey with the fae. Do you think the war has ended?*

Mori shook her head. "With Yorn defeated, we still need to go after Dairus, or history will repeat itself. This war is far from over, but I'm a lot more prepared for the ending."

Faust walked off while Mori walked over to Lorem and the badly injured fae folk. By the time everyone was healed enough to walk, Faust and Duncan had left with the others, and Mori was even more fatigued than when she'd started. She was actually starting to wonder if the royal magic had a limit. There would be plenty of time to think about it while they recovered. For now, she opened a portal to the fairy territory and waited for everyone to go through before following behind.

Chapter Twenty-Six

After returning to the fairy territory, Mori collapsed the moment her feet touched the grass on the other side of the portal, which disappeared instantly. The battle had taken a lot out of her, and she managed to stay awake until everyone had been rescued. Though, unlike the last times she pushed herself too far, she didn't pass out.

"Mori!" Duncan called, and sprinted to her aid, helping her sit up.

"I'm OK, just really tired." With Duncan's help, she managed to stand on shaky legs. "I need to sleep. I think I used too much magic."

"Let me help." In one swift motion, the elf picked up Mori and princess-carried her to the guest mushroom and laid her down on the bed. He helped her remove her armor so she was in the more comfortable underlayers before pulling the covers over her body. "I will make sure Faust can join you when he's finished with his work."

"Thanks, Duncan. I'm really glad we met." A smile formed on her lips before it fell as she passed out.

Upon waking up, she blinked her vision back into focus before scanning the room. Faust was at her feet with his head on her shin. Then she noticed she was in different clothes, ones meant for sleeping. She propped herself up on her elbows, her movement stirring her companion awake.

You are awake. How are you feeling? he asked as he lifted his head to look at her.

"A lot less tired, but still groggy. How long was I out this time?"
Only a day.

"That's good." She plopped back down on the bed with an exhausted sigh. "Where are Duncan and Lorem?"

They are helping the former prisoners return to their homes, the ones who were strong enough to travel. They should be back within a day or two.

That's good. They'll be back soon, and then we can get to some real magic training, she thought.

Faust's ears turned backward before his head swiveled toward the door just before Queen Sophie walked in. "Oh good, you're awake." A smile tugged at the corners of her lips as she stepped inside, closing the door behind her. "How are you feeling?" The fairy queen made her way to a nearby chair and pulled it over to the bed to sit down. Mori sat up and gave her a small smile.

"I have a minor headache, but that's about it. I'm glad for the sleep. How is everyone doing?" She spoke softly, her voice feeling heavy in her dry throat.

"Everyone has returned here for treatment, and escorts have been sent to safely return the former prisoners to their home," Sophie explained as she reached out to gently place her hand on top of Mori's. "You did a good thing by defeating the false king. Everyone is thankful you didn't give up on us, myself included."

"I appreciate you telling me that. I was worried I would still be treated as an outsider. While I didn't do this for the recognition, it's hard to want to save people who are jerks back, but I'll do it. For the forest and the nice fae I've met along the way." Mori looked down sheepishly, trying her best not to let her intrusive thoughts control the narrative of how others felt about her.

"I'm sure they'll treat you well, even the people who were rude to you before. Just give them some time to heal." Sophie's words struck Mori deeply. A lot of fae had been traumatized by the war that had been going on for over a hundred years. Because Viviana was not able to stop the raiders, a lot of the fae had lost confidence in their royal. That kind of deep-seated distrust ran through their veins as smoothly as their blood. It wasn't about to go away so easily or quickly.

"Thanks, Sophie. I will keep that in mind." Mori nodded, but her mind was quickly retreating to safety like it always did. After everything she'd been through, she was tired of running. She'd faced her fear of Bob, faced her fear of rejection, and stood up to Yorn. So why did she feel like she needed to run away from the forest again? Run away from her battle with Dairus?

Faust moved to lie beside her and put his front leg around her. *What worries you?* the wolf asked her, leaning forward to lick her cheek a few times. Feeling the wet tongue on her cheek, imagining them being his own version of kisses, always cheered her up. This time was no different.

I don't know if I can face Dairus. He's really strong, and every time I go up against him, I only win because he leaves. If I want this war to end, I need to make it so he can't disappear before the final blow. Mori used the mental link this time, not wanting Sophie to know her fears. It could be seen as shrugging off her duties just as she was starting to prove her worth.

I do not think you have any reason to fear Dairus. We will come up with a plan to stop him, just as we did Yorn. Focus on resting for now. There will be time for planning.

Mori shook her head. "No, I need to get started on the plan. There's too much to do to sit around in bed all day." She spoke out loud this time, earning a look from the fairy queen.

"I will leave you to your thoughts, deary. Let me know if there's anything we can do to help. Remember, we must learn from the past to protect the future. Your first plan against Yorn worked well.

I'm sure you'll come up with something just as good." Sophie stood up and gave Faust a light pet before taking her leave.

Learn from the past to protect the future. I think I know what she's getting at.

"Faust, can you go get me something to eat, please? I'm really hungry." Growling erupted from her stomach, making her arms cover it quickly. The wolf climbed off the bed and turned to look at her.

I will be back shortly with lunch, he said, and turned to walk out the door, which had been left cracked open for him.

There, he was gone. She would be able to do what she needed to do without interruptions, or looking weirder than she already was to everyone. Now that she was alone, she crossed her legs and closed her eyes as her hands rested on her lap. Summoning the royal magic, and those who resided inside, she found herself opening her eyes inside the oak tree house, which was undamaged and beautiful. She felt the soft cushion on the sofa she was sitting on. Her mother, Viviana, was sitting on the desk chair, facing her.

"Hi, Mom." She smiled, having to fight back tears at the sight of her mother, whom she'd barely had the chance to get to know before her untimely demise.

"Hello, Moriana. I'm glad to see you." Her smile lit up the whole tree house much brighter than the lights. She was radiant and filled with life in this form. Mori really was the spitting image of her mother, just with higher cheekbones and different royal freckles. "I know you didn't call for me to catch up. I sense turmoil inside you. Tell me what's on your mind." She crossed her right leg over her left as she sat politely and waited.

After wiping her eyes, Mori was able to speak. "I defeated Yorn, but he wasn't the one pulling the strings. Dairus is."

Vi nodded in understanding. "I suspected as much, but I never met Dairus. I only knew him by name. I fought Yorn several times, but his skills with a sword outmatched my own. He had much longer than me to learn how to fight." Viviana grimaced as her emerald eyes looked down. "I was a failure as a queen."

Mori shook her head. "No you weren't, Mom. You inspired a lot of fae to stand up and fight. I only won because I was able to find Fae'ohtan, thanks to you." A reassuring smile curled her lips as her mother looked up at her.

"I tried for a long time to find it but was unsuccessful. Where was it hidden?"

"A false cave on Scuttle Island. To make it there, I had to get past King Avarisha's ghost ship and free his spirit. No one went there because the ship would always show up and kill everyone," she explained, pushing some of her long hair out of her face. "The outside was covered in blooming lavender flowers, just like the poem you told me. And lavender is always in bloom."

"What was inside the cave?" Vi asked, leaning forward a bit as she waited for the answer with bated breath.

"A crystal that took me to a sacred grove. It had statues of the first three royals. I don't know the names of the first two, but it was guarded by the third's soul that was ripped away from the royal magic. Her name's Vedia. She was very helpful and made sure I got my royal name before she'd allow me to have it." A small snort escaped Mori. "I was named The Bridge because I'm half-human."

Viviana burst out laughing. "That's so fitting! I hope you like your name. I loved the one I received."

"Not one bit. I was actually very mad about it, but I think I'm getting used to it. Though I don't know how to be a bridge between humans and fae. We live in two different realms, and seeing each other is nearly impossible. Besides, all the raiders are dead. Well, all but two."

"Only two?" Vi raised an eyebrow.

"Tim and Tom. They never wanted to be raiders and asked to join me. I'm keeping them on a tight leash because they're also the ones who kidnapped me. Though now I see it was for the better." The image of Faust and Duncan crossed her mind, a small smile forming on her lips.

"You made friends. That's wonderful! I'm glad things worked out."

"They're my first friends I ever made. Humans ran from me and fae sneered at me. So it was nice to be wanted for a change." Mori fidgeted with the hem of her shirt as she looked down. "They're the only people who I didn't feel the need to run from when things got tough."

"Like how you ran away when Faust died?" Vi pointed out.

Mori's eyes snapped up to her mother, her brows pushed together a bit as the left corner of her lip rose. She couldn't believe her mother had just said that. "Rude."

Vi shrugged. "I want you to learn from your mistakes. You run when things get hard-"

"I didn't run from Yorn! I kicked his butt real good," she interrupted, and punched the air at an imaginary punching bag. "Completely liquefied his insides with Fae'ohtan."

Light giggling came from the previous queen, her lips smiling in a way that reached her eyes. She settled down before speaking. "You still ran away when things were hard, when you were needed. I want you to learn from this, learn to stay even when every fiber of your being is telling you to run."

Mori dropped her hands into her lap and huffed. "I'm not going to run from Dairus. He has to be stopped. That's all there is to it. It seems so simple, but it doesn't *feel* simple. I've fought him twice and couldn't land a single blow the entire time. And he always disappears right before my hammer makes contact."

"That is troublesome. Can't kill what you can't hit." Vi mulled over everything as she leaned against the back of the chair, her legs uncrossing. "Restraints?"

"Doesn't hold," Mori said with a sigh.

"Have you tried pulling him underground?"

"Yup. And tried using his own red bull against him. We ganged up on him. Nothing holds him still, and he uses his wind powers to blow us all back. It's hard just getting close." She slumped back against the couch, staring at the floor with unseeing eyes. There was something she was missing about him—she could feel it in her gut—but she had no idea what it was.

"I wish I could be more helpful. How old is Dairus?" Vi asked.

"I'm not sure. A lot of the fairies said he's been around longer than Sophie." Mori shrugged one shoulder.

"What about Duncan?"

"He remembers seeing Dairus when he was a child. Said he hasn't aged a day, just the same as himself. So I think he's older than Duncan." She looked up at her mother. "Where are you getting at with this?"

"I think you need to talk to someone much older than Duncan." Vi smiled, her eyes soft yet determined.

"What do you mean?"

"You must speak with Bob. He's the oldest fae here. The royal journals mention him at least once by every single ruler. Though he didn't always go by the name Bob in their writing. Before Elissa, he was simply called the skull-headed beast, or the monster with the deer skull head. She was the one who first used the name." Vi looked up at nothing in particular, her hand moving some of her hair from her face. "I believe she called him that because everyone would shout 'beware of beast' whenever he got close. So she shortened it to Bob." Her eyes returned to her daughter, uncertainty crossing her features.

"Would that name actually translate well? I mean, beware of beast is an English term, but I don't know what it would be in fae."

"Well, it's different in the fae language, but the name they gave him sounded the same. Probably spelled differently. I had a knack for picking up languages, so learning English to talk to your father was easy. I learned many languages during my time as queen."

"Is that why others can understand me even though I'm speaking English?" Mori asked.

Vi nodded. "The royal magic translates your words for them, something it learned from me." She sat up straight and puffed out her chest a little.

"Is that why I can understand Bob when he talks? Duncan said he only growled at me."

"Yup, that's why. And he can understand you because your magic translates for him." She reached a hand out and gently placed it on her daughter's knee. "Mori, words hold power, but action is much stronger. You can tell the fae you'll protect them until you're blue in the face, but until you prove it through action by ending this war, you will never earn their respect. They will never allow you to rule over them."

That made a lot of sense. Telling the fae she was going to protect them and actually doing it were two very different things. "I killed Yorn. Doesn't that count for something?"

"Yes, it does, but it may not be enough. By now, the fae know Dairus is a threat as well, and he will keep the war going long after Yorn is gone." Vi pulled her hand back before standing up to sit on the couch next to Mori.

"Just how old is Bob for him to be older than the royals? Older than Dairus?"

"Alder, the second royal, mentions seeing the beast as a child and hearing stories of his father's youth running from him. I think he's older than the first royal."

"Who was the first royal?" Mori looked up at her mother, a curious spark in her eyes to know more.

"His name was Oberon. He's the one who created Fae'ohtan." Vi smiled and put her arm around her daughter to hug her. "He was fearless but took his duties as king too far. Power consumed him and ultimately led to his demise."

"There are stories in the human world about Oberon saying he was king of the fae, but they depict him as benevolent, not some power-hungry dictator." Mori looked back at the floor. "I've learned that's not the case, but humans have a much different impression of him."

"That's the thing about history. Documents depict the point of view of the writer, and if only one writer's work survives the ages, that's all people will believe. I'm not sure where his image of kindness came from, but he wasn't kind when he returned to the forest from the human world. He was hell-bent on destroying everything. I think something in the human world changed him, and not for the better."

That would make sense. Humans were known for their war and destruction. A violent race, for sure.

"I should go, and you need to return. Faust is approaching." Vi stood up, making Mori follow suit, and the two hugged tightly.

"Thanks for the help, Mom. I will make sure to call you to catch up instead of asking for advice, but I have a war to end first."

"I will always be here, my darling Moriana." Viviana placed a kiss upon her forehead, and Mori closed her eyes to enjoy the comfort that one simple gesture brought to her. When she opened them again, she was back in bed inside the fairy territory. Faust came in not long after.

Everything all right? he asked as he came inside with a basket of food.

"Yes, everything's fine, Faust. Thank you for the food."

Chapter Twenty-Seven

The forest was eerily quiet at this time of night, not that Mori had any way to know the exact time by human standards, but it was definitely dark enough for her to spot what she was looking for. Through all the trees, she saw a glowing red orb about fifteen feet up from the ground.

"There you are," she breathed, glad to find her target before something else found her. The red orb shifted a bit before a second one appeared beside it. A low growl reverberated off the trees between them as those bright lights grew in size. Despite her quickened heartbeat and shallow breaths, Mori refused to step back. Instead, the grass beneath her rapidly grew to raise her up to his height, knowing he wouldn't bend down.

Bob stopped in front of her, the smell of rotting flesh making her stomach almost eject her dinner. He cocked his head to the side as if to inspect her before opening his mouth. That long, blood-covered tongue looked ready to rip the flesh from her bones, but she still held firm.

"Don't make me bring out Fae'ohtan." Her nostrils flared, her gaze refusing to back down as her hands rested on her hips. The skull-headed beast closed his mouth and snorted before standing to his full height.

Good, he knows the name of my hammer.

"I know I'm the last person you want to see, but you're the oldest fae around," Mori began, her hands falling to her sides as her shoulders relaxed.

"Not fae," Bob's husky voice responded, making the queen roll her eyes.

"I don't know what you are, but whatever. Beast, then. You're the oldest beast in the forest." She took his silence as agreement, or it could have been indifference. It didn't really matter which. "I have to confront and kill Dairus. You know who that is, right?" The beast nodded once. "Have you ever fought him?" Again, another nod.

Mori opened her mouth to speak again, but the words were caught in her throat. Wait, he fought Dairus and *lived*? Just how strong is he? She ran a hand through her long, curly hair as she exhaled slowly. Bob just cocked his head to the other side.

"Ask."

Her eyes snapped up to meet his gaze as she sharply inhaled. She finally decided to ask the burning question she had been wondering for a month now.

"How do I kill him? Can he be killed?" She held her breath, not daring to let her ragged breathing make her miss any of his words. His silence was killing her, as all she could hear was the slight wind moving the leaves of the trees. After what felt like minutes—but was really seconds—Bob spoke the words she was hoping for.

"He dies with hammer." That long tongue of his darted out to lick a small crack that was now on the side of his snout. "Power makes pain. No win for me."

Mori inspected the crack before slowly reaching out her hand as his tongue retreated inside his mouth. She hesitated slightly and then proceeded to track her fingers from the top of his tooth up the crack that stopped just past the midpoint of his muzzle. A green light bled from the crack and sealed it up completely. Even without face muscles to make expressions, he seemed just as shocked as she was.

"Not fae? Are you sure about that?" she asked, a smirk tugging at her lips as she crossed her arms. Bob nodded his head once. "I guess my magic works on whatever was born in the forest, or something like that." She shrugged, not wanting to dwell on the semantics of the royal magic. "Anyway, you said Dairus can be defeated by Fae'ohtan, right? But I can't get him to hold still long enough to hit him with it. He's too fast, and that wind power of his keeps blowing me away." Her arms fell to her sides and her shoulders hung low with her head. Victory seemed so out of reach at this point that she was willing to try anything.

"Wind power?" Bob questioned, and Mori nodded. He was silent for a few moments before speaking again. "No air, no wind."

"No Dairus . . ." Mori finished, and looked up at the beast. "Wouldn't he suffocate if I took away the air?" He nodded once. "That's a hell of a way to go," she said under her breath as she gazed off in the distance with unseeing eyes. "I don't know if I have it in me to do that. It's inhumane."

His skull turned upward to look at the starry sky above them. Mori's head tilted back to try to see what he was looking at. "Dairus bad man, hurt many. No mercy for the wicked." His skull tilted back to her. "Queen must be merciless."

Her own gaze found his once more before dropping down at nothing in particular. Was there really no way to stop him? She knew she would have no problem killing him after he'd hurt so many, but to be able to hold him down long enough to deliver the final blow was the biggest challenge she had.

"He can disappear into a puff of smoke and teleport away. I don't know how to stop someone with that kind of power." A defeated sigh escaped her as she looked to the side, her arms crossing to hold herself.

"Not teleport," he said as he reached out a handful of claws and used one of them to gently lift her head back up to meet his. "Invisible."

Mori blinked rapidly before confusion was replaced by understanding. "Are you saying he can't teleport, but instead just turns invisible?" Bob nodded once. "But how did he escape my hammer during our last battle at the compound?"

The beast let out a breath of air that Mori could only assume was a sigh. "Fire make smoke. Wind push him." His hand pulled back as he straightened up to his full height.

"Wouldn't I just be able to restrain him if that were the case?" Mori quirked an eyebrow, her arms crossing over her chest.

Shaking his head, Bob sat down on the grass, his silence making Mori fidget with the hem of her shirt with every passing second. His red eyes disappeared, leaving a hollow space in the sockets. Did he just close his eyes?

Those red orbs reappeared just as he let out another breath.

"Am I annoying you, Bob?" she finally asked, brows pinched and a hint of teasing staining her words.

"Always. Knows nothing," he commented, his large hands digging slightly into the dirt between his spread legs.

"You're the oldest creature here. No one else alive was around when Dairus showed up. We still don't know *what* he is, let alone how to beat him." Her arms fell from her chest to rest on her hips. "Help me out here. If he isn't stopped, he will eventually turn his sights on you."

Silence blanketed them as they stared at each other, each unwilling to move first, but Bob was the one who relented first. He cocked his head from one side to the other before finally speaking.

"Dairus ancient. Use ancient magic." He paused as if to collect his thoughts. "Wind cuts binds."

"Even metal?"

He nodded once. "Stop wind, stop him."

Mori's fingers rubbed at her chin as her arm rested on her other crossed arm, her eyes unfocused toward the ground. "If I can make it so he can't use wind magic, then he can't propel himself away from my blows. It's going to be tough to do, but I think I can work with that." She looked back up at the beast before her. "Thank you for that information. I think I know how to end the war."

Bob groaned. "Less food."

Her stomach did backflips at that comment, but she was more focused on not turning green. "I get it, but do you even need to eat?"

He shrugged once before standing up. "Invisible, hard to see. Need Seer," he growled out.

"Need Seer?" She mulled it over for a moment. "Oh, Leana. Well, I guess I will have to talk to her again. Wait . . ." She looked up at him. "How do you know about her?"

"People talk much," he responded, and turned to the side. "I leave." He hesitated a moment, his red eyes focused on her, before walking off into the trees.

"Not the most helpful, but at least it was something I can work with. I don't think I'll ever get used to being around him." She let out a breath. "At least I got some good information. Thanks, Bob. I will keep all of this in mind if you ever need the favor repaid."

Stepping out of the portal into the vibrant throne room, Mori looked around. Not much had changed since her failed coronation. Everything was still alive and beautiful, just the same as that day. However, it was more peaceful without the crowd of fae folk booing her out the door.

"That was a bad day . . ." She mumbled to herself before turning toward the lit crystal throne. After a deep breath, she ascended the steps and touched the armrest, prompting the chair to move out of the way and reveal the stairs.

The inside seemed to be a little brighter this time around, though it was still difficult to see. At the bottom sat a figure with her hood up to hide her face. Mori walked over and sat down in front of her so they were eye level.

"I knew you would be back." Leana chuckled.

"I knew you would be here," Mori retorted.

"What makes you so sure about that, girlie?"

"Because I need you, and you said you would only be available if you were needed. Since I need your ability to see the unseen, I knew you would be here. However, I also know part of your soul doesn't reside within the royal magic. When I talked with the past royals, they all showed themselves to me, except the first four and the eighth royals were nowhere to be found." Mori crossed her arms, not feeling up to the games Leana liked to play. "I already met Avarisha and Vedia and learned why their souls were pulled from the magic."

"You're smarter than you look, Bridge." Her head lifted enough for her smiling mouth to be visible in the dim light. "Yes, I knew you would need my help with Dairus. I already foresaw everything."

"Why didn't you give me the power before? Why wait until now to offer it to me?" Her hands gripped her pants, her words reflecting the hurt she felt.

"You were not ready to wield the power I possessed at the time. You needed to grow into your role, gain access to Fae'ohtan, and defeat Yorn. If I had given it to you when we met the first time, you would have grown cocky and allowed him to kill you. No, my dear sweet child, you were not ready for the type of power I possess. It would have allowed you to see things you were never meant to see." Leana lifted her head to look up at Mori fully.

"I wasn't ready to see the invisible?" She groaned. "I could have killed Dairus ages ago if I had known he couldn't actually teleport, and if I could see him when he turned invisible, then he'd already be dead."

"Then that would have led to your downfall."

"How so?"

"Yorn would have taken revenge on you by doing a full assault on the birch tree house while you were unprepared. The palace and everyone in it would have perished." Leana leaned forward. "I have seen it."

"I get it, you can see the future." Mori rolled her eyes. "But that still doesn't mean I couldn't have handled him. You don't know what I can do."

"Actually, I do. I can see everything. Past, present, future, it's all connected."

"Then why not change anything?" Mori stared at Leana, her nostrils flaring. "You could have saved my mother, but you chose to hide from her!" The anger in her voice reverberated all around the two women, her voice bouncing off the walls of the small room.

"Just because I can *see* what happens, doesn't mean I can *change* what happens. Seeing is not always enough, and your mother knew that. When she came to find me a second time, she was asking for the hammer. I could not tell her where it was, as she was not worthy of wielding it." Leana leaned back, hunching her back as she stared at the girl.

"Not worthy?" Mori shouted. "What do you mean she wasn't worthy? She was willing to do whatever it took to stop Yorn and Dairus and you didn't help her at all!" Her voice echoed all around them, her shouts full of spite. "You didn't lift a finger to help her, yet you sit here and judge her for not being good enough. What gives you the right to do that?"

Leana held up her hand to silence the queen, waiting for the steam of anger to calm. "She went to the human world, something that is against our laws."

"That was an accident!"

"Is that what she told you?" The woman cackled. "It was no accident. She ran from her responsibilities, and because of that, hundreds of fae died. She ran away in the middle of a battle with Yorn." The Seer smirked. "Like mother, like daughter."

Those were fighting words, but this was neither the time nor the place for it. A growl rumbled in Mori's throat. Her hands clenched into fists that bleached her knuckles. "So that gives you the right to judge her? Be her judge, jury, and executioner?"

The old woman shook her head. "Not at all. She made those decisions on her own, but I foresaw what would happen if she claimed Fae'ohtan. The whole forest would have been in danger. She did not have the strength to wield such power."

"And I do?"

"Yes," she said bluntly. "Being half-human allows you to not be consumed by its rule. Fae'ohtan may be a warhammer on the outside, but it possesses something similar to sentience on the inside. It knows when it can corrupt the one who commands it, but it also knows when to back down. Fae are susceptible to its influence, while humans are not." Leana's eyes were glassy and stared unseeingly at Mori.

"Alder, the second royal. He was corrupted by the hammer?"

Leana nodded once. "Indeed. Fae'ohtan also corrupted its own creator. After the war with the humans, he returned to the forest a changed man. The magic inside was too powerful for him to wield and consumed his very soul."

"Will that happen to me too? It was locked away by Vedia because of its power."

"No. Your human half keeps you out of its reach and allows you to channel its magic rather than its magic consuming you. Your mother was a strong warrior with the sword, but not with the mind. She fell for a human after a few simple, sweet words. Enough to bring him back."

"My father is a good man. He's helped me ever since I rescued him." Mori's hand unclenched, but her racing heart was still ready to fight.

"I know he is, but that doesn't excuse the fact that Viviana ran in the middle of a battle that destroyed an entire territory. That was something she did frequently. She could have easily been influenced by Fae'ohtan into doing much worse things."

That made more sense to Mori than she wanted to admit. Her shoulders relaxed as she looked down at the hammer around her wrist. Was it really trying to control her and failing? Did she really take after her mother when it came to running from her problems? All she could do was run when she was in the human world. The bullies were much bigger and had more power, but that wasn't the case anymore. Mori wasn't in the human world anymore, and she wasn't powerless against her enemies.

Clenching her fist, she looked up at Leana. A new flame ignited within her to keep going, to keep protecting those she cared about, even if they didn't care about her.

"I'm ready for the power, Leana," she said, her hand relaxing in her lap.

A smirk crossed The Seer's face as she reached out a hand, palm facing the young girl. Purple ribbons of light shot out and wrapped around Mori. The light was beautiful and looked like fairy dust from movies Mori would watch as a child. One particular fairy in green with blonde hair came to mind.

Her body began to feel lighter than a feather as her eyes suddenly started to glow green. She could see it, the past, *her* past. How she was left on the porch of Missy and Jason's house, learning to walk, going to school, and discovering she had magic when running from her kidnappers. Her whole life flashed before her eyes until it reached this very moment. Mori, sitting in front of Leana and watching all of this unfold. Then it kept going.

The vision had her looking through a bird's eyes as it flew east over the Faenor Mountains. To her right, she saw what was left of the raiders' base, smoke now gone and the place lively with fae. The old prison building had been replaced with many smaller homes, with smoke coming from their chimneys from lit fireplaces. Looking straight ahead, she saw the Ursamong Peninsula. Though she had never been there before, she could see the vast trees that covered the area like a large patio umbrella. Waves from the sea crashing on the shore to the left of it, but that wasn't what the vision wanted to show her. It was beyond that shore that was important. An island, one she had yet to hear about, was not far off the shore of the mainland, but appeared to be a grassland with only a small hill to one side.

The island started getting closer as the bird Mori was seeing through took a nosedive toward the island, getting so close that she gasped as her sight went dark the moment it touched the ground. Her eyes stopped glowing, and she was now back in the room with Leana, panting hard as her heart tried to break out of her rib cage.

"What was that?" she asked, feeling beads of sweat drip down her face.

"That is Ursamong Island. It's forbidden, even to the royals. It's believed to hold something ancient that predates the first royal. No one knows what it is, not even me, but I believe that's where Dairus has been hiding."

"Has he been able to find whatever it is?"

"Not as of yet, but I presume he's close. You must go there and stop him."

"I will gather the troops and head there now." Mori uncurled her legs to stand, but Leana held out a hand to stop her before returning it to her lap. Mori sat back down, an eyebrow raised. "What?"

"You must wait. Now is not the time. He will not be there," The Seer said.

"Then why am I being shown it now?"

"To prepare. He will be there in two weeks. Gather what you need for backup and head there in two weeks. Then you will catch him where, and *when*, you need to."

"Why must I wait? Why can't I just go there now?"

"If you do, you'll die. The visions you see may be out of order. It will be up to you to put what you see in the correct order. Right now, the base you just destroyed is still smoking and full of the dead. What did you see in your vision?" Leana clarified, leaning forward with anticipation.

"The building had been rebuilt and there were fae folks everywhere. They looked happy."

"Exactly. Time has passed between now and that vision." The woman sat up, her bright green eyes shining in the dim light as she looked at Mori. "My work here is done. Return when you finish with Dairus. I expect to get my power back when you finish. Until then, I will not be available."

In the blink of an eye, Leana vanished. Mori sighed and leaned back on her hands to look up at the small light coming through the opening to the stairs. "I have to put the visions in order based on the clues it shows me. That's going to be hard to do without any context to how things look now." She chuckled. "Guess I will have to assemble the army again to go after Dairus, now that I know where he is."

Chapter Twenty-Eight

The high noon sun brought much warmer temperatures than Mori was used to. Blazing down on the forest, it felt like it was trying to cook her inside her light clothing of a simple white shirt and brown pants. Glancing to the side when she heard someone grunt, she watched as Tim and Tom were put to work tending the fields. They seemed to love manual labor and gardening more than fighting or hurting anyone. Seeing their smiling faces gave Mori hope for their future, even if their past wasn't all sunshine and rainbows.

The two former raiders looked up and waved at her, bright smiles plastered all over their faces. She waved back to them, not as enthusiastically, of course.

"We're picking the vegetables for tonight's dinner!" Tom shouted, the bigger man picking up his trowel to start digging again.

"Sounds good. Keep up the good work," she called back as she approached the fungus building where her father was staying.

"Dad, can I talk to you?" Mori asked as she walked into her father's room, closing the door behind her. The guest mushroom wasn't decorated with personal items. Just a bed, dresser, kitchen, and couch. Walking to the couch, she sat down and turned to face her father as he leaned against the back.

"Of course, Mori. What can I help you with?" A smile formed on his lips, and his eyes were soft and kind.

"Do you know anything about Ursamong Island?"

Ren blinked a few times as he raised both brows. "Oh, wow. How did you hear about that place?"

"I went to see Leana again to gain her seer abilities."

"Were you able to get them?"

Mori nodded. "Yes. I was looking through the eyes of a bird over the mountains and saw a small island close to the peninsula. It was grassy and flat except for a small hill. I'm not sure why I was shown that, but I think Dairus will be there in the future." Her gaze became unfocused at the floorboards, and she hoped she wasn't asking about a sensitive topic. When her eyes finally managed to pull away to glance up at her father, he was rubbing his chin with his fingers while staring off into space.

"That's a tough question. From what I've been able to learn, it's off-limits to everyone, even the royals. It's believed to be older than the first royal," he explained.

"Oberon. That's the name of the first royal."

Ren nodded. "That would make sense. He's in a lot of lore back in the human world. Known for his generosity and protective nature of the forest." He glanced over at Mori. She was shaking her head.

"Reality is quite the opposite. He started out kind, but when the humans attacked the forest, he did the best he could to fight back. That's when he made this." She raised her wrist to show the small hammer charm dangling from her bracelet. "This grows much bigger. It's a warhammer named Fae'ohtan, the Hammer of the Royals."

Ren's eyes grew wide as he leaned forward to inspect it. "I read about it in some of the royal journals, but I never thought I would ever be able to see it in person." Reaching out, his fingers lightly glided over the crystal and rose-gold-colored handle before he lay back, his hand returning to his lap. "That's incredible. What happened next?"

"Oberon went through the portal to the human world with an army to seek revenge, but you know how humans are. War and violence are what we do best." Mori rolled her eyes.

"That is unfortunately true." Ren shook his head before refocusing his attention back to her.

"Humans fought the fae army back through the portal, but from what I learned, he was changed. He sought out to destroy the forest. From my understanding, Fae'ohtan can corrupt fae with its magic, but I'm not entirely sure how." She looked at her wrist that was back in her lap. "Leana said my human half will protect me from its corruption, but I'm still skeptical. What if I'm corrupted anyway and try to destroy the forest after eight months of trying to save it?"

A hand touched her shoulder, making her turn her gaze to her father. "That's never going to happen, Mori. You're a strong woman, and I have no doubt that there's not a single soul or power that can control you. The prisoners spread rumors whenever they overheard the guards. I knew within a week of your arrival that you were here. I could only hope you'd find me before my time came." He smiled softly. "I was right to hope that."

Mori placed her hand on top of her father's wrinkled one. "I will always come to your rescue. With the power I have, I will find my way to you if anything were to happen."

"Good to know." He chuckled, his sleeve sliding down his arm to show just how much better he was doing. When Mori had found him, he was skin and bones, barely alive from lack of food. Now, he was at a much better weight, but still had a long way to go to being healthy.

"Dad, I don't know if I can stop Dairus. Even though I now know how his powers work, I still haven't been able to come up with a way to hit him with my hammer." Her head fell backward to rest on the back of the couch as she stared up at the ceiling.

"I have watched you train so hard since coming here. You're ready to take him on and end the war. You should never doubt the skills you've gained from all your time with Duncan, Lorem, and Sophie." Ren pulled his hand back and smiled fondly at his daughter. "You have come a long way from the stories I've heard of you barely being able to grow a flower."

"What?" Mori fake-gasped and clutched at imaginary pearls. "Who told you such nonsense?" She chuckled, looking over at her father as he laughed as well.

"Duncan, actually. I asked him about what you were like when you first met, and he was more than willing to tell me, but the one thing that always came up was how brave you were. Even without the knowledge and experience you have now, you still managed to stand your ground and take every enemy head-on."

"Did he tell you how many times I ran away? How I ran back to Missy and Jason when Faust was killed?" Her face fell, and she looked down at her lap, her fingers now fidgeting with the hem of her shirt.

"He did, but you came back. That's what matters."

"Not really. I have been running from my problems my whole life. I've only stayed as long as I have because Faust is here."

"Your best friend. Definitely worth staying for." Ren nodded. "What about Duncan? Wouldn't you want to stay here for him?"

"He and I don't always see eye to eye. He keeps me at a distance and won't open up to me, so I stopped opening up to him. Don't get me wrong, he is my best friend, but I don't have that same bond that I do with Faust."

"I see. That's a valid reason."

"When Faust died, I felt there was nothing left to keep me, so I went home. It took Mom coming to me one night and talking to me. Something about destiny and whatnot, but none of that made me want to return. It was seeing Faust alive and waiting that convinced me I had to come back." She shook her head, tears starting to fall as her fists gripped her shirt hem tightly. "I'm a failure as a queen. Even after defeating Yorn and rescuing so many fae, they still hate me. They still look at me differently, like I'm an outcast. Nothing's changed."

The couch shifted beside her as arms wrapped around her body to pull her into a hug. Mori released her shirt and grabbed on to her father's, holding on tightly as she cried all the tears she'd been holding in since coming to Albright Forest. The tears for her lost mother, the tears for her rejection by the fae, and the tears for never being good enough to stop the one person who would keep this war going forever. Everything she worked so hard for was crashing down around her, and there was nothing she could do to stop it.

"There there, my sweet girl. No one hates you. The fairies have been treating you with nothing but kindness." Ren petted her head to soothe her, but to no avail. Her tears would not stop running.

"I talked to some pixies this morning, and they threw rocks at me. Called me all sorts of names that I don't want to repeat. They don't translate well from Pixish." The queen pulled away from her father enough to wipe her eyes with her sleeves, allowing the older man to see her.

"It sounds like they're still bitter about you not being Titania."

"Of course I'm not her. She's been dead for a long time, but it's not like they believe me. None of them do. They think I'll die within the first five minutes of my fight with Dairus." Leaning back, she looked up at her father with puffy red eyes. "I don't want to fail them, or myself."

Ren gently moved some hair from her face and wrapped it around the back of her ears. "Mori, it doesn't matter if they believe in you, as long as you believe in yourself. And if anything, you have me, Faust, and Duncan who believe in you no matter what. If after everything you've done doesn't show just how ready you are to take your mother's place, then there's nothing in this world that will. You have done some amazing things since coming here, and I'm glad I get the chance to watch you grow into your role as queen and show everyone the kind-hearted daughter I always knew you would be." He placed a soft kiss upon her forehead, making Mori close her eyes and enjoy the tenderness her father was showing her. He was right, she didn't need anyone else to believe in her, only herself.

"I have something for you." Ren reached into the drawer beside him and pulled out several pouches that were connected and tied off.

She gently took the pouches, noticing the loops on the back to be strung up by a belt. "Thank you, but what is it?"

"This holds many seeds from several different carnivorous plants from both the human world and the fae world. You can toss them on the ground and grow them with your magic," he explained, a soft smile on his face.

"It's beautiful! Thank you, Dad." After looping it through her belt and putting the belt back around her waist, she smiled up at him.

"I think it's time we knock Dairus off his high horse and show him who the real queen is here." He chuckled.

"You're right. We have two weeks to plan an attack, and I fully intend to teach Dairus a lesson that will stay with him the rest of his life."

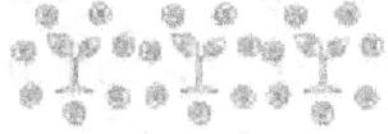

Mori gathered up the leaders of groups that had been established over the last week, consisting of Sophie, Lorem, Duncan, and Orian, to lead groups of fae toward the assault location. Faust and Renfred had joined in the meeting room with the others to provide insight.

"According to my vision from The Seer's magic, Dairus will be on Ursamong Island in a week. That means we have until then to come up with a plan. I don't fully know what he's doing there, but—"

"Sorry to interrupt," Tom said as he and Tim walked into the gathering mushroom. Everyone looked up at them.

"This is a meeting for leadership only," Sophie said, walking over to usher them out, but both men put up their hands.

"Hold on! We have information!" Tim got out before Sophie could force them out of the room.

"Wait," Mori commanded, walking around the table to stand in front of them as Sophie returned to her seat. "Information about what?"

"Dairus and his master plan." Tim put his hands down as he spoke, Tom following his lead.

"There's something on Ursamong Island that he's after. He claims it can destroy the entire forest, like a reset of everything."

Mori's eyes narrowed as she crossed her arms over her chest. "A reset of everything? Are you sure about that?"

"Positive," Tom said, nodding to reaffirm himself.

"Keep talking." The queen walked around the table and returned to her place at the head as Tim and Tom stepped up to the round table where there was space.

"There is a legend that was passed down through the generations among our people."

"Humans?" Mori asked.

"We're close to humans, but most of us are a mix of different fae species with the appearance of humans since that's how our ancestors started out," Tom continued.

"That would explain why my healing magic doesn't work on you. You're part-human and don't originate from the forest. I tried to heal a man who abandoned Yorn months ago, but he succumbed to his injuries from a pack of wolves."

"Yes." Tim nodded. "My ancestors were taken as prisoners of war by the first royal. We lived on the eastern side of the mountains for a long time. According to the stories my grandmother told me, my family managed to survive inside a cave with a very narrow entryway, which is how predators stayed out. Yorn was part of a nearby settlement. The stories of him being a descendant of Jerro are very much true, though Jerro was an illegitimate child born of adultery and never ascended the throne, even though his father was the previous royal." He crossed his arms and shook his head. "I wouldn't be surprised if that's why he wasn't chosen to be the next royal. I don't know how that works, but I'm glad he wasn't."

"The stories go on to say Jerro had a very troubled childhood, where Silvana was the golden child who was raised to be queen. She was the one born with the royal freckles; he wasn't. That was the whole reason their parents had a second child. Jerro resented that, and when he was old enough, he tried to claim he was royalty, but without the magic to mark him as such, no one followed him. From the texts he left behind, he traveled with Silvana, exacting his revenge in the only way he was allowed to—doing her dirty work. Anyone who defied her was dealt with. That's all we really know about them." Tom glanced around at everyone when he finished speaking, his hands playing with the belt tied around his tunic.

"I heard Jerro did some awful things while with Silvana, not that she would admit it to me herself." Mori sighed and crossed her arms.

"How could Silvana tell you herself? She's been dead for ages," the skinnier former raider said, glancing at Tom as if he had the answers before his eyes trailed back to Mori.

"I can speak to almost all the past royals. The first three and the eighth are not part of the royal magic. The fourth is not as well, but she has a place I can go to talk with her if I need to, same with the third," she explained, letting her arms fall so she could lean on the table with her hands.

"I didn't know there was royal magic. Is it different from regular magic?"

"Very different," Duncan chimed in. "It's sentient and chooses who it passes itself on to. That's why Silvana was chosen for the throne. It had nothing to do with the previous royal and everything to do with whomever the magic wanted to command it."

"That's pretty cool and also makes a lot of sense." Tim blew a few stands of his brown hair out of his face before continuing. "I didn't know there was such a thing."

"Back to the task at hand, we need to come up with a plan. Right now, we only have the fairies on our side. We lost a lot of good people during the battle with Yorn, but we still have a lot of strong fighters. I will be available for healing throughout the battle, so make sure your group knows if they need healing to call out to me. I will do my best to keep everyone alive." Mori pushed some red hair from her face, still feeling like shit for not being able to bring back their fallen friends. Most had been dead too long, and their souls had passed on before the battle ended. She did manage to bring back a few of them with Titania's help, but it was a fraction of those who had given their lives to protect the forest.

"I think we need a full assault on him. With the raiders dead, he won't have anyone to fight by his side. He will be alone. There's no way he can take us all on." Mori glared down at the map that was laid out on the table. It marked the territory of all the fae creatures, and outlines marked the borders to their provinces. The writing was all in a common fae language that Mori didn't know, but her magic translated for her like having English text under Japanese characters in a sub-anime.

"I don't know if that will work this time." Lorem crossed her arms, her eyes trained on the map, and her ears twitched. "He knows that's something we'd do again. As much as I love going in swords swinging, I think a little more stealth is needed. Whatever is on that island is still unknown, and taking the entire army over could be bad. I think half the army should stay on the mainland by the shore in case backup is needed."

"That's a good idea, Lorem," Orian said. "That way if he does manage to get his hands on whatever's there, all our forces won't be in one spot. Mori can teleport them to our location if we need them."

Mori nodded in agreement. "I've already asked the fairies to put their lives on the line more times than I should have. I can't ask for them to keep doing it, because no one else will help."

"Don't worry," Sophie said, waving her hand back and forth. "We have your back no matter what. Call upon us whenever you need. If it weren't for you, we wouldn't even have an army. So don't fuss about us. We will be there to fight for the forest."

That was a relief, for sure. At least she had a few people who would stand by her side while she fought for everyone. Mori couldn't have asked for better allies.

Tim spoke up as Tom pointed to himself. "We want to go too."

"Why? You both aren't fighters." Duncan looked at the two with interest.

"We may not be much help in a fight, but we want to support everyone else. Be the backup they need if they drop their sword or get sent flying. I'm a great cushion for breaking falls," Tom said with a light laugh.

"I can confirm that. Saved bones by landing on him when I fell out of a tree." Tim nodded.

"Fine, the two of you can come with us." Mori waved her hand to signal the end of that part of the discussion. "Now, let's talk about this plan. We have one week to get this right. I don't plan on walking away until that man is dead."

Chapter Twenty-Nine

"There he is," Duncan said as the three of them approached the island. The land was mostly flat, with grass and a few flowers despite its size, and a small hill toward the center. Dairus was standing on the shore, staring at them with crossed arms.

Mori narrowed her eyes and snarled as their boat came to a halt in the sand, followed by several other boats holding those who couldn't fly. Duncan got out to pull it onto shore while Faust growled at their enemy. Standing next to the evil man was Eclipsativa. She purred as her tail flicked behind her.

"Hush now, puppy. No need to get so snippy with us," she said, jumping up to Dairus's shoulders and rubbing against him.

"I suspected you were working with him. Spying on us to see if we'd reveal our plans. Well, you failed! We knew we couldn't trust you from the moment we met you." Mori took a step closer to the two of them, extending her hammer and resting it on her shoulder while her wolf bared his fangs.

I have not liked that cat since the very beginning, he growled.

"No one knows what you're saying. But I'm sure it was something threatening." He scoffed, crossing his arms over his chest. "You three are so predictable. Coming after me so soon after killing Yorn with the army that barely survived. You really think you can stop me?"

"I'm not as predictable as I used to be. I know your tricks now, so you're in for a treat." Mori smirked as she lunged at Dairus and

Eclipse, swinging her hammer to the side. The cat disappeared as Dairus evaded the attack.

Duncan charged from one side while Faust pounced from the other, both meeting right above Dairus, who blew them back with wind. "You're never going to get close to me with those cheap tricks!" Laughter erupted from him as he levitated into the air, a tornado of air beneath him. A group of fairies dove from above, their swords stretched out toward Dairus, but they were too slow. A tornado whipped up around them, catching them all in its fast winds, leaving them suspended in the air and swirling around out of control.

"Let them go!" Mori yelled, dashing around to avoid flying rocks and debris before launching herself off the ground toward the evil man.

Dairus smirked. "Gladly." The tornado shifted into a funnel and shot each fairy out toward her. Most of the fairies were able to recover before crashing into her, but one of them was not so lucky. He hit her square in the chest and sent them both crashing down to the ground, a small pit forming around the crystal of the hammer.

"Are you OK, Mori?" the warrior asked as he scrambled to his feet and helped her to her's.

"I'm fine. it's not your fault." Rubbing the pain from her head away, she looked up at Dairus to see him throwing fairies around like playthings. "This isn't good. We won't win at this rate. He's throwing us around like rag dolls."

Faust landed beside her, skidding to a stop on all four paws. *What should we do? None of us can get close enough to hit him.*

Mori surveyed the battlefield as the fight continued above her, seeing nothing but grass and a few flowers on a small hill. There was no real reason for it, but she knew the fact that it was there meant something. "Keep him busy. I have to check something out," she called out to her team before sprinting toward the mound.

Looking around frantically for something—anything—she could use against the enemy, she realized that she was seeing without *seeing*.

Eyes now glowing green, she looked at the hill once more. Down below the mound of dirt and plants was a ball of glowing blue energy that was very slowly spinning on a vertical axis. It was beautiful, the way it sparked like electricity searching for something to zap. The air above its location was not void of activity. With The Seer's magic on her side and active, she could see the flow of rainbow colors all around her, intertwining among each other.

"This must be the ambient magic everyone talks about," she said softly to herself, a small grin tugging at her mouth to show teeth. "It's beautiful." Stepping closer to the hill, she watched as ribbons of sparkling magic swirled around in a circle like a tornado. The Seer's magic was showing her where to stand to get the power below her feet, but before she could take another step, she was suddenly yanked backward. Hitting the ground with a thud and a cry of pain, she opened her no-longer-glowing eyes to see Dairus sprinting toward the location of the magic tornado and standing in the center of where it would be.

"Thank you for pointing out where it is. I have been searching for this for far too long."

"What even is it?" Mori asked as Duncan rushed over to help her to her feet.

"That, my dear, is Fae'tori'atta. It was born when the forest was created. Ambient magic couldn't harmonize with its surroundings, so it hid itself here. With it, I can enhance my own power and destroy this realm once and for all." A sinister grin spread on his face as he was lifted into the air. Activating The Seer's power, Mori watched the swirls of magic light gravitate toward Dairus, circling around him as he rose into the air.

"We have to do something!" Duncan said, but Mori didn't move. She turned her glowing eyes toward her friend.

"I don't know if there's anything we can do. That's very powerful, very ancient magic. I don't have the means to stop it." She turned her gaze back to Dairus, who was now being struck by the blue magic seeping out of the ground from the large ball of energy below.

"Can't you hit him with Fae'ohtan and put an end to this?" he asked.

"I'll try, but that magic predates my hammer." Kneeling, Mori channeled her magic into her legs and took off, soaring through the air at Dairus with her hammer ready. The moment she was in range, she swung the weapon, but it was stopped by the tornado of power that circled the man. He cackled wickedly as the force from the impact sent Mori flying right toward Faust, who wasted no time enlarging his body to catch her and take the brunt of the impact.

Mori groaned from the pain as she got to her feet and turned her attention to her companion. "Are you OK?" she asked as Faust stood up and shook off the dirt that clung to his fur.

I am fine. We need to stop him from absorbing the magic.

"I know, but there isn't anything I can do. My magic is weak compared to that." Her heart raced, but not from the physical exertion. Blood rushed to her legs, the urge to run kicking in. There was no winning this. She wouldn't be able to survive if she stayed, and there was no stopping him.

The magic continued to pelt Dairus in the chest as he laughed between grunts of pain. His body grew in size with each hit as it absorbed more and more magic.

"We need to be ready. His power will be increased tenfold. More than likely taking him to god-tier levels of strength."

"I don't know how we're going to stop that. We could barely take him on when he was at his normal strength." Duncan readied his sword as Dairus started to lower toward the ground.

"Everyone, take your positions! Don't lose focus!" Lorem shouted right before charging at the man with her longsword. Dairus saw her coming and pushed her back into Orian with his newly enhanced wind powers. Duncan and Mori dug their weapons into the ground to keep their balance as Faust stood beside her so she could hold on to him in his smaller form. When the wind subsided, she pulled her hammer from the dirt.

"Charge!" she shouted, war cries releasing all around her as the army rushed their enemy. Swords swiped through the air as arrows soared into the sky to rain down on Dairus, but nothing struck him. The energy he now possessed acted as a shield to the incoming attacks.

"You're all clearly blind if you can't see how weak you really are!" the man shouted as another laugh erupted. "With this power, no one will be able to stop me! Not even your precious hammer!" As he held out his hand, palm facing Mori, electricity shot out. It struck the hammer's crystal, shocking the queen in the process. She screamed out as agonizing pain overstimulated every nerve in her body. What felt like hours of torture for her was really only a few seconds before it released her and dropped her body to the ground as smoke drifted away with the light breeze.

"Mori!" Duncan and Lorem called at the same time, both rushing to her side. Lorem scooped the girl up as she opened her eyes.

"Everything's really blurry," she managed to mumble out.

"Hang in there. Your magic should heal you quickly." Just as Duncan finished speaking, Mori blinked her vision back into focus and sat up on her own.

"Damn that hurt." She rubbed her head with her hand before looking up at Dairus. He was much bulkier now, with glowing blue eyes that radiated the same energy as the magic he had just absorbed.

Back on her feet, she picked up Fae'ohtan and held it at the ready. "We gotta stop him somehow."

"How? He repels everything we throw at him," Duncan said as they all watched the other warriors attempt to get close but were constantly repelled.

"I'm still working on that part. For now, let's give it our all." Mori charged at Dairus once more, dodging the electricity striking the island and launching herself at him again, allowing the heart on top of Fae'ohtan to point directly at him.

"As if you can touch me, little girl!" Unhinged laughter bellowed from his wide-open mouth just as Mori was pushed back to the ground with a hard crash, displacing the earth around her. Before she had a chance to stand up, she had to roll out of the way of fire that Dairus shot at her.

Lorem jumped into the air at the floating man, just to be pushed back by his wind and another cackle of cockiness.

"I think we should take this somewhere more dangerous." Dairus slashed his arm through the air, forcing the wind to pick up. Fairies were blown backward toward the water and some were sent flying even further than that. Duncan and Lorem dug their swords into the ground to hang on, but even that proved futile as they were soon ripped away from the earth and sent flying back toward the mainland. Mori had followed suit with her hammer and managed to hang on much longer, but the dirt gave way and she was forced backward, making it all the way back across the water.

"Is everyone OK?" she called out, getting to her feet quickly to look around the area. While most people were groaning, none of them appeared badly injured.

"Why were we tossed back here?" Orian asked, checking his wings for damage before picking up his sword from the ground.

"I'm not sure, but I have a feeling it won't be anything good. Stay on guard." Mori watched as Faust walked out of the water and shook as much of it out of his fur as he could.

I am unharmed, just wet, he communicated to her before making his way to her side where he belonged. With a nod, she adjusted her focus back toward the island in time to see Dairus hover over the water to them.

"I had no idea what true power was like until I was enhanced by something so ancient and raw. It's unlike anything I've ever felt." An idea flashed through his eyes as his lips curled upward into a wicked grin. "I have just the idea for testing out my new abilities. Nighty night." He held out his hand, and blue flashed out over the entire army, blinding everyone. Mori lifted her arms to cover her face as she clenched her eyes tightly. Everything was silent, and the light through her eyelids had faded before she attempted to open them.

Chapter Thirty

When she awoke, she was no longer on the shore by the island. She was back at the demolished oak tree house with all her things scattered where they had lain since the destruction originally happened. Everything her mother had ever left for her to discover had been destroyed. It was much worse now than it had been when the destruction happened. Her chest tightened at the sight of losing something so precious as the traumatic memory flooded back.

Spinning on her heels, she took off running, tears running down her cheeks as light sobs escaped between her panting. Her legs took her back to the cliff she had slid down that second day she was in the forest, the one where Duncan was captured and dragged away. The moment the memory flashed in her mind, Duncan appeared with several raiders. They jumped on top of him and cuffed him as he shouted toward her. No, it was a memory of her, the one sliding down the crag as she cried out for the elf. It was surreal watching herself fall like that and then watching as Duncan continued to struggle as the restraints were pulled taut around his wrists.

"Let me go!" he shouted at his captors, headbutting one of them before kicking another behind him.

"Don't be that way, Duncy. It will only make it that much more satisfying now that I have you," Memory Dairus said with a grin, watching as the elf was dragged away. She ran after them and tried to pull the men off, but her hands went right through them, just the same as they had when she'd discovered the fake cave guarding the sacred grove.

Pulling her hands back, she inspected them before turning her gaze back up to the others. "Why am I seeing this?" Mori asked softly, though she knew there would be no answer. This was only a memory, not what was actually happening. Walking over to the cliff, she peered down at herself, unconscious, wet, and covered in mud.

The forest around her began to dissolve, causing her to spin frantically as her surroundings changed. When the scene finished constructing itself, she was staring at Faust's dead body with his entire chest and stomach exposed, the chunk of flesh ripped away. Bob had been chasing them while her beloved wolf's body laid on the ground, growing colder with every passing moment. Tears rolled down her cheeks the moment she laid eyes on the scene.

"No . . ." she breathed, her chest squeezing tightly as it became harder to draw in air. A figure ran past her, the curly red hair a dead giveaway as to who it was. Mori watched herself and her elf friend talk before fleeing the area, heading straight for a portal. Duncan called after her, but the portal closed shut behind her. Falling to the ground and slamming a fist onto the dirt, he cursed in his native elf language words the royal magic refused to translate.

"Dairus! Show yourself!" she called into the forest, but she was answered with only silence. "Coward," she grumbled before she walked over to her wolf. Kneeling beside him, she sighed heavily, tears still running and turning her eyes red and puffy. "I should never have left you, Faust. You wouldn't have abandoned me, but I abandoned you. I can never make up for what I did, but I try my best every day."

When she reached out a hand to touch his fur, it went right through him as if he were not there, but she didn't care. She wanted to be there for him this time, even if she could never go back in time and make things right or change how she ran from him.

Just as quickly as before, the scene changed again, but this time, she was back in the human world. She watched herself run past as two familiar raiders chased her through a park. Tim was doing his best to keep up, and Tom was panting hard, stopping to catch his breath as he doubled over.

"She's fast," he said, his voice hoarse from the physical exertion.

"We still have to catch her or the boss will kill us." Tim rushed to his partner's side to help him up.

"I don't even want to catch her. I don't understand why she's a target, and I want nothing to do with this." The larger man shook his head while he spoke, swinging his arms in front of him like they were cutting something, but it was more commonly used to gesture not wanting to continue what they were doing.

"I know, I feel the same, but we don't have much choice. It's her or us." The taller raider tapped his companion on the shoulder to get his attention. "Come on, we have to get her." The two raiders ran off after her again, but Mori knew they'd lost her by this point. She had made it home, and they couldn't find her again until she ran away at the mall.

"They were chasing me and they didn't even want to. But why am I being shown all of this?" While she thought about it, the park disappeared and was replaced with the backyard of Missy and Jason's house.

Little eight-year-old Mori was chasing her friends around on the other side of the yard while real Mori stood beside the picnic table. A couple of her childhood friends were talking amongst themselves.

"She's so weird. Why are we here?" a blonde girl by the name of Michelle asked the other two girls.

"Free cake and free babysitting. That's what my mom told me." Another girl, Ariana, pushed her hair behind her shoulder while speaking, her nose in the air like she was better than everyone else. That was exactly how Mori remembered her, snobby and spoiled rotten. After this party, Ariana went on to bully her for years with the third girl at the table, Nissa.

The girls who were playing with the younger version of herself all gathered around the table for cake when Missy brought it out. A few of the girls sang happy birthday, but not all of them. After eight-year-old Mori blew out the candles, Missy removed them just in time for Ariana to force her head down into the cake, making all the other girls laugh. Even though her adopted mother scolded the young girl, Mori still ran inside the house crying, with cake falling out of her hair and sliding off her face.

"I hated that party. It was the start of the bullying," real Mori grumbled.

"Why would you do such a thing?" Missy questioned, her voice stern as she worked on cleaning up the mess.

"She's weird! She has giant hair and weird freckles! That's not normal!" Ariana shouted, venom in her tone as she stood up. "I want to go home. Call my mom."

"Gladly." Missy finished cleaning up and went inside. Jason was helping the young girl clean cake off her face and out of her hair when Missy walked inside, real Mori following behind.

I remember this conversation. I never had a birthday party again after this.

The scene around her changed once more, putting her back in the forest, but this time, she was surrounded by all her friends. Faust, Duncan, Lorem, Orian, Sophie, and Renfred, all of them were in a circle around her.

"Running away again, Mori?" Duncan asked as he looked down his nose at her. "It's just like you to run when things get tough."

"Yeah. You're such a useless queen. I don't even know why we bother training you at all. You're lousy with a sword and worse with a hammer." Lorem shrugged, tilting her head to one side nonchalantly.

I cannot believe I let you ride me like a steed. I am a mighty direwolf, not a horse. You are not worthy to be in my presence. If I could kill you, I would have done it back in the cave, Faust chimed in, sitting on the grass with his nose in the air. *You left me behind when I was killed and eaten by Bob. Death would have been preferable to being your friend.*

"What are you talking about? We're best friends. All of you are my best friends." Mori spun around, listening to their laughter as their faces contorted into sneers and grins.

"As if any of us would want a halfling to be our queen, let alone our friend," Sophie said, making Mori stop her spinning to stare at her, mouth hanging open and tears falling from her eyes. "All you've done is get my people killed over and over. There's no way we could support someone who just wants us all dead and then deserts us in our time of need."

"That's not true! I'm doing my best to protect you, to protect everyone!" Sobbing replaced her shouts as she looked around once more at all her friends.

Why would you do this to us, then? You let me die and ran away. When Mori turned to Faust, the chunk of flesh Bob had bit off was missing. *You let me die when Bob ate me. You claimed to be my friend, yet you left me to be eaten by the thing you're afraid of.*

"Faust . . ." A waterfall of tears cascaded down her cheeks as she fell to her knees. "I didn't mean to . . ."

I watched you leave. You packed a bag and left.

Mori buried her face in her hands, unable to control the overwhelming depression that blanketed her, weighing her down as every bad thing was spewed out by all her friends. From running away when things got tough, to how weird her freckles looked compared to the other royals, to how much curlier her hair was compared to her mother's, the hate continued to pummel her just like the bullies used to do in middle school.

The more she thought about all the people who had hurt her, the more they showed up to tell her more awful things. Ariana, Nissa, and even her adopted parents appeared to tell her how bad of a person she was. Then her mother showed up in the crowd, stepping forward with her hands on her hips.

"I'm so glad I gave you up. My life got infinitely better once I no longer had to take care of you. I never wanted a child, but I had no choice as a royal. The bloodline had to continue." Viviana shrugged nonchalantly.

"That's not true! My mother wanted me, but she couldn't keep me! It was for my own good!" she shouted back at the image of Viviana. "You're not my mother!"

"Is that what I told you?" Vi laughed. "As if I would want a useless daughter like you. You didn't receive the proper training to become queen, which makes you unworthy of the title. A pathetic excuse for a queen who can barely wield a sword. *You're* the real coward here." Vi smirked, crossing her arms over her chest as she looked down her nose at her own daughter. "The only reason the royal magic chose you is because I couldn't conceive another child. You were it."

Even through all of this, Mori still refused to give up on any of her friends. Refused to lie there and allow Dairus to take them out one by one, but what was she supposed to do? Where was she supposed to go to break out of this? Tears still stained her cheeks as she looked around and slowly stood up. As she spun herself around, the images of her friends were replaced with images of herself. Every fake Mori sneered at her, each at a different level of injury to show the many ways the people around her had died in the past.

"This is your fault!" one of them shouted.

"You're the reason we're dead!"

"You're the reason we will die here today!"

"No!" Mori found her hammer and started swinging it around, trying to make the clones of herself shut up. Anything for peace and quiet, to make the voices stop telling her how she'd messed everything up. To silence them from reminding her of everything she had ever done wrong in her life, and everything that was wrong with her. How she destroyed so many peoples' lives.

As Fae'ohtan sliced through each fake Mori, two more took its place, saying the same things over and over. "Stop it!" she screamed, her voice cracking. "I'm not that person anymore!" Mist drifted around her, blocking her view of all the fakes, but their voices, their words, never stopped.

Just as the voices were beginning to overwhelm her, the hammer suddenly stopped slicing the air. A clawed black hand had grabbed the handle just above her hands, gripping it tightly it was like trying to move a sturdy brick wall with her bare hands. Through the thick fog, she saw two glowing red orbs staring at her. They moved closer to show the deer skull head they were attached to breaking through the gloom.

"Focus."

Chapter Thirty-One

The deep, guttural voice that rang out could only belong to one beast. Looking up at the skull-headed creature, Mori's breath hitched. Silence filled the air, the voices no longer haunting her as she slowly lowered her hammer at the same time that Bob let go of it. All the clones of herself had vanished; all their chanting had ended. This battle was over, but there was still a war.

"Everyone crazy," he growled, though she couldn't see anyone. Using her gifted magic, she saw everyone in their own trance, standing around like mannequins with their eyes glossed over. "What happened?" Bob asked, standing to his full height to look around.

"We were fighting Dairus and were blown back to the mainland from the island with his wind magic." She turned to face the beast. "He got the magic. The one that enhances his own power." Tears threatened to well up again, but her eyes were dry. There were no more tears left to shed for the things she can no longer control.

Bob nodded once before walking over to Duncan and lightly pushing him, but he did nothing but catch his balance and stand still.

"I'm not sure that will work. We need something to scare them, like a jolt. Kinda like you did with me," she said, releasing a breath she had held in too long.

Turning his head to face her, the beast let out a huff. "You escaped on your own. You moved, they didn't."

Mori arched a brow. Has she really overcome anything? She had been flailing around trying to kill images of herself. She wouldn't exactly call that therapeutic or healthy. "If you say so, but I don't think I escaped. You snapped me out of it somehow. Maybe it's because I'm afraid of you."

"No." He shook his head. "Not afraid of me. Afraid to lose them." Using his head, he gestured toward the others who were still in their trance. That made the most sense to her. She had been fighting these last several months to keep them safe. Now she was just standing around, talking to Bob instead of finding a way to help them.

"You're right. I am afraid to lose them. I have friends for the first time in my life, and I'm not going to run away. Not this time." Something large caught the corner of her eye. Turning toward it, she flinched at how massive and ugly the thing was. It looked like an overgrown, mutated cockroach with crab claws for hands. The crustacean-like creatures were much larger than Mori had expected, having seen them in a few of her books on the fae, but she couldn't remember what they were called.

"Meenlocks." Bob hunched over, ready to charge at the creature. "Bigger."

"Agreed. They're much bigger than the books say they are. Two feet, yeah right." Pointing her hammer at it, she took aim before the skull-headed beast's claw blocked her path.

"Mine." Bob pulled his claw back before letting out an ear-splitting roar and charging at the overgrown crab.

"It's all yours! Eat it!" Mori cheered on, watching as it took no time for the creature to become food for her new friend. Groans from the others pulled her attention to her friends. Without asking, she lifted her hands to heal the army back to health before she turned toward Dairus, who was now approaching.

"Oh, you managed to escape my pet's spell. Well, damn." He scoffed, crossing his arms as he landed on the ground. "You couldn't have waited until I was here to kill you before becoming aware of my meenlock?" He glanced over at Bob, who was now cracking open the meenlock's shell and eating the meat. "And eating it?"

"As if you wouldn't have broken the spell too."

Dairus shrugged. "Got me there, but I doubt you can do this." A wide grin spread across his face as he held his hands out, palms down. Magic flowed from his core through his arms and down to the ground. The earth beneath them began to quake, making her lose her balance and fall forward onto her front. Just then, a hand shot up from the ground right in front of her face, a scream releasing from her throat as she scrambled back to her feet and took a few steps back. Faust placed himself between the queen and the hand as he growled at the undead fairy that pulled itself out of the ground. "I didn't come alone." Dairus laughed as more undead fey creatures emerged from their unmarked graves.

"Where are these things coming from?" Mori asked, having to move out of the way of an undead leprechaun so he couldn't grab her ankle.

"There was a battle here several royals ago. All the dead were left behind while the living fled," Duncan explained before stabbing a zombie fairy through the chest, but it continued to try to grab him. "How do we kill these things?" After pulling his sword back, the elf ducked under a swipe of the zombie's claws and jumped out of its reach.

"They're zombies. We have to destroy their brain," Mori called out as she brought her hammer down onto the leprechaun's head, smashing his entire body into a flat disk of flesh and blood.

"What the hell are zombies?" Lorem asked as she stabbed her longsword through the forehead of an undead yeth hound.

"They're the undead. In the human world, they come back to eat brains, but I imagine these ones just want to eat our flesh." The queen knocked a zombie pixie to the ground and stepped on it, digging it into the ground under her boot. "Keep fighting!"

"It's hard not to!" the satyress called back as she decapitated another zombie whose flesh had rotted away so much it was unrecognizable. "There's too many of them!"

Sounds of bones breaking and bodies dropping to the ground ran out across the battlefield. There were so many different kinds of undead fey that Mori couldn't name all of them, nor could she see an end to their numbers. The fog was already lifting, so she didn't have to rely solely on The Seer's powers.

As the fight raged on, Mori backed up more and more, trying not to get cornered. She ended up running into Duncan just as Faust and Orian joined them in a circle, their backs to each other. They were completely surrounded, as were the rest of their small army.

"We have to stop them." Sophie shot a fireball at a zombie that was getting close to her. "We need to get to Dairus and put an end to this."

Mori shook her head. "I don't see how." Groans from their troops echoed out, the fog gone so she could see the entire battleground. There were undead aaxte, hags, blink dogs, redcaps, and more fey she couldn't name as far as she could see. "We're severely outnumbered and most of us are tired and wounded."

"Not any longer." The high-pitched voice of Queen Astalla sounded from above as a swarm of pixies came down, each dressed for battle and holding small weapons. Each one dive-bombed the undead creatures, attacking their heads directly to cave in their skulls and destroy the brain. Behind them, a horde of leprechauns, naiad warrior women on kelpies, and a few others that Mori didn't recognize came riding in alongside their respective leaders.

"We're here teh join teh fight," the assumed leader of the leprechauns said with an accent, and pointed a small rapier toward the undead. "For our home!" The leprechauns charged forward, each one shouting their own catch phrase or war cry with their swords and axes toward the enemies.

"For Titania!" Queen Astalla shouted as the pixies rushed a group of redcap goblins, attacking the undead soldiers to dismantle them however they could. Their limbs fell to the ground once they were detached from the unflinching creatures.

"For Albright Forest!" the rest called out before charging as well.

Mori couldn't believe it. The fae she had gone to see during her travels were there to help. They were there to protect her, their home, and were even helping Bob rip apart the larger undead fey.

"It seems our efforts were not in vain," Duncan said with a smile as he patted her on the shoulder. Mori was still staring in disbelief with her mouth hanging open. They had all come, even when they'd repeatedly told her in their own way to piss off.

"They came to help me? I thought they all hated me."

"We don't hate you, Mori. You saved us from the raiders and healed our wounded," the naiad leader said as she stood beside the queen and guard captain.

"Queen Adairria," Mori said softly.

"You may not 'ave saved us when Dairus destroyed our home, but thanks to you, we didn't 'ave teh return to ruins and corpses. There was greenery and homes we could live in, and our dead received proper burials. You brought life back to our province. You didn't just set us free that day, you gave us hope." The leprechaun leader walked up to them. "I'm Sullivan, king of teh leprechauns, and we came to help yee fight. We 'ave yer back." He smiled.

Mori glanced from Adairria to Astalla and then to Sullivan, wanting to cry with relief, but refraining. "Thank you all for coming to help." She held up her hammer and smirked. "We should end this now. For our future and our forest!" she shouted the last part, making the leaders cheer before they all joined the fight.

A group of hags lunged at the small group of leaders, but with one swing of Fae'ohtan, Mori sent their bodies, now turned to ash, flying into the wind. Bob ripped apart a fomorian as he boomed out a bloodthirsty cry before assaulting another. These giants were covered in rotting flesh and foliage from where their graves rested, releasing a pungent odor that could curl nose hairs. Orian had flown over to help the skull-headed beast take on the larger undead fey to keep them from claiming more victims.

Faust was fighting off a pack of undead wolves alongside Lorem, who expertly wielded her longsword to decapitate the fiends from a distance. Sophie was obliterating undead goblins with her magic, easily ripping their heads from their bodies and crushing them. Mori was rather proud of her team. Each one with their own unique set of skills being utilized in the forest's time of need.

"I think it's time we kick things up a notch." Reaching into one of her pouches, she pulled out some seeds and scattered them over the ground, her magic fueling the plants' rapid growth into massive cape sundews. Sticky, tentacle-like green bodies flailed as they grew bigger and bigger, their long red bristles sprouting and producing the sweet sugar water lure. Now grown to giant proportions, each one swept over the battlefield to capture as many zombies as possible before curling up to squish and digest them. These carnivorous plants swept up and killed—for a second time—a massive number of enemies before the undead fae had a chance to fully leave the ground. There was no telling just how many had lost their lives here during the fight a long time ago, but it appeared to be in the thousands, judging by the number of undead.

"Nice thinking, Mori," Duncan called as he slashed another undead fairy, making it drop to the ground with an audible thud.

Dairus snarled as he let loose his magic, electrocuting several fae warriors, some of them dying while others were knocked unconscious. Fireballs followed the electricity, burning all the plants Mori had just grown, as well as the grass around them.

"I refuse to lose any more people." Jamming the handle of Fae'ohtan into the ground, she activated a barrier that would prevent the lost souls from escaping, her eyes lighting up as Titania took control. With the Hammer of the Royals to amplify the power, the fallen soldiers' bodies were healed and their souls returned to the flesh they belonged to. Each one stood up, grabbed their weapon, and returned to the battle.

"Keep it up, Mori! We're finally winning!" Orian called over the sounds of metal clanking together and grunts of pain. As each of her army fell, they were resurrected within ten seconds of their death.

"Winning? Well, we can't have that, now can we?" Dairus's eyes glowed blue as bolts of lightning struck the ground all around both armies. He didn't care which side he electrocuted.

"We have to stop him from killing more people!" Sophie yelled over the thunderous booms of attacks.

"That's kind of the point of this whole battle, Sophie." Mori rolled to the side to dodge an incoming attack before kicking the goblin directly into the awaiting sword of Duncan.

"We need a plan!" Duncan shouted as he slashed another undead goblin to kill it before dashing to the side to avoid being stepped on by a fomorian. Bob and the giant had a death grip on each other's shoulders, trying to pull each other down to get the upper hand. The skull-headed beast opened his large maw and took a chunk of flesh from the undead's arm before spitting it out. Leaning his head back, the large creature headbutted the zombie, an antler piercing the skull and brain. With a cry of pain, the undead giant went limp and fell to the ground, crushing a few zombies and none of the living. Bob boomed out a victorious warcry before charging at another fomorian, antlers first.

Rushing over to a nearby soldier, Mori punched the undead redcap back, bones cracking under her heightened blow. Using the momentum, she spun 180 degrees and uppercut another undead fairy, ripping its head from its neck, making it fall to the ground. She then stomped on it to break the skull completely.

"Thanks. I would have been a goner," the fairy man said before blocking another incoming attack with his sword.

"If I can't protect my people, then I'm not worthy of being queen." Mori roundhouse kicked another zombie who got way too close for comfort. Grunting and thumping from large feet smashing into the ground grabbed her attention just in time to jump to the side to avoid being crushed by Bob as he fell over. "Bob! Are you OK?" she called, only receiving a low growl in return as the beast stood up and lunged at the giant.

"I have an idea! Mori, grab Fae'ohtan. We're gonna need it to take him down," Duncan said, making his way over to her to help her to her feet.

"What about our people? I don't want any more of them to die. If I remove Fae'ohtan—"

"They knew what could happen when they came here, but their deaths will be in vain if we don't win this war," the elf interrupted, lightly pushing her toward the hammer that was still working its magic.

Mori nodded and rushed over to grab Fae'ohtan, dodging several attacks before making it to her weapon. Twirling it in her hands, she stood tall, having an idea of what her guard captain was planning. "All leaders on me! We're going to end this once and for all!"

Chapter Thirty-Two

Was this really how things were going to end? An all-out assault on Dairus? Would that even work?

Only one way to find out.

Duncan charged at the man, sword downward to the side for a slash. Mori tossed seeds in his path, growing large pitcher plants of varying sizes to form a staircase for the elf. Stepping on each plant's lid, he made it all the way up and swung his sword. The blade sliced a few strands of hair as Dairus leaned back, but he couldn't dodge the tackle. Duncan sent them both to the ground and rolled out of the way just in time to avoid Lorem's longsword stabbing down into Dairus's shoulder.

Dairus yelled from the gushing pain before pushing her off with a strong gust of wind, pulling her sword out, and using it to block the downward strike from Orian's own weapon. Using fire, the man pushed the fairy off him, burning his face, clothes, arm, and shoulder. Stumbling backward, Orian quickly put out the fire as Mori ran over to him to heal his injuries.

Grabbing a mix of seeds, she twirled herself around to scatter them as far as she could from her position. She closed her eyes as she concentrated on growing more cape sundews to replace the ones that had gotten caught up in Dairus's inferno. The tentacle-like plants set to work on fighting off the undead just as the ones before them had. Venus flytraps broke through the earth and snapped closed around some undead, while the bigger ones tried to bite Dairus. One managed to catch him in its mouth, the hairs along the edge keeping him from escaping.

"Think that did the trick?" Lorem asked, her longsword back in her hands.

"I doubt it. There's no way a plant will be able to contain him." Sophie helped Duncan to his feet after healing his bruised ribs, his hand still clutching his side.

"Don't let your guard down. Dairus will break out, and when he does, we need to focus on him. Let the army take care of the undead." Mori gripped her hammer tightly, ready for the right moment. The bulb of the flytrap shook violently before ripping apart, pieces of it and its digestive enzyme covering the area around it.

"That little trick won't work on me! I refuse to be eaten alive!" Fire erupted from his outstretched hands, instantly catching everything Mori had just grown. The sundews curled up as they turned black, the sweet smell of their nectar filling the air and their noses. Pitcher plants folded in on themselves, charring as their own digestive acid ate away what remained of their bodies. The venus flytraps expanded from the intense heat and exploded as the fire burned away what remained. "Not so tough without your plants." He snickered, lowering himself until his feet touched the ground in the center of his wildfire.

Without another word, the queen moved swiftly to avoid the ashes that rained down from her beautiful plants. Grabbing two seeds from her pouch, one in each hand, she grew very long stems filled with thorns from a blackberry bush. These whiplike weapons trailed behind her before she took her stance and flung them forward, the left one gouging Dairus's chest while the right wrapped around his neck, his hand grabbing it in an effort to pull it away.

Mori pulled the whip tightly, forcing the man to fall to his knees as Duncan and Orian launched Lorem into the air, her longsword raised high and the pointed end aimed downward. Letting gravity be her force, she plunged the sword toward Dairus, striking him through the arm and leg. The man shrieked in agony as blood spilled from the new wounds, a smirk crossing the satyress's face.

"Wipe that smirk off your face!" When he grabbed the whip, it began to glow red as the intense heat finally burned through the stem and thorns, allowing him to break free and pull the rest of the whip off his neck. Wind pushed Lorem away from her weapon, and she crashed into Orian, sending them both backward. Dairus took hold of the longsword and pulled it out of his arm and leg, grunting from the pain as he tossed it to the side. "You haven't won yet!" Holding his hands at his sides, he turned invisible with a small puff of smoke, but Mori was ready for this.

Activating The Seer's powers, she could see the blue-and-red colors of magic within Dairus flowing together, mixing as he moved around.

"Oh no you don't!" She scattered oak and birch tree seeds everywhere, forcing them to grow big and tall before using her hammer's air cutter ability to shake the pollen loose. The yellow particles blanketed everything, including his invisible form. "Your old tricks won't work anymore. I can see you while you're invisible." She smirked, shrinking the trees to clear the battlefield of them. She had never been more thankful that she didn't have any allergies.

"Don't celebrate too early. You never know if you're going to actually win or lo—" Eclipse had shown up just in time for Faust to grab her around the neck with his mouth and snap it. The cat's body became limp as he placed a paw over it and ripped the head right off.

We will win. I have every faith in Mori that we will. Faust dropped the head onto the ground before lunging at Dairus, only to be blown to the side, landing on his paws as he slid to a stop. *We cannot get close enough to strike him all the time. We have to catch him off guard.*

"Agreed. We need to catch him off guard in order to get close," Mori said, having discarded the whips as they burned and returned to using Fae'ohtan. Faust ran up beside her, allowing her to jump on his back and ride him back into battle, the leaders behind her.

Adairria commanded the waters from the shore to come to her, using the seawater as her own whips as she wrapped them around Dairus. Astalla flew down to lend her power to Sophie as they both commanded the earth around them to reach up and grab their enemy in a tightly packed soil cocoon. Sullivan launched himself into the air and landed on top of the new prison, reinforcing the strength of the metal residing within the dirt.

"Now's the time, Mori! End this!" Duncan shouted.

Jumping off Faust when she was close enough, the queen lifted her hammer above her head. "I'm ending this now!" she bellowed as she brought the crystal down, but before it could make contact, the vibrating dirt pod detonated, throwing Mori back against her wolf. Sophie and Astalla were thrown into Adairria, where all three of them were shot into the water with a loud splash.

Dairus hovered above the ground, his eyes still glowing blue as he panted. His disheveled hair and clothes were covered in mud from the attempted capture. "I'm not that easy to kill, girl!" Using his wind powers, he threw fast fireballs at all the leaders and several unsuspecting fae in the army, setting the whole battlefield on fire. The undead had been defeated except for the last fomorian Bob was going claw to claw with. Naiads had climbed the giant's body and were doing everything they could to disable its senses.

The queen threw her body over her wolf just as a fireball came flying at them. It ignited her clothes and singed her hair as she cried out, the smell of burning flesh filling her nose. Mori quickly lay on the ground and started to roll, putting the fire out as fast as she could, but it still gave her third-degree burns. Every cauterized nerve sent pain throughout her body. The royal magic took the time to heal her skin but could do nothing about her clothing.

Mori, are you all right? The wolf moved in front of her, trying to be a comfort. *You should not have done that. I would have come back if it had killed me. You will not be revived.*

A smirk crossed her pained expression. "I couldn't let my best friend die again. I won't put you through that." With her back healed, she stood up, gripping her weapon tightly.

"Hold him down with everything you've got!" she shouted as her fellow leaders continued to strike, not letting up for a moment.

What do you plan to do? Growling as he moved to stand beside her, Faust was ready to get back in the fight.

"Do everything you can to help the others restrain him. I can feel my magic depleting quickly. I'm gonna give this my all, and there's no room for error. I can't miss."

Do not do something that will get you killed.

"I don't care if this kills me or not, as long as it kills him. You have your orders, Faust." She gave a small smile as she looked at him. "You are my best friend. I couldn't have asked for a better reason to put my life on the line, as long as it protects you." Kneeling, she threw her arms around his neck, hugging him close. "I'll see you on the other side."

Pulling back, Mori stood once more. Faust didn't know what else to say, so he took off running to assist. Massive boulders pushed up from the ground as more electricity shot out, striking her briefly, but enough to drop her to her knees.

A ringing sound rang in her ears, cutting off the sounds of her friends fighting. With blurry vision and shaking legs, she tried to stand up but stumbled and fell once more. The pounding headache was throwing off her balance, and her heart hurt from how hard and fast it was pounding in her chest. Staggering to her feet, she watched as the large boulders smashed against Dairus's sides, and metal from Sullivan curled around them to keep them securely in place. Large plants had grown from Astalla's powers to block his wind magic from blowing all of them away. Just when they thought he wouldn't be able to move, the man shot lightning out of his eyes, carving deep trenches into the dirt as it made its way up toward her.

Mori cried out as she was struck by the lightning again, every nerve feeling like it was being tortured before she fell to her knees, scraping them badly. Her kneecap cracked from the impact. Sweat poured down her face, dripping onto the grass as blood leaked from her nose and knees, staining her clothes. She wiped the fluids from her face away on her sleeve before standing up, her legs threatening to give out.

"This ends right here, right now. I won't risk anyone else's lives any longer." Plunging the hammer handle down into the dirt, she glared up at the man who was hell-bent on destroying her forest. As she gripped it tightly, her knuckles turning white, the crystal of Fae'ohtan began to glow a bright teal, like a beacon. The amount of magic Mori had within her was running dry, but she was still determined to end things here. All she could do was push every spark of power she had left into this one last attack. If she couldn't stop him here and now, there was never going to be a way to stop him. She would never win, and everyone would lose hope of ever having peace.

I don't have enough. He'll be able to survive the blast with the amount I have.

"You don't have to do this alone," Viviana's voice rang out as she placed her hands over her daughter's.

"You will never have to be alone again, Mori." Titania grabbed the handle of Fae'ohtan with both hands. Another pair of hands, Leana's, gripped the handle, followed by Elissa and Silvana. Remus and Avarisha followed suit, along with several other pairs of hands, all past royals. If they couldn't reach the hammer, they placed their hands on the shoulders of the royal in front of them.

Looking around at everyone, Mori found more tears to shed, but this time, they were happy ones. This whole battle, she was never alone. Faust, Duncan, and so many others had fought by her side against the illusions, the undead, and Dairus. They were still taking him on while she charged up as much power as she could for one last final blow. This time, to kill.

"Everybody, hang on!" she shouted as the crystal's light grew brighter until it blinded everyone, making them all shut their eyes. Her friends moved out of the way, allowing all the plants, metal, and boulders to restrain the struggling man. With one solid pure-white beam of energy, it shot out at the bound Dairus, his screams of pain starting off loud, but getting quieter as his flesh was ripped away from his bones. Every organ was shredded before disintegrating, every vein and piece of muscle torn apart. His wails grew silent as he met his end.

As the beam's light grew dimmer, Mori opened her eyes to see what had happened. If it weren't for his charred bones, she would have believed he'd escaped that blast. Slowly rising to her feet, Mori and all the royals watched as the remains of their greatest enemy turned to dust and fell away from the restraints to the grass below. Where he used to be was a glowing ball of blue energy, the same one she had seen before he'd absorbed it and turned its power against them.

After pulling her hammer out of the ground, she slowly walked over to the ball of light, examining it instead of touching it.

"Be careful," Duncan said, keeping his distance just in case.

"What will you do with that power, Mori?" Adairria asked, holding her daughter close to her body.

Turning to face her army and the spirits of the past royals, she gave a small smile. "I'm returning it to where it belongs. On an island where everyone is forbidden to go, including me." She glanced back at the blue light. "There's no reason anyone should have this much power. It's too great of a responsibility for any one person to shoulder. So no one will have it." Shrinking the plants around the ball and pushing the boulders to the side with magic, Mori lifted Fae'ohtan like a baseball bat ready to strike. "Go back to the island and rest. You were abused by an evil man. You deserve peace. As long as I'm alive, no one will come near you again." She knew there would be no response, but she'd learned a long time ago that everything here had a consciousness, and everything deserved to be happy. She swung her hammer as hard as she could, and the crystal made contact with the power, sending it flying toward the island. Using the power of The Seer, she watched it return to its hill and sink below the grass to its former resting place. Turning back to the royals, she beamed. "Thank you for your help, everyone. Get some rest, and we shall talk again soon. I couldn't have done it without you."

"We're glad the war is finally over," Viviana said. "I love you, my dear Moriana. I know you will do great things as the forest queen." With a small wave, all the royals faded away.

Mori dropped her hammer before falling to her broken knees and collapsing to the side. The last thing she heard and saw was Duncan and Lorem calling her name and rushing to her side with Faust on their tail.

She'd done it. The war was over.

Chapter Thirty-Three

Waking up in the large bed inside the birch tree house, Mori groaned from the intense headache she felt. The sun was too bright through the window, making her pull the covers over her head.

"She's awake! Get Duncan and Sophie!" Lorem's voice echoed slightly in the large room. Something large jumped onto the bed and lay beside her. She would recognize that furry body anywhere. Faust pulled the sheets away and licked her face repeatedly while she laughed and pretended to push him away.

"Hello to you too, Faust." She reached an aching arm to scratch behind his ear with her fingers. The movement sent shocks of pain through her sore muscles. "How long was I out? And why does my body hurt so much?" she asked, her voice hoarse and gravely.

"You were out for a week," Duncan said as he walked into the room, Sophie right behind him. "Not surprising after the amount of magic you used." He stopped by the bed with the fairy queen next to him.

"It is to me. I thought I was past this." Mori sighed, staring up at the ceiling.

"It doesn't matter if you think you're past this or not. You put every scrap of power the royal magic gave you into that final attack on top of continually bringing back those we lost," Sophie explained, softly smiling at the young queen. "We didn't lose a single person because of you."

"And Titania. She's the one who can bring people back, and she was more than happy to do so." Mori laughed as Faust returned to licking her face.

I was worried you would not wake up. He nuzzled her affectionately, his tail wagging behind him as she petted his head.

"I will always wake up, buddy. Who else is going to scratch your ears and give you belly rubs? Duncan?" Mori laughed as the elf held up his hands as panic crossed his features. Faust growled at him, showing some of his teeth.

"I'm not touching you like that!"

Good. Only Mori can pet me like a common house dog. He stopped snarling and turned back to Mori, his ears perked up as he panted happily. She couldn't help but laugh.

"I'm pretty sure I don't want to know what he said." Duncan let out a breath.

"Nope." She petted Faust for a little longer. "Sophie, do you think I have enough magic to make a portal? There's something I need to do." The queen looked up at the fairy woman, waiting for the answer.

"I suppose you can, but I wouldn't recommend it. What's so important that you can't wait until you're fully recovered?" Sophie asked, crossing her arms over her chest as she narrowed her eyes suspiciously.

"It's complicated, but I do need to go." Moving her aching muscles to climb off the bed, Mori looked down at the clothes she was wearing. A white puffy shirt and her sleep pants. "Who changed me?" she asked, narrowing her eyes at everyone in the room.

Lorem raised her hand. "That would be me. You were drenched in sweat and dirt. I had to clean you up and dress you in clean clothes. Your hair was a mess, but I have experience with taming wild curls from decades with your mother." The satyress puffed out her chest with her fists on her hips, proud of her cleanup job.

"At least it was you and not one of the guys who might get handsy," the queen grumbled as she made her way to the wardrobe to find something else to wear. "Clear the room," she called out before looking over her shoulder. "Faust can stay." The wolf wagged his tail happily while the others left the room, Sophie closing the door behind them. After getting changed into something more fitting to be worn outside, she made her way down the hall, only to run into the one person she thought she'd never see again—Pettil.

"Your Majesty," she said as she bowed. Her short black hair, now longer since the last time they'd seen each other, covered her face before settling back into place as she straightened up.

Mori couldn't help but cross her arms. "Are you gonna tell me I'm not your queen and disappear again?" She narrowed her eyes, not trusting the so-called royal advisor, but the dryad shook her head.

"I accept you as my queen. I will serve you faithfully."

"What do you do, exactly?"

"I'm connected with the forest, so I can receive summon requests from all the different fae. I also keep track of your schedule to make sure we can visit all of them and determine which celebrations you must attend as the queen." Pettil pulled out a leaf that acted as a clipboard and looked it over. "Right now, you don't have much going on. Duncan has requested that you spend a week recovering after the battle took so much out of you."

"That's not going to happen right now. I have somewhere to be, so for now, stay here. I will return within the hour." Mori didn't need a hitchhiker to come with her just to stand around in the throne room since no one else was allowed in Leana's chamber.

"As you wish." Pettil bowed and moved to the side so the queen could pass. Once outside, she opened a portal and stepped through it.

"The throne room is as lively as ever." She chuckled as she stepped into the massive room. The flowers were in full bloom and the vines had grown longer since she had last been there gaining the ability of Leana. Now it was time to give it back.

Making her way to the throne, she opened up the stairway and walked down. This time, the room was empty. Still, the queen walked to where she usually sat and crossed her legs.

"It's time I return what was borrowed." Holding her hands up, palms skyward, she closed her eyes for a brief moment before opening them. Their glow illuminated the dimly lit room as trails of purple and green light floated to the cushion Leana always sat on. Sparkles of light formed her outline as more filled the details until The Seer was whole again, her solid body fully materializing.

"Ah, better," Leana said as she stretched her body. "Your joints get stiff when trapped in the same spot for too long."

"Aren't you a spirit?" Mori smirked, but lost it when Leana flicked her forehead. "Ow."

"That real enough for ya?" The woman cackled, having a good laugh before calming down. "Thank you for returning my soul back to my rightful place."

"Thank you for letting me borrow your power. It was very interesting to see the ambient magic around here, and the ancient one on the island, but I don't want to see that all the time." She shook her head as she spoke. "Not for me. I will stick with swinging a hammer.

"It suits you well, Mori." Leana smiled softly. "The war has ended, but there is still much to do. Many homes to repair and lives to rebuild, but you will get there. You are The Bridge. There is no telling where it will take you."

"Just like a bridge over water," the young queen said, looking down at her hands with a light smile. "I met my mother, found my father, and made friends for the first time. I can freely go back to see Missy and Jason because I have the ability to open a portal, just like my mother." Her eyes trailed back up to the older woman. "I didn't quite understand why you gave me that name when we first met, but it's really grown on me. I could do some real good here, and I want to help people. I think I will continue my plant studies here and send shipments of tea leaves back to my parents so they can help those who need relief from ailments."

"Like I said, you will be the bridge between humans and fae. This war has ended, but your story is just beginning." Leana lifted her hand, the sapling insignia glowing purple on her palm. "It seems you have officially been accepted by all as the fifty-ninth royal."

Mori stared at the sapling with wide eyes before looking down at her own hand. The same sapling was glowing green on her right palm, radiant in the dark room and pulsing with magic.

"The royal magic has fully accepted you. It seems it unlocked its true potential and is completely yours to command," the old woman commented.

"Wait . . ." Mori looked up at The Seer, her eyes even wider than before. "What do you mean it's *completely* unlocked? Wasn't it already mine to command?"

Leana cackled more as she almost fell backward. "My dear Mori, you still have so much to learn. Everything has a consciousness, even magic. The royal magic first has to determine if you're worthy to fully command its immense power. There's a reason it stays within the bloodline."

"What about the past royals who abused it?"

"Have you not read all the journals? Those who abused the power, like Asani and Alder, could feel their connection with the royal magic diminish with time. It didn't deem them worthy and was able to slowly pull away from them, then disappeared completely when an heir was born so they couldn't hurt the child. It's a miracle the Albright bloodline has lasted as long as it has." The Seer lowered her hand, resting it in her lap while she spoke.

"I have been training to end the war, but now that it's over, I'm going to sit down and read all the books I can from the oak tree house."

"That sounds like a good plan. Shall you need guidance again, I will be here if you truly need me." With a little wave, Leana's body turned into little shimmering lights before fading away.

"Thanks again, and I will come to visit sometime."

The past week brought recovery from the battle with Dairus. Duncan, Faust, and Pettil stepped out of the portal into the pixie territory to offer their aid. The little fae were busy rebuilding after Bob had run through their homes a few months back. It was slow going because their homes were grown, just like the fairies'.

"Queen Mori, how are you feeling? We heard you were under the weather," Astalla said as she flew over and hovered before her.

"I'm doing much better. Thank you for asking, Astalla." Mori beamed before looking around. "Do you need any help rebuilding? I know you've been waiting for your new homes to grow. I can speed things along."

"That would be wonderful!" The pixie queen looked down and glared at something. "Starbug, don't steal from your queen!"

Mori looked down and quickly closed the pouch the little yellow pixie was trying to get into. Starbug backed off with a sheepish smile before hovering next to Astalla.

"Sorry. I was really curious about what you have in the pouches."

A small laugh escaped Mori, even though she was trying not to. Opening the pouch and pulling out a seed, she showed it to the little one without giving it to her. "This is the seed of a plant back in the human world. It's called a cape sundew. With long green stems and bright red bristles that produce sugar water, it can attract insects to eat. It's a carnivorous plant that typically grows in harsh conditions and in soil with very little nutrients."

The little pixie's eyes widened as they ooh'ed. "That's really cool! Can I have it?"

"I'm afraid not. These can't be collected here in the forest. I have to travel to the human world for them, and they can be difficult to track down. Besides, I need them to keep everyone safe." Mori dropped the seed back in the pouch it came from and pulled the string taut.

"Thanks for showing me," Starbug said before taking off to join her friends.

"She's very curious, but I can't blame her. She's young, only about six months old." Astalla chuckled lightly.

"Wow, pixies grow fast." Mori put her hands on her hips.

"All fae generally grow up fast due to the conditions of the forest. For pixies, six months means adulthood," Pettil informed her, taking a step back after speaking to be next to Duncan.

"Thank you, Pettil. That's useful information. Well, I better get to work." Being careful where she stepped, she made her way over to the bulk of where the new homes were being grown and held out her hands. Ribbons of magic twinkled around each plant as it grew to the size it needed to be to become a new home. The trees shot upward in size and hollowed themselves out before forming a door to allow access to its tunnels. In a matter of seconds, all the new pixie homes were ready to be inhabited.

"Thank you, Mori. That would have taken several more months or even years to do!" Astalla flew over to a new tree home and opened the door to check out the inside. "Very spacious, I like it." The little pixie queen turned back to the forest queen and bowed.

"I'm glad I was able to help. If there's anything else you need, please feel free to send a message to Pettil. She will relay the message to me so I can come assist any way that I can." A smile formed on her lips. She was glad she was finally having a decent conversation with the pixies for the first time.

Now that their homes were complete, Mori opened another portal, and the four of them stepped inside.

When they exited the portal, they were with the naiads. "Why are we here again?" Mori asked, watching as the women went about their usual day-to-day lives.

"I requested it," Duncan said as he took a few steps toward three women who were each holding a baby naiad. Mori recognized the women as the ones Duncan had had some fun with during the festival they had been invited to.

"Wait, Duncan, are you a dad?"

"Of course! I've helped the naiads repopulate for a long time. Finding elves and fairies to mate with can be difficult due to their location, so I do what I can to keep the population from shrinking," the elf explained as he took one of the little girls from her mother and kissed her forehead. "I hunt and bring back treasures every chance I get." Pulling a shell necklace from his pocket, he looped it over the little girl's head, making her laugh happily, her gills flapping excitedly. "I love every single child I father, and I keep track of their lives. Listening to their stories every time I visit, which will be easier to do with your portal magic." He looked up at Mori. "If that's alright with you, Mori."

"I don't mind helping you out. You were my first friend here, after all. Besides, I think it's beautiful to have so many children." A thought occurred to her, spiking her curiosity. "What happened to the elves? Why haven't we come across any that can help with the population?"

"During the war the second royal started, they were the primary soldiers of his army. When Vedia locked away the hammer and took her place as queen, the elves went through a portal to leave the fae realm. A few stayed, like me, but they're scattered all over the forest in hiding. They're very good at illusion magic, so finding them will be difficult."

"That makes a lot of sense to me." She nodded in understanding. "I hope future royals will learn from the past and prevent wars instead of starting them."

Will you mother any children? Faust asked her, nudging her hand as he stood beside her.

"I haven't thought about it. I'm still only eighteen, which is young for humans. I think I will have them much later in life, if I can find someone I can actually stand to be around all the time." She laughed, petting her wolf's head. "I read that my mother had me when she was 164 years old. That's pretty old by human standards."

"We don't go by human standards here. Her life equates to around eighty-two years in the human world. Then she lived eighteen years longer before passing. As far as royal standards go, that's very young. Our oldest royal was about 466 by the time he passed." Duncan thought for a moment. "I would say roughly 233 years in the human world, give or take a few." He handed back the child and pulled out two more necklaces before putting them over the heads of the two other babies.

"That's still pretty old." Mori laughed. "I don't know if I can make it to that age since I'm half-human. We typically live to be about eighty years old."

"I think it's doable, but we've never had a half-breed for a royal," Pettil said.

"Don't call me that." Mori turned to glare at her advisor. "I'm a hybrid, not a half-breed, not a halfling, hybrid. Got it?" she said sternly.

"Yes, Your Majesty." The advisor shrank in on herself, backing away quickly.

"I thought you hated being called that." Duncan quirked a brow.

Mori shrugged. "Only when my friends call me that. *She* is not my friend. She still has to prove herself to me after our first meeting." The queen's words made Pettil shrink more, partially hiding behind a bush with a saddened expression.

We should head to the next area. It seems the naiads do not need our help, as they did not lose anyone during the battle. No one did. Faust looked up at Mori, meeting her gaze as she smiled.

"You're right, buddy. We should head to the next place." Looking back at the women with their daughters, she couldn't help but think of her own. They looked so happy, and it made Mori imagine Viviana holding her like that and playing. Missy said she received Mori when she was only a month old. "Let's get going. I still need to check on the leprechauns. I think they will need the most help." Opening a portal, she waited for her two friends and royal advisor to step through before following behind.

The leprechaun territory was in ruins under the foliage Mori had made for them. Charred framework peeked through the dying leaves. The soil's nutrients had been burned in the fire and could not sustain the plants' needs.

"Queen Mori," Sullivan called as he walked over to her, waving his hand in the air to get her attention. "We're glad to see ya, lass. We are in a wee bit o' a pickle here. None of teh plants are alive anymore. They all died as we returned from teh battle with Dairus."

"I can see that." Mori walked over to a burned structure to examine the frame before pushing on it with her finger. The whole thing buckled when the wood gave out under her pressure, causing it to collapse, and Mori had to jump back to avoid being hit or inhaling any of the ash that danced in the air. "I can't repair the already destroyed structures, but I can help you make new ones. Have your people gather all the things they wish to keep and remove them from the temporary homes. I have to bury all of it to nurture the soil back to health before I can grow new trees." Turning to Duncan and Pettil, she continued. "You two start gathering branches that fell nearby. I can use them as a base component for the new trees, but I want to make sure I can do what I'm hoping I can do for them."

Duncan and Pettil both nodded before walking off to do as they were told. Sullivan had already spread word of what was needed of his people. There were so few of them left since Dairus had killed so many of them. Her heart ached for them, wishing she could bring back the dead like she had during the battles with Dairus she'd fought over the last couple months.

Returning with some sticks, Mori took them from her companions and channeled her magic through the wood and bark, making it bend while holding strong.

"You needed a stick just to bend it?" Pettil narrowed her eyes, trying to figure out what the queen was doing.

Mori chuckled. "You have a lot to learn about me, Pettil. Watch and learn your first lesson." Turning toward the remains of the leprechaun territory, she slowly raised her hands. The ground beneath them quaked, a few screams coming from the group of civilians as the soil opened to swallow the burnt wood and dead plants. With the area cleared of the building remains, the queen reached into her end pouch and pulled out several seeds before scattering them all around, making sure to get every location a house used to be and then some. Beads of sweat lined her temples as she kept her hands out in front of her, palms down, and slowly raised them. Saplings sprouted and rapidly grew, but not into tall trees. Instead, they twisted and turned to form houses, complete with doors and openings for windows. Leaves covered the roofs to prevent rain from entering. During this process, her eyes began to glow green as the royal magic gave her a helping hand, along with one of the royals she didn't recognize.

The trees stopped growing once the houses were fully formed, allowing Mori to cut the connection with the wood and fall to her knees. Faust was there to catch her and keep her from falling further onto the ground.

"Thanks, buddy," she said weakly, catching her breath as she stood up, trying not to fall again as she stabilized herself.

You do not need to push yourself too hard right now. You are still recovering from your battle.

"I'm fine, Faust. You're such a worrywart." Mori laughed.

I do not know what a "worrywart" is, but I do not think I am one of them. Once she was steady on her feet, the wolf took a step to the side.

"Thank yee, Queen. We are forever grateful yee was willing to do this fer us," Sullivan said as they all watched the small leprechauns enter their new homes with their belongings and set to work on decorating.

"I'm glad I was here to help. All of you came to my rescue when I needed it most. This is the least I can do. And if there's anything that can be done to help your population grow again, please don't hesitate to reach out. Pettil will get your message and let me know, and I will be here in a jiffy." A fond smile crossed her features as she watched the families. It made her miss her own parents, Missy and Jason.

Duncan and Pettil had wandered off to help the leprechauns while Faust played with the children. This gave her the chance to slip away into the forest and pull out her smartphone. She hadn't looked at it or even turned it on since the day she'd left their house to return to the forest. Thankfully, she had charged it before leaving, so when she turned it on, it had a full battery.

"I hope this works." Opening a portal against a tree, she watched as the rivers of purples, greens, and blues all swam together. She tapped on the screen of her phone before putting it to her ear, listening to the ring as she sighed with relief. It worked.

"Mori!" Missy's voice came through the speaker, making Mori huff out a breath as she cried.

"Missy!" she breathed, relief washing over her that she had a way to talk to them. "It's good to hear your voice. I have so much to tell you."

"I'm glad to hear from you, too. Jason's here with me. Tell us everything that's been going on."

Epilogue

"**A**re you *actually* sure I'm ready for this?" Mori asked her companions as her hands smoothed out the green cloth that covered her torso.

"You are definitely ready for this," Ren told her, a soft smile on his lips.

"It's been two months since we stopped the raiders and killed Dairus. You're ready for this." Duncan adjusted the lavender flower in Mori's hair so it was a little more in place.

This has been a long time coming. I think you are ready, Mori, Faust said before the queen knelt to adjust the bow tie around his neck.

"Thanks, Faust. What would I do without you?" She stood up and turned to look in the mirror. Instead of the flowing green dress she wore the first time, she was dressed in a royal uniform with pants adorned with crystals of varying colors, different kinds of flowers, and green leaves. She felt it was more fitting for herself than a dress. With a quick adjustment of the leaves that decorated the chest piece and fixing up her curly red hair that was still in a neat braid going down her back, she felt like she could take on the world.

Duncan brushed her green slacks and pulled them taut so they were straight and even over her black boots before standing up.

"Whoever said a queen can't wear pants has never met you before." Ren chuckled as he admired his daughter. "I'm so proud of you, Mori."

A flutter of warmth flooded her whole body as she turned to face her father. It felt wonderful to get to know him better these last few months. To hear those words from him meant the world.

"Thanks, Dad." Hearing Mori call him Dad always brought a tear to his eye that he had to wipe away. He missed her entire childhood, so she had a feeling he was trying to make up for lost time. She embraced her father in a tight hug; feeling the tightness of his arms around her brought her comfort. A bell rang above them, and the two parted.

"It's time. See you out there." Duncan put his hand on Mori's shoulder as he gave a reassuring smile and walked off with Faust in tow.

Ren stood in front of Mori and gently grabbed her arms with his hands. "You are ready for this. We have been preparing you for this for months, and you have earned this. While you haven't been here for a long time, I think you belong here, just like your old man." He smiled gently.

"I won't let you down." She chortled. "I feel like I belong here too. I felt out of place back in Ohio, like I was different from everyone else. Now it all makes sense." Her emerald-green eyes met his brown ones. "I'm half-fae, and I'm damn proud of it."

"I'm glad. When Vi told me she was pregnant, I was worried what our half-human child would think when they found out their father was human. I couldn't have asked for a more perfect daughter. I love you, and I'll see you out there." With one last hug, Ren left the back room to take his place with the others.

Mori turned and took one last look at herself in the mirror and sighed. "We did it, Mom. I will finally officially be the queen of Albright Forest. Just took a little longer than we were both expecting." Spinning on her heels, she shook out her nerves and made her way to where she needed to stand before Duncan motioned her to walk inside.

The walk down the aisle was just as nerve-wracking as the first time. The fae who had gathered were staring at her with intensity as she kept her chin up and eyes forward. However, the difference this time is who sat before her. She was told the Seelie and Unseelie Courts would be in attendance this time, and she was nervous about who they were and how much power they actually had. She didn't dare look up at them as she walked, knowing she needed to keep her eyes forward. She caught a glimpse of Missy and Jason as she passed the front row, their eyes full of proud tears, both beaming at her. It wasn't easy to get them to the fae realm, but she wanted them with her for this moment. Besides, what good was it being the bridge between the two worlds if she couldn't have all her favorite people together on the most important day of her life? Duncan, Faust, Lorem, and Orian, along with several territory leaders, were all waiting at the front for her. Everyone important to her was there, celebrating with her and showing her their support as she stepped into her new role.

Upon reaching the bottom of the steps, she stood directly in front of Duncan.

"While there will never be enough time to mourn the death of Forest Queen Viviana Albright, we will now be able to do so in safety. Today, we celebrate the official arrival of Forest Queen Moriana Albright. She has been deemed worthy by the royal magic and will take her rightful place as the fifty-ninth royal and our queen," Duncan started, his voice echoing in the large room. "We have all gathered here to show our support and our trust in Mori, just as she did for us. As a stranger to this world, she had no real reason to protect us from the raiders, but not only did she defeat the raiders and kill the false king, she also defeated Dairus so history cannot repeat itself. We are able to continue our lives without fear due to her bravery and actions." The elf looked around the room before looking back at her, the room still silent enough to hear a pin drop. The new queen trembled in her boots as her heart pounded against her rib cage, worried they would boo her right out the door again. "Mori, you have been given the name The Bridge by The Seer. You are the bridge between fae and humans. You even found the Hammer of the Royals, Fae'ohtan, and spent the last two months hunting down the last of the raiders. I am pleased to say that they have all been accounted for and brought to justice."

Mori smiled, feeling like she had finally done some good with her life. Behind her, the crowd cheered at his words until they grew silent once more so Duncan could continue. Duncan walked down the steps, knowing that was her cue to kneel, so she did.

"Do you, Moriana Albright, swear to put the forest before your own needs, to put the needs of your people before your own, and to always do whatever it takes to keep us safe?"

Green eyes trailed up the elf's body until she was looking him in the eyes, a smile on her lips. "I swear."

Duncan gave her a nod before she stood up and turned to face the fae. "I present to you our forest queen, Moriana!" Raising her hand, she showed off the green sapling insignia that shined brightly, proving she was worthy.

The fae cheered and clapped with whatever hands, hooves, or fins they had. The entire room was buzzing with life, and every inch of seating and air space was filled with different fae creatures. From the fairies to the remaining leprechauns, and even several naiads had made the journey to the throne room for the occasion. Lavender flower petals rained down from the ceiling as the queen let out the breath, happy tears welling up in her eyes and threatening to run. Faust nudged her and took his place beside her. Lorem stepped forward and put her arm around the queen's shoulders.

"Well done, Queenie, and congratulations," Lorem said.

"Congratulations, Your Majesty." Duncan smiled.

A chuckle escaped Mori. "Don't call me that," she joked, remembering all the times she used to say that to him whenever he slipped up.

Ready to head back out there, Queen? Faust asked, his tail wagging frantically behind her.

"Definitely." Mori looked around the room full of fae once more before her gaze locked on to a dark figure in the very back just beyond the doors. Two bright red eyes stared right at her, unmoving and unblinking. He gave a single slow nod before standing up and disappearing behind the wall. Mori hadn't known he was there, as she had not seen him when she originally entered through that door, but she was glad he was able to attend. She had a new appreciation for the skull-headed beast.

Faust grew in size and Mori climbed onto his back as they walked back down the aisle and out the door. "What if I'm not good enough to be queen? Just because I ended a war doesn't mean I'm qualified to be queen. What if I mess up again and cause more problems?"

I do not recommend dwelling on it. We can figure things out as we go. Learning how to rule over a realm will always take time, but you will never have to do it alone, Faust told her through their mental link.

Those words made Mori smile as her focus shifted down to him. "Thanks, Faust. As much as it hurt, I'm glad I fell down that cliff and met you." She petted her wolf's back a bit as they continued on. "Let's head to the oak tree. There's something I need to do there."

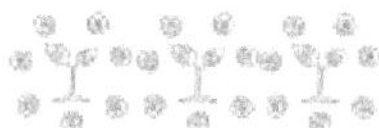

Duncan caught up with Mori and Faust at the broken oak tree house. Its pieces had begun to rot, and bugs had claimed them as their home. A lot of the things that were exposed to the elements had become drenched and molded as time went on. She feared nothing could be saved.

Why did you want to come here? Faust asked as he cocked his head.

"There is something about the hammer that had me really thinking," she said as she climbed off him and went to examine the pieces.

"It's a good thing you think a lot. What idea do you have in mind?" Duncan walked over to the stump of the tree house and grimaced.

"Well . . ." Mori trailed off as she pulled the hammer off her bracelet and let it grow to its full size. Looking down at the gold plate, she ran her fingers over the words from the ancient language it was written in. "This part here. It says, 'Swing once to topple an empire, swing twice to build one,' and it made me think back to the battle with the raiders and Dairus. When I was swinging it, it only took one hit to destroy their compound building, their gate, their walls, and their lives. So what is the second part supposed to mean?" She looked up at the destroyed oak tree that used to be their home.

I do not understand what you are getting at. Faust sat down as he cocked his head to the side.

"That look he has is one I share." Duncan gestured toward the wolf. "What are you talking about?" He sat on the grass as he watched with interested eyes.

Mori glanced at the two before looking back to the tree house and then down to the hammer. Something about this weapon told her she needed to do things twice. She lifted it to the side and swung her hammer at the tree house and hit it. Just as quickly, she raised the hammer above her head and brought it down on the tree trunk, hitting it as hard as she could with the crystal hammerhead.

Duncan jumped to his feet instantly, and Faust lowered himself to the ground as if ready to run.

The crystal hammer began to glow its bright teal color as green light burst out from it. Chunks of the oak tree went flying toward the broken stump, each putting itself back together like puzzle pieces. Trails of magic flowed through the wood as the oak tree grew taller than it had before. With the tree complete, it began to regrow its leaves, each one a bright green color. Mori lifted the hammer off the oak and took a step back, Fae'ohtan at her side just in case. With every splinter of wood returned to its rightful place, the sapling insignia reappeared, carved into the bark just as it had been before.

"I can't believe it. The hammer's motto is actually instructions on how it works. I haven't seen the hammer for so long that I forgot." Duncan walked up to the tree and ran his fingers along the rough bark. "Can you open it?"

Mori returned her hammer to its bracelet form and placed her hand on the sapling, channeling her magic into it, and it revealed the door and windows just like it used to. With no hesitation, she grabbed the handle and yanked the door open, her eyes growing wide as a big grin had her mouth opening. Other than the mess of books, jars, and blankets, everything was exactly how it used to be. Stepping inside, she looked around as most of her things were whole again. The mattress had sustained a lot of damage and was even ripped in two, but now it was repaired as if nothing had happened.

"I missed this bed. It's soooo comfortable." She giggled, tears running down her cheeks that she wiped away with her sleeve. Faust walked up to her and rubbed his side against her body.

Duncan closed the door and sat down on the couch. "We just need to clean up and get things back inside that we saved, and it will be like it was never destroyed."

Mori and Faust nodded before stepping out of the tree house with Duncan so she could close it up, but something caught her eye. "You two go on ahead. I will catch up in a few minutes." A portal opened on the tree house trunk.

"Are you sure?" Faust asked, trying to see what she was looking at, but made no indication he could see it.

"I'm sure. Don't worry, buddy, I'll be fine."

Her two best friends went through the portal to the birch tree house. Once they were through, the portal closed behind them, and she looked over into the distance at the two red eyes looking right back at her. The energy in the air gave away what it was, but she was no longer afraid when she walked over to Bob. He had removed all the arrows sticking out of his body, and the missing patches of fur had grown in fully and looked as though they'd been brushed recently.

"Not a bad queen," he growled out.

"You're right, Bob. I'm not a bad queen, just inexperienced, but I plan to work hard to get better." She smiled.

The skull-headed beast shook his head. "You experienced now. Stopped war." He looked over at the repaired tree house, his head cocking to the side. "Repaired?"

"Thanks for that. And yes, Fae'ohtan doesn't just destroy, it can repair." Mori lifted her wrist to look down at the small hammer charm before adjusting her focus back up at him when she heard him speak.

"First royal took eye. Broke promise and kept it. Hate royals since." He looked down at her. "Until you."

"I'm nothing like the first royal. He sounds like a villain to me. When I make a promise, I intend to keep it. You kept your end of the deal and even went beyond it to help defeat Dairus, so I needed to keep mine. I hope we can work together again in the future if the need arises. For now, I won't tell you what to do with your time or who you can"—she cleared her throat into her fist—"kill, but do try not to cause too much trouble for me. I hear a lot of complaints about you."

Bob stared at Mori with a blank expression for a few moments before answering, his large claws and shoulders rising and falling.

Was that a shrug? Or at least an attempt at one?

His arms lowered back to the ground as his shoulders relaxed, and he brought his head down to be more eye level with her. "Understood, but I won't stop being who I am."

Being so close to the beast and not being afraid of being eaten was still a new experience, but a welcome one. There was nothing for her to fear anymore, and she had no reason to run away.

"Be you, but be a version of you who keeps himself in check. If you have any problems you can't deal with on your own, come to me. I can sense your presence when you're nearby. I will seek you out." Mori reached up to touch his skull, but he lifted his head out of her reach and stood up again.

"Understood."

"Do you think I can ask you something while you're here?" She looked up at Bob, meeting his gaze as he gave a single nod. "Why did you keep trying to eat me?"

His silence made her nervous. "You royal. Hate royal."

"But now you think I'm different, right?" A nod from the beast calmed her racing heart.

"Good different. Won't eat."

She was going to miss hearing that guttural voice full of gravel and the deep rumble that reverberated in her chest. She watched as he turned to the left and started to walk away. Shaking her head with a light laugh, she crossed her arms and huffed out a breath.

"Your strongest ally is also your greatest fear. That is definitely going in the royal journal." She breathed out a small laugh before turning back to the oak tree house and opening a portal to the birch tree house. The first thing she wanted to do was record everything that had happened in the journal so future royals could learn from her mistakes. The second thing she was going to do was open her own tea shop here in the fae realm. Royal-Teas had a new meaning to go along with this new area.

Leaving the birch tree house the next day, the four of them—Pettil joining them—made their way to the fairy territory. While they didn't need the help, Sophie had requested Mori's attendance for something big. She had no clue what it was since their homes were rebuilt ages ago and all their people were still alive after the battle, thanks to Titania.

"Oh good! You made it!" Sophie said as she fluttered over to them, letting her wings relax when her feet touched the ground.

"Pettil said you had something important for me to do. What seems to be the issue? Is it Bob? I know he's been around this area lately." Mori extended her hammer and looked around at the trees, searching for the skull-headed beast. Sophie laughed as she shook her head.

"No, no, nothing like that. Besides, we can handle that brute just fine." Fae'ohtan returned to its bracelet size as Mori slowly lowered her arms, her eyes narrowing at the fairy queen.

"What did you call me here for?" Flower petals rained down from above them, covering the five of them in several different colors of vibrant corollas. Looking up at the two fairies above her, she couldn't help but smile. "What are you two doing?" Bursts of laughter rang out from Mori and Duncan as Faust panted happily with his tail wagging.

"It's the spring celebration! We welcome in the flowers and have a week-long festival to give thanks to those who bring us a bountiful harvest," one of the fairies said as she landed beside Sophie.

"Since you were the one who ended the war and nurtured the soil to full health so we could have more food than we know what to do with, we decided to send the excess to neighboring fae territories and use the rest for a feast!" Sophie clapped her hands together once. "Let the festivities begin!"

Over the course of the next few hours, Mori was thanked by many fae, even non fairies, who attended the spring celebration. There was food, dancing, music, and lots of flowers. Several fairies had made flower crowns and necklaces for Mori and her friends. Faust didn't seem to mind being dressed up in flowers, which made her happy to see. Everything was well and alive. She got to talk to her mom, help the fae rebuild, get to know Bob, and make friends during her travels. Even Tim and Tom had done their best to earn the trust of everyone and were enjoying their time with the fairies. This forest might not have been her home for long, but she intended to stay and continue to make it a home worth fighting for.

Map of Albright Forest